MURDER IN THE CASTLE

A 1920s Cozy Mystery

A Lady Felicity Quick Mystery
Book 9

ROSIE HUNT

ISBN: 978-90-834331-7-2

With thanks to early readers Renee Brown, Michelle Clegg, Kelly Hodgkins, Dawn House, Lorraine Terrell, Nancy R. Willis, and others

Cover art by DLR Cover Designs

For the cousin
who once knew me best.

A Note on Language

This book is written in British English. There are two reasons for this:

- the story is set in England, and
- I, the author, am British.

Part of my British writing style is the use of s where z is used in American English. For example: hospitalise instead of hospitalize, and immortalise instead of immortalize.

However, you may have noticed that in the blurbs and marketing for this book, it's called a cozy mystery and not a cosy mystery.

This is because the American spelling is standard for the genre. Spelling it this way helps people (and algorithms) recognise my book more easily.

But outside of book genres, it's cosy all the way.

Cast of Characters

Quick family

Lady Felicity Quick, journalist and detective

Lord Jasper Quick, Earl of Denbury, editor-in-chief of the Western Daily News and Felicity's brother

Lady Henrietta Quick, Dowager Countess of Denbury, grandmother to Felicity and Jasper

Pip, Felicity's Yorkshire Terrier

Cullingslock family

Lady Winnifred Cullingslock, Dowager Baroness and Felicity's great-aunt

Lord Tristan Cullingslock, Baron of Cullingslock, Winnifred's son

Lady Philippa Cullingslock, Baroness of Cullingslock, Tristan's wife

Mr Peregrine Cullingslock, Tristan and Philippa's son

Mrs Elfrida Brand, Winnifred's daughter

Miss Audrey Brand, Elfrida's daughter

Other inhabitants of Cullingslock Castle

Mrs Cornelia Imrie, assistant to Winnifred

Miss Rhoda Hartley, assistant to Winnifred

Mr Jeffrey Silkstede, researcher

Mr Harold Kemp, land agent

Mr Jonathan Timpson, butler

Mrs Mary Wiseley, cook

Mr Jacob Reid, footman

Others

Mr Alexander Cooper, reporter for the Western Daily News and Felicity's fiancé

Mr Brian Pope, Winnifred's solicitor

Dr Marsh, local physician

Sergeant Norris, local police sergeant

Constable Fielding, senior local constable

Constable Dinsdale, junior local constable

Animals

Solomon, Tristan's Border Collie

Lionheart, Mr Kemp's Old English Sheepdog

Thoth and Ra, Winnifred's cats

Extract from a private letter to Lady Katherine Cullingslock from her father, Lord Edmund Cullingslock, dated September 1642

Your brother's zealous devotion to the King's cause makes him careless of the ruin it might bring. He sees honour where I fear disaster.

So I entrust to you what I cannot place in his keeping. Upon your marriage, as detailed in the enclosed agreement, you will inherit the Cullingslock Wastes — five hundred acres of moorland, the name chosen to avoid your brother's objections. This is not from want of love for him, but from a deep trust in your prudence and in the gentleman you have accepted as your husband.

These lands have sustained us through plague and hunger. They must not feed the fires of war. Survival oft requires yielding, not breaking, a fact you grasp while your brother does not.

To spare him shame — and worse, indignation — this condition shall stand henceforth: that the so-called Wastes shall always pass to the younger woman who weds before her older brother. Let it seem a rule born of tradition, not judgement, and so preserve harmony among kin.

Extract from the Empire Examiner, 1922

Letter From the Grave! Ghostly Plea Stuns Devon!

MANCHESTER, 3 September — An astonishing letter has arrived at our newsroom, said to be penned by a spirit from beyond the veil!

The message, linked to the recent tragedy at Cullingslock Castle, was delivered anonymously and has left our reporters shaken.

Who sent it? And what does the dead man wish to say?

Turn to Page 3 to read the missive in full!

Chapter One

EXMOOR, NORTH DEVON, AUGUST 1922

Arriving at Cullingslock Castle towards nightfall had not been part of Lady Felicity Quick's plan. Road closures from landslides following heavy rain and a poorly signposted detour had seen to that. Felicity's grip tightened on the steering wheel as the imposing hilltop fortress appeared above the trees, sending a chill up her spine. Yet didn't the bats flitting around the crumbling, ivy-covered towers against the purple sky bring forth a forlorn, almost romantic beauty?

The distant screech of quarrelling foxes was rather less charming.

"Care to remind me again why you need to be here?"

Mr Alexander Cooper flashed a wry smile from the passenger seat as Felicity guided the white two-seater Alvis up the steep, winding drive. With deep blue eyes, dark blond hair, and strong jaw, Alex looked dashing in his smartly tailored tweed jacket. It contrasted sharply with Felicity's pale blue linen motoring coat, her auburn curls peeking out from under a matching cloche, the ensemble feeling increasingly unsuitable for the rugged terrain.

Between the trees, another view of the castle revealed a large curtain wall partially collapsed, its red sandstone gushing like a frozen waterfall down the hillside.

Alex sucked in a breath. “I know these old places cost a fair bit to look after, but what would the bill be for those repairs?”

“That section might be beyond saving.” Felicity winced, happy to side-step his earlier rather sarcastic question.

Alex knew perfectly well why they’d come to Exmoor.

An eccentric family tradition tied to inheriting five-hundred acres of apparently worthless moorland — charmingly named the Cullingslock Wastes — had been activated by Felicity and Alex’s desire to marry. The triggering of the tradition also revealed a hitherto estranged branch of Felicity’s family, and it was the prospect of exploring these new connections that had prompted the visit.

But while she hadn’t left Devon, Felicity was beginning to feel awfully far from home.

“I’m sure some sections are liveable.” Perhaps sensing her apprehension, Alex’s tone was suddenly bright with unwarranted optimism.

“Let’s hope so.” Felicity hadn’t explicitly requested Alex’s company, but she was immensely glad to have him at her side. She had little information about the relatives she was to visit, and the task’s daunting nature increased with every glimpse of the fortress.

The castle approach had quite a different effect on Pip, however.

The Yorkshire terrier stood with hind legs on Alex’s lap and front paws on the dashboard, tail wagging, nose lifted to the earthy scents streaming through the open windows. Unlike Alex, Pip hadn’t chosen to accompany Felicity. He had whined when Felicity’s grandmother, Lady Henrietta, departed for a plant society expedition to Cornwall. The following day, when Felicity packed the Yorkie into her Alvis, the terrier perked up, though his tartan travel bed hadn’t been used since Alex’s lap became available after Exeter. After a lacklustre start all those months ago, the two were becoming firm friends.

“It’s only right I meet your relatives.” Alex steadied the excited dog as Felicity steered around a tight bend, the engine’s purr echoing against the rocky hillside.

Felicity smiled, buoyed by their enthusiasm. “I’m rather curious to know them, too. There's not been any contact since that old falling-out."

The Cullingslock branch, which was on her mother's side, had cut all communication following a severe disagreement generations ago over Felicity's great-grandmother's progressive educational pursuits. Her great-grandfather had supported women's education, but her great-great-grandfather objected strongly. An educated woman was hardly scandalous in 1922, but in the Victorian age it could be.

"It won't hurt to have a few extra faces on the bride's side of the church, will it?" Felicity's circle of living relatives was rather limited. Following the passing of both her parents, she felt obligated and personally driven to maintain or rekindle familial ties wherever possible.

"Whatever the outcome of your visit, I invariably cherish time spent with my future wife." Alex's smile was warm, his hand touching Felicity's on the gearstick.

"Just as I'm always happy to keep company with you." She returned his smile. The castle's foreboding exterior didn't mean its inhabitants would be equally intimidating, did it?

Felicity ducked to look out of the window. Through the trees, gently undulating hills swathed in purple heather with bright touches of yellow gorse rolled towards the sparkling sea.

"Stunning, isn't it?"

"Do you believe we'll ever get to holiday together?" Alex raised his brow teasingly, the scar on his forehead more prominent.

Felicity couldn't suppress the joy in her voice. "We have our honeymoon to look forward to, do we not?" They had slid into this mutual understanding of their upcoming union in a most gentle and delicious way. A smooth resolution to the matter of the family tradition and land inheritance would pave the way for their wedding day, which was guaranteed to happen even if a precise date hadn't been set.

As the driveway flattened and the trees became sparse, a knot tightened in Felicity's stomach. With no telephone connection at the castle, calling ahead when they realised they would arrive late hadn't been possible.

Alex gently swatted at Pip's tail as it brushed his nose. "Have you given our honeymoon destination much thought?"

Felicity's fingers tightened on the wheel. "I suppose we ought to settle the matter of the wedding's location first. Grandmama is already thinking about decorations for the great hall at Bradley Court." She cast a sideways glance at Alex. "But what of your family? Your parents rarely venture beyond Covent Garden, let alone London."

Persuading Alex's parents to stroll into the neighbouring parish during a recent city visit had proved challenging. The chance of the hard-working couple abandoning their market stall for more than a day seemed remote. Marrying without their presence was, however, unthinkable.

Alex stroked his clean-shaven jaw. "It can indeed be difficult to convince them of the merits of time off work. Aha. There's the welcome party."

A small group waited at the castle's monumental arched entrance, above which was etched an enormous family crest featuring a rampant wolf and crossed swords in weathered limestone. Around it, the red sandstone glowed like old embers in the dying light.

"Oh dear," whispered Felicity. The solemn expressions thoroughly distracted from any wedding planning concerns. "I do hope we're not causing a disturbance by arriving so late."

"They could be furious, and it wouldn't matter." Alex swept his hair back and placed his hat on his head as the Alvis halted. "They'll be beguiled by you in no time."

Less assured of her captivating abilities, Felicity smoothed her travel-rumpled skirt and reminded herself of her mission. To decline, gently and politely, the land she was supposed to inherit — for between sleuthing, journalism, and planning a wedding, life was quite complicated enough — and to build bridges between the estranged family sides. Compared to recent undertakings, this North Devon mission was refreshingly straightforward.

The elderly woman's expression at the head of the group didn't soften as Felicity and Alex approached. Under Felicity's arm, Pip's tail wagged hard, the terrier oblivious to the frosty welcome.

"Are you Felicity?"

A puff of grey hair in an outdated Edwardian style sat around the elderly woman's head like a halo. Great swathes of silk and organza, purple like the darkening sky, draped her small figure. Beads and chains adorned her neck, bracelets clinked at her wrists, and rings glinted on her fingers, including a heavy Egyptian scarab of lapis lazuli on her left hand, while her right remained partially concealed by a flowing sleeve. With chin raised, her bearing was that of a woman accustomed to commanding rather than requesting.

"Great-Aunt Winnifred?" Who else could it be? Felicity's brother had never met the woman but had created a vivid portrait of the Cullingslock matriarch in Felicity's mind.

Bats swooped overhead and trees rustled in the sea-scented breeze as Winnifred and her entourage regarded Felicity with stern carefulness. Two were household staff. The butler, a dignified silver-haired figure, had an impressively waxed moustache that quivered slightly, while a much younger footman had ears protruding prominently from his closely cropped head. Both wore smartly pressed black livery yet mirrored Winnifred's scrutinising attitude.

The two women accompanying Felicity's great-aunt were a stark contrast.

One was petite with a curvaceous figure, dressed in a simple blush-pink frock, her brown hair bobbed with a slight wave. Her inquisitive eyes sparkled as she regarded Felicity and Alex. The taller woman was pale-skinned in a flowing blue gown, her thick blonde hair gathered in a tight chignon. Her large, deep-set eyes looked not at Felicity but through her.

Winnifred had a son and daughter. Might one of the women be Felicity's first cousin once removed?

"It's an honour to visit you." Breaking the awkward silence, Felicity's greeting was vague enough to avoid embarrassment, given she wasn't entirely sure whom she was addressing. From Alex's gentle smile, Pip's enthusiasm, and Winnifred's party's calm, perhaps Felicity alone felt nervous. Still, she stood with the poise befitting an earl's daughter.

"Timpson?" The older woman kept her eyes on Felicity.

The butler's spine straightened. "M'lady?"

Winnifred waved the hand with the scarab ring. "See that my great-niece is established comfortably in the Rose Suite. Her companion should be made at ease in rooms overlooking the old keep."

"Very well, m'lady." With a slight incline of his distinguished head, Timpson signalled to the footman, and the pair collected Felicity and Alex's luggage while Winnifred and her female companions remained statue-like.

The warm welcome Felicity had dared dream about was clearly out of the question, but decades of separation couldn't melt into friendship in moments. Patience was required. Patience and a touch of charm.

"It's incredibly kind of you to welcome Mr Cooper and myself into your home, Great-Aunt. If indeed 'Great-Aunt' is how you wish me to address you?"

Winnifred closed her eyes and inhaled deeply, as if trying to catch Felicity's scent. The two women beside her did the same. Pip whimpered and wriggled as she and Alex exchanged looks. The butler and footman continued moving the luggage without looking up.

Winnifred's bright blue eyes sprang open. She stepped forward with such urgency Felicity nearly recoiled, but she stood her ground as Winnifred advanced. The resulting embrace was a complete surprise. Winnifred's arms were stiff yet warm, her jewellery clinking and her amber perfume powerful as the softness of her bosom pressed against Felicity.

With Felicity too stunned to react, the two women came to Winnifred's side and joined in, encircling both of them in a large and overly familiar hug.

Felicity met Alex's gaze with wide eyes. She'd wanted a warm welcome, but this was too much. There had not even been any formal introductions.

Stifling a chuckle, Alex offered a shrug.

Yip!

A bark from under the layers of limbs and clothing reminded the huggers that Pip was struggling for space.

Winnifred eased her grasp, and the younger women stepped away. She rested a bejewelled hand on Felicity's shoulder, a smile on her wrinkled lips as Felicity maintained her composure.

"You must call me whatever you wish to, my child." Winnifred's tone was affectionate, her blue gaze roving over Felicity's features as though admiring a painting. "This is Mrs Cornelia Imrie." She gestured towards the willowy blonde.

"How do you do?" Mrs Imrie spoke primly and with a Scottish lilt.

"And this is Miss Rhoda Hartley."

"Truly a pleasure to meet you." The curvy brunette's eyes sparkled as she warmly shook Felicity and Alex's hands.

"Mrs Imrie and Miss Hartley will assist me this evening." Winnifred lifted her chin. "Now, come inside. There's a whole gathering quite desperate to meet you." She released Felicity's arm and turned towards the entrance, her movements fluid but measured. The two younger women fell in line as though choreographed.

Calming Pip with reassuring strokes, Felicity exchanged an eyebrow lift with Alex. The welcome had been unorthodox, but the worry pressing on her chest was lifting. Bridges were already being built.

In the coolness of the vast entrance hall, dusky twilight glowed through leaded windows high above a vaulted staircase. Thick candles burned in an enormous chandelier of crude medieval ironwork. Tapestries depicting hunting scenes and mythological beasts, their colours muted by age, hung beside paintings and framed photographs. Ornate wooden chests and armour stands jostled with cabinets of curiosities along the perimeter. Their footsteps echoed on the large, worn flagstones.

"You shall get your chance at a run outside," whispered Felicity to the wriggling Pip. "Have patience, please."

Ahead was a lit doorway, warm lamplight revealing perhaps half a dozen people standing or leaning forward on sofas. Their expressions ranged from an imperious raised eyebrow from a woman of about forty, to calm appraisal from a fresh-faced gentleman with military bearing. Were they concerned about the Cullingslock Wastes being transferred to her? Felicity was ready to reassure them.

She straightened and smiled, meeting everyone's eye with kindness and respect. Family could not be taken for granted. Bridges may be built, but they must also be maintained.

Grrr. Baff!

Pip continued struggling vigorously. Felicity's choice became either to drop him or set him down with control.

"Why, you..." she began under her breath.

As soon as his paws touched the floor, the Yorkie skittered across the flags towards the lit room.

"Pip!" called Felicity with dismay and to no effect. Winnifred and her followers turned to watch the little dog fly past.

Alex shook his head. How was he still smiling?

From behind a sofa, a black-and-white Border Collie sprang into action, adopting a pose of head lowered, haunches high, ready to play.

"Steady now, Solomon." The gentle voice belonged to a tall, slender gentleman in a single-breasted fawn suit with a scholarly air.

"No, Lionheart. Sit." The sharp command came from a square-jawed, ruddy-faced man in country tweeds and riding boots.

As Felicity considered how to explain Pip's lack of manners, Winnifred took a sharp turn away, her female followers close behind. She was heading upstairs.

Was the lit room full of waiting people not their destination?

Felicity glanced at Alex, confused. He raised a doubtful eyebrow.

Yip!

The tall fellow in the fawn suit approached, his footsteps echoing in the vast hall. He was about forty, with thinning reddish-blond hair and a long neck in which bobbed a prominent Adam's apple. In his slender hands, he held a wriggling Yorkshire Terrier.

"I thought you might wish to have your dog back," he mumbled apologetically as he slid the Yorkie back into Felicity's arms. At his side trotted the Collie, its gait calm and perfectly in line with its master's, its dark, intelligent eyes flicking with excitement towards the wayward terrier.

"Thank you," said Felicity. "I can only apologise."

The man smiled briefly. His tallness gave him a fragile air. "No need. Although Solomon's rather large to be his playmate." He glanced affectionately at his Collie.

"Good evening. I don't believe we've met?" A small but powerful woman with a heart-shaped face bustled forward, hand already extended. She had dark shoulder-length hair and wore a smartly tailored suit in lightweight burgundy wool. Her gold jewellery was subtle yet of high quality.

Winnifred slapped a hand on the banister of the staircase and let out a loud sigh. The two women who had been ascending behind her paused and switched their attention to the scene.

"I'm Lady Philippa Cullingslock," continued the woman in burgundy, giving Felicity and Alex's hands a firm shake, "and this rather too modest fellow—" She tugged at the tall, delicate-looking man's arm and peered up at him with a chastising yet tender smile. "—is the baron himself, Lord Tristan Cullingslock, who also happens to be my husband."

Felicity gave Pip a tickle under the chin. Thanks to the terrier, she'd now met one of her first cousins once removed. "Very pleased to meet you both."

"Philippa, please." Tristan looked uneasily at his wife between apologetic smiles in Felicity and Alex's direction.

"And I should like to present my son to you as well." Philippa's gaze darted about as though expecting someone else to have joined her. "Perry?" Her voice echoed through the hall, but no one came.

Tristan's shoulders hunched as though he wished to shrink away.

"My mother clearly has plans for the evening. Let's not hold things up."

"Oh." Philippa's lips parted as if surprised. She leaned forward to catch Winnifred's gaze from the staircase. "My apologies, Dowager Baroness. Are we interrupting?"

The older woman's eyes fluttered skywards with a hint of exasperation. When she spoke, however, her tone was warm. "It's quite all right, though if you're done, there are others waiting to meet our guest."

"Yes, yes." Philippa offered a courteous smile to both Felicity and Alex. "I suppose the family introductions can wait."

"Come, my child." Winnifred beckoned to Felicity as she resumed her progress up the stairs, the chandelier's flickering candlelight sending shadows dancing over her features. "They really are quite desperate to meet you."

Chapter Two

Leaving behind a room full of people seemingly curious to meet her wasn't the oddest thing to have happened since Felicity's arrival at Cullingslock. At Winnifred's request, she'd also left Alex behind, which would have been worse had he not seemed so relaxed about the whole situation. Felicity wasn't entirely without support as she followed Winnifred upstairs, however. Pip was still tucked under her arm, his wet little nose twitching as the route through the castle became increasingly interesting.

Richly decorated corridors with framed paintings and photographs on the walls and thick carpets underfoot gave way to bare stone, with unravelling tapestries and painted leather hangings stretched across walls to combat the chill. The occasional arrow slit allowed the moorland breeze to whistle through the hallways as gas-lit wall sconces cast eerie, elongated shadows.

Winnifred led the party, followed by Mrs Imrie and Miss Hartley. Felicity and Pip brought up the rear.

"May I ask where we're headed, Great-Aunt?"

Winnifred paused midway up a stone staircase, shifting her weight. Though of advanced age, she moved with remarkable determination. Mrs Imrie and Miss Hartley also ceased their advance, maintaining a respectful distance from Felicity's great-aunt.

"Patience, my child," said Winnifred warmly and a little breathlessly. "All shall be revealed."

Silence fell as they continued upwards. Felicity had promised herself she would be as accommodating as possible towards her estranged relatives, with the goal of rekindling the family connection. But it wasn't unreasonable to wish to know where one was going.

"Please don't consider me impertinent, Great-Aunt, but may I know who we're meeting?"

Winnifred merely continued climbing, the silver threads in the drapes of her outfit shimmering in the dim light.

"Is this about the Cullingslock Wastes? Are we perhaps meeting your solicitor?"

Felicity had been told by her brother, Lord Jasper Quick — who had done an excellent job of keeping the estranged Cullingslock family branch a secret from her for a number of years — that Winnifred was the land's current trustee. Though it would be unusual to go straight into discussions of legal matters, it was only natural that Winnifred should wish to smooth out such issues straight away. If Felicity took on the land, which was absolutely not her intention, then it would be the first time in generations it would leave the hands of the castle's residents.

"Here we are," announced Winnifred as they reached the top of a narrow, winding staircase, her voice betraying only slight breathlessness and offering no answer to Felicity's questions.

Accommodating. Felicity had promised herself she would be accommodating of her newfound relatives.

They passed through a squat doorway into a surprisingly vast tower room, two storeys tall. Remnants of former floors were still visible in the bare stone walls, which were partially covered by long velvet drapes. The floor was blanketed with overlapping Oriental rugs, which muffled all sound. At the room's centre stood a round table with high-backed Gothic chairs, surrounded by tall silver candelabra casting pools of golden light. The room's single window offered a breathtaking view. Stars spangled the night sky, and moonlight silvered the distant sea beyond the dark silhouette of

Exmoor's hills, but Felicity's wonder was cut short. The butler, who had reached the tower room ahead of Winnifred and her entourage, promptly closed the velvet curtains across the window, sealing them from the outside world.

A young girl with a sturdy build and a button nose emerged from behind a heavy curtain. She wore a practical pinafore dress, her freckled face framed by reddish hair. Though perhaps only fifteen or so, her robust form suggested someone accustomed to physical work, yet her movements were gentle. She seemed nervous or perhaps excited.

Winnifred kissed the girl firmly on the cheek. "Thank you, Audrey. Now go and join your mother," the older woman instructed, already turning towards her butler.

The girl blinked. "Yes, Grandmama," she said, heading obediently for the door.

Grandmama?

Winnifred suddenly pivoted. "Thoth and Ra are already downstairs, aren't they?"

"Of course, Grandmama," Audrey confirmed.

As she passed her, Felicity attempted to smile at the young woman. The girl's cheeks flushed as she hurried away, her eyes on the floor, but it didn't matter. There would be ample time for proper introductions with all family members later.

Miss Hartley approached the table carrying a tray with an unusual collection of items. There was a feather, a dark mirror with a burnished brass frame, and a porcelain bowl filled with water. Miss Hartley smiled warmly as she gestured Felicity to a seat.

"May I ask what's going on?" asked Felicity quietly as she sat and tucked Pip onto her lap.

"The Reverend One wishes to contact the other side," said Miss Hartley cheerily but in equally low tones as she set the tray of items on the table.

The Reverend One?

Felicity swallowed. She felt a sudden chill. Her brother had mentioned Winnifred's interest in spiritualist practices, but she hadn't expected to be thrust into them so quickly. And certainly not without any introduction or warning.

A gentleman with wire-framed spectacles and a pointed grey beard approached the table. His frock coat and button boots, though well-maintained, belonged to another era.

"Not like that," he murmured to Miss Hartley, gently adjusting the feather's position.

Miss Hartley giggled. "Oh, Mr Silkstede. Where would we be without your expertise?"

"Heaven forbid I should take any credit," he said, doing precisely that. He turned to Felicity with a satisfied smile. "Please, no need to stand, your ladyship. Mr Jeffrey Silkstede at your service." He offered a slight bow.

"How do you do, Mr Silkstede? Are you also one of my great-aunt's assistants?" The question was perhaps a little forward, but Felicity was becoming rather desperate for information about what exactly was going on.

"Erm." The fellow hesitated, wincing slightly. "I'm actually collaborating with the dowager baroness — your great-aunt — on her latest book." He stroked his beard, his self-assurance restored. "I expect you're familiar with her works?"

"I'm afraid not." Goodness, Felicity's brother had been extremely lean on detail when sharing what he knew about Winnifred and her tribe. Either that or Jasper simply hadn't been aware himself.

"Aha," said Mr Silkstede, his eyes brightening. "So I deduce that you're not a spiritualist. Otherwise you would surely have a tome or two by the dowager baroness on your shelves." He chuckled a little, glancing over his shoulder for Winnifred's reaction. "We all do."

Winnifred showed no acknowledgment of Mr Silkstede's fawning. She stood before an ornate basin on a small hexagonal table, carefully removing her rings and bracelets before she washed her hands. The candlelight revealed faint scarring along her right wrist, which was quickly recovered by her flowing sleeve.

Felicity stroked Pip's back, the little dog a reassuring presence amid the strange surroundings. "I'm indeed not a spiritualist."

Mrs Imrie approached, concern etching her pale features, her cheeks deep hollows in the candlelight. "You're not a spiritualist? Yet you're joining us this evening?" She glanced at the others. "Must we not ensure that we're surrounded only by receptive souls?"

"Mrs Imrie, really." Winnifred didn't look up as she replaced her jewellery. "How many times must I tell you? Such anxiety impedes communication with the other side."

Mrs Imrie blinked hard, her gaze darting accusingly towards Felicity. "Apologies, Reverend One."

The butler finished lighting the candles at the edges of the room. "Will that be all, m'lady?"

Winnifred nodded. "Thank you, Timpson."

As the servant departed, drawing a heavy velvet curtain across the doorway, Felicity found herself alone with Winnifred, Mr Silkstede, Mrs Imrie, and Miss Hartley. Pip was there physically, though the Yorkie had fallen asleep on Felicity's lap. A séance was clearly imminent — the setting impressively theatrical — and Felicity's participation was expected. She'd never attended such an event, though spiritualism had helped many cope with losses from the Great War.

She took a deep breath. This could be endured, couldn't it? Hopefully, Alex was having an easier time downstairs.

Mr Silkstede and Miss Hartley took their places while Mrs Imrie draped a gold-threaded shawl around Winnifred's shoulders. As they settled, Mrs Imrie struck a match and lit a cone of incense resting on a small silver dish at the side of the room, releasing a potent musk scent. A draught stirred the curtains and made the candle flames dance.

Winnifred inhaled sharply, bringing her fingertips to her forehead, her eyes closed. Everyone's attention went to the dowager baroness, including Pip's, the little dog having been awoken, nose twitching, by the powerful odour of the incense.

"Do we have the mirror of truth?" Winnifred's voice deepened dramatically.

"Yes, Reverend One," intoned her two helpers in unison.

"And the feather of Horus?"

"Yes, Reverend One."

"And has divine water been blessed and prepared so that I might see all there is to see?"

"Yes, Reverend One."

"Then we may begin." Winnifred extended her hands to her sides. The others followed suit. A circle of held hands was forming around the table.

Felicity hesitated. She could refuse to participate, but what would that accomplish? Her purpose was to mend a family rift, not to create new tensions.

She took the offered hands. Mrs Imrie's grip was bony and cool, while Mr Silkstede managed a touch that was properly respectful without being overly familiar.

It's theatre, Felicity told herself. *Nothing more.*

"Let us close our eyes," Winnifred commanded. "Let us seal ourselves from the human realm."

Felicity watched as all eyes closed around the table. She would have preferred to have kept her own open. The purpose of her visit was harmony, however, and she didn't wish to offend. She closed her eyes.

A sound between humming and groaning grew around the table. Mrs Imrie's grip tightened.

Shwush!

A sound like a sabre slicing through the air silenced the humming. Felicity peeked through one eye but saw only the gently swaying curtains and the séance participants, all perfectly still. Pip remained quiet in her lap, though his nose was twitching with enthusiasm.

She closed her eyes again.

"Lady Katherine. Are you there?" Winnifred's deepened voice warbled slightly.

There was a pause. "I am." The response came from somewhere beyond the table.

Felicity didn't recognise the voice, though it was distinctly female.

Someone in the room had to be a ventriloquist. Where had the response come from otherwise?

"I have with me your distant descendant, Lady Felicity Quick. Is she capable?"

Another pause. "She is."

"Thank you, Lady Katherine. Lady Elinor, are you there?"

Felicity opened one eye again slightly. There was no Elinor present — who would answer?

"I am." It was another female voice, from a slightly different location.

"Do you consider Lady Felicity Quick capable of upholding the traditions of Cullingslock?"

"I do," said the voice, but Felicity saw neither Mrs Imrie nor Miss Hartley's lips move even remotely. Perhaps there were speaking tubes hidden in the walls?

Pip chose that moment to spring from Felicity's lap towards one of the velvet curtains. She watched helplessly as he sniffed along its edge, where it touched the floor. Felicity couldn't call him back without disrupting the séance. The Yorkie seemed interested in something behind the heavy fabric. Hopefully, he wouldn't cause a scene.

"Lady Aphra, I sense your presence also," Winnifred continued.

Pip's ears perked up, and he turned towards a specific section of curtain, his head cocked curiously.

"Do you approve of our guest?"

A pause. "I do," came yet another distinct voice.

Were there hidden assistants? Perhaps even mechanical devices? There had to be a logical explanation for the disembodied voices. It was an impressive performance but a performance nonetheless.

Miss Hartley shifted, clearing her throat softly. Felicity quickly lowered her gaze, feigning closed eyes. The puzzle of the voices was one thing. But who were Katherine, Elinor, and Aphra? Felicity would ask her great-aunt just as soon as she got the chance.

Humm, humm, ha. Humm, humm, ha.

The two assistants began chanting. It went on for an

uncomfortably long time, long enough for Pip to make his way towards the curtain at the entrance to the room. If he slipped out and got lost in the castle's countless stairways and corridors, it might be days before anyone found him again.

Shwush!

The same air-cutting sabre sound repeated itself, though Felicity couldn't see where it came from. Thankfully, however, it distracted Pip from making an escape from the room.

Winnifred's eyes opened, her bright blue gaze focused intensely on Felicity.

Felicity smiled weakly. Had she been found out? Was peeking at a séance such a terrible offence?

"I have made my decision," intoned Winnifred, her voice less theatrical now.

The circle of hands around the table was released. The assistants and Mr Silkstede mumbled their approval.

Felicity stood up and moved swiftly to collect Pip. "What decision would that be, Great-Aunt?" Unless she had misunderstood, it wasn't up to Winnifred what happened to the land. The dowager baroness was merely the trustee. It was up to Felicity whether she wished to follow the ancient tradition and become the owner of the Cullingslock Wastes.

Winnifred's smile was warm, almost indulgent. "I'm afraid I've tired myself, my child. I shall make my announcement tomorrow."

"Very good, Reverend One," said Mrs Imrie, nodding.

"We support your decision," added Miss Hartley, "whatever it may be."

Felicity opened her mouth, about to ask for further clarification, but Winnifred cut her off with a wave of her palm.

"Tomorrow at lunch, my child."

Chapter Three

The séance finished late, and most of the house had already gone to bed. With the footman and butler waiting with flickering candles to show Felicity and Alex their way to their separate chambers, there wouldn't be much opportunity for a discussion until the following morning.

Eager to exchange impressions with Alex, Felicity rose early. She donned a cotton day dress in pale lilac with delicate embroidery at the collar and cuffs, pairing it with sensible cream walking shoes and a light cardigan against the morning chill that lingered in the castle's many miles of ancient corridors. On her first attempt to locate Alex, the labyrinth of the castle got the better of her, but in a sunny hallway lined with framed etchings and floating with dust motes that danced like fairies in the slanting light, Felicity came across a woman of about forty with long reddish hair, slender features, and a white apron.

Felicity asked if the woman, presumably some member of the household staff, knew where she might find the guest rooms in which Alex was staying.

"Did you have breakfast yet?" The woman's tone carried a heavy dose of weary resignation.

Felicity hesitated for a second, a little confused about having her question answered with a question. "I hoped Mr Cooper and I might take my dog for a walk before the first meal of the day," she said as Pip wiggled under her arm.

The woman smiled with something between amusement and irritation. "The breakfast room ceiling was damaged by a water leak back in the spring, and it hasn't been fixed yet. Perhaps it never will be. In any case, breakfast has been served in our rooms ever since." The woman continued along the passageway, her footsteps echoing softly against the worn stone floor. "If you're keen to eat before starting the day, I would suggest you return to your room. Otherwise you might miss it."

"But might you still tell me..." began Felicity, but the woman continued briskly onward without looking back.

A sensation prickled uncomfortably at the nape of Felicity's neck. She gave herself a little shake. There was no need to overreact. The woman's brusqueness could be due to a myriad of factors unrelated to the encounter with Felicity.

Still unable to find her way to Alex, Felicity located a patch of outside space overgrown with coarse grasses and surrounded by crenellations jutting from the castle's high walls like broken teeth. After Pip went about his business, she found her way back to her room, where she waited for an absolute age before the elfin-eared footman arrived with her breakfast on a tray.

Felicity's reaction was swift.

She wrapped several pieces of toast and multiple rashers of bacon in a napkin before the servant could even set the tray down, then insisted the footman bring her to where Alex was staying. They followed winding passageways and narrow stairs, past dozens of framed photographs and prints and the occasional suit of armour half-collapsed in shadowy alcoves.

The footman paused before a studded door with an iron ring pull. "This is Mr Cooper's room, your ladyship."

Felicity summoned Alex with a rapid knock, unafraid of waking him because it was now mid-morning, and she was more than desperate to share her thoughts with someone other than herself.

"Did you sleep well?" asked Felicity as Alex pulled on a

lightweight jacket of soft brown tweed that complemented his fair colouring and spread across his broad shoulders perfectly.

"No," he said flatly, some of yesterday's buoyancy gone from his voice as he placed a straw Panama on his slicked blond hair, adjusting it until it sat at just the right angle. "Barely a wink."

"Me neither." Felicity turned to the slightly nervous young footman who had continued to linger in the corridor, awaiting further instruction. "Mr Cooper and I wish to take my dog for a stroll in the grounds. Where would be an appropriate location for such an outing?"

Navigating yet more twisty staircases and long corridors spread with Persian runners of varying stages of threadbareness, the footman brought Felicity and Alex back to the castle's front entrance and opened the doors of the grand arched entryway. The surrounding trees were lit by the pale morning sunshine, and the intense twittering of birds filled the air as cool, earth-scented dampness rose from the grass beyond the gravel forecourt. With Pip leading the way, Felicity and Alex headed for the trees and created enough distance from the castle to offer an amount of privacy, at least in terms of being overheard. The castle's many windows meant they were certainly overlooked.

Felicity was careful about her facial expressions as she relayed her experiences with Winnifred and her spiritualist supporters from the evening before. A night's sleep hadn't done much to ease the growing feeling that her brother had perhaps been right when he'd advised her to stay at Bradley Court and to allow the matter of the Cullingslock Wastes to be arranged via each party's respective solicitor.

Alex already looked a little solemn from lack of sleep. As Felicity told him of her unwitting role in a séance in which her 'capabilities' were discussed with various spirits, his expression grew very grave indeed.

"That's going rather too far," he said, his jaw tightening with a protectiveness that warmed Felicity despite her own assessment that she had handled her first evening at Cullingslock rather well, all things considered.

They hung back as Pip sniffed intently at the base of a tall conifer.

"There seemed to be a relative of mine present, albeit only briefly." Felicity looked up at the treetops, which were silhouetted against the pale blue of the morning sky. "A young woman who called my great-aunt 'Grandmama', which I believe would make her my second cousin, although I can't say for certain. Sadly, we weren't introduced."

Alex found Felicity's hand, his warm fingers entwining with hers. "I met a character or two myself yesterday evening."

"Were they spiritualists, too?" asked Felicity, though she sincerely hoped not. She was almost desperate to hear something that would counter the creeping feeling that coming to Cullingslock Castle had been a mistake.

Alex shook his head. "Doesn't seem like it. I spoke to Winnifred's son — the tall fellow who caught Master Pip — and her daughter. They both live here at the castle. They each have a child. Winnifred's son has a wife that lives here with him. There's also some kind of estate manager who seems pretty integrated into the group." Alex lifted the brim of his hat and looked up at the swaying treetops. "I can't say I've made any firm friends yet. A couple of them were pleasant enough, but there was something of a chill in the air." A wry smile touched his lips. "Although there was a pleasing absence of outright hostility towards me."

"That's heartening." Though Felicity's mind had been preoccupied with the unnerving experience of the séance, that ordeal now lay behind her. The prospect of meeting the rest of the family loomed close. A flutter of excitement mixed with a knot of nervousness settled in her stomach.

"But then I'm not the one who might claim the castle's land, am I?" Alex's dark blue gaze was calm and honest. He wasn't the sort who sweet-talked and offered reassurance when there was none to be had, and Felicity appreciated that. But she wasn't keen on the idea of returning to Bradley Court earlier than expected. Missing the chance to reconnect with family would be one thing. Her brother's smugness over the soundness of his advice would be quite something else.

"I shall make my intentions clear as soon as is appropriate," said Felicity. "No contracts have been signed yet."

"Funny you should mention contracts. Winnifred's solicitor is in attendance, as well."

"Really?" Felicity still struggled to understand how Winnifred's priority for her great-niece's visit had been to involve her in a séance.

There was a rustling in the undergrowth ahead. Perhaps a mouse or a vole. Pip had noticed it too. Before the little dog could dash away in joyful yet ultimately disappointing pursuit, Felicity scooped the terrier under her arm, his fur moist from the wet grass against her lilac dress. A damp patch, however, was the least of the matters on her mind.

"I wouldn't mind a word with the solicitor."

"Not a terrible idea," agreed Alex.

"Ideally, before I meet the family." Felicity met Alex's gaze with determination. "And certainly before Great-Aunt Winnifred makes any announcement over lunch."

Chapter Four

Wishing to speak with the solicitor was one thing. Locating him was another matter entirely. It was only after an appeal to the castle's butler that Felicity, Alex, and Pip were brought directly to him.

The solicitor was a portly gentleman with thinning grey hair slicked with excessive pomade. He sported a rumpled three-piece suit and circular wire-rimmed spectacles perched on a bulbous nose. He lounged with a cigar and a crystal tumbler in what the butler had referred to as the castle's library, its large bay window offering a view across treetops touched by golden sunshine. Though the library may have once been impressive, many of the oak shelves now stood empty.

"Burned." The solicitor rose from his battered armchair, its leather cracking in protest as he shifted his considerable weight. "One terrible winter last century. Cut off by heavy snow. It was that or freeze to death. The dowager baroness has attempted to replenish the shelves, which will become apparent if you look closely. All that mumbo jumbo stuff, of course."

Felicity and Alex continued to peruse the shelves as Pip sniffed the library's faded carpet. The scattered tomes were indeed mainly on the topic of spiritualism. Among them, positioned with apparent pride of place, were multiple copies of books with *Lady Winnifred*

Cullingslock given as the author. Their titles included *Whispers from Beyond the Curtain*, *Thoughts on the Invisible World*, *Our Boys Beyond the Veil*, and *He Still Walks With Me*. On one of the shelves stood a framed photograph of a younger Winnifred in an ornate Egyptian-inspired costume and thick make-up on what might have been a theatre stage, her eyes closed and her arms outstretched, as if summoning spirits from beyond.

The solicitor gave a little gasp, followed by a poorly suppressed hiccough. "Apologies. I spoke too quickly."

Felicity waved a gentle hand. "You've not offended me. Indeed, I appreciate your candour, Mr...?"

"Pope. Mr Brian Pope at your service, your ladyship," he replied with a slight bow that made his watch chain jingle against his substantial middle.

Unlike Mr Silkstede, who had offered his services the night before, Mr Pope was actually someone from whose expertise Felicity could benefit.

She folded her arms across her chest. "Are you here to assist with the matter of the Cullingslock Wastes and the 1642 settlement?"

Mr Pope nodded enthusiastically. "Exactly that. Thankfully, the entailment itself was kept at our offices, otherwise it might also have been thrown on the fire."

Alex glanced at the table with the cigar still smoking in the ashtray and the empty crystal tumbler. "Is it usual for a solicitor to be entertained as a guest by his client?" Alex's directness was essential for his work as an investigative journalist. Such candour could be less helpful in social situations, but on this occasion, his challenge was valid.

The solicitor chuckled. "The castle is rather remote, as you may already have noticed, and the dowager baroness and her family are long-standing and highly valued customers of my practice. Admittedly, a busy man such as myself benefits from a rest now and then. All work and no play and all that." His eyes drifted momentarily to the empty tumbler with barely concealed longing.

"I've several questions about the Cullingslock Wastes, if I may," asked Felicity as Alex came to stand beside her. "I've heard some information from my brother, who received the details from my father ahead of his passing not long after the war. It was, however, my mother who had the direct line to the Cullingslocks. She passed when I was just an infant, so my understanding of the situation may not be complete."

"Please, your ladyship. I am here to help."

"I'm not obliged to take on the land, am I?"

The solicitor gave a little frown. "Of course not."

"And what would happen to the Wastes if I didn't take them on?"

"Well, nothing at all. It would remain in trust with your great-aunt as the trustee. Matters would continue very much as they do now."

"And how is it that matters continue now?" asked Alex, watching Pip out of the corner of his eye as the Yorkie approached the library's slightly tattered damask curtains.

"Mr Kemp — whom you met yesterday, Mr Cooper — sees to the running of the lands and the dowager baroness, as specified in the entailment, looks after the proceeds." Mr Pope knowingly arched his eyebrow. "Not that there are many proceeds of which to speak. Although Mr Kemp is rather a confident gentleman." His tone was low, as if speaking in confidence to just Alex. "Especially around the ladies, if you take my meaning."

"Mr Kemp is the estate's manager?" Felicity was certain neither she nor Alex had any interest in the personal commentary Mr Pope wished to relay about the fellow.

"His focus is on the land rather than the castle, so he's referred to as a 'land agent', but he's certainly a manager of sorts." The solicitor cast a glance over the empty library shelves. "And if the castle were to fall under his remit as well, then things might look a little different around here."

It was an intriguing remark, but the solicitor's opinions on the land agent were off-topic in terms of what Felicity wished to have settled before lunch, which was fast approaching given the late start to the day.

"My great-aunt — the dowager baroness — said yesterday that she would make an announcement at lunchtime, yet the settling of the land is not her decision to make if I understand correctly?" Felicity's tone was gently insistent.

"You understand correctly, your ladyship."

Felicity glanced at Alex. She was starting to feel more at ease, increasingly reassured marriage wouldn't saddle her with the burden of landownership on top of an already well-occupied life.

"It's a family tradition," continued Mr Pope, a professional demeanour displacing his earlier relaxed attitude. "It's well-established in legal documents, with a trust and contracts dating back to 1642, as you rightly pointed out. But you cannot be forced to become the land's owner."

Had Felicity encountered a relative or two from that particular time period at the séance yesterday evening? She chased the thought from her mind. Of course she hadn't. It had been a theatrical performance. Nothing more. What mattered was that her position on the Wastes could be swiftly and clearly established, leaving ample room for the building of bridges between family members.

Alex frowned a little as Pip pawed at the damask in order to slip behind the curtains. "Might you know why the land is called 'the Wastes'?"

"Pah. Mr Kemp might have you believe otherwise, but the land is as good as worthless."

Felicity returned her attention to the sparsely populated bookshelves. "Are you aware of any documents detailing the family history that I might peruse?"

The solicitor shook his head slowly. "As I said, the contents of the library were entirely burned some hundred years ago. You would need to speak to your family members for their view on the lineage. The dowager baroness is not as strong as she used to be, of course, but her memory for family matters remains quite remarkable."

Felicity turned to look at Alex. He raised his brow encouragingly. Not being in any way obliged to take on the land rather simplified matters, although Felicity felt a pang of disappointment that there was no documentation about the family tree. But one mustn't be greedy. There were still living relatives at the castle she was yet to meet.

The solicitor steepled his fingers before him in a gesture of polite interest. "Do I understand, your ladyship, that you are erring on the side of turning down the opportunity to take on the land from the trust?"

"I wish to speak to my great-aunt before luncheon," was all Felicity would say in reply. It wasn't right to share her position with the solicitor before discussing matters with Winnifred. And despite the discomfort she'd endured at the séance, Felicity had no desire for her great-aunt to embarrass herself at lunch.

Chapter Five

"I'm afraid that won't be possible, your ladyship."

That was the butler's answer to Felicity's request for an audience with her great-aunt ahead of lunch, his waxed moustache quivering with dutiful rigidity.

They were in the great entrance hall with its medieval chandelier, the candles unlit as sunlight streamed through the high windows, casting elongated diamonds of light across the worn flagstones. The castle's residents were beginning to gather, awaiting the luncheon gong, their voices creating a gentle murmur that echoed against the stone walls.

Felicity gripped Pip tightly to her chest and kept her tone low. "But the dowager baroness said last night that she would make an announcement at luncheon. I have information that might affect that announcement—" She lowered her voice further. "—and the last thing I want is for my great-aunt to be undermined in any way."

A flicker of discomfort in the butler's features indicated Felicity had chosen the right angle of attack. Timpson was clearly unflinchingly loyal.

"I'm afraid I am under strict instructions to protect my mistress's peace until the gong," he replied with quiet firmness, adding after a moment's hesitation, "The dowager baroness finds mornings particularly taxing on her constitution."

Felicity nodded. She could push no further, but it meant there was a rather awkward moment to come in the dining room. The prospect of publicly contradicting her great-aunt — with whom Felicity had only recently made acquaintance — tightened her chest with etiquette-related dread.

As the butler withdrew to continue the preparations for lunch, Felicity swept away a curl that had fallen across her forehead. "I suppose I should at least introduce myself to my relatives," she said quietly to Alex, "before making a scene at the dining table."

"Understandable." Alex's one-word answer conveyed both sympathy and a touch of the dry humour that had first drawn Felicity to him.

The freckled girl with reddish hair seen in the tower room prior to the séance loitered near the dining room doors, which were closed. On a lacquered cabinet beside her perched a pair of identical cats with long smoke-grey fur. One of the felines had its eyes blissfully closed as the girl tickled it under the chin. Though sturdily built, the young woman's movements had a gentle grace.

As Felicity approached with Alex, the girl sharply turned her attention away from the cats and blinked at the guests, a mixture of wariness and wonder in her eyes.

Felicity offered a warm smile. "You're Miss Audrey, are you not?"

The girl continued to blink, her long lashes almost touching her freckled cheeks. "I am." Her voice was soft and clear. It was also nothing like any of the disembodied voices heard during the séance.

"We met awfully briefly yesterday evening and haven't yet been properly introduced. I'm Lady Felicity Quick." Such formalities might seem unnecessary to a young girl, but Felicity was determined to establish a sound connection with this newfound relative.

The girl nodded eagerly, a flush of pink appearing beneath her freckles. "I know who you are."

"This is my companion, Mr Alexander Cooper," Felicity continued, gesturing towards Alex, who gave a little bow of greeting.

The light caught his dark blond hair as he moved, giving him a golden appearance that reminded Felicity how her own grandmother occasionally referred to him as 'that handsome young man' rather than by his name.

"And who is this?" The girl extended her hand to where Pip was tucked under Felicity's elbow, so that the little dog could sniff her fingers.

"Oh." While the Yorkie had been a companion on many adventures, Felicity wasn't accustomed to introducing him. "This is Pip."

"Master Pip," added Alex, the corners of his eyes crinkling with amusement.

Pip licked Audrey's finger, his tail wagging with enthusiastic approval. Audrey giggled.

"He seems to like you. He can be a little choosy about his friends." Felicity eyed Alex, remembering Pip's indifferent first impression of him.

Sssshhh!

One of the cats arched its back and hissed at Pip, its smoky fur standing on end like a miniature thundercloud.

"Thoth, do be nice." Audrey reached into her pocket, then held out her hand to the irritated feline. The cat's attention went immediately to the girl's palm, its arched back relaxing.

Felicity smiled. "Is the other named Ra?" The mention of the deities had been one of the many oddities at last night's séance. Egyptian gods seemed a peculiar choice for household pets, though perhaps not surprising in a home like Cullingslock.

Audrey nodded and smiled affectionately at the cats, reaching out to further calm the irritated Thoth while Ra sat in a ball, his eyes almost closed. "I'm sure they do their best, but I'm afraid they don't always live up to their divine namesakes."

"May I know your full name?" Felicity felt both charmed by and curious about her young relative.

Audrey looked at Felicity with wide eyes, as if surprised someone would be interested in her.

"Her full name is Miss Audrey Beatrix Brand."

Felicity turned. The aproned woman she'd encountered earlier that morning and who had informed her about the castle's breakfast rituals was approaching, though she no longer had an apron tied at her waist. She wore a sophisticated dropped-waist dress in sapphire blue with a thin belt of navy ribbon. Her reddish hair, which was precisely the same shade as Audrey's, was swept into an elegant twist at the nape of her neck, though a few rebellious tendrils had escaped to frame the woman's slender, faintly freckled features.

"And Audrey is my daughter." She placed a hand on the girl's sturdy shoulder. Aside from their colouring, the pair were rather unalike, the mother slim and of average height, the daughter sturdily built and a little taller than her mother.

Felicity's stomach sank like a stone. "You're my great-aunt's daughter?"

A smile played on the woman's lips as she extended a hand, shaking both Felicity's and Alex's in greeting. "That's right. I'm Elfrida. Elfrida Brand, although I used to be a Cullingslock. And I believe we're first cousins once removed, your ladyship." There was a lively intelligence in her eyes and no trace of ill-feeling.

It did nothing to prevent a flush of embarrassment from warming Felicity's cheeks. "Heavens. Do call me Felicity, although I've doubtlessly made a horrid first impression on you. When I came across you in the corridor earlier this morning, I simply assumed you were a member of the household staff."

Elfrida sighed. "An understandable mistake. And I'm sorry that I wasn't in the right frame of mind to introduce myself properly. We haven't truly had time to make impressions on one another, good or bad, wouldn't you say? Although I've no doubt my mother has already made quite an impact on you. Actually, my money would've been on you not making it through the night. When I saw that sweet little white car of yours still parked on the drive this morning, I thought now that's a lady with some gumption." Though decidedly dry, there was a warmth and openness to Elfrida's manner. It was an enormous relief not to have made a terrible first impression on her.

"Felicity has no shortage of gumption," agreed Alex a little cheekily and with a dash of pride.

"Ah," said Elfrida. "A man who can appreciate a woman's strength. Such a rare thing."

"Please," said Felicity, combining a smile and a frown as she looked between Elfrida and Alex. "Great-Aunt Winnifred has done her best to make me feel welcome."

Elfrida raised a doubtful eyebrow. "That's kind of you to think so."

Audrey was half-watching the conversation, though she was rather distracted by Pip, whose small body was wriggling under Felicity's arm with the determination of a prisoner set on escape. Before he could succeed in breaking free, Thoth and Ra jumped down from the cabinet and slunk off in the direction of the stairs, smoky tails held high.

Audrey reached out and touched Pip's paw. The gesture seemed to calm him.

Felicity saw an opportunity. "Might you like to hold Master Pip?"

The girl's eyes sparkled with excitement. "May I?"

As Felicity gratefully slipped the restless Yorkie into the girl's arms, the little dog lifted his nose to rub his cheek against hers. It was something close to love at first sight between the pair.

"As you've already noticed," said Elfrida wearily but with affection, "Audrey is utterly crazy about animals. But if I may nudge us onto another topic—" She tipped her head. "—may I be so bold as to enquire what brought you to visit us here at Cullingslock?"

Felicity glanced at Alex. They exchanged smiles, Felicity's more nervous than her beau's. "The trigger is that Mr Cooper and I are intent on marriage."

Elfrida lifted an eyebrow, her face otherwise composed. "Congratulations."

"Thank you." Felicity felt a little flustered. She wished to make a good impression, but were there misgivings in the household regarding her right to the Cullingslock Wastes? "Because my nuptials are planned to take place before my older brother finds himself a bride—"

"Oh, yes." Elfrida waved a hand. "I know all that. I also know you're rather in demand as both a journalist and a detective — far be it upon any woman in our lineage to choose a 'normal' path through life. What I don't understand is why you didn't allow your solicitor to take care of the issue on your behalf?"

Felicity's forehead creased. Had she really made a mistake by coming to the castle? As much as she would have liked to have enquired about the paths chosen by her female ancestors, Elfrida's challenge had to be answered.

"I imagined it might be a nice opportunity to rebuild the connection between our family down at Bradley Court and the household here at Cullingslock."

"Oh, really?" Elfrida looked genuinely surprised. "That's rather brave of you." Lifting her chin, she raised her arm and made a beckoning motion. "Say, you didn't meet my brother yet, did you?" She beckoned ever more insistently, the exasperation in her expression growing.

"Actually, I did." Felicity turned to see to whom Elfrida was signalling. "Albeit rather briefly," she added quietly, her introduction at the castle having been anything but standard thus far.

"Ah. Tristan." Elfrida folded her arms over her chest and gave a narrow-eyed smile. "How kind of you to join us at last."

The man Elfrida was addressing was the same Tristan to whom Felicity had been fleetingly introduced while on her way to the séance. His reddish hair was the same colour as Elfrida's and her daughter's, though it was paler and thinner. He was dressed in a lightweight linen suit, a cravat tied loosely at his neck, his long awkward arms pressed in at his sides. He would not have looked out of place in a college quadrangle in Oxford or Cambridge.

He lifted a hand and gave Felicity and Alex an awkward little wave, his long fingers fluttering briefly before retreating to the safety of his trouser pocket. "Hullo again."

At the man's side was Solomon, the black-and-white Border

Collie for whom Pip had developed a fondness the evening before. The dog's ears and eyes were bright with interest towards the Yorkie now in Audrey's arms, but he remained seated calmly at his master's side. Pip, meanwhile, was entirely distracted by Audrey, who was now cradling the little dog on his back and whispering endearments.

"Shouldn't you be in the lead in entertaining our guests?" Elfrida's eyes danced with mischief. "You are the lord of this splendid manor, after all."

"Now." Tristan's Adam's apple bobbed, and he rubbed the back of his neck. "Well, yes. But that's not actually—"

"Lady Felicity." Philippa was advancing towards them dressed in a suit of navy twill with a cream silk blouse, a young gentleman of barely eighteen in tow. "How pleasing to see you again. May I introduce my son?"

The young man stepped forward and offered a broad-palmed hand. He was as tall as Tristan but with wider shoulders and a powerful aura more similar to that of his mother. He had the same reddish hair as Tristan, Elfrida, and Audrey, and an incredibly upright posture, his shoulders squared beneath a set of lightweight tweeds. Freckles dappled his long, elegant nose. His expression was serious.

"How do you do, your ladyship?" The depth of his voice gave it an effortless weight.

"Please, there's no need for formalities." Felicity smiled at the young man. She had now made the acquaintance of two second cousins, two first cousins once removed, and one great-aunt, all of whom she'd not even known existed until just a few weeks ago. It warmed her to envisage an increased number of guests at her and Alex's wedding.

"Oh, I think Philippa rather enjoys the formalities," said Elfrida, needling her sister-in-law somewhat. "Don't you, Baroness?"

Philippa didn't look at Elfrida. "Peregrine is about to enter Sandhurst," she said, blazing with pride.

"How splendid," said Felicity as Alex nodded his acknowledgement of the achievement. Gaining a place at the prestigious military college was quite something. Philippa had every right to be proud.

"I say." Tristan smiled tentatively but again, touching the back of his neck. "If you would like a tour of the land that's to be yours, then I would be more than happy to show you around."

"On the matter of the land—" began Felicity, but her attempt to clarify was cut short.

Elfrida addressed her brother, her brow pinched. "You're not going gallivanting across the wilderness before Felicity has had a thorough tour of the castle. Or what's left of it, in any case."

Philippa laughed, though it sounded somewhat forced. "Come now, you make it sound as if we live in a pile of ruins."

Elfrida cocked her head. "Have you not visited the East Wing recently?"

"A tour of the land, you say?"

The booming voice caused everyone to turn.

Striding across the entrance hall was a powerfully built yet elegant fellow dressed in a rough tweed jacket, tan breeches, and sturdy boots. His ruddy complexion suggested long hours in the open air, though his full head of thick brown hair showed no sign of discolouration from the sun. Trotting at his side on a rather tight lead was an Old English Sheepdog with flowing white and grey fur, its eyes obscured by a long fringe. Its mouth was open, tongue pink and lolling, the creature panting as though having just come in from a run.

"I would be more than happy to lead such a tour. We've met, haven't we?" The fellow stopped before Felicity and thrust his hand in her direction, the palm calloused and the grip unnervingly firm. "Harry Kemp, land agent. At your service." The introduction was delivered with the self-assurance of a man who considered himself indispensable.

"I believe we're only being introduced just now." Felicity's tone was polite, but she had little need for anyone's service, despite being offered it by Mr Silkstede, Mr Pope, and now Mr Kemp.

"I work for the dowager baroness, but I understand you'll be the new owner of the land I oversee," continued Mr Kemp. "I would, therefore, be extremely interested in explaining matters to you." His smile flashed bright white, creating a startling contrast to his weather-beaten face. "There's an awful lot of potential out there."

Felicity glanced at Alex. How much explaining would a tract distinguished as 'wastes' possibly need? While it was quite wonderful to meet the household, especially her relatives, there was an issue that needed nipping in the bud before matters got out of hand.

"About my claim on the land," Felicity began, preparing to untangle the misunderstanding with as much delicacy as she could muster.

"I do think Mr Kemp is best placed to explain matters to you, your ladyship." Philippa gazed with dark-eyed intensity at the land agent and Felicity. "Isn't that right, Tristan?"

"Well, I was thinking," began Tristan. "Ought we not—"

"Splendid." Elfrida clapped her hands. "So we're getting into this rather thorny territory even before lunch. I, however, remain firm in my position that it makes sense for Felicity to understand the castle before seeing the land."

"You're inheriting the castle?" The land agent frowned at Felicity.

"Goodness, no." Felicity tried to keep her tone light, though she felt rather like a tennis ball being batted between increasingly determined players. "And as for the land, nothing has yet been—"

Bonnnngggg!

The gong in the hall's corner had been struck with the force of a battering ram. Pip and Mr Kemp's Old English Sheepdog whimpered as the air reverberated with the wobbling, echoing sound. Standing beside the instrument with the mallet in her hand was a decrepit-looking woman in a white cook's cap.

"Lunch is served," she called out in a strong North Devon accent as she hung the mallet back in its place and shuffled towards the baize-covered swing door connecting to the staff corridors.

As the gathering redirected itself towards the dining room doorway, Felicity's opportunity to make a statement about her lack of desire to take over the land had come to nought. Her stomach tightened at the idea of Winnifred's announcement.

Alex gently squeezed Felicity's hand as they followed the family group and the land agent into the dining room. "As long as you know yourself what it is you want, then everything will fall into place."

"I'm certain that I wish to marry you," she whispered to Alex, firming her grip on his palm, "and I should like to establish bonds with my newfound relatives, if possible."

"But you're worried about making a scene over lunch?" There was a hint of amusement in Alex's tone.

"It can irritate that you know me so well."

Alex briefly brought Felicity's hand to his mouth and kissed it. "You knew it wouldn't be easy coming here. You can rise to the challenge."

Felicity took a deep breath. She dearly wished to believe him.

Chapter Six

Lunch at Cullingslock was served beneath a hammer-beamed ceiling darkened by centuries of smoke from a large granite-framed hearth. With the fire unlit and despite the sunshine outside, a chill cooled the air, which was scented with a blend of beeswax and the musty smell of old stone. At the far end of the hall, a silver-banded shepherd's crook stood propped beside a squat figurine with outstretched arms, its eyes inlaid with turquoise, incongruous against a backdrop of medieval England.

At the head of the long polished table sat Great-Aunt Winnifred, Mrs Imrie and Miss Hartley flanking her like devoted sentries. Seated beside Miss Hartley, Mr Silkstede bent over his notebook, a hand stroking his pointed beard as he wrote. Mr Pope, the solicitor, who had the seat next to Mrs Imrie, nursed a dose of amber liquid in his crystal tumbler. The rest of the party found their places with ease, the Border Collie and Old English Sheepdog settling beside their masters, Pip curled contentedly in Audrey's lap. The butler and footman moved with quiet efficiency at the sideboard.

As everyone took their seats, Felicity approached Winnifred. She would whisper in her ear for a private word, then deliver to her the news that she would not be taking on the land. That would save

Winnifred from the embarrassment of making an announcement Felicity would have to contradict. But as Felicity arrived at the head of the table, Winnifred took the hands of Mrs Imrie and Miss Hartley, and the three women began softly chanting, their heads bowed. The rest of the diners continued as if nothing odd was going on.

As Felicity returned to her seat, Alex leaned in, his tone gentle. "You've navigated situations more awkward than this. And this will soon be over."

Felicity gave him a brave smile. He was right, of course. He usually was.

The chanting ceased with the serving of the first course. The simple celery soup had a fresh green aroma and was well-prepared but plainly presented, served in matching white porcelain bowls with little adornment. Felicity and Alex were seated close to Tristan, his wife, and the land agent. They chatted about the contrasts between South and North Devon — the south with its gentle hills and red earth, the north wilder, with moorland and a rugged coast — and between London and the countryside, the city crowded and grimy but rich in culture and opportunity, the countryside cleaner and healthier, if a little old-fashioned.

It was all pleasant enough, although rather superficial, which was understandable seeing as Felicity and Alex were just getting to know everyone. As the main course of roasted leg of lamb with a thin mint sauce and carrots arrived, Mr Kemp seemed to have grown in comfort and confidence in the group and had no qualms about dominating the conversation, which was a pity. Felicity would have liked to have heard more from her first cousin once removed.

"Flock's looking healthy," said the land agent as he carved into the meat on his plate. "Should be an excellent clip. I'm expecting very good returns, even with wool prices being what they are these days. The tenant farmers are a stubborn lot. Trying to get them to turn over a few acres to field beans or beet can be like getting blood out of a stone. But if the yields come in as expected, they'll not be grumbling for long."

Philippa listened intently as Alex tucked into his meal and Felicity kept watch from a distance on Winnifred. She considered leaving her seat and attempting another private conversation, but the scene would then be of Felicity's making. And how might that affect her chances of building bridges with the household?

"And you're expecting to make a profit this year, are you not?" Philippa's eyes were bright with interest.

Mr Kemp nodded as he chewed on his meat. "There's money to be made on the estate, that's for certain."

"There's not quite as much heather this year though, is there?" said Tristan quietly, his eyes dipped to his plate.

Felicity caught her great-aunt's gaze. She smiled warmly at Felicity and closed her eyes slowly, like a contented cat. Felicity returned the smile, though a vague nervousness clutched at her stomach. By the end of the meal, the awkwardness would have passed. There was at least that to look forward to.

"Heather doesn't make money, does it?" Mr Kemp carved off another slice of lamb. "Then there's the hunt later this month. It's rather a big event. Not just for Cullingslock but the whole area."

"Is the land making money, then?" asked Alex between bites of lamb.

"Is it?" The estate manager spluttered sarcastically. "It'll soon be making even more money now than it did during the war, when the government was purchasing any resources that weren't nailed down."

Felicity's attention was suddenly firmly back on her end of the table.

"It's not making money now, though, is it?" pressed Alex.

"Enough to cover expenses," replied the land agent. "But it'll very soon be far more than that."

Alex subtly raised an eyebrow in Felicity's direction. Jasper had told her that the land was worthless. The term 'wastes' had also supported the assessment, as the solicitor had underlined. Had she arrived at the castle with some significant misapprehensions?

"Quite the windfall for you, your ladyship." Mr Kemp grinned as he tucked heartily into his meat.

Felicity frowned a little. She remained quiet as she considered the new information. Even with potential profits, Felicity still wasn't interested in owning land. Was she?

Philippa, who was seated beside her son, grimaced. "Why would it be a windfall for Lady Felicity?"

Tristan sighed deeply.

Philippa looked between her husband and the land agent. "Is there something I'm missing?"

"I believe there's been a misunderstanding," said Felicity. "I should like to clarify that—"

Ting-ting-ting!

Miss Hartley tapped her glass to gain the room's attention. As the butler and footman cleared the plates from the main course, Winnifred rose steadily from her seat.

It was too late. It was happening.

Philippa turned worried eyes on Felicity, but Felicity could say no more. She smiled apologetically. It was time for Winnifred's announcement.

"Friends," she began, looking warmly at the spiritualists seated closest to her. The solicitor also seemed to be captured in this address. "Relatives," she said, looking at Elfrida and Tristan and their families. Elfrida appeared slightly bored. Audrey's attention was mainly on Pip, who seemed thoroughly contented with his new friend. Philippa was beginning to look alarmed, her gaze seeking her husband's, but Tristan kept his eyes on the table as if embarrassed. Their son had a calm, almost blank expression.

"As you will have noticed, there are guests among us." Winnifred held out a bejewelled hand in Felicity's direction. "This is Lady Felicity Quick. She is the daughter of my niece. And beside her is seated Mr Alexander Cooper, a close companion of Lady Felicity's."

Felicity smiled as all eyes settled upon her and Alex. The introduction was a little tardy, but there seemed to be no quarrelling with Winnifred's way of doing things.

"Lady Felicity is with us because of an ancestral obligation." Winnifred's theatrical tone carried easily across the hushed dining hall. "The land surrounding our castle, the Cullingslock Wastes, has been held in trust since my dear husband departed for the other world. I am the land's current trustee."

"What exactly is going on?" Philippa's whisper was sharp. Her jaw clenched as Tristan leaned close, his shoulders curving inward. Whatever reassurance he mumbled into her ear failed to calm his wife's mounting agitation.

Further along the table, Elfrida propped her head on her knuckles while Audrey continued her fascination with Pip, her fingers creating cowlicks in his silky fur. The spiritualists remained serenely attentive, as though Winnifred's pronouncements held divine significance.

"For those unfamiliar with our arrangements," Winnifred continued with growing authority, "the trust ensures land ownership passes to female descendants when they marry ahead of elder male siblings. Our ancestors demonstrated remarkable foresight regarding feminine capability while maintaining practical necessity. This tradition originates from the Civil War, when diplomatic restraint prevented needless bloodshed in our district. At that crucial moment, the responsibility fell to Lady Katherine, the first female owner of the Wastes, whose wisdom preserved peace where her brother's rashness might have invited catastrophe."

Lady Katherine had been one of the names from the séance, but now was not the time for ancestral enquiries. Felicity's hands were gripped tight in her lap as she prepared herself. The stand she had to make against her great-aunt must be gentle and extremely polite.

Elfrida's fingers pressed against her temple with exaggerated despair. "Mother, if you could reach your point." Her whisper carried admirably.

Winnifred continued, unperturbed. "Though I descend from a different branch, having married into the Cullingslock family, I'm proud to say that Lady Katherine proved formidable, as have subsequent generations of women in the family. Lady Felicity herself exemplifies this tradition, given her widely acknowledged accomplishments as both a journalist and a detective."

Felicity continued to smile but shrank slightly. Public recognition remained her particular torment. Mr Kemp's hitherto stony expression transformed into obvious admiration. Even Elfrida's brow quirked. The spiritualists nodded with devoted approval while Mr Silkstede continued his industrious note-taking.

"As trustee, I must ensure traditional preservation and proper stewardship. Having conducted thorough investigation—" Winnifred gestured towards her assistants, who responded with more solemn nodding. "—Lady Felicity emerges as the ideal candidate. I shall therefore meet with Mr Pope this afternoon to complete the necessary documentation."

Mr Pope's eyes had drifted closed, but the solicitor startled awake at his name's mention. "Yes, yes. Of course. Yes."

Expressions around the table varied dramatically. Philippa's confusion and worry had crystallised into acute frustration, though her anger seemed directed more towards Tristan. Peregrine's brow creased slightly in his mother's direction.

Felicity couldn't fully assess all the reactions around the table. It was time to act.

She rose from her seat with determination. "Great-Aunt Winnifred, please excuse my interruption, but I've already consulted Mr Pope regarding this matter."

Winnifred raised an imperious hand. "I know, my child. I know everything."

Felicity rather doubted that claim. "I must reassure everyone that my intentions—"

"Please, resume your seat. Everything is proceeding according to plan."

"I fear a significant misunderstanding—"

"Please." Winnifred's voice became more commanding. "Do sit down, my child. Everything is exactly as it should be."

Felicity drew in a deep breath. It wasn't fair on the family to allow the misunderstanding to continue any further. It also wasn't fair on Felicity. "My apologies, Great-Aunt, but I would like to state clearly that I shall not accept the land. The decision is mine to take, as Mr Pope can confirm from our previous discussion."

Philippa's bewilderment deepened visibly. Tristan glanced upwards with obvious confusion.

Mr Kemp chuckled appreciatively. "Never a tedious moment."

"Well, that arrangement seems rather impossible," Elfrida observed to no one in particular.

Winnifred blinked once at Felicity, then glanced sharply towards Mr Pope. Quickly regaining her composure, she returned a gentle gaze to Felicity. "Please, my child, do sit. All shall be resolved satisfactorily."

Having delivered her declaration to a universally attentive audience, had Felicity not made herself clear? What more could she possibly do?

As Winnifred sat back down, Felicity, too, resumed her seat. Was the situation now resolved? The awkwardness seemed to have intensified rather than dissipated. She offered Alex an apologetic glance. Their expedition to Cullingslock Castle had perhaps been rather misguided.

Alex's warm hand found hers beneath the tablecloth as he leaned in to whisper in her ear. "At a minimum, no one shall forget your debut family luncheon for quite some time."

Felicity had to smile. He was right. And no one could force her signature onto any contract.

"Does this mean the land remains with the castle?" Philippa sounded hopeful, throwing the question to the whole table.

"It's never been with the castle," Elfrida muttered, though her brother remained quiet.

Felicity, at present, was ignorant of the trust's precise mechanisms. "I shall clarify matters with my great-aunt and Mr Pope directly after the meal. But I can assure you, it's not my intention to become the owner of any land, whether here on Exmoor or elsewhere."

Philippa put a hand to her chest and smiled at Felicity. She looked relieved, though rather drained.

A quiet word from the butler to Elfrida prompted both mother and daughter to rise. Audrey returned Pip with noticeable reluctance. "He has such a gentle soul," she said as she transferred the drowsy Yorkie back to Felicity's care.

"Thank you." The little dog whined quietly as Felicity placed him on her lap. "He certainly adores your company."

Mother and daughter withdrew from the dining hall, Elfrida's lips pressed into a line that suggested she had more to say but chose not to. Winnifred entered a hushed consultation with her devoted followers. Mr Kemp's attention focused on restraining his enthusiastic sheepdog, who seemed excited by Pip's presence. Tristan's Border Collie maintained discipline despite sharing the sheepdog's interest in the Yorkie.

Peregrine shook his head and placed a broad hand flat on the polished oak of the table. "I confess myself thoroughly bewildered," he announced in his resonant baritone.

"You possess considerable company in that sentiment," replied Felicity, "though I intend to swiftly remedy the confusion. Directly after lunch." There was still at least a dessert course to follow.

"Then why venture to Cullingslock at all?" A tremor of concern had returned to Philippa's voice. "If not for this inheritance everyone assumes you'll claim?"

"Pippa, please." Tristan's brow was creased, but he dared only glance at his wife. "Lady Felicity remains our guest."

"Forgive me." Philippa put a hand to the lace collar of her blouse. "I mean no discourtesy, your ladyship. I'm simply... I'm utterly at sea."

"In truth, the land matter did bring me here," Felicity acknowledged. "But only because I would never even have heard of Cullingslock otherwise. Accepting ownership of the land was never my intention."

Mr Kemp's swagger appeared deflated. "You're not to be the land's new owner?"

Felicity glanced towards Alex, who somehow maintained admirable composure.

"I came here simply to meet you," she admitted, addressing Tristan primarily. "I've only a small circle of living relatives and, well, I wish to know my family."

The land agent's laughter rang with genuine amusement. "But instead you encountered that circus act." He nodded towards Winnifred's spiritualist circle. "Rather regretting your expedition after enduring yesterday evening's entertainment, I imagine?"

Felicity declined to comment on Winnifred's supernatural pursuits. The division between mystic devotees and sceptics made for treacherous conversational terrain, which was best avoided until proper assessment of everyone's allegiances had been conducted.

As Elfrida and Audrey returned bearing plates, the arrival of dessert proved both a distraction and a revelation. The apple and blackberry crumble's golden-brown surface released clouds of cinnamon-scented steam as thick Devon custard pooled like yellow silk around each generous portion. Audrey managed the service with endearing awkwardness — china rattling ominously though mercifully unbroken — while Elfrida moved with grace but an empty expression, as though her mind was elsewhere or absent entirely. The sight of a dowager baroness's daughter reduced to domestic servitude wasn't the strangest thing so far encountered at the castle, but it was something of a curiosity.

After distributing the plates, mother and daughter retook their seats.

Felicity savoured her first spoonful of crumble — the tart apples provided a soft texture beneath the crumbly topping while sweet blackberries burst with earthy flavour. Sometimes the simplest of dishes were the best.

"Mr Kemp, perhaps you'd enlighten us regarding this month's hunting expedition?" Though such sports held minimal appeal for her, Felicity was keen to move the conversation onwards, and the land agent seemed capable of monopolising the discussion throughout dessert.

Mr Kemp required no further encouragement. "Magnificent

stags this season — broad antlers, full weight. You'll doubtless observe several during our upcoming tour."

Tristan's glance conveyed mild irritation at the land agent's appropriation of his offer of a tour, though he remained diplomatically silent. Felicity likewise avoided correction. It might be best to avoid such a tour, seeing as there was already confusion about her intentions towards the land. Might it even be wise to leave Cullingslock after the discussion with Winnifred and her solicitor, and delay the building of bonds between estranged relatives for a time when the question of the Cullingslock Wastes had been fully settled?

"Any hunting parties confirmed?" Philippa enquired.

"A number of prestigious bookings." Mr Kemp's tone radiated satisfaction.

Tristan cleared his throat. "Several curlew pairs nest on the moorland currently." His tone was stiff. "Are you implementing measures to minimise disruption to them from the hunting?" His question targeted the land agent, but his gaze fluttered to the table.

Peregrine observed the exchange with keen attention.

Mr Kemp's smile was reminiscent of a father indulging a wayward child. "Care to explain what practical benefit ground-nesting curlews provide to estate operations?"

Philippa straightened in her seat. "Have I ever seen a curlew?"

Tristan sighed deeply. "Gladly. But where to begin?"

Ack!

The hideous sound erupted from the table's far end.

Aaaaack!

Winnifred clutched her throat, her complexion draining to an alarming pallor, her right arm floundering.

"Reverend One?" Mrs Imrie's voice trembled.

The footman stood paralysed beside the sideboard. Mrs Imrie and Miss Hartley rose from their seats. Mr Silkstede half-stood from his chair, notebook forgotten, while Mr Pope lurched towards consciousness with startled confusion.

Elfrida pushed back from the table but did not stand up.

"Grandmama?" Audrey leaned forward to get a view of her grandmother.

Felicity and Alex began moving towards the head of the table, but Tristan had already reached his mother's side with surprising alacrity. Mr Kemp followed, his usual swagger replaced by disquiet.

With a glance at one another, Felicity and Alex hung back.

"Mother, what's happening?" Tristan demanded, his gentle demeanour now full of desperation.

"Possible choking," the land manager suggested, moving to lift Winnifred from her chair.

"Careful!" Mrs Imrie's cry was fierce. Miss Hartley had gone white as bone china, with one hand pressed to her mouth. Mr Silkstede frowned deeply.

Peregrine approached, uncertainty flickering beneath his calm facade. He hung back with Felicity and Alex and watched as the others went to work.

"Grandmama!" Audrey's distress verged on tears, but Elfrida's firm grip on her arm prevented the girl from going to her grandmother's side.

Ack!

Winnifred's struggles intensified, her complexion assuming greyish tones. Felicity wished to take action — which was not necessary, given her lack of medical knowledge and the number of people already involved — or at least to reassure, which wasn't possible without knowing first what was wrong with her great-aunt. There was nothing she could do but watch.

Philippa approached the footman. "Tell Timpson to summon Dr Marsh immediately," she commanded with crisp authority.

The footman's rapid departure offered minimal comfort. Given the castle's isolation and lack of telephone communication, medical assistance would be desperately distant, even by Devonian standards.

"Might we be able to assist?" suggested Alex. "Perhaps reach the doctor in the Alvis?"

Philippa shook her head, her mouth down-turned as she watched her mother-in-law writhe with discomfort. “There’s a motor. The butler can drive.”

With the assistance of Tristan and Mr Kemp, Mrs Imrie supervised Winnifred’s careful repositioning on the floor.

“Reverend One, what do you perceive?” Mrs Imrie knelt beside her mistress as the terrible sounds continued. “What visions come to you?”

Winnifred’s mouth worked soundlessly, her eyes rolling upwards.

Then came one massive, shuddering breath.

Chapter Seven

It was by bicycle that the footman departed for the doctor's surgery in Brackenfold village. The butler insisted on remaining at Winnifred's side once he witnessed her distress, assuring everyone that the young footman on his bike would be quicker on the downhill track than the castle's hulking old Napier. Dr Marsh arrived with commendable swiftness in his dark grey Humber and was, mercifully, able to administer immediate care. With Philippa orchestrating the arrangements, the family and spiritualists were ushered into an elongated and faintly musty drawing room to await the physician's assessment.

Afternoon light filtered through the drawing room's tall windows, which were draped in faded burgundy velvet. Chippendale chairs with fraying silk seats flanked a marble-topped table bearing an exquisite Ming vase marred by a chip on its rim, while Persian carpets — their once-vivid patterns now muted — covered polished wood floors. Felicity and Alex joined the vigil to await the doctor's news, their exchanged glances heavy with concern. The idea of leaving lingered in Felicity's thoughts, but the moment was far from apt. The afternoon had deviated spectacularly from any plan Felicity might have entertained. With Winnifred's alarming collapse, practical discussions regarding land contracts seemed not merely improper but positively vulgar. It might be appropriate to leave only after Dr Marsh's update.

The spiritualists had claimed the drawing room's most distant corner, clustering around a mahogany side table like conspirators. The remaining assembly — Tristan, his formidable wife, and stalwart son, Elfrida and her capable daughter, plus the land agent, solicitor, and Felicity and Alex — arranged themselves uneasily before the cold hearth. Audrey had settled cross-legged on a thinning rug beside Solomon, the Border Collie's intelligent eyes bright with anticipation as she produced a seemingly endless supply of treats from her pinafore pocket. Now and then she wrapped her arms around the dog's neck, hugging the canine close for comfort, a gesture to which Tristan did not object. The Old English Sheepdog observed proceedings, his panting revealing nervousness rather than exertion. Felicity perched on the edge of a lumpy sofa upholstered in faded damask, Alex standing protectively beside her. From Felicity's lap, Pip watched Audrey and Solomon with rapt attention.

Considering his efforts on his bicycle, the footman materialised alongside the butler with undimmed enthusiasm for his role, bringing silver trays laden with bone china and refreshments capable of conquering any crisis. The Earl Grey's familiar bergamot perfume mingled with the sweet aroma of shortbread biscuits, while delicate cucumber sandwiches spoke of a determination to maintain civilised standards despite the afternoon's dramatic turn and an increasing disquiet. The physician's delayed emergence suggested Winnifred's condition required thorough evaluation — a realisation that settled upon the gathering with the steady tick of the old bracket clock above the fireplace.

Following refills to teacups, a second round of sandwiches, and many entreaties to the butler regarding an audience with Winnifred — each politely but firmly rebuffed while the doctor continued his work — the spiritualist trio began their strategic withdrawal from the drawing room.

"Where might you be going?" Philippa enquired, her voice carrying the strain of someone desperately attempting to maintain authority over the situation. "Do you not wish to await news of the dowager baroness's condition?"

"We cannot simply sit idle while our Reverend One suffers," Mrs Imrie replied in her soft Scottish lilt, her pale hands clasped before her as though in prayer. "If we invoke Brigid and Airmid, perhaps their influence might reach her."

"A healing circle ritual would indeed be most beneficial," suggested Mr Silkstede, already moving to hold the drawing room doors open for Miss Hartley to pass through.

"Oh, what a splendid notion," Miss Hartley breathed. "You always have such good ideas, Mr Silkstede."

"I shall gather the necessary implements." Mrs Imrie spoke with brisk efficiency. "The energies must be channelled properly."

Philippa's shoulders sagged with resignation, yet it was obvious even to newcomers at the castle that Winnifred's spiritualist followers operated in a different sphere to the rest of the household.

Elfrida regarded the departing spiritualists with fond bemusement. "If their ritual provides comfort, surely there's no harm in the endeavour."

Philippa's laugh was brittle. "Comfort, perhaps — but at what expense? Have you seen the guide prices for those 'necessary implements' in the catalogues for the auction houses where they were procured?"

"Oh!" Elfrida put a hand to her cheek with mock surprise. "So it's money you'd like to discuss, for a change."

Peregrine's gaze flew sharply to his aunt, but he said nothing.

"Pippa." Tristan interjected in a quiet, weary tone. His pallor had intensified. "Not while Mother lies ill." He looked almost sick himself.

Philippa's fingers flew to her lace collar. "You're absolutely right. My apologies. It's simply... Your mother has always possessed such vitality, such strength. To witness her so suddenly diminished... It's just such a shock."

"Age claims us all eventually, doesn't it?" The observation emerged from behind Mr Kemp's copy of a periodical titled *The*

Rural Ledger and was delivered with the casual indifference of someone commenting on the weather. The land agent's substantial frame filled a leather wingback chair that had seen better decades, his weathered hands turning the pages with unhurried ease.

Tristan's features tightened. He sat up straighter, though not to his full height. "I'm rather uncertain what you mean to suggest."

Mr Kemp's attention remained fixed on the printed pages as he responded. "Old age. Death."

The words hung in the air like the smoke of a particularly unpleasant cigarette.

Audrey's hands stilled upon Solomon's silky coat, her wide eyes swinging towards her mother.

Elfrida didn't react to her daughter's apparent need for reassurance. She was watching the land agent.

The solicitor — whose crystal tumbler had somehow acquired a fresh measure of amber liquid despite the afternoon's drama — occupied a fraying armchair that looked to have a dubious capacity for holding such weight. "Mr Kemp isn't wrong," he said, implying either philosophical resignation or merely the lubricating effects of good brandy upon one's capacity for harsh truths.

"That would be my mother — and your employer — you're discussing with such touching concern." Elfrida's tone was icy but with a hint of amusement.

Mr Kemp lowered his periodical just enough to reveal a satisfied smile. "Surely you recognise my genuine fondness for your mother? Just as you must acknowledge your own deep affection for her." His tone possessed a surprising familiarity — or perhaps presumption. "I'm merely providing the sort of realistic perspective for which your mother employs me. Heaven knows this whole ruddy place requires substantial doses of practical thinking."

"But your job isn't the whole castle, is it, Mr Kemp?" Philippa reacted quickly and forthrightly. "Is it, Tristan?" She turned to her husband, her tone wavering.

Peregrine also seemed invested in what his father might say.

"Mr Kemp is at liberty to express his opinions," mumbled Tristan.

A line appeared between Philippa's eyebrows, her hands clutched tightly in her lap. She said nothing more.

Felicity glanced at Alex. He returned Felicity's gaze with a look of concern but also of calm. He was no longer amused by the situation at Cullingslock, but he didn't seem desperate to leave. His patience for Felicity's family and her endeavours generally seemed limitless, but his serenity didn't make her feel less guilty about having dragged him into the situation.

She gave him an apologetic smile. Even if it was dark by the time the doctor's update came, Felicity would still be keen to leave, and not just for Alex's sake — if the outcome was the very worst, it would make sense for her to withdraw and give the household the peace to deal with the situation.

Regarding the Cullingslock Wastes, however, her position remained unchanged. Profitable or not, she would decline the inheritance entirely, most likely via her solicitor. Her brother might urge her to reconsider now that it appeared the land had the potential for income. In Felicity's view, however, given the evident financial concerns at the castle, it was even more of a reason to leave the Wastes unclaimed.

"Expressing opinions requires no particular gift," Elfrida observed. "Recognising when such expressions might prove inadvisable, however, demands rather more sophisticated judgement — a capability I fear Mr Kemp may lack."

Mr Kemp's response emerged as a grunt from behind his periodical. Elfrida smiled victoriously.

"Given all that has happened," began Philippa, "should we not endeavour to treat one another as kindly as possible?" Her tone was verging on desperate as she eyed Elfrida and Mr Kemp.

"I quite agree," said Tristan, flashing a glare at his sister but doing nothing further by way of correction. He may have been lord of the Cullingslock estate, but he seemed to have no authority over the household.

Pip chose this moment to stage a minor rebellion, writhing with determined energy towards infinitely preferable company. Given that the atmosphere in the salon was already awkward enough, Felicity surrendered, releasing the Yorkie to career across the carpet towards Audrey, where he bestowed enthusiastic canine kisses upon her freckled cheek.

"My apologies." Felicity rose from her seat. "Shall I reclaim him?"

"Oh no, your ladyship," Audrey replied, her smile radiant. "I'm perfectly content." The girl's natural ease with the animals added a hint of warmth to the drawing room's tense atmosphere. Even Elfrida's gaze softened maternally towards her daughter.

"Thank you, Miss Audrey." Felicity settled back on the sofa with relief. "Master Pip seems to prefer your company at the moment."

"I rather suspect you didn't anticipate encountering this particular situation when you decided to visit Cullingslock," Elfrida observed, turning her gaze towards Felicity.

"Certainly not," Felicity confessed, her gaze briefly seeking Alex's steadying presence. "And might I express our profound regret—" She included her beau with a graceful gesture. "—that Great-Aunt Winnifred should suffer such distressing circumstances." The words felt inadequate even as she spoke them. Their status as relative strangers to this domestic crisis felt increasingly apparent with each passing moment.

Elfrida's dismissive wave implied she was accustomed to family dramas. "My mother possesses the constitution of a moorland pony and twice the stubbornness. You'll discover she rather relishes being the centre of attention."

Mr Kemp's periodical descended with dramatic suddenness, revealing an expression of astonishment. "You rather forcefully criticised my supposedly inappropriate remarks not five minutes past."

Elfrida cocked her head at the land agent. "And what precisely do you propose to do about such inconsistency?"

The solicitor's shoulders shook with mirth, while Peregrine

regarded the scene with the sort of appalled fascination one might reserve for a motoring accident.

Philippa clasped her hands before her chest. "How gracious of you to express such concern, your ladyship." Her response to Felicity scrupulously side-stepped Elfrida. "Would you not agree, Tristan?"

Tristan managed a distracted nod. "Indeed. Quite thoughtful."

"Grandmama shall recover, surely?" Peregrine's freckled features were clouded, either with fear of loss or perhaps with confusion regarding appropriate responses.

"You need not worry, Perry." Tristan's reassurance carried undertones of grave concern rather than hope.

Philippa moved to her son's side and placed a hand on his shoulder. "Whatever circumstances arise, we shall manage admirably. Shall we not, Tristan?"

Her husband's gaze travelled between wife and son before settling on his own lap. "Naturally."

Another round of tea delivered by Timpson and the footman provided a welcome distraction. The late afternoon light caught the steam rising from delicate teacups. Felicity sought refuge at the window, drawn by the golden sunshine and the promise of tranquil vistas beyond the castle's charged atmosphere. Exmoor's wild beauty spread before her like a living watercolour, its rolling hills clothed in purple heather and yellow gorse, while the distant sea merged with a dusky blue sky. A small herd of red deer moved gracefully across an open field, their forms burnished copper in the declining light. The leaves of the trees surrounding the castle shimmered like scattered coins.

Alex joined Felicity in silent contemplation for a spell. "Rather magnificent, isn't it?"

Felicity smiled and nodded, absorbing the vista with growing wonder. What might it mean to claim stewardship over such untamed beauty? Such romantic notions demanded swift dismissal. Every indication suggested that Cullingslock Castle harboured complexities far beyond even Felicity's capacity to navigate or resolve. Yet she refused to consider her visit a complete disaster. Her intentions had been admirable, and she was already steeling herself against Jasper's inevitable satisfaction at her retreat. Building family connections had seemed a worthy endeavour, but she would not linger and further expose Alex to whatever currents of discord flowed beneath the household's surface.

There was an urgent knock at the drawing room door, followed immediately by the physician's entrance.

"Dr Marsh." Elfrida's casual composure evaporated as she rose with sudden urgency, concern finally piercing her detachment. "How does Mother fare?"

Tristan also stood, his long limbs unfolding swiftly.

Philippa rose at his side. "What news have you?"

The land agent closed his periodical, while the solicitor maintained his position in the rickety-looking armchair. Audrey looked up from where she'd been coaching Pip through the same repertoire of tricks that Solomon executed with Border Collie precision. Peregrine straightened in his seat but did not stand.

Dr Marsh spoke with measured authority, the evening light glinting on his balding head. "The dowager baroness remains stable and doing well, considering the circumstances."

Elfrida hugged herself. "What's wrong with her?"

Dr Marsh pressed his lips together for a moment. "I'm afraid the dowager baroness is suffering from severe gastric distress. It's rather more serious than simple indigestion, though not quite a danger to her life. Such conditions can prove taxing for someone of her years, especially given that her constitution has been somewhat compromised by previous health challenges."

"Gastric distress?" There was scepticism in Elfrida's tone. "We all ate the same food at lunch. Why should Mother alone suffer such consequences?"

Dr Marsh nodded patiently. He was accustomed to such interrogations. "Often these episodes result from individual sensitivity to particular ingredients rather than wholesale contamination. The custard served with the apple crumble, for instance, contained eggs, which, as I'm sure you're all aware, can occasionally cause trouble. It's also possible there was browning in the fruit that might prove irksome to someone with a delicate constitution."

Felicity and Alex exchanged a meaningful glance. Elfrida had made an excellent point. Despite the physician's reassurances, how likely was it to have a single person fall ill from a meal everyone ate?

"Thank you for updating us, Dr Marsh." Philippa sounded relieved.

Tristan nodded, his hands stuffed in his pockets. "Thank you."

The assembled company appeared to accept the doctor's professional assessment. Felicity and Alex swapped another look. Given their experiences of criminal investigations, were they simply too prone to a certain way of thinking?

"The patient remains weak but stable," the physician continued, "though I have advised complete rest and freedom from disturbance until my return tomorrow morning."

"Is it truly possible that a bit of egg might make a person so violently ill so very quickly?" Alex's question had been on Felicity's mind as well. She was thankful he was bold enough to challenge the doctor.

The physician nodded with understanding. "It's quite possible, yes. Especially in a sensitive patient."

"Might we not visit her briefly?" Philippa's enquiry carried a hopeful note.

Dr Marsh shook his head with gentle firmness. "I fear I must advise against such intrusions." A weary sigh escaped him. "The dowager baroness being rather determined in her preferences has insisted upon a specific audience, however."

Elfrida stepped forward with the expectant bearing of dutiful daughters everywhere. "Tristan," she called to her brother, already positioning herself for departure from the drawing room.

"With a certain Lady Felicity Quick," Dr Marsh added.

The room's collective attention swivelled towards Felicity.

"With me?" The words emerged with rather less composure than she might have preferred.

Alex quirked an eyebrow.

Elfrida's graceful advance towards the drawing room doors halted abruptly. "With Felicity?"

Philippa and Tristan regarded her with a series of expressions ranging from bewilderment to concern. The land agent and solicitor maintained their positions as interested observers of yet another fascinating chapter in the ongoing Cullingslock family drama.

"Indeed," Dr Marsh confirmed with resignation. "The dowager baroness proved remarkably persuasive in her insistence, withholding cooperation with my prescribed treatment until I agreed to convey this particular invitation. She also maintains that she must speak to her ladyship with considerable urgency."

Felicity met Alex's gaze. At a time such as this, what could possibly be urgent?

Chapter Eight

Without Pip and, even more regrettably, without Alex, neither of which the doctor would allow to accompany Felicity for fear of overexerting his patient, Felicity followed Timpson through the winding labyrinth of the castle's corridors and staircases. Felicity occasionally shivered as a cool, earthy breeze whispered through arrow slits unfitted with glass.

They passed Miss Hartley, carrying with her a brass censer still trailing wisps of incense, her pert cheeks flushed with exertion as she hurried along. She stopped, wide eyed, and watched the butler and Felicity proceeding past, her expression shifting from surprise to annoyance.

"You told us no visitors," she said to the butler, presumably aware of the route towards Winnifred's quarters.

"Her ladyship has been summoned by the dowager baroness." Timpson's reply was delivered with professional neutrality, but it left Miss Hartley unsatisfied. Her eyebrows lowered dramatically, and she gave a little huff as she continued on her way, leaving a thin trail of sandalwood smoke in the corridor.

Felicity resumed following the butler, but she would gladly have allowed Miss Hartley or anyone else to take her place if it would make them happy. Not that she had no wish to speak to her great-aunt, but the castle was rife with discontent at her summoning. Felicity was only beginning to grasp the considerable resentments and rivalries at play.

"Here we are, your ladyship." Timpson unlatched a heavy wood-panelled door and stood aside.

"Thank you, Mr Timpson."

The chamber Felicity stepped into was similar to the room in which the séance had taken place. Situated in a turret, the walls were curved with heavy drapes covering the bare stone and a patchwork of different rugs enveloping the floor. The aroma of old incense had soaked into the room's fabrics. The space differed, however, in atmosphere. Dark oak beams crossed overhead, a simple chandelier of curled ironwork at their centre. A rudimentary gas supply reached some areas of the castle, and the lighting in the bedroom glowed with a soft amber warmth, the jets in the sconces hissing faintly. Against the far wall stood a magnificent four-poster bed, dense with curtains and blankets. The hues of the abundant fabrics were warm — reds, browns, and hints of gold — creating a cosy, if slightly shambolic, sanctuary.

What was less cosy, however, was the bewildering array of curiosities scattered across the room's vast stone mantelpiece and over every other available surface. A gathering of iridescent peacock and dark raven feathers had been fashioned into a sort of fan. An old sword with rust on its blade had a pommel studded with what might have been rubies beneath the tarnish. Collections of dried herbs tied with black ribbon hung about the place. In pride of place above the hearth, there was a shoe in faded red silk and gold ribbon that wouldn't have looked out of place at a Stuart court.

On a side table, partially obscured by a crystal decanter, sat a silver-framed photograph that caught Felicity's eye — a younger Winnifred in an ornate Egypt-inspired costume surrounded by what appeared to be fellow performers, their faces frozen in dramatic poses. Winnifred had undoubtedly led a colourful life, one Felicity might hear about one day. But not now. To avoid further irking the household, this encounter must be kept brief. And for Alex's sake, their departure from the castle must not be further delayed.

Felicity hung back as the butler went to the bedside. The curtains around the four-poster meant Felicity could not yet see Winnifred, nor could she hear the words she exchanged with the butler. The only window in the room had its shutters drawn, but Felicity could hear rain beginning to patter against the glass beyond, a gentle drumming that echoed the unease in her chest. She and Alex would drive home not only in the dark but in the rain. It wasn't ideal, but Felicity and, more importantly, Alex had already suffered enough discomfort.

When the butler withdrew from the room, he merely nodded to Felicity as he closed the door gently behind him.

"My child, don't be scared. You may approach." Winnifred's voice was surprisingly firm despite its tremor.

Felicity duly advanced. A flicker of unease danced along her spine — not fear, precisely, but the sort of wariness one might feel approaching a wounded animal that might either accept help or lash out. Yet Felicity's plan was clear. She would hear what Winnifred wished to tell her, say her own piece, then leave. The path to reconciliation with her previously estranged relatives could be resumed on another occasion should Felicity return to Cullingslock Castle.

"Please, my child, take a seat." Winnifred nodded towards a worn wooden stool positioned at the side of the bed. She was propped against a mountain of pillows in a white frilly nightgown, the lace at her throat slightly ragged with age. Her grey hair was spread as wild as storm-tossed waves on the goose-down fortress supporting her. Her necklaces and bracelets were gone, but she still wore her rings, the scarab beetle prominent on her left hand while her right hand lay beneath the coverlet. The two smoke-coloured cats lay either side of Winnifred's legs, their amber eyes regarding Felicity with feline disdain. It felt like an audience with royalty in their private chambers, as once was the tradition.

Felicity settled carefully onto the stool. "How are you feeling,

Great-Aunt?" Although she wished to keep this interaction brief, she was genuinely concerned for Winnifred.

The older woman heaved a sigh, her left hand fluttering dramatically. "We have rather a lot to talk about, don't we?" She seemed rather more recovered than the doctor had indicated. Was there a chance to resolve the matter of the land before returning to Bradley Court?

"We do indeed," agreed Felicity gently. "And I'm glad to have this opportunity to apologise. It wasn't my intention to contradict you so openly at luncheon. I tried to find you ahead of your announcement to inform you of my decision privately. It's a decision I maintain, incidentally."

Winnifred's face contorted, creating a map of wrinkles. "What's that, my child?"

Felicity straightened on the stool. "The land I'm supposed to inherit. The land of which you are the trustee."

"The land?" The lines around Winnifred's lips and brow deepened like crevasses in the flickering gaslight. "Goodness, my child, that couldn't be further from my mind."

It was Felicity's turn to adopt an expression of bewilderment. "Then... Why have you summoned me?"

Winnifred's eyes widened into a look of genuine fear, then narrowed into wariness. Her left hand gripped the coverlet. "I," she whispered, pausing for dramatic effect, "have been..." She leaned forward as far as her condition would allow. "Poisoned."

Felicity's chest tightened sharply.

The suspicion had crossed her mind even as Winnifred lay on the dining hall floor, but it was in Felicity's nature to think such things. She never expected it to be true. Or that her visit to Cullingslock could become even more complicated.

"Poisoned by bad ingredients in the food, you mean?" Felicity kept her tone neutral, though her detective's instincts were already flying ahead.

Winnifred drew herself up against the pillows with affronted dignity. "My illness was no accident, my child. But you would not be the first person I have encountered with a tendency to disbelieve me."

The accusation landed between them like a dropped vase. Both cats raised their heads as if sensing the shift in atmosphere.

Felicity suppressed the urge to swallow lest it encourage Winnifred's taste for the dramatic. She had been closer than many to various unfortunate circumstances that resulted in the permanent extinguishing of a life. Yet something about her great-aunt's quiet revelation proved unnerving. Had Felicity overlooked a poisoner in residence?

"Apologies, Great-Aunt. I mean no disrespect. The situation you describe is extremely grave indeed. How can we be certain someone meant you harm?"

Winnifred studied Felicity with a steady gaze. "Do you consider me prone to untruths?"

Felicity's hands tensed in her lap. Communing with spirits could be viewed as a sham, yet it certainly wasn't the moment for that discussion. "Of course not, Great-Aunt. I'm just a little confused because Dr Marsh said you suffered from gastric distress caused by bad ingredients."

Winnifred chuckled. "My child, you know maybe better than most that deliberate poisonings often go undetected. Is that not the case?"

Felicity had to agree. Certain poisons like arsenic could be distinguished through testing, but many plant-based toxins remained undetectable. The symptoms Winnifred had displayed — sudden gastric distress, weakness, and pallor — could indeed result from several substances growing wild on the moors or found in household preparations. Without sophisticated laboratory analysis, which was hardly available in rural Devon, distinguishing deliberate poisoning from accidental food contamination might prove impossible.

"In Dr Marsh's view, an accidental cause would be the most likely explanation. And I can't fault the man for doing his job in the best way he knows how. He is a professional through and through. But he doesn't know this household, my child. Not like I do."

"Did you not suggest to him that it might have been a deliberate poisoning?"

"Might? Do you still not believe me?" The accusation in Winnifred's tone came more from disappointment than indignation.

It prompted a pang of guilt in Felicity. Her experience at the séance had perhaps rather coloured her perception of Winnifred's pronouncements. The sight of photographs hinting at a theatrical past had also helped develop the impression that her great-aunt was something of a show-woman. But that was a dangerous prejudice to maintain, wasn't it? What if there actually was someone with murder on their mind at the castle? Who knew what they might be capable of?

"I believe you, Great-Aunt."

"And would you have had the doctor go downstairs and announce to the whole household, including whoever did it, 'We have an attempted murder on our hands'? What effect do you suppose that would have had?"

"It would indeed not have been an ideal situation," agreed Felicity, reflecting on the remoteness of the castle and the tensions already bubbling among its inhabitants. "The police can be informed discreetly. Mr Cooper and I shall—"

"The police?" Winnifred's eyes lit up with mirth and fury. "I will not have those barbarian oafs involved here."

Felicity raised an eyebrow. She had not always had a smooth experience with the Devon County Constabulary, but 'barbarian oafs' was going rather far.

"If it's a question of murder, Great-Aunt, the police are best placed to help."

"No." The older woman's nostrils flared. "I will not involve the police. They are not welcome at this castle. Not after what they did the last time. And that is my final word on the topic."

Felicity regarded Winnifred. It was becoming apparent why she had been summoned to her great-aunt's chamber. The pieces were falling into place with uncomfortable clarity. "Then what do you propose should be done?"

Winnifred remained quiet for a moment. "You've noticed it, haven't you?"

"Noticed what?"

"The tensions sizzling between everyone here."

Felicity took a steadying breath. "There seems to be quite a gulf between your spiritualist supporters and the rest of the household."

"By Jove, no." Winnifred reacted with surprising vehemence. "I'm not talking about Mrs Imrie or Miss Hartley or even Mr Silkstede. You couldn't find more loyal, trustworthy friends. No, no, no. Not them. They would never hurt me."

Felicity frowned. "You believe your own family would?" Against her better judgement, she had already begun cataloguing suspects. It had been Elfrida and Audrey who had served the apple crumble, and it seemed to have been the dessert that had such a devastating effect upon Winnifred.

"Surely you've seen enough to have your own ideas on the matter, my child."

Winnifred was correct, but Felicity maintained a carefully neutral bearing. "If you believe that someone made an attempt on your life, then we should contact the police." She would not propose her services as a detective, even if that's what Winnifred wanted. Not when police intervention was the better option.

Winnifred pressed her lips together hard. Her right hand twitched beneath the coverlet as though she wished to gesture but couldn't. "Very well. I see how this ends. I'm thankful for you coming here, my child. I'm very glad we met. I'm pleased we had the opportunity to know one another. We all are." Winnifred closed her eyes with the finality of a curtain falling. "Please, send Mr Timpson along."

It was difficult to tell who Winnifred meant by 'we', but that was the least of the awkwardness of the discussion, which seemed decisively over. Was she insinuating that she might perish if Felicity didn't take action? Felicity had never been blackmailed into investigating before, though her grandmother had certainly employed similar tactics for Felicity's participation in various charity and social events.

On this occasion, however, Felicity would not be coerced into acting against her will. She had wished to reunite with the estranged side of her family, but practically speaking, she owed Winnifred nothing, did she? And it was her great-aunt's decision to involve the police or not.

Felicity's time at Cullingslock Castle had reached its conclusion.

She rose from her stool. "I hope you recover swiftly, Great-Aunt," she said with measured politeness, "but it remains my strong advice that you contact the police."

Winnifred said nothing as the cats watched Felicity's departure with knowing eyes, as though they, too, understood the game being played.

Chapter Nine

It was dark by the time Felicity was reunited with Alex. The rain having stopped, they slipped outside on the pretext of walking Pip. At long last, they could have a private discussion.

The castle's surprisingly well-maintained flower garden, enclosed by ancient stone walls, was the venue for the outing. Moonlight silvered the gravel paths while gaslight from the corridor windows cast amber pools between the shadows. Felicity relayed the unexpected developments of the discussion in her great-aunt's bedchamber as Pip bounced ahead under roses and honeysuckle that climbed trellised archways, their damp blooms releasing waves of perfume into the cool night air.

Alex's arm pressed against Felicity's as they strolled close to one another. His voice was a whisper. "Do you really think someone would try to do away with your great-aunt in your presence?"

"My presence hasn't deterred murderers in the past."

"But this is a small household and everyone knows you're a successful detective. Why wait until you're here to make a move?"

It was a fair point that Felicity might not have been pompous enough to make herself. But it wasn't the only measure of doubt about the situation. "The doctor didn't seem to have any suspicions."

Their feet crunched gently on the gravel as they followed Pip, his nose twitching at long fronds of lavender and catmint. The garden was so well-kept it might even have delighted Felicity's grandmother. It was a surprising contrast to the less well-tended areas of the castle.

Moonlight caught the dark blue of Alex's eyes. "Are you adamant about leaving?"

Felicity halted and looked at him. "I've tried to imagine how I might feel if I left a murderer to end my great-aunt's life, but I can't quite picture it."

Alex stopped alongside her, his hands on his hips, his jacket tucked back. "But isn't a potentially poisoned apple crumble precisely your area of expertise?"

Felicity tucked her chin and gave him a look.

He held up a hand. "Not to imply that you're indiscriminate in your choice of cases."

Felicity gave a little sigh. "I realise I usually have difficulty keeping my nose out of precisely this kind of situation, but yes, my resolve is to depart first thing." It was really too late to leave now. If she rolled up to Bradley Court with the cockcrow, she would never hear the end from her grandmother. She planned to ask Timpson to arrange for an early breakfast for herself and Alex. "I'm not a contrarian, but my great-aunt's attempt to pressure me into investigating has had exactly the opposite effect. If her suspicions are serious, it's unfathomable that she wouldn't contact the police."

"So you have no theories about the case whatsoever?" Alex flashed a little smile.

She narrowed her eyes at him. He knew her too well.

There was Elfrida and Audrey's handling of the dessert course, although she couldn't match either the mother or the daughter to wishing an end to Winnifred's life, at least not from what had so far been witnessed. There was also the discussion of the castle's finances while waiting for news from the doctor. The source of the discontent seemed mainly to have been Philippa — but how normal was it to deliver poison to one's victim then openly discuss one's motives?

"I don't wish to voice anything aloud, not here and not now."

Alex's smile broadened slightly. "I thought as much." His

expression returned to seriousness. "Although I'm, of course, happy to leave any time you wish."

"I can quite imagine. And I can only apologise for dragging you out here."

"No need." His hand found hers in the darkness. "It was my decision to accompany you, and with all this talk of complicated families, it makes one wonder about our own wedding arrangements."

Felicity's chest tightened slightly. They'd been discussing the matter in the Alvis but had been interrupted by their arrival at the castle. She'd been utterly distracted from the topic since. "I understand your family would find it difficult to leave London. We should most certainly take steps to ensure they're included in the celebration."

"That's my problem to address." His thumb stroked the back of her hand. "What's important to me is that you and your family are comfortable with the arrangements. Whatever is decided will be more than acceptable to me. I promise." Alex's tone was gentle and warm, but there seemed to be more to it.

Felicity tipped her head and regarded him carefully.

Crunch!

The little Yorkie had bitten off the head of a crimson dahlia.

"Pip!" Felicity grabbed the wayward dog and tucked him under her arm before he could cause more destruction.

"Lady Felicity?"

The butler materialised from the shadows near the door through which Felicity and Alex had accessed the little garden. In the mingled moon and gaslight, his moustache gleamed like polished pewter. Had he been listening in? Not that there was much that the staff missed in a house, and the butler definitely seemed very close to Winnifred. Felicity hoped he at least hadn't noticed Pip taking a bite from the herbaceous border.

"Yes, Mr Timpson?"

"Telegram for you, your ladyship. Apologies for the late delivery.

With everything that's happened today, I'm afraid it got rather delayed."

Pip struggled in Felicity's arms.

"I can watch him," offered Alex.

"You're too kind," she said, setting the little dog on the ground well away from any plants. Pip and Alex's relationship had developed tremendously from the earlier days of wary looks and the thorough sniffing of shoes.

She unfolded the piece of paper and went to the light of the doorway to read it. The telegram was from her brother Jasper:

> URGENT STOP ARTICLE ON CORNISH SMUGGLING REVIVAL NEEDED STOP ALEX IDEALLY PLACED STOP CAN HE RETURN IMMEDIATELY QUERY STOP HOPE ALL WELL STOP.

So the Western Daily News, the Quick family newspaper of which Jasper was editor-in-chief, was missing Alex's investigative skills. The sign-off also hinted that Jasper might be concerned about Felicity's welfare, though he gave her more of a free rein these days.

The butler had retreated into the corridor, his hands clasped patiently behind his back. "Would you like to send a message in reply, your ladyship?"

"When would it be sent?"

"The footman will be at Brackenfold post office tomorrow just before lunchtime, your ladyship."

"Alex," she called softly. "Jasper has an assignment that requires your immediate attention. Something about Cornish smugglers."

Alex approached, Pip trotting beside him with a suspicious bulge in his cheeks. So much for keeping an eye on the terrier. They were partners in crime.

Alex read over Felicity's shoulder. "Sounds intriguing. Though I suspect my idea of 'immediate' differs from your brother's."

"Well, we're leaving first thing in the morning. I'm not sure how more immediate our return could be than that."

Alex lifted an eyebrow as if to say, *Are you sure about dashing off?*

Yes. Felicity was sure.

She turned to Timpson. "Thank you, but a telegram in reply won't be necessary. I was actually hoping you might arrange for our early departure. Perhaps a light breakfast at half-past six and our luggage brought down?"

The butler inclined his head. "Very good, your ladyship. I shall see to the arrangements."

As Timpson turned to leave, something in the corridor caught Felicity's eye. It was an old photograph, its sepia tones faded but still clear behind glass that bore the patina of age. There were many figures captured in the image, including animals and children. Hardly anyone was smiling, but when did they ever in Victorian portraiture? It was still clearly a convivial gathering.

The butler hesitated as Felicity stepped forward and examined the photograph. Silk dresses with intricate beadwork, gentlemen in perfectly tailored morning coats, children in velvet and lace that must have cost a small fortune. The image had been taken at the front of the castle, when the sharpness of the carved family crest was still proudly maintained. A ringleted girl of perhaps seven years sat in the front row, her hands on a pair of Springer Spaniels.

"Mr Timpson, how long have you been here at Cullingslock?"

The butler gave a soft chuckle. "I wouldn't dare say, your ladyship. I began here as a hall boy, if that helps?"

"Were you here when this photograph was taken?

"I was, your ladyship."

"And do you know who the people are?"

"Of course, your ladyship. It was a visit of Lord Wolfe and his wife and children to the castle here at Cullingslock."

"Lord Wolfe... My mother was Adelaide Wolfe before she married."

The butler permitted himself a knowing smile. "That's Lord Wolfe there, your ladyship."

Felicity peered closely at the man. She hadn't known either of her maternal grandparents. It was difficult to draw conclusions from merely a picture, but beyond the stiffness of the morning coat, necktie, and old-fashioned sideburns, he had the eyes of a man who was kind.

"And I believe that's young Miss Adelaide seated with the dogs."

Felicity pressed her fingertips against the cool glass, forgetting any earlier caution. The ringleted little girl wore a pale muslin dress with puffed sleeves and a straw bonnet. She was the only one in the picture who was smiling.

"That's my mother," she murmured as Alex arrived at her side to join her in peering at the picture, Pip now tucked under his arm.

"Yes, your ladyship. Do you wish me to point out the dowager baroness?"

"Please do." So Winnifred had known Felicity's mother, albeit when she was just a child.

"She's that figure there, your ladyship."

Had the butler not pointed at Winnifred, Felicity never would have recognised her. Her face was slender and fine-boned, her posture upright. There were no trappings of spiritualism or theatrics. She wore a high-necked gown of obvious quality, jet beads at her throat, every inch the respectable Victorian matron.

"And that's Lord Cullingslock." He pointed to the tall, handsome but pale man standing beside Winnifred. "He sadly left us too young." The butler sounded genuinely sorrowful. "We lost him just two years after this photograph was taken."

"How terrible. What took him?"

"Consumption."

"Goodness." Felicity glanced at Alex. Consumption was a painful way to watch a loved one disappear.

Winnifred had a hand on the shoulders of two boys standing before her, a gangly boy of perhaps twelve and another slightly younger fellow. Beside them stood a girl with rather a serious gaze for her age. She was perhaps only six.

"I can see Tristan," said Felicity, pointing to the taller boy, "and Elfrida," she added, pointing to the solemn-faced girl.

"Indeed, your ladyship. The young master was always tall for his age, and Miss Elfrida had that same determined set to her chin even then."

"And who's this?" Felicity put a finger on the boy standing beside Tristan.

"That's young Master Alaric, your ladyship."

Felicity turned to the butler. "And where is he now?"

"With the angels, your ladyship. He left us shortly after his father did."

"Heavens."

The loss the family had endured — a father and his young son — cast Winnifred's spiritual beliefs in a different light. Perhaps it wasn't merely showmanship but a desperate attempt to maintain a connection with those she'd lost. The photograph showed a conventional Victorian family, complete and proper. How dramatically time had transformed them all.

"Is there anything else I might do for you, your ladyship?"

Felicity hesitated, her resolve wavering.

Alex regarded her with a neutral expression, though she knew what he was thinking.

"Please cancel the plans for our early departure, Mr Timpson," said Felicity.

Alex's smile of approval was a little too triumphant. Pip's tail wagged.

"We shall still leave tomorrow, but we shan't rush off so early," she added, half frowning at both her companions.

As the butler withdrew, his footsteps practically silent on the corridor's stone floor, Felicity, Alex, and Pip went back outside. Alex went to put the Yorkie down.

Felicity scooped him up before his paws touched the gravel. "Not here."

Alex raised his brow in genuine dismay. "Have I failed you?"

"No." She plucked a petal from the little dog's beard. "But he has."

"I shall do better next time." Alex's smile returned, less triumphant this time. "So we're extending our stay?"

"For a short while." Felicity took Alex's hand as they strolled along the moonlit, flower-scented path. "For all her eccentricities, Great-Aunt Winnifred is family. She deserves whatever help I can offer."

Alex squeezed her palm. "I sense an investigation coming on."

"Let's not call it that." She smiled at him. "But it can't hurt to extend our visit, can it?"

Chapter Ten

The next morning at the castle dawned clear, sunlight dancing through the lace curtains and warming the oak floorboards of Felicity's chamber. The footman arrived with her breakfast promptly, and Felicity made quick work of her meal. Donning a pale blue linen dress with flutter sleeves and seizing a triangle of toast and strawberry jam for the journey, she clamped Pip under her arm and wound along the meandering corridors and sinuous staircases to the neighbouring wing, where she rapped on Alex's door.

He appeared bleary-eyed in the doorway. "Morning. How are you both?" he asked, offering Pip a scratch under the chin.

"Did you not sleep well?" asked Felicity, noting the shadows beneath his eyes.

Alex stifled a yawn as he pulled on a lightweight jacket in pale beige. "I hope you won't take this the wrong way, because I adore living in Devon, but there's a difference between sleeping in a city like Exeter and trying to get some kip in a place like this."

Felicity tilted her head. "It's quieter here, isn't it? Surely that's better for sleep?"

Alex gave a rueful chuckle. "It's too quiet. My mind gets overactive." He lowered his voice, though the narrow corridor stretched empty in both directions. "Don't tell the spiritualists, but I thought I heard voices at one stage."

Felicity raised her brow. "I do hope you're joking."

"I wish I were. I might ask the butler if he has a wireless or something to help me sleep tonight."

"If you would like to leave—"

"With a potential murder plot to unravel? Leaving now would be like walking out of a dance before the band warmed up. The Cornish smugglers can wait."

"I'm glad you find merriment in my great-aunt's potential brush with death."

Alex tucked his chin. "I thought you doubted her story."

Felicity narrowed her eyes. He'd caught her out. While she still felt Winnifred's poisoning self-diagnosis to be dubious, by asking a few subtle questions here and there, she intended to depart the castle with a clean conscience. "Let's go."

From Alex's room, they navigated with increasing confidence to the grand entrance hall, where the morning light glinted off the medieval chandelier's iron curves. They didn't have to wait long before encountering the footman, who proved admirably efficient in locating Elfrida.

Winnifred's daughter was Felicity's first target of the day for several reasons. She possessed a refreshingly candid perspective on matters that promised actual conversation rather than mere pleasantries. She had also offered Felicity a tour of the castle, providing the perfect excuse for extended discourse. Most pressing, however, was the matter of Elfrida's handling of the apple crumble that had apparently so severely affected her mother. The challenge lay in probing without appearing to do so — but it was a skill Felicity had honed through many similar situations.

"But I must go! I can't stay. It's never happened before, and it can never happen again. And I don't even know how it happened."

The lamenting female voice carried up the staircase that descended into the castle basement and its kitchens, the stone steps hollowed by generations of feet.

"Mrs Wiseley, please." The butler's voice was patient but firm. "You are not talking rationally."

"But how can I carry on? It's all my fault. I made the lunch all by myself. I didn't want to bother you, Mrs Brand. You do so much for us all already."

"Take a seat, Mrs Wiseley." Elfrida's tone was remarkably gentle, though there was a hint of underlying weariness.

Felicity and Alex, with Pip nestled contentedly under Felicity's arm, didn't wish to interrupt, but nor did they wish to conceal their approach. As they descended the stairs, the kitchen came into view. An enormous fireplace built in vast blocks of stone — where several hogs might once have been roasted — was now partially filled by a Victorian wood-fired range, its brass fittings polished to military brightness. Aged and dented yet perfectly serviceable pots and pans hung neatly along the walls. Sunlight slanted through high windows set deep in the stone walls, illuminating the honey-coloured grain of the enormous oak table at the centre of the room. The faint smell of baked bread mingled with the aromas of dried herbs and wood smoke.

Beside the table knelt Elfrida, comforting the cook, her white cap clutched in trembling hands. The woman appeared frailer than Winnifred, her spine curved like a question mark from decades of work. The butler stood nearby, his face grave yet maintaining a respectful distance, allowing Elfrida — a white apron over her dusky plum day dress with a pin-tucked bodice, her reddish hair swept into a practical bun — to manage the delicate situation.

"It's no one's fault that Mother is ill, Mrs Wiseley," soothed Elfrida, her hand resting on the cook's arm. "These things happen. It might have been an ingredient from a supplier or something Audrey collected from the garden."

"Don't say that, Mrs Brand." The cook took Elfrida's hand in both of hers, her knuckles large and rough. "I don't want your girl getting into any sort of trouble. I shall go. It's for the best."

"Mrs Wiseley, please. Far more damage would be done by your leaving than your staying. Isn't that right, Mr Timpson?"

The butler nodded without hesitation. "Most certainly. Please remember, Mrs Wiseley, the dowager baroness has weathered far worse than a touch of gastric distress."

"And I'm really not sure I have the talents required to feed everyone here," continued Elfrida, the exhaustion in her voice increasingly clear. "I'd probably end up poisoning people daily without your guidance, Mrs Wiseley. Please, I promise you. My mother isn't angry with you in the slightest."

The cook sniffed and looked up at Elfrida. "She's not?"

"Of course not. She adores you. She depends on you. We all do."

The cook straightened a little, her weathered face crumpling with relief. "I only want to do my best for the baroness. That's all I've ever wanted to do."

"And by staying, you will continue to do so," suggested Timpson, his moustache quivering.

"Now," said Elfrida, rising to her feet. "What is it we're preparing for lunch?"

Mrs Wiseley wiped her eyes and replaced her cap, transforming from distraught wrongdoer to capable cook with admirable speed. "Cold roast beef sandwiches with horseradish cream, a barley soup, and gooseberry fool for pudding."

"And what can I do to help?" offered Elfrida.

With the worst of the rather desperate scene in the kitchen having passed, Felicity stepped forward from her vantage point in the doorway, making their presence known — though she suspected the butler had been aware of them all along.

"Your ladyship." Timpson approached, his professional composure restored, any trace of worry gone from his brow. "Mr Cooper. How may I be of assistance?"

"Good morning, Mr Timpson. Thank you, but I'm actually here to speak with Mrs Brand."

"Oh?" Elfrida turned with interest at the mention of her name. "Will you be able to do without me for a spell, Mrs Wiseley?"

The cook was already busying herself. "Most definitely, Mrs Brand."

Approaching Felicity, Elfrida folded her arms over the pleated bodice of her dress, a little smile playing on her lips. "You've not been scared away yet, then?"

Felicity caught Alex's eye. "Is there a reason I ought to be afraid?"

"Well, first the séance, then my mother's dramatics at lunch. And I'm sure what you heard of our household bickering in the drawing room didn't help."

Felicity had to smile. She somehow appreciated Elfrida's biting candour. It made it difficult to imagine her as a poisoner.

Elfrida quirked an eyebrow. "Not everyone has the stomach for Cullingslock's particular type of chaos."

"I can happily report that we haven't yet been given reason to flee."

"Not yet," added Alex, matching Elfrida's dryness.

"You mentioned a tour of the castle," continued Felicity. "Does that offer still stand?"

"Most definitely." The corner of Elfrida's mouth tugged upwards as she began untying her apron, her expression suggesting she found something amusing in the request. "Although I hope you have on comfortable walking shoes. We'll be climbing more stairs than a bell-ringer on Christmas morning."

Felicity glanced at her neatly laced cream Oxfords and Alex's polished brogues. She smiled. "It seems we do."

Chapter Eleven

Elfrida's tour of the castle was swift and efficient, understandably so given the vastness of the edifice. To potter along might have taken days.

Felicity absorbed every detail as Elfrida explained the castle's origins. It started as a motte-and-bailey in Norman times and expanded through various architectural periods — a great hall added during the thirteenth century, Tudor renovations that included larger windows on the ground floor, and Victorian modifications that brought gas lighting — all built from local stone and timber, though the Exmoor sandstone sadly proved rather too vulnerable to the extremes of weather blowing in from the Atlantic.

She was refreshingly candid in pointing out areas where the castle needed repair, from water damage to ceilings to missing panes in windows.

"When is the work expected to be done?" asked Alex.

Elfrida chuckled mirthlessly. "You'd have to ask my mother about that."

The castle was grander than Bradley Court both in scope — there were three drawing rooms to Bradley Court's one and an entire wing that had once housed a full garrison but now lay abandoned to time and decay — and in ornamentation, which, though faded, remained remarkably detailed. Paintings, photographs, and etchings covered the walls, and every available surface groaned with antiques, artefacts, and trinkets, some of which could not be ignored.

"May I ask about this?" said Felicity, her brow creasing as she pointed to what appeared to be a statue of a woman with a cat's head draped in real clothing. They had seen perhaps a dozen rooms by now and were in a curious little salon with an odd hexagonal footprint, a low slung table and two chairs with worn mahogany arms at its centre. A single window provided a view of the front drive, the rugged moorland beyond stretching towards the sea. Like many of the castle's rooms, the faint smell of exotic incense hung in the air.

Elfrida, who had maintained the energy of a professional guide throughout the tour, suddenly sighed. "I'm afraid I can't give you details beyond assuring you this is a purchase made by my mother for mystical reasons. This room is used mainly for readings."

"I don't see any books." Alex looked about as Pip sniffed the deep Persian carpet.

"Not that kind of reading." Elfrida's smile was sardonic.

"Your mother has quite a profile in that area, does she not?" asked Felicity, thinking back to the books in the library and the photographs of Winnifred dressed as though appearing on stage.

"She used to." Elfrida's face clouded slightly. "Much less so now, although I suppose it can be hard for a person to accept that one is past one's prime."

"Her powers aren't what they used to be?" suggested Alex a little obliquely.

"Oh, it's not a question of 'powers'. It's the ability to attract an audience. Not only attract it but keep it."

"Is that something you're involved in at all?" Felicity posed the question as though she hadn't been waiting for the right moment to ask things that might seem a little ignorant or rude if they were asked without time first to build trust.

Elfrida tucked her chin. "Am I involved in spiritualism do you mean?"

Felicity nodded.

"I've dabbled. I tried speaking to my husband once." Sadness touched Elfrida's tone. "But I didn't like what he had to say." Her impish smile returned.

"Your husband is..." Felicity began.

Elfrida nodded. "Lost in the war."

"I'm so sorry," said Felicity.

"My sincere condolences," added Alex.

Elfrida sighed. "He was an artist, so I assumed he'd be a pacifist. How wrong I was." She was quiet for a moment before continuing, "It could be worse. I might not have had a home to go to. My mother and brother were understanding. Despite everything."

Felicity raised her brow. "Everything?"

Elfrida waved a hand. "Oh, you know. Nothing's ever straightforward, is it? Not when it comes to family."

"Does that explain why you're so active in the kitchen here?"

Elfrida blinked. "I'm not sure I follow."

Felicity caught Alex's eye. Her attempts at natural conversation were perhaps not as natural as she had hoped. Had she misread Elfrida's warmth?

"I mean," continued Felicity, more carefully this time, "is that how you show your gratitude to your mother and brother? By helping in the kitchen?"

Elfrida's face hardened momentarily. "You have a brother, do you not?"

"I do," confirmed Felicity, sensing a shift in atmosphere.

"And did you find that your male sibling was mollycoddled by your mother while she behaved rather more strictly towards you?" Something flickered in Elfrida's eyes. Frustration, anger, resentment? Enough to slip something into that apple crumble?

"My mother actually passed away before I truly knew her."

Elfrida turned from Felicity, shaking her head. "Of course. How silly of me. Do forgive me."

"It's quite all right," said Felicity. The mistake gave her something of a conversational upper hand. "Your brother was mollycoddled?"

Elfrida laughed sharply. "Still is. Haven't you noticed?"

Felicity glanced at Alex, who shrugged. They had seen little interaction between Winnifred and Tristan. Indeed, Winnifred and her spiritualist supporters seemed to operate separately from the rest of the household.

"I can't say I have," said Felicity.

"Tristan is lord of this castle. He's the Baron of Cullingslock, but you wouldn't guess it, would you? Not from how he behaves."

Felicity blinked. With Winnifred's husband gone, it made perfect sense that Tristan, as the only living son, had inherited the title and the castle. Yet he did not act as though he held any authority in the household. Felicity had certainly gained the impression she and Alex were Winnifred's guests, not Tristan's.

Elfrida turned back. "My mother still very much rules the roost." Her sardonic smile returned. "And my brother is powerless to object."

Felicity's investigative senses tingled. A son undermined by his mother — was it another possible motive against the castle's matriarch?

"Would Lord Cullingslock's objections fail because of his own inability to stand firm or because of your mother's dominance?" Alex's question was incisive, but Elfrida seemed unperturbed by it.

She glanced out of the window. "Both. Or perhaps neither." She smiled wistfully. "I'm not sure anyone truly knows what's going on in that head of his these days. Our father passed when we were rather young. Our mother took on the responsibilities before Tristan was old enough. She simply never gave them up."

"He has never tried to take them from her?" enquired Felicity.

Hurried footsteps echoed up the stairs leading to the little reading room.

Elfrida tilted her head, narrowing her eyes playfully. "You can ask him yourself if you like. Although if you asked his wife, you'd get quite a different assessment."

Felicity and Alex exchanged glances. They would do well to speak to both Tristan and his wife.

"Mummy, are you giving the castle tour to Lady Felicity?" Audrey arrived, breathless, a flush under her freckles. She was clutching the skirt of her loose-fitting smock-style dress with a blue-and-white dotted print. "You said you wouldn't do so without me."

Pip gave a delighted yip and flew to Audrey. As the girl picked him up, her frustration melted away.

Felicity and Alex's time alone with Elfrida had been cut short. They perhaps had not burrowed into the very heart of the woman's frustrations with her mother, but her honesty about her irritations didn't seem to match the evasive movements of a would-be murderer. There was also a kindness that lay beneath her cynical humour. Winnifred's claim of poisoning remained doubtful.

"I've not done the gardens, if that's what you're worried about." Elfrida put her hands on her hips but had a smile on her face as she watched her daughter fuss the Yorkie into submission.

"Jolly good." Audrey looked up at Felicity. "Can I show you the gardens? Would you like to see them now?"

"That's awfully kind," said Felicity, glancing at Elfrida, "but I'm not sure if your mother was finished with her tour." There was a hint of hope in her voice. It wasn't essential information for the possible poisoning, but she was curious to know why Elfrida's husband's passing made her so grateful towards Winnifred and Tristan.

"We could spend days touring this place. I think our guests would appreciate a breath of fresh air." Elfrida quirked an eyebrow. "Would you not?"

Felicity smiled. She caught something in Elfrida's expression — perhaps a flicker of relief at being spared further questions. "Yes, I believe Pip would appreciate a stroll outside as well."

Audrey stood but kept her attention on the Yorkie. "The castle's to be yours, isn't it, Lady Felicity?"

"Audrey, that's not what I—" Elfrida sounded sharp.

"Absolutely not." Felicity's reaction was prompt yet gentle. "Where did you get that idea?"

Audrey looked bewildered. "But you're taking the Wastes from us, aren't you?"

Elfrida gasped. "Audrey, really." She sounded agitated. "It's not our land for anyone to 'take' from us — we've discussed this." The colour rose in her cheeks. Was this merely the girl's misunderstanding of the situation, or were there misguided rumours swirling about Felicity's intentions?

"Please, I'm not taking anything from anyone," said Felicity, remaining quite calm. "I merely came to Cullingslock to meet you all and to emphasise that I wish to lay no claim to the land."

Elfrida spun towards Felicity, arms folded over her chest. "Hmm. I would've thought Mother would've told you by now."

Felicity frowned. "Told me what?"

Elfrida lowered her voice. She leaned in. "About the curse."

Chapter Twelve

"Mother was just teasing."

With Pip trotting alongside her, Audrey led Felicity and Alex into the brightness of one of the castle's interior courtyards. It was the neat and pretty flower garden where Felicity and Alex had their outdoor discussion the night before, though the doorway Audrey used wasn't the same one beside which hung the Victorian family photograph. Bees and butterflies flitted across a rainbow palette of blooms. The perfume from the roses and honeysuckle was even stronger now in the August sunshine.

"Mother tells me frequently that we don't believe in curses or spirits or anything magical." Audrey ran her hand through a bouncing patch of lavender, releasing a waft of scent into the air as Pip dashed ahead. Would he behave himself for Audrey? Only time would tell.

"So she made the story up?" There was concern in Alex's voice. Even if he didn't believe in curses, his protective instincts were heightened.

Before Elfrida returned to the kitchen, she told Felicity that an ancestor of theirs — a woman who wed before her elder brother, just as Felicity would — had refused to take on the Cullingslock Wastes. She had enough to think about with running a whole new household on the other side of the county. The curse she suffered was that her relationship with the duke she had married soured quickly and irrevocably. Each ended up living alone and quite miserable.

"Oh, it's a true story. Mother didn't make it up." Audrey paused, withdrawing shining clippers from the pocket of her dotted smock dress. "It was my great-great-great-grandmother, if I remember correctly." She kneeled and collected a few flower stems, the Yorkie's nose following her every move. "Mind your whiskers, Master Pip." He was truly on his best behaviour.

Felicity cast Alex a doubtful glance and gave a light shake of her head. Normally, it was Alex offering Felicity reassurance, but the idea of a curse upon their marriage seemed to have affected him while Felicity was impervious. They didn't believe in spirits. Why should they believe in a curse? There were more realistic threats about which to worry.

Audrey stood up and held out the little floral bouquet. "For you," she said to Felicity, her freckled face lighting up with a smile.

Felicity accepted the delicate posy, which contained aromatic herbs as well as summer flowers. "Thank you," she said, lifting it to her nose and sniffing, the rosemary's pine-like fragrance mingling with the sweet floral notes of the lavender. "It smells quite delightful." She handed it to Alex.

Audrey watched with satisfaction as Alex's face lit up with surprise at the lovely smell of the little bouquet. "What's that lemony note?"

"Thyme. It's said to be good for the chest and breathing. It used to be added to love potions." Audrey giggled as she turned and continued along the gravel path.

Alex smiled at Felicity with a blend of charm and amusement that made her heart skip. "I'd like to think we're past needing love potions," he whispered.

Felicity smiled back at him playfully as they set off after their tour guide. "If you find me doubting my choices on the morning of our wedding, go outside and gather some herbs."

Further along the path, Audrey had stopped beside a patch of tall, heavily scented phlox. With accuracy and efficiency, she pinched away the spent flowers. Pip sniffed at the base of the plants but kept his jaws closed.

"Did you create this garden by yourself?" asked Felicity.

"It was planted up many generations ago. I just maintain it."

"How did you learn to do so?" asked Alex.

"My mother showed me a few things," answered Audrey, her attention still on the pruning, "but then she let me take over. She said I have the greenest fingers. I've a few books in my room from Christmas and birthdays. My uncle also has a lot of knowledge. I've learned so much from him about growth cycles and soil."

Felicity looked around the little garden. It was as perfect as a painting. All the plants looked healthy and lush. The contrast between this thriving space and the castle's crumbling walls was stark. "Are the herbs used in the kitchen?"

Audrey nodded. "Mrs Wiseley gives me a list and I come and collect what she needs. We've a kitchen garden, too, with fruit and vegetables. It's been quite productive this year." There was the faintest hint of pride in the girl's voice.

Felicity's detective instincts prickled. Audrey handled the kitchen herbs daily. She knew which plants could help or harm — and she and Elfrida had served that potentially deadly apple crumble. Felicity had been charmed into underestimating innocent-seeming young women before. It was a mistake that, if repeated, might prove fatal.

"Are any of the plants poisonous?" Alex posed the question with just the right amount of city-dweller ignorance.

Audrey laughed. "Many of them, if you eat enough." She gestured towards a shadowy corner. "Foxglove and monkshood are beautiful but deadly. Grandmama insists we keep them for their appearance, though I'd rather not." She stroked Pip's head. "I hate to think of the animals accidentally eating any of them."

A chill ran down Felicity's spine. So readily available, so easily accessed. Yet was Audrey capable of such a crime, and against her own grandmother, no less? It would call for a rather desperate motivation, and Felicity hadn't yet detected even a hint of animosity from Audrey towards any of her family members.

Perhaps imagining no one was looking his way, Pip slowly opened his jaws around the head of a frilly yellow marigold.

Felicity snatched him up and tucked him under her arm. "Miss Audrey puts a lot of effort into maintaining her garden. Let's not ruin it for her, Master Pip."

"Or poison yourself," said Alex, his eyes a little wide with genuine alarm.

Audrey smiled. "I'm quite certain marigold won't hurt him, but you can check with my uncle if you like. He's got rather specific knowledge." Her gaze wandered across the flowerbeds. "About many things, actually."

"I should indeed like to speak with your Uncle Tristan," said Felicity, although she wouldn't ask him about the effects of marigolds on Yorkshire Terriers. If she was to continue to take her great-aunt's suspicions even remotely seriously, far more pressing questions must be posed.

"Do you want to see the vegetable garden?" said Audrey, bouncing slightly on her toes.

Felicity's brow lifted. "Certainly." If there would ever be a need for the Cullingslocks to charm Felicity's own garden-obsessed grandmother, she would put Audrey on the front line.

They headed back inside and navigated the draughty corridors of the castle's interior maze. They passed Mrs Imrie and Miss Hartley, the former in a pale blue wool dress that seemed to drain what little colour she possessed, the latter cheerful in rose-printed cotton and a flowing chiffon scarf. The two women had trays laden with delicate sandwiches and a steaming teapot with them, perhaps sustenance for a reading or a séance. As Felicity, Alex, and Audrey passed them, polite greetings were exchanged.

Mrs Imrie stopped and turned sharply towards Felicity.

"We know what you're doing for the Reverend One," she whispered, her gentle Scottish accent lending the words an almost prophetic quality, "and we are immensely thankful."

Felicity's posture stiffened. The woman's pale eyes held gratitude, and something else — concern? Fear? She resumed a look of studied serenity and turned to follow Miss Hartley down the corridor.

Felicity looked at Alex. His jaw tightened. The extension of their visit at the castle had not escaped notice. Felicity's great-aunt and her followers had taken it as tacit acceptance of Winnifred's request for help.

"Would it be too much to presume that the spiritualists know about the poisoning," whispered Alex as they followed Audrey along the corridor, Pip held at her side. "And that they know that you're investigating?"

Audrey hopefully hadn't heard the interaction with Mrs Imrie. Seeking clarification about a suspected poisoning under the pretence of getting to know one's family members was one thing. Being unwittingly exposed while doing so was quite something else.

"I don't like it," said Felicity, her voice low. "I don't like it at all." Had Winnifred indeed convinced her supporters that someone in her own family meant her harm? Were there not already enough tensions at the castle?

Rearranging their faces into polite smiles, Felicity and Alex followed Audrey's invitation back out into the sunshine of another courtyard with gravel paths. It had the same layout as the flower garden, but instead of scented blooms there were upright rows of leeks and onions, bright green sprays of young summer spinach, and even tomato vines in various stages of ripening, soaking in the warmth from the stone walls against which they grew. Runner beans climbed wooden tripods, their scarlet flowers alive with bees, while rows of cabbages and cauliflowers stood like sentinels in rich, dark soil.

"Goodness," breathed Felicity. It was even more impressive than what the gardeners achieved at Bradley Court under Lady Henrietta's instruction.

Cluck, cluck, cluck.

"Edna, Dolores, Sally-Ann. How are you, my dears?"

Audrey was crouching, Pip sitting patiently beside her, his tail wagging excitedly as three frilly chickens, small but with large decorative tails and feathers around their legs, dashed towards Audrey. She fed them from her pocket.

Felicity smiled. "I wasn't expecting to see chickens in the castle."

Audrey kept her attention on the birds, managing the interaction with Pip, whom she encouraged to be gentle. "It was my uncle's idea. They help me with the caterpillars, and Mrs Wiseley loves their eggs. They're not the only—" Audrey stumbled over her words. "They're not the only animals at the castle, of course."

"Certainly not," said Felicity. "I've counted at least two dogs and two cats. And now three chickens."

Audrey giggled nervously as the chickens pecked at her palm.

"The gardens certainly look beautiful," continued Felicity. She hoped she'd not somehow made Audrey uncomfortable. There were still questions to ask.

Alex tipped his hat back to appraise an enormous marrow. "Very impressive indeed." With his background at the market in Covent Garden, he knew a thing or two about produce.

"I get some help with the digging from the footman. And my uncle brings the seeds," she said, still petting the chickens. "I do so love living here. I don't want me and Mother to be homeless again."

Felicity's heart constricted. The loss of Elfrida's husband in the war had been hard enough. Finding herself homeless with her daughter was another blow entirely. The grandeur of the castle — faded though it was — must have felt like salvation after such hardship.

"Why would you worry about being homeless again?" asked Felicity carefully.

Audrey looked over her shoulder at Felicity. "I thought you would take ownership of the castle, but apparently, I misunderstood."

"I'm pleased to confirm that you did indeed misunderstand," said Felicity gently. "And even if I ever were to take over a castle, I'd certainly not want to make anybody homeless."

Alex wore a look of concern. "Under what circumstances did you become homeless?"

"After Daddy left to fight."

Felicity felt a blend of sadness and confusion. The war years had certainly been difficult for many, but government and community support meant women whose husbands were sent to the front hardly ended up on the street. "Were you not offered any help?"

Still petting the chickens, Audrey shook her head. "They said we didn't deserve any."

"Why on earth not?" Alex sounded somewhat angry on the girl's behalf.

Her voice grew thin. "Because Daddy was German," she said, still petting the chickens and the Yorkie.

Felicity felt winded by the revelation. Brand — Elfrida and Audrey's surname — could be both English and German, but it now made sense that Elfrida felt so grateful to her family for taking her in. Women in her position, abandoned by German husbands wishing to fight for their fatherland, could end up shunned by society, even if they had no say in their husband's actions.

"I'm so sorry that happened to you," said Felicity softly.

Audrey rose suddenly to her feet, her eyes wide and blinking.

Felicity turned.

In the doorway to the little vegetable garden stood Peregrine Cullingslock, his bearing as rigid as a sergeant-major's. He was smartly dressed in well-cut tweeds, every inch the future officer despite his youth. He stared at Audrey in a way that transformed her from fun-loving to fully alert.

"My father is looking for you," he announced, his baritone flat and carrying a hint of displeasure — at being sent on an errand, or at his present company?

"Uncle wishes to see me?" said Audrey, sounding hopeful.

"No." He nodded in Felicity's and Alex's direction. "The guests," he said, his tone cool. Perhaps he'd overheard the conversation and was the sort of fellow whose mood darkened at merely hearing the word 'German'. The young man was rather difficult to read.

"That's convenient," said Felicity, matching his coolness with gentle enthusiasm, "as I would quite enjoy the opportunity to speak with your father." She turned to Audrey. "Thank you so much for showing us your gardens. They're most beautiful. You obviously have a talent for gardening."

The girl's cheeks flushed a little. "Thank you," she said shyly.

"Got any riding gear with you?" asked Peregrine matter-of-factly.

Felicity exchanged glances with Alex. She knew how to ride, of course, but hadn't expected doing so while at the castle. Alex's ability to ride was a different matter entirely, and his slight grimace suggested her concerns were well-founded.

"I don't, I'm afraid," said Felicity. "Perhaps we might take a motor instead?"

Peregrine's lips thinned. "Father insists on horses."

Felicity and Alex looked at one another. Investigating Winnifred's suspicions certainly involved speaking to her son. What choice was there but to saddle up?

Chapter Thirteen

With the main entrance hall as the basis from which to follow Audrey's directions, it was not too difficult to find the stables. They were on the other side of the castle from the entrance and separate from the fortress itself, although still within the confines of the medieval curtain wall.

The ramparts at the back of the castle looked too crumbly and unstable to walk along, but the plants blooming in pink and yellow that pushed through the cracks tipped the atmosphere more towards the romantic than the dilapidated. From the stable yard, Cullingslock Castle loomed behind them, its towers piercing the morning sky. The air carried salt from the distant sea mingled with the earthy sweetness of hay and leather polish.

The heels of Felicity's tightly laced Oxfords clicked over the cobbles, the sharp sound echoing against the stone walls. She'd been up to her room to change into a walking skirt that reached past mid-calf and a crisp cotton blouse. Her cloche hat was pinned firmly to her head. She also had with her the soft leather gloves that she used for driving. It certainly wasn't a typical riding outfit, but it would do.

Alex still had on his pale linen suit. Although finely cut and very attractive on him, it was entirely inappropriate for a ride out, which was just as well. He had little experience on horseback and didn't want a gallop over several hundred acres of rough moorland to be among his first riding experiences.

If Felicity wished to know Winnifred's son better and understand the tensions between him as the castle's lord and his mother as running the place, then she would have to do so alone.

"Are you quite certain you're comfortable with this?" Alex asked quietly as Pip trotted ahead of them towards the slate-roofed stable building nestled against the outer wall.

"Comfort aside," said Felicity, who would rather have been wearing jodhpurs, "I don't believe I'm putting myself in danger. I'm not fully convinced there's a would-be killer at the castle. Even if Tristan wishes to do away with his mother, what opportunity did he have yesterday to slip poison into her lunch?"

"None," confirmed Alex. Tristan had been seated towards Felicity and Alex's end of the table. "Everyone besides Audrey and her mother remained in their seats for the duration of the meal."

"And was there anything about Elfrida or Audrey this morning that hinted at murderous intentions towards my great-aunt?" Felicity's question was somewhat rhetorical. There had been nothing about their behaviour to indicate they were part of a poison plot, either separately or together. "It's certainly possible to misread people, especially if one doesn't know them well, and I accept that we're new to the castle. Yet my assessment remains that my great-aunt is mistaken and there has been no wrongdoing."

"But you continue to investigate?" poked Alex.

The question was fair. Felicity rolled it around her mind for a moment. "It would be a satisfying rounding-off to matters if I could reassure my great-aunt that no one in her family is plotting her demise."

In the cool, hay-scented shadows of the stable, they came across Tristan. He was brushing a sturdy chestnut mare who seemed to enjoy his attention, the horse leaning into his strokes with contented snorts. He had on riding breeches, a tweed waistcoat, and a cream-coloured shirt with the sleeves rolled up to the elbows. His pale reddish hair, usually pomaded into submission, fell boyishly across his forehead. When dressed in more formal attire, his frame seemed swamped and rather weedy. Now active with the animals, his wiry physique appeared more powerful and in its element, the muscles in his arms sinewy like ship's ropes as he worked the brush over the horse's flanks.

He stood up straight and smiled awkwardly when he saw Felicity approaching. A flush of colour touched his pale cheeks. Whether from exertion or social discomfort, it was hard to determine. He shook hands with Felicity and Alex, his grip surprisingly firm despite the tremor of nervousness in his voice as they exchanged greetings. He even gave Pip a pat on the head, although the Yorkie was promptly off to the corner of the stable where Solomon was asleep on a hessian sack. The Collie was delighted to be woken by the Yorkie, and the two dogs engaged in a frolicking round of play.

"I'm ready for a tour of the land," said Felicity.

Tristan nodded, his shoulders tensing slightly, but he continued to smile. "Wonderful. Will Mr Cooper be joining us?"

Alex held up a hand with polite refusal. "I'm afraid I'm not much of a rider, and I shouldn't like to slow you down. I gather there's a lot of ground to cover."

"Indeed there is," confirmed Tristan, a little solemnly.

"Mr Cooper doesn't mind being left behind," said Felicity, turning to Alex. "Do you, Mr Cooper?"

"I have a book with me." He produced a copy of F Scott Fitzgerald's latest. "I shall be quite happy keeping watch over Master Pip and finding a spot of sunshine in which to relax."

Alex smiled knowingly at Felicity. Relaxing was the last thing Alex would do as long as there was even a whiff of a potential murder scheme to uncover at the castle. He would do his best to gather information, just as Felicity would do on horseback with Tristan.

"Very well." Tristan headed for the saddle rack, his movements betraying an eager energy. "Let's take the horses out for a run."

"Splendid," said Felicity, although her enthusiasm wilted as

Tristan fetched a rather antique-looking sidesaddle from the rack. She was not the keenest of riders at the best of times. Would the outing be worth it, or would she end up tossed into one of Exmoor's countless boggy mires?

The chestnut mare on which Tristan rode and Felicity's dappled grey gelding thundered across the heathland, the tiny purple flowers frothing beneath them, the scent of the sea on the wind and the warble of the skylark in the air.

Felicity was seated comfortably in the sidesaddle, her walking skirt, Oxfords, and gloves holding up well to the experience. White and grey clouds whipped across the bright blue sky. Why did she have it in her head that horse riding was not something she was terribly keen on? The experience was exhilarating.

Solomon did a commendable job of keeping up with the horses, his tongue lolling as he ran into the wind. It was difficult to have much of a conversation while flying along at such a pace, but as had been discussed at the stables, five-hundred acres was an awful lot of ground to cover and they wouldn't see it all that day. Yet Tristan was keen to show Felicity what he could, his initial reserve melting away as he pointed out boundary markers and ancient rights of way with boyish enthusiasm.

"These moors have sustained people for centuries," Tristan called over the galloping hooves, his voice carrying surprising passion. "The peat cutting rights alone date back to the Domesday Book. And the heather—" He gestured expansively at the purple carpet stretching to the horizon. "—provides grazing for the sheep and shelter for the red grouse. Without proper management, all this wildness would be lost to bracken and scrub."

"It's quite beautiful," replied Felicity, raising her voice over the thunder of the horses, though 'beautiful' seemed inadequate for the raw majesty surrounding them. "Why on earth call it the 'Wastes'?"

Tristan gave her a little smile. "One must look closely to understand the true value of it."

Eventually, they slowed at the edge of a forest. A nearby pond, its surface mirror-smooth save for the ripples where dragonflies hunted, allowed the horses and Border Collie to recover and drink. The weather was quite warm and the air rather heavy, filled with moisture from the Atlantic.

Felicity and Tristan stood in the shade of ancient oaks whose gnarled branches had weathered centuries of coastal storms. The ride had been thrilling, but it had also been — Felicity was only now realising — rather exhausting, especially hanging on in sidesaddle. She was beginning to recall why she didn't gravitate towards riding as a pastime. Her legs would doubtlessly ache the next day, but she might as well enjoy it for the moment. Not that enjoyment was her reason for taking the tour with Tristan.

"The woods are extremely important and rare. Some of these oaks are over four hundred years old. And the rowan there — locals still hang branches over their doors for protection." His voice dropped to something almost reverential. "The oaks shelter dormice and purple hairstreak butterflies. In spring, the forest floor becomes a dense carpet of bluebells." Tristan looked a little drained from the ride but also very alive and interested. He stood with his hands on his hips and looked up into the trees, the leaves in the wind hissing like river water, a woodpecker's rhythmic tapping emanating from somewhere in the lush, green canopy.

"You know an awful lot about this land," Felicity observed, genuinely impressed by the depth of his knowledge.

Tristan blinked at her. "Am I boring you?"

Felicity's eyebrows shot up. His reaction suggested he was accustomed to scorn. "Not at all." She was happy Tristan felt so able to speak to her, albeit so far only about land-oriented topics. "How do you know so much?"

"I studied agriculture at Oxford." His expression shifted, becoming more sullen. "Mother was disappointed, of course. She would've preferred me to study something more esoteric. History at the very least." He forced a little chuckle. "Or better yet, follow her interests into the metaphysical."

The mismatch of a parent's expectations and the child's own desires was a common familial narrative, but this example didn't seem fraught enough to induce deadly consequences.

"I thought studying at Oxford would help me, you know, run this place." Tristan quickly held up a hand. "Although please trust me that I always knew there was the risk that I wouldn't become the next trustee after my mother. I mean, we're very aware that the land doesn't belong to us. But we've a duty to take proper care of it."

As beautiful as it was, Felicity still couldn't envisage a scenario in which she'd wish to become the owner of the Wastes. "It's quite all right," she said, genuinely unbothered by the talk of the land's ownership. "I can imagine agriculture was a very interesting topic to study."

Tristan nodded, some of his earlier enthusiasm returning. "Came in handy in the war. They called me up to Whitehall. Helped them with food production strategies and so on. But I felt too guilty about not fighting, so I went to the trenches in the end." His Adam's apple bobbed. "When I came back, everything was so... Different. I still love coming out here, though." He cast a gaze upwards into the trees as the wind set the leaves dancing.

Felicity nodded. The memories and reflections of veterans could be delicate. That Tristan had volunteered to fight despite playing an important role in keeping the country fed during the U-boat blockade implied a tendency towards action based on both thoughtful conviction and deep feeling. He didn't appear to be the kind of son to wish harm on his mother.

Felicity joined Tristan in gazing up at the trees. "The land doesn't judge or demand explanations, does it?"

He said nothing.

"May I ask what was so different when you returned?"

A hint of darkness flickered across his features. "Mr Kemp had been engaged by my mother to oversee the Wastes. He has a... He has a rather different way of going about things."

"Mr Kemp seems already rather proud of the profits the land will soon make," said Felicity carefully. "If I understood him correctly, it was possible to make money during the war due to the demand for resources, but it's been a struggle to generate income since."

Tristan narrowed his eyes. "But at what cost?"

"I'm not sure I follow."

"Has he told you how much he expects a year?"

Felicity blinked and shook her head.

"Do you not wish to know?"

"Actually, I don't." Felicity had considered the Wastes's ability to generate income. It didn't make a difference to her view on owning the land, but it certainly seemed like a source of tension at the castle. "Although I am curious about what happens to the proceeds."

Tristan's forehead creased. "The wording of the ancient trust documents is unfortunately not very specific about what should be done with the land's revenue while in trust. With the way things stand now, the best approach would be reinvestment."

"Has that not happened?"

Tristan turned away with his hands on his hips. He looked out across the hills. On the moorland in the distance, a flock of sheep grazed its way over an open patch of bright green grass, their woolly forms like scattered clouds. "Partially, although I believe the money made during wartime has nearly run out. Beyond setting up his specific schemes, Mr Kemp hasn't seen the need for reinvestment, and Mother has other priorities. She believes the spiritual world requires as much investment as the physical one."

"Do you not have a say in matters?" suggested Felicity gently. She was perhaps prodding rather hard with someone she barely knew. But Elfrida had described her brother as 'powerless' without explaining exactly why. "You're the Baron of Cullingslock, aren't you?"

Tristan turned to look at Felicity. She expected him to be vexed by her comment, but the tension in his face had dissipated. "It perhaps comes across as odd to you. I know others who struggle with it. But my mother has been through rather a lot. She can be commanding and difficult and has held onto the reins for far too long. I see that as much as anyone else. But she has suffered and continues to suffer."

Felicity remembered the photograph in the corridor. The husband and son that Winnifred had lost. The mere notion of such grief continued to prompt sympathy in her. To have witnessed his mother's pain first-hand would have made a deep impression on her remaining son.

"The accident changed her, you see. She's never been quite the same since that dreadful business."

Felicity's senses sharpened. "What accident?"

Tristan blinked rapidly. Had he said too much? "Look," he said, his tone denoting a change of topic. "I'm not a proud man. I will not undermine my mother and make her life even more difficult than it has been. My time will come." He looked out over the land. "As will my son's. For we must always have an eye on the future, must we not?"

Felicity quirked an eyebrow. "Indeed." Discussion of Winnifred's accident could be saved for another time, but Tristan's words weren't those of a man who would attempt to do away with his own mother, let alone in front of an audience through a poisoning at lunch.

He cleared his throat. "Are you truly serious when you say you won't take on the land? Do you really not care if there's an income from which you might benefit? I hope I'm not being too blunt in asking that. The decision is yours, and I don't intend to influence you." He looked solemn, his brow drawn low. "I only wish to know."

Felicity appreciated her relative's honesty, but she studied him with fresh eyes. Here was a man clinging to something about which he cared deeply that might be snatched away. Yet it had no bearing on the possible poison in the apple crumble, did it?

"I don't wish to become a landowner," confirmed Felicity, batting away any thought of the supposed curse Elfrida had delighted in mentioning. "I'm simply waiting for the opportunity to sit down with your mother — when she's recovered — and with her solicitor so that we can arrange things."

Tristan nodded and sighed, his angular frame deflating slightly. "I suppose that would be it for my lifetime, at least. After my mother, the trusteeship would come to me. Not much of a chance of that blasted clause being triggered again as long as I live." He ruffled a hand through his thin hair, his shoulders once again tense. "Please excuse my language, and if I've said anything objectionable, I can only apologise. I suppose I'm getting rather het up about matters. Philippa has always said I over-react to the smallest of things."

Was Tristan, by his own admission, inclined to lose his head occasionally? Their isolation pressed upon Felicity's awareness. They were miles from any help, the castle a distant silhouette on the horizon.

"The threat of losing land you love is no small thing," she suggested gently.

Tristan's brow creased deeply. "If you'd been serious about taking the land for yourself, then I would've probably offered you the castle."

Felicity drew in a breath, surprised by the desperation in his tone. "I do hope you're joking." The castle was home to many, not just Tristan and his family. It reminded Felicity of what Audrey had said about being made homeless again.

Tristan smiled sheepishly. "I suppose I am. But that's the attachment a man can have to land. It's not the same as what one feels for a building. Buildings come and go. The land remains."

Toot, toot! Toot, toot!

A rudimentary road wound through the Wastes. A large motor car, unmistakably the castle's old-fashioned Napier limousine, its landaulet top pulled open, was making its way steadily over the rolling hills. The afternoon sun glinted off its nickel-plated fittings. From beside the pond, it was possible to make out several figures within.

Toot, toot!

Tristan sighed deeply as Felicity squinted into the sunshine. There came a distant but unmistakable yapping. Pip's excited bark carried across the moorland air. Solomon's ears pricked, but he remained beside his master.

The motor had stopped. Someone was standing in the back seat and waving. Beckoning.

"Is that...?" began Felicity.

Tristan began stalking towards the horses, his expression grim. "Indeed. We have company."

Chapter Fourteen

The contents of the charmingly old-fashioned Napier made Felicity grimace slightly, then smile as she and Tristan grew closer on their horses. The land agent, Mr Harry Kemp, was behind the wheel, but next to him sat Alex with Pip on his lap. In the backseat, wearing a large sun hat with a pale blue ribbon fluttering in the strong breeze, was Tristan's wife, Philippa. She wore a tailored travelling suit of dove-grey serge, its city sophistication setting her apart from the windswept riders approaching. Polite greetings were exchanged between Tristan and his wife and the land agent, but he was quick to turn down an invitation to join the group in the car. It was impractical because of the horses.

"I thought Lady Felicity would want to see some of the progress we've been making over the past couple of years," said Mr Kemp to Tristan, who looked less than happy about his own tour being interrupted.

"Mr Kemp does manage these lands, Tristan," said Philippa a little pleadingly, her hands folded tightly in her lap, but Tristan's downcast expression didn't change.

"You can follow along with the horses if you like," said Mr Kemp dismissively to Tristan as Felicity took her place in the back of the

Napier, the leather seat creaking beneath her and releasing the scent of beeswax polish. She was loath to leave Tristan, but she had heard enough from her relative to be quite certain he hadn't attempted to poison his own mother. She was also disinclined to leave Alex alone in facing the overpowering presence of Mr Kemp.

Alex twisted in his seat as Pip scrambled onto the back bench to join Felicity. "How was the ride out?" The meaningful lift of his eyebrows indicated he had found an interesting titbit or two of information that he would share with her later.

"Exhausting but quite interesting," said Felicity, subtly indicating that she, too, was eager for an exchange with Alex, although it could certainly wait till they were alone. She smiled at the passenger seated next to her. "Are you much of a rider, Lady Cullingslock?" said Felicity, maintaining the formal politeness Philippa seemed to prefer. As hoped, Felicity was steadily working her way through the family, searching for a convincing motive to do away with Winnifred that she was quite certain she wouldn't find.

Philippa's posture remained rigidly upright despite the jolting movements as the motor rolled forward. How might she express herself without her husband present?

Philippa smiled with a touch of melancholy. "If only I were a rider. I might see a little more of my husband then," she said, casting a glance towards Tristan as the baron set off on his chestnut mare, galloping with intensity, Felicity's mount on a leading rein, Solomon bounding through the heather after them.

"Will we be meeting Lord Cullingslock further ahead?" enquired Felicity of Mr Kemp as he wrestled with the old Napier's gears. The engine's roar competed with the whistle of the coastal wind, while dust from the rough trackway and petrol fumes from the motor mingled in the air.

"I can't promise that," said Mr Kemp, "but I'm sure you'll be impressed by what I have to show you."

Felicity would've liked to have swapped a meaningful glance with Alex in response to the man's pompousness, but Alex was facing ahead in the front seat and Felicity had only Philippa and the little Yorkie on the back bench for company.

She maintained a polite smile. “I very much look forward to it, Mr Kemp,” she said, raising her voice above the engine.

Philippa seemed satisfied with Felicity’s attitude, although a shadow of doubt rippled across her features. “I imagine my husband had much to say about the land you are to inherit.”

“Lady Cullingslock.” Felicity’s tone was polite yet firm. Her protestations about landownership seemed to have fallen on deaf ears. “Please allow me to reassure you that I have no intention of taking on the Wastes — or any other tract of land, for that matter.”

Philippa held up a hand with courteous authority. “Lady Felicity, with all due respect, I appreciate very much your commitment to your position, but you are reaching a conclusion without having all the facts. Mr Kemp will be able to explain precisely how the land is used and its value. I don’t think it’s fair that such information should be hidden from you, but there is a high risk that once you understand the land’s potential, your mind will be changed.” Philippa sounded earnest yet concerned. “It would not be good for Cullingslock if you discover the truth of things further down the line, then change your mind and take all of us by surprise in doing so. You must consider matters fully so that the issue may be directly resolved.”

“Are you referring to the income from the land?” asked Felicity.

The question was perhaps too head-on for Philippa’s tastes. Her cheeks coloured slightly. “Well, yes. I suppose it’s fair to say that’s the nub.”

Felicity tipped her head. “That’s very kind of you to ensure that I have the facts. But I already touched on that topic with your husband. And I can reassure you just as I reassured him — I shan’t change my mind.” It would have been churlish to say aloud, but the Quicks had enough income from which to live, and Felicity had enough on her plate without the extra responsibility of landownership.

Philippa gave a tight nod. “If you say so.” She didn’t sound convinced. “You know, it’s rather remarkable that you came to the castle and that you’re still here with us now.” She gave an apologetic smile. “Forgive me if that sounds presumptuous of me, for I realise we’re barely acquainted, but I know what it is to be an outsider in this family — in this entire area, in fact, as I was born down in Plymouth. The manner in which the castle is run is unconventional, to say the least. Your apparent desire to reunite the estranged branches of the family is admirable. If anything would benefit Cullingslock, it would be more contact with the outside world.” A wistful expression crossed her face. She gazed out at the landscape for a moment, the swallows riding bursts of wind above the heather, the castle’s towers rising from their hilltop perch in the distance. “Beyond even Exmoor, I mean.”

Felicity smiled warmly at her co-passenger. “If you believe I could be of some benefit to the household in that regard, then I’d be happy to fill that role,” she said, recalling her original intention for her visit to Cullingslock.

The wind gusted powerfully as the motor bumped over the uneven track, each jolt sending tremors through the old vehicle’s frame, its springs protesting with metallic groans. Felicity kept a steady hand on Pip’s silky back, but she didn’t have to grab onto her cloche. It had been pinned in place for the horse riding. Philippa, meanwhile, caught the ribbons from her hat and fastened them under her chin. With eyes as dark as onyx set among delicate features, she was an attractive but also clearly very practical woman. She and Tristan seemed well suited to one another with their level-headed natures, yet there was something of a gulf between them.

“Curse it!” The land agent’s exasperation was obvious as the motor hesitated and lurched while he searched for the correct gear towards the brow of a hill. At the side of the trackway, small tortoiseshell butterflies danced between daisy-like heads of golden ragwort in the salt-touched breeze.

“Your husband gave me excellent insight into the flora and fauna of the area,” said Felicity.

Philippa swept a wayward ribbon from her cheek. “Of course he did.” Her tone was hard. “He was always interested, but when he came back from the war, he was quite changed. Towards me, towards Peregrine. He seemed to have left his devotion to his family somewhere in the mud of Flanders.” She turned sharply to Felicity. “Did he tell you he sent himself out there? That no one asked him to go? It wasn’t as if he had no use here in England. He was working for the Ministry of Food.”

Many relatives sounded proud of the contributions made to the war effort by their loved ones. Philippa sounded almost disdainful.

“He did tell me, yes,” said Felicity gently.

Philippa thrust her gaze back to the moorland, her hands clutched tightly in her lap. “When he came back, he spent an awful lot of time outdoors, even when the weather was terrible. It became an obsession. He used to manage the estate, you know.” Her voice was brittle, as if trying to maintain composure. “He did a very good job of it. I mean, not in the same way that Mr Kemp is doing his work.” She cast the land agent a little glance, her jaw tightening as if reluctant to admit the pompous man’s prowess. “But he was making money. The dowager baroness only brought Mr Kemp in to manage matters while Tristan was away. But when my husband came back, he had such different priorities. The war had changed something about his character. It would’ve been dangerous to hand him back the reins.”

It wasn’t unusual for men to return from war with a different outlook on life, but how might this translate to land management — and Tristan’s temperament?

“How was your husband different?”

“You’ve witnessed him talk about the moors. He knows the name for everything. Every plant. Every bird and insect.” Philippa broke off, fingertips massaging her temple. “Good gracious, why am I telling you all this?” She turned towards Felicity. “I’m so sorry, your ladyship. I am blathering on, aren’t I?”

Felicity smiled at Philippa with sympathy and understanding. The woman somehow still felt she was an outsider at the castle, and there were clear strains on her marriage. Felicity's appearance at Cullingslock was perhaps an opportunity to express emotions that propriety demanded Philippa keep very much bottled up. But what was coming through was more frustration at Tristan than any significant misgivings about Winnifred, the supposed victim of an attempted poisoning.

"I'm listening," Felicity said. Even if she was not related by blood to Philippa, she was still a relative.

Philippa looked mildly ashamed but also relieved. "You'll keep my confidence, won't you? About what I've said regarding my husband?"

"Naturally."

"I just want you to understand the situation here. Did my husband tell you how important the land has become for the upkeep of the castle?"

Felicity gave a little frown. "He did not."

"The place would be in an even worse state if it weren't for the income Mr Kemp generated from the Wastes during the war — if a worse state is possible to imagine." Philippa's laugh held an edge of desperation. "But then my husband is the baron. The castle is his, yet he continues to allow his mother to run things, to set her own priorities. He has difficulty seeing the reality of the situation and taking control. I know the war changed him, and we must all be thankful for his sacrifice. I can bear the coldness he has developed towards me, but he seems to forget that we have a son. A son who will inherit."

Felicity maintained a polite neutrality. Tristan's allowing his mother to keep hold of the reins was, according to him, quite deliberate. He had also expressed concerns about the future and for his son, yet she was keen to hear his wife's view on matters.

"You've seen the state of the castle," continued Philippa. "You've seen what Tristan's mother has spent the money on. Even if Mr Kemp can generate further profits, as long as the dowager baroness is in charge, it's doubtful the castle will benefit."

Felicity sat up straighter. Was this a motive for wanting Winnifred gone? To stop the continued disintegration of the castle and preserve Peregrine's inheritance?

"What has my great-aunt spent the money on?"

"Ha!" Philippa's laugh was mirthless. The raw honesty of her reactions undermined Felicity's ability to imagine her as a calculating poisoner. "Don't tell me you haven't noticed all those statues and headdresses and mirrors and goodness knows what, all of them said to have mystical powers." The tone she used for 'mystical powers' implied she believed in no such thing. "I witnessed that fellow Silkstede, who is supposedly writing a book about the dowager baroness, bringing such pieces and convincing her to pay exorbitant prices. And he might not be the only one of them at it. I have no idea what kind of money they're making off her."

Felicity raised an eyebrow. According to her great-aunt, her supporters were beyond reproach. What dangers was Winnifred potentially blind to?

"I've tried to talk to Tristan about it, but he won't listen, and his sister has detested me since the beginning. I can't speak to her. So I'm stuck watching it happen, watching our son's inheritance being frittered away." Philippa fetched a handkerchief from her pocket and dabbed at her eyes, the wind whipping the ribbons of her hat about her neck. The handkerchief was edged with delicate lace and monogrammed with her initials in fine embroidery, perhaps a relic of more prosperous times. "I'm so sorry, your ladyship. I don't know what came over me. You don't need to hear all this. You just need to know about the land and make up your own mind about what to do regarding it."

Moved by the display of emotion, Felicity reached out and took Philippa's hand. There was a tremor in the woman's fingers. "Don't apologise. I'm keen to learn as much as I can, and not just about the land. Tristan is family, and by extension you are, too. What might I do to help?"

A flash of hope, tempered by embarrassment, lit Philippa's dark eyes as she looked at Felicity. "You must feel free to make your own decision. You must have all the facts in order to do so." She paused, seeming to gather herself. A shadow crossed her features, as though remembering something painful. "The dowager baroness has endured terrible losses, you know. Her husband, then her son..."

"I am aware."

Philippa swallowed and nodded. "It's perhaps what drives her to seek comfort in the spiritual realm, but understanding her grief doesn't make it easier to watch our resources disappear. Although they're not our resources, of course. The Wastes belong to you, should you wish to claim them."

Felicity patted the back of Philippa's hand. "Please, you've no need to worry," she said, a hint of coolness creeping into her gentle tone. She'd felt genuinely moved by Philippa's display of emotion, but what if that was precisely the point? Felicity wasn't infallible when it came to misdirection. What if everything Philippa had put forward was designed to prompt Felicity's pity for Philippa and her family?

Screech!

"Blasted thing!"

The motor had come to a sudden halt, almost throwing Pip from Felicity's lap. Luckily, she had hold of him.

Philippa sat up straight, her hands gripping the seat, her eyes wide with worry. "What's happening? What's wrong?"

No answer came, but the land agent had already snatched up a rifle from beside his seat. He slung it over his shoulder and sprung out of the vehicle with the agility of a rabbit.

The Old English Sheepdog, which must have been at rest in the driver's footwell until that point, also went to jump down from the motor.

"No, Lionheart!" bellowed the land agent, pointing a finger at the dog. "Stay! You hear me? Stay!"

The big grey-and-white dog whimpered and sank onto the driver's seat as Mr Kemp went dashing off through the heather.

"I'd advise to stay low," Alex said to Felicity and Philippa as he craned his neck to get a look at where Mr Kemp had vanished.

"What's going on?" whispered Philippa.

Felicity dared a peek over the side of the vehicle. The moorland had grown suddenly still.

"Get down!" cried Alex as he ducked.

Crack! Crack!

Felicity thrust herself towards the seat, covering Pip as bullets flew above the motor, her heart hammering against her ribs as the acrid scent of gunpowder drifted on the air.

Chapter Fifteen

"Blasted thing!"

Crack!

The land agent fired another shot from his rifle. Felicity, Philippa, and Alex crouched low in the Napier as the motor continued to idle. Lionheart sat frozen on the driver's seat, his shaggy coat shuddering with each report of the rifle. Keeping a tight grip on Pip, who was more curious about the situation than afraid, Felicity shot a look of concern at Alex. His eyes scanned the surrounding moorland, but he didn't seem shaken. He had a clearer view of whatever had prompted the land agent to seize his gun and leave the vehicle.

"What's going on?" asked Felicity.

"The man's a—" Alex glanced at Philippa and changed his mind about sharing his assessment of Mr Kemp. "Are you both all right?"

The women nodded, although Philippa's knuckles were white where she gripped the leather seat.

"It's best if you both remain low." Alex leaned an elbow over the door. "Are you quite finished?" he called out with measured authority to Mr Kemp. It was wise not to rail against a man holding a loaded weapon, but irritation edged Alex's tone.

The land agent ejected the spent cartridges with habitual ease and strode back to the vehicle. He was smiling a little, but his jaw worked with annoyance. "Almost got him."

Alex shook his head. "Got what? That scrawny fox that ran across the track?"

"Filthy blighters. Carry disease, they do. Lost several sheep to the rot last month. I thought the fencing would keep them out, but we've got the foxes and the badgers burrowing under it." The land agent vaulted over the motor's door with unnecessary vigour and stowed his weapon beside his seat. Lionheart scrambled back down into the footwell as his master settled. "We've got the hunting parties coming later this month, though. That'll get things back under control."

"Thank goodness," said Philippa, her voice thin. She gazed out across the moors as though wary that an aggressive fox might reappear for revenge.

The vehicle set off again, bumping over the uneven, hilly trackway. The intimacy between Philippa and Felicity had been shattered by the discharge of Mr Kemp's weapon. The scent of gunpowder still hung in the air, mixing unpleasantly with the leather and motor oil. Felicity and Alex exchanged several meaningful glances. It was far from ideal to be in the company of someone reckless and in charge of a gun, but there wasn't much choice. Tristan and his horses had long disappeared from view.

The Napier slowed in front of a cottage constructed from the local red sandstone, the slate on its roof grey and weathered. The cottage was small, but there were other buildings scattered around, including a pigsty and a little lean-to, its weathered wooden door open to reveal rudimentary tools. A battered old tractor sat under a covering, likely to protect it from the salty sea winds. A pile of peat blocks stood ready for winter fuel, while chicken wire enclosed a small run where several hens pecked industriously at the ground. At the front of the cottage there was a neat little vegetable garden and rows of bright marigolds that nodded in the breeze. The air had a tang of manure to it, plus the rich aroma of something like beef and onions, presumably dinner cooking in the cottage's little kitchen.

The dwelling and its yard bore all the hallmarks of a working tenant farm — neat but modest, with everything serving a practical purpose.

Before the vehicle came to a halt, a man in a flat cap and a stout woman emerged from the cottage, both closer to Winnifred's age than Felicity's. The woman wore a checked apron over a faded blue dress, the man a collarless shirt and a woollen waistcoat. They positioned themselves beside the trackway like a miniature welcoming committee.

"Good day to you, Mr Kemp." The man removed his cap and squeezed it in his thick-knuckled hands, the lines in his face deepening with an obsequious yet rather hollow smile. "I haven't been able to get the beet seed in the ground yet after all the rain we had last week." The man's accent was strong but similar to that of Felicity's area of Devon. She could easily follow him, although from Alex's expression, he was having difficulty keeping up. "The ground's been washing away. I've never seen anything like it. Proper chaungy weather we've been having. Mr Higgins over at Pleasant's Farm said he had the same problem as well." The man spoke hurriedly, as if keen to make his case.

The land agent slung his rifle over his shoulder as he alighted from the vehicle. Was it absolutely necessary to take the weapon with him for a visit to a tenant farmer? Might he fire off a shot at any moment? Lionheart slunk after his master, staying very much at heel. Felicity stuck closely beside Alex and did her best to position herself to avoid accidentally being caught in the line of fire should Mr Kemp suddenly take a potshot at some unsuspecting animal. Philippa hovered near Mr Kemp. She offered a gentle greeting to the couple from the cottage, shaking both their hands, although there was an uneasiness on both sides. As concerned as she was for Felicity's deeper understanding of the land, this wasn't Philippa's natural habitat.

"Alright, Mr Crocker." Mr Kemp positioned himself with his hands on his hips in front of the ageing farmer and his wife. "We can discuss the new crops some other time, but I'll have you know I won't stand for malingering. You can't hide from the future. Change is always inevitable. Now. This here is Lady Felicity Quick." He gestured to Felicity with a jab that almost made her recoil. "She'll be the new owner of this land."

"Mr Kemp?" said Felicity, attempting to interrupt.

The farmer's wife clutched her husband's arm, eyes growing wide. "A new owner? Will that mean more changes?"

Mr Kemp laughed. "You don't have to worry about that. I'm not going anywhere."

The reassurance failed to make the farmer or his wife look relieved. Mrs Crocker's grip on her husband's arm tightened. They seemed almost frightened of him.

A flush of annoyance rose in Felicity's chest. She was a little irritated by the land agent's attitude. More than a little, in fact.

"I believe we've yet to discuss the matter of who I would employ as a land agent, Mr Kemp," said Felicity with crisp authority. There seemed no point in revisiting her lack of desire to own the land, which almost everyone seemed set on ignoring.

Her comment caused Alex to raise an eyebrow and Philippa to look somewhat fearful. The land agent frowned at Felicity not with irritation but with bewilderment, as if there couldn't be any doubt that he would continue as the land agent, regardless of who was trustee or owner of the property.

"Tell her ladyship about the success we're expecting with the new crops, Mr Crocker," said Mr Kemp, thrusting his chin at the elderly farmer. "As the new owner of the Wastes, her ladyship needs to understand what we're achieving here." The land agent's use of 'we' rang somewhat false. Pressuring other people into doing one's bidding did not count as collaboration.

"Please," Philippa stepped forward. "Lady Felicity indeed needs to know what she would gain by accepting ownership of the Wastes." So the visit to the little farm was partly Philippa's idea as well.

"Oh. Well. Yes." Flustered, the farmer shifted his weight. His wife patted his arm encouragingly. It was admirable that the land agent wanted Felicity to hear directly from the tenants that farmed the Wastes, but he was putting more pressure on the elderly couple than was comfortable. If Mr Kemp was trying to impress Felicity, he was failing.

"We planted the beans. Didn't we?" said the woman, her voice strengthening as she looked at her husband. "They're practically ready to bring in."

"Beans?" echoed Felicity gently with a glance at Alex. "How interesting," she said as Alex nodded agreeably. She wanted to be respectful and encouraging of the Crockers, but in reality she had little understanding of farming, and the mention of the crop didn't mean a great deal to her.

"First time field beans have been cultivated up on these hills," Mr Kemp cut in. "People told me it wouldn't work, but it's been a roaring success, hasn't it?"

The farmer hesitated, then nodded. "Yes, sir. If you say so." A flash of something — disagreement or perhaps fear — crossed Mr Crocker's weatherworn features before he lowered his gaze.

Mr Kemp put his hands on his hips. He surveyed his surroundings as if realising the little farm and the anxious farmer weren't the best illustration of whatever he was trying to show Felicity — that he was extremely capable in his role? That the profits to come would be significant? Either way, it was of little consequence to Felicity.

"We could see some of the land that's been recently turned over to cultivation. It wasn't doing much before that — the sheep were grazing it, but they were mostly skin and bone, and they're getting much better feed now. And better prices." Mr Kemp narrowed his eyes towards the rise of a nearby hill. "This way." He strode off at a commanding pace, taking a wooden stile in the wall at the side of the dwelling and forging through tall stalks bearing bean pods and drying leaves towards the brow of the hill.

Lionheart trotted along obediently. Philippa followed, gathering her skirt to scramble uneasily over the stile. Alex stepped forward and offered a hand, which she gladly took. Pip squeezed under the stile and went bounding off through the bean crop, jumping about and enjoying himself, although Felicity was careful to ensure that he didn't get too close to Mr Kemp. The land agent still had his loaded weapon with him.

The bean crop was rather sparse, with fallen stalks between those ready to harvest. Shallow crevasses indicated where rain water had flushed the land bare. Was this the 'roaring success' Mr Kemp had been talking about?

Eventually, the little party caught up with him, leaving the farmer and his wife still standing outside their cottage, uncertain of whether the visit had concluded. The land agent stood on the brow of the hill with his hands on his hips, his dog commanded to sit beside his feet, the canine's grey-and-white coat blowing in the wind. The view extended towards the rugged coastline, the water a silvery blue disappearing into a milky sky. The beauty of it was staggering. Then Felicity's breath caught.

Below them rolled moorland and forest, all draped like silk across the land, but with patches sliced away, square, sharp, and unnatural looking. New fields had been created and fenced off. In some, there were sheep or cattle. In others, crops were growing. There was even a section of woodland that had been recently felled, the stumps still visible in the ground, the stripped and de-branched trees neatly piled up. Scattered about the hills were cottages much like the one beside which Mr and Mrs Crocker still stood, their inhabitants perhaps awaiting or even fearing further instruction from the land agent, the hills their families had farmed for centuries changing before their eyes.

"The dowager baroness isn't half as silly as she makes out," said Mr Kemp, staring down at the newly created fields, which looked like wounds on an otherwise unblemished visage. "In giving me free rein, we've made the type of progress this area has long been crying out for." His brash confidence seemed to waver, as if deeply moved by his own achievements.

Philippa nodded in agreement. Neither Mr Kemp nor Tristan's wife appeared to hold Winnifred in especially high regard, but would either of them do away with her? It felt terribly unlikely, but Felicity couldn't turn a blind eye to their attitudes.

"My great-aunt doesn't seem remotely silly to me," said Felicity rather pointedly, looking at Mr Kemp and at Philippa as she spoke.

Philippa averted her gaze, a hint of shame in her eyes.

The land agent chuckled as though Felicity had told a joke. "She hired me to look after this land, and when she saw what I was doing, she kept me on. It'll be making money for the first time since the war, and good money at that."

With a hand on her hat, Philippa looked up at the land agent. "It's money the castle sorely needs."

Felicity and Alex exchanged glances. Money was something of a sore point at Cullingslock. But whatever Mr Kemp's abilities in terms of generating a profit from the land might be, his achievements were undermined by his attitude.

Felicity's patience was growing thin. "What point did you bring me here to make, Mr Kemp?"

The agent turned to Felicity. There was something condescending in his grin. "That money will be yours when you take over the land. Yours to do what you like with."

Philippa swallowed. Her fingers worried the ribbons of her hat. She no longer looked so impressed with Mr Kemp, but she didn't interrupt him, even though it would have been her right to do so. She was the wife of the baron, and even if Mr Kemp ranked above the household staff, he was still a paid employee of the family, even if he reported to Winnifred as the land's trustee rather than to Philippa or her husband. The land agent had no right to take Felicity and Alex out into the Wastes and say whatever he wanted to them.

"I believe I've already made it quite clear that I have no desire to become a landowner," said Felicity.

Mr Kemp continued to smile knowingly. "I haven't told you how much money it'll make yet."

"And I shan't be asking," said Felicity firmly.

A tremor in the ground made everyone turn.

Tristan had galloped up to the top of the hill. With him was the horse Felicity had ridden, its saddle still empty, but there was a third horse now — a powerful bay gelding with a white blaze down its face.

Peregrine sat upright on the beast's back. Despite his youth, he rode with natural grace, though his expression held none of a horseman's usual ease. His jaw was set, his face drawn with an emotion that was hard to place.

Father and son looked down at the land agent. They'd appeared so unalike until that moment. Peregrine's withdrawn tension now echoed his father's quiet intensity.

As Solomon sprang forward to play with Pip, Lionheart stirred at his master's heels. A sharp reprimand from Mr Kemp caused him to remain in place.

"Father, tell him, won't you?" The young man's baritone shook slightly, not from anger but from something closer to desperation.

Tristan regarded the land agent. "Have you spoken about the damage that's been done?"

Mr Kemp frowned and laughed a little. "The damage that was done by ignoring the need for the land to make money, you mean?"

"Peregrine, please," said Philippa. Her voice carried a sharp edge. "There's no need for you to be involved in any of this."

The young man turned to his mother. His shoulders sagged slightly, his military bearing crumbling for just a moment. He looked vaguely upset — not hurt from being chastised, but perhaps injured by the possibility he'd done wrong in her eyes. "Father should say his piece, though, shouldn't he?"

Philippa's attention snapped to Tristan. "Why must you choose now of all occasions to speak out?" The words emerged with barely suppressed frustration.

Tristan's horse shifted restlessly beneath him. "I can show you, if you like," he said, addressing Felicity now. His voice held the same quiet passion she'd heard when he'd spoken of the ancient oaks. "The real consequences of what Mr Kemp has done."

Philippa frowned deeply. She looked enormously uncomfortable. She glanced at Felicity as if to gauge what she might be thinking but was unable to hold her gaze for long.

Felicity looked at Alex. Her investigation — or, more likely, the wild goose chase — into who might have poisoned Winnifred would be complete when she'd spoken to each member of the Cullingslock family, and Felicity had yet to interview Peregrine.

Alex understood perfectly. He gave her a brief nod. They would compare notes regarding their separate experiences later on.

She approached the horse with the empty saddle. The gelding snorted gently, its breath warm against her outstretched hand. "Show me," she said to Tristan and his son.

As Tristan dismounted and helped Felicity climb back into the sidesaddle, she caught a glimpse of Mr Kemp's expression. The land agent's knowing smile had finally faltered, replaced by something harder, his grip tight on the strap of his rifle. Was it reckless to irk him? Perhaps. But Felicity so hated to see arrogance go unanswered.

Chapter Sixteen

The wind gusted harder, the shadows of clouds racing across the landscape as Felicity accompanied Tristan and his son towards the patch of recently felled trees. As they descended from their horses, both Tristan and Peregrine assisting Felicity out of the sidesaddle, the smell of sap and freshly cut wood assaulted her senses, sharp and resinous. The once dense forest looked violated, the surviving trees displaying vulnerably bare trunks and branches where they had been accustomed to shelter from their neighbours now cut down.

"He says he wants to plant turnips. But he won't be able to do so until the stumps have been cleared. He'll probably set light to them, and that might catch the heather." Tristan stood with his hands on his hips as he stared at the devastation.

Peregrine hung back near the horses, while Solomon sniffed around the tree trunks. The Border Collie seemed subdued, as if sensing the wrongness of the scene.

Felicity hugged herself as the wind cut through her cotton blouse despite the sunshine. Raw earth and splintered wood stretched before them where once had stood rowan, oak, and ash. The sight made her chest tighten. But what did she know about land management? Her family's estate at Bradley Court was mainly landscaped parkland, the upkeep of which was overseen by Lady Henrietta for aesthetic purposes more than anything else.

"I understand Mr Kemp's priority to be the generation of income. Is that not what he's trying to achieve in doing this?"

Tristan lifted his hat and dragged his fingers through his thinning, reddish hair. He had been so placid indoors, almost shy. Outside, on the land, he seemed a different person. "He has had some success in the past, and he might bring more money in for the short-term, but these woodlands have been here for hundreds of years. He's only thinking about the next five years before he moves onto an even bigger estate. He's thinking only of his own career."

Felicity cocked her head. There were certainly some tensions in the Cullingslock household, but contrary to Winnifred's beliefs, the dowager baroness didn't seem to elicit the strongest of reactions. "What did Mr Kemp do before coming to Cullingslock?"

"Managed a farm's estate with lands just a fraction of the size of these down in Dorset."

"Did he have success there as well?"

Tristan stared at Felicity, his pale eyes hardening. "It depends on how you define success."

"Your mother seemed impressed enough with him to take him on and keep him," Felicity observed.

Tristan sighed. The mention of Winnifred seemed to deflate him. "She has her own priorities. I don't wish to come across as heartless, but she won't be around forever."

Felicity quirked an eyebrow. "What would your priorities be for the land?"

Tristan glared at her. "The restoration of the natural habitats for the animals and insects. Space and time would be needed for them to recover, but once the balance is restored, the tenant farmers won't have to struggle to achieve the yields needed for the land to make money. The rain won't wash the ground away so easily. There'll be fewer pests on the crops. They would work with nature rather than against it."

Felicity nodded. Coming from a well-studied and experienced

agricultural expert, Tristan's argument was convincing, even if it didn't sound as immediately profitable as Mr Kemp's approach. "Does my great-aunt not agree with your view on things?"

"As I said," replied Tristan. "My mother has her own priorities."

"Grandma's not taking good care of the castle though, is she, Pa?"

Despite the gusting wind, the question somehow hung in the air. Peregrine's voice carried none of his usual stiff bearing — there was something unguarded in his tone, his fingers worrying his horse's reins.

"It's not up to your grandmother to take care of the castle." Tristan began stalking back to his horse, each step crunching through fallen twigs and scattered sawdust. "It's up to me."

Peregrine opened his mouth as if to speak, then closed it again. Had Felicity not been present, might they have dug into the matter a little further? The interaction reflected Philippa's concerns about Tristan's lack of regard for Peregrine's inheritance. Peregrine was young, but he perhaps wasn't as oblivious as Audrey. Was he frustrated at watching his inheritance crumble away?

The visit to the felled forest was swiftly over. Even the horses shifted restlessly, eager to leave. Felicity wasn't sure if her reaction to the destruction had been what Tristan had hoped for, but he certainly didn't seem happy. He rode off with Solomon racing behind before Felicity had managed to mount her horse. Peregrine was gentlemanly in assisting her back into her sidesaddle.

"Did I upset your father?" she enquired of the young man as he climbed back onto his own mount.

"No." Peregrine watched his father galloping through the heather. "I believe I did."

They set off at a gentle pace, the castle rising into view as they followed the contour of the land upwards from the sea, the fresh wind gusting at their backs.

"I'm sure it's not your fault," Felicity said, studying Peregrine's profile, the freckles scattered over his long, elegant nose. "It seems there's rather a lot on your father's mind at the moment, and I'm not sure my arrival at the castle has helped."

Peregrine glanced at Felicity. Something warm flickered in his eyes — gratitude, perhaps, or relief at being understood. "They were like this before you came."

"Mr Kemp and your father?"

"My father and my mother."

Felicity's heart squeezed with sympathy for the boy. His parents' troubles were obviously affecting him. "Are they having difficulties getting on with one another?"

"My mother wishes my father would take on more responsibility. My father wishes to do things in his own way."

They rode in silence for a few moments, Felicity waiting in case the boy wished to say more of his own accord. As tiny butterflies danced above the purple flowers of the heather and white clouds continued to streak above, a mournful cry echoed across the moor. The striking sound was hard to ignore.

"A curlew," said Felicity. "How lovely."

Peregrine's mouth hooked into a smile. "Close. A whimbrel. An early one at that."

"I'm not sure I've ever heard of a whimbrel." Felicity smiled at the boy. "Did you learn that from your father?"

"Yes." Peregrine's smile fell. He straightened on his mount, his eyes ahead. "But it shan't be of use to me at Sandhurst."

"Have you always dreamed of a career in the military?" Felicity ventured.

"I suppose so. Doesn't every young man?"

They rode on again in silence. Ahead, Peregrine's father and the Border Collie were waiting where the rough moorland track met the more established road back to the castle.

Felicity's time alone with Tristan's son would soon be over.

"And what's your opinion on the situation between your father and your mother?" She spoke gently, as though simply continuing an ongoing discussion.

"My opinion?" Peregrine straightened in his saddle, as if the question had caught him off-guard.

"Is it odd that I should ask for your opinion?"

There was a pause. "No."

"Do you have any notion of what might be the source of the tension between them?" Felicity would have liked to have mentioned the boy's grandmother specifically, but she didn't wish to encourage animosity where there perhaps was none.

Peregrine looked ahead, his jaw set, his youthful features hardening like a warrior preparing for battle. "I must keep my focus on my army career."

Chapter Seventeen

"There is discontent and tension. Sadness and regret. All the usual ingredients, actually."

Felicity and Alex's chosen meeting place was tucked away close to Alex's rooms. In defiance of the sunshine outdoors, the abandoned spiral staircase with its smoothly worn narrow steps held the chill of centuries, the heavy wooden door at its base hanging slightly ajar. Above them, the door at the top of the stairs was padlocked shut, rust bleeding down the ancient iron of the mechanism. They could hear the footsteps of anyone coming up towards them, but they still kept their voices low, their words barely disturbing the dust that danced in a shaft of light from a narrow window slit.

Felicity sat on a cold stone step with Pip on her lap, the terrier's small body radiating a welcome warmth. He was tired after all the fresh air on the moors.

Felicity continued. "But are there murderous intentions towards my great-aunt? And more specifically, is there someone among the family group who has already taken action to end her life? Perhaps I'm overlooking something, but I'm afraid I can't see it."

"The motivations are there, though, aren't they?" Alex sat one step below her, close enough that she could feel his warmth. He had his hat on his knee, a lock of his dark blond hair fallen onto his scarred forehead as he looked up at her.

"In theory, yes. Elfrida and her daughter are treated like servants. Tristan is dominated by his mother. Philippa is frustrated at the ruination of the castle and what might be left of it for her son. Peregrine himself seems to reflect this concern. But they've all been relatively open with me about their feelings on these topics, and none of it is hatred or resentment that burns hotly enough to generate action of the violent sort. And we haven't even discussed the risks that the potential murderer would've taken by slipping poison into a portion of the apple crumble at luncheon."

Alex raised his brow and was about to speak.

Felicity held up a hand. "Very well — and in front of a renowned lady detective."

"Thank you," said Alex with obvious satisfaction.

"Then there's the logistics of it. Aside from the servants — and do remember how the cook seemed ready to throw herself off the battlements for her unwitting role in Winnifred's illness — it seems only Elfrida and Audrey had access to Winnifred's food ahead of her eating it. Can you imagine Audrey harming anyone, let alone her own grandmother?"

"Just because I can't imagine it, doesn't mean it didn't happen."

Felicity tutted. Alex had a point, but she would finish making hers. "Elfrida has complicated emotions towards her mother, just as Tristan does, but I wouldn't say she felt driven to matricide."

Alex narrowed his eyes at Felicity. "So your great-aunt was just imagining things?"

Felicity let out a sigh and shifted her seat, her hip a little sore from the sidesaddle. "I don't wish to be dismissive or intolerant of spiritualism, but it wouldn't be her first flight of fancy, would it?"

Alex rubbed his jaw. "What if someone paid a member of the household staff to add the poison to your great-aunt's food? Perhaps even blackmailed them?"

Felicity gave her head a little shake. "Are you losing your faith in my ability to draw valuable and relevant conclusions from what I observe?"

"My faith in you is unshakeable," he said without a hint of humour. "But since when am I not allowed to ask questions?"

Felicity narrowed her eyes at her husband-to-be. "Paying or even blackmailing a servant takes a lot of forethought and planning. So why organise it when a famous sleuth has come to stay?" She said the words 'famous sleuth' in a way that made it clear she was being ironic.

Alex gently pushed his shoulder into her knee. "I'm delighted to hear you acknowledging your status."

Felicity harrumphed, though the effect was undermined by the warmth in her expression.

"And you're absolutely right," continued Alex. "It makes little sense."

Somewhere in the castle's depths, a door creaked.

Felicity lowered her voice further. "I would say it's rather a good thing if the poisoning is purely a figment of my great-aunt's imagination."

"And what an imagination," said Alex. "Will you report back to Winnifred to that effect?"

"Not exactly in those words, but I believe I have some things she ought to hear. I would also like to draw a line under this land ownership question, although I don't think the situation is as straightforward as I imagined it would be."

Alex shifted closer, his warmth a comfort against the cool stone. "The income, you mean?"

"Not that."

Alex's eyes widened with worry. "The curse?"

Felicity frowned. "Of course not. I thought it would be easy for everyone if I just turned down ownership of the land. But I was thinking about why Tristan was so eager for me to tour the Wastes and witness what he perceives as the destruction of its value, even if it means more money when Mr Kemp clears space for more crops and grazing."

Alex nodded. His expression grew thoughtful in the dim light of the narrow staircase. "He wants you to take the land off his mother."

Felicity shifted her bruised hip on the stone step. Pip stirred briefly, then settled back into gentle snoring.

"He seems to go to great lengths to avoid confrontation with his mother, even to the point of potentially damaging his relationship with his wife and son. It's easy to overlook him as the lord of the castle, yet he is not without his interests and passions. He seems to care more about the land than anything. I'm beginning to suspect he would be satisfied if I took on the land and dismissed the land agent."

Alex quirked a brow. "Would you be interested in doing that?"

Felicity hesitated. "I feel for Tristan, but I also feel for Philippa. She seems to desire precisely the opposite — that I leave the land with the trustee for the money to come in, hoping it would one day be reinvested in the castle."

"So you're considering becoming a landowner?"

"Not exactly, but I wonder if there might be an opportunity for me to help smooth matters out between the various parties."

"You mean you'd like to become even more embroiled in the drama of this place than you already are?"

Felicity smiled down at Alex. "Perhaps." She hadn't thought the idea quite through. In the half-light, his features held both concern and affection. "Dramatic or not, they are family. I say." It was time for a change of subject. "Did you hear anything about an accident my great-aunt might have had at some point?" she asked, recalling what Tristan had divulged but refused to explain.

Alex shook his head. "Not that I recall. Why? Is it significant?"

"If the poisoning is, as I suspect, something of a fantasy, then understanding her past might help us understand what led my great-aunt to imagine it."

Alex smiled with amusement. "Suppose you invite them all to our wedding and Winnifred has a funny turn, then insists you investigate."

Felicity knocked his shoulder with her knee. "I'm already very much looking forward to our first investigation as newlyweds." Her stomach tightened a little. "But if you'd rather I'd not invite the Cullingslock contingent—"

Alex twisted to face her. "I was only joking. You can invite whoever you like."

Felicity tried to smile, but it quickly faded. "Do you not have any strong opinions on what our wedding should be like?" It was a topic she'd already attempted to broach since arriving at Cullingslock. She didn't wish to push, but nor did she want to make assumptions about the event without Alex's proper input.

Alex took Felicity's hand and brought it to his lips. "I should like you to be there."

Felicity couldn't help but smile. "But might your family not find it difficult to attend the event if we hold it in Devon?"

Alex frowned. "Where else do you propose we hold it?"

"London?" Felicity suggested, somewhat meekly. She'd never envisaged it for herself, but it wasn't unusual for aristocratic young women to tie the knot at a prominent church in the city.

Alex looked perplexed. His hand loosened from her palm. "Do you want that?"

"I wish to know what you want."

The look Alex gave her made Felicity's stomach clench. How had she, in so few words, managed to displease him?

Tap, tap, tap, tap.

There were footsteps on the staircase below them.

Letting go of Alex's hand, Felicity rose promptly from her seat and tucked Pip under her arm. Alex replaced his hat on his head as he stood. They gazed at one another for a moment but said nothing. Alex smiled a little sadly. She'd disappointed him, hadn't she?

Tap, tap, tap, tap.

The footsteps continued towards them.

Alex glanced at Felicity before starting down the steps. What had she said to upset him?

It was Audrey who appeared around the staircase's bend. She'd been smiling to herself, but her smile fell when she saw Felicity and Alex.

"Lady Felicity," she said, some of the colour waning behind her freckles. "Mr Cooper."

Felicity smiled brightly. "Hello, Audrey. It seems we took a wrong turn," she said, using lines upon which she and Alex had agreed before taking their seats on the stone steps. "I was hoping to find your grandmother's chambers."

The girl's gaze danced from Felicity to Alex. "M-my grandmother's in the other wing."

"She is?" said Felicity, retaining the most spirited tone she could muster. "Then my bearings are worse than I thought. Might you be able to tell us how to get there?"

"Of course," said Audrey. "I can take you there, if you like?"

"That would be most kind of you," smiled Felicity.

As they set off after the girl, Alex's fingers found Felicity's and gave a discreet squeeze. She looked into his eyes, but his expression remained grave. It was a gut-wrenching moment to cease their private talk. It was clear they still had matters to discuss.

Chapter Eighteen

Timpson was standing guard at the dowager baroness's door when Felicity and Alex arrived. He was extremely polite but most firm in admitting Felicity only, citing her ladyship's need to rest in turning Alex and Pip away.

"Good luck," whispered Alex as Felicity slipped the Yorkie into his arms.

She gave a firm nod, appreciating the sentiment but doubting that luck was required. It was quite obvious what needed to be reported to Winnifred.

The dowager baroness was still resting in her four-poster with her two cats seated beside her like silver-furred sphinxes when Felicity was led into the room by the butler. Through the diamond-paned window, the sun had ducked behind a bank of silver-white cloud above the wind-bent treetops that surrounded the castle. The scent of incense — sandalwood, perhaps, with a touch of amber — mingled with something sharper, camphor, most likely, and a faint, cloying trace of laudanum.

"Your great-niece wishes a word with you, m'lady," said Timpson gently to the castle's matriarch.

The older woman's eyes fluttered open with visible effort. "Hmm? Oh yes, of course. Come, my child, sit with me," she said, struggling to raise herself up in bed, a grimace of pain flickering across her features before she composed herself. Thoth and Ra stretched languidly but remained in place as Winnifred shifted, the butler assisting her in rearranging her pillows without having to be asked to do so.

"Leave us, please." Winnifred directed the command across the room. Tucked behind the door through which Felicity had entered were Mrs Imrie and Miss Hartley. Various glass vials, dried herbs, and crystals had been arranged on the cabinet top, suggesting the preparation of a remedy or healing ritual.

"Yes, Reverend One."

The two women withdrew from the room shortly after the butler, who quietly closed the door behind them, leaving Felicity alone with Winnifred.

"Please, my child, do sit." Winnifred watched as Felicity lowered herself onto the stool beside the bed. A ringed hand stroked the soft fur of one of the cats, his eyes closed with feline satisfaction. On the rosewood table beside her bed, a candle flickered. The wax of the candle had been coloured purple, and it had a green ribbon tied around it. Dried leaves — rosemary, by the scent — were strewn about the candleholder.

It wasn't how Felicity would have decorated her own room had she been confined by illness, but the atmosphere was undeniably soothing.

"How are you feeling, Great-Aunt?" asked Felicity quietly. Even if the act of poisoning had been a fantasy, Winnifred's illness — as attested by Dr Marsh — had not.

"Better." She smiled faintly. "Ever so much better."

"I'm happy to hear that."

"And I should be happy to hear from you, my child. What have you discovered?"

Felicity had considered carefully how she might present her findings in the most effective way possible. "I have spoken to all your relatives in the household — to your son and your daughter, to their children, and also to your son's wife."

Winnifred nodded knowingly. "I am assuming you heard bad words said about me?"

Felicity paused. The directness didn't surprise her. Winnifred possessed the sort of dramatic honesty that might have disarmed less prepared opponents. "Do you wish me to speak frankly?"

"Of course."

"They see your faults. They see them clearly through their own lenses, each with their own concerns."

Winnifred fixed at Felicity with a sharp gaze, her blue eyes widening. Had she expected denial rather than confirmation?

Felicity continued. "But they also regard you with an enormous amount of affection. They know what you've been through." She lowered her tone a little. "About your losses." The loss of her husband and her young son was clearly a delicate topic. Felicity hadn't heard it from Winnifred herself, but it was not a secret. "Your family understands what has led you to where you are now."

Winnifred's left hand trembled slightly on the cat's fur, while her right remained motionless. Her stern gaze crumpled slightly. She perhaps hadn't expected Felicity to refer to her past.

"In short," continued Felicity, buoyed that she seemed to have an advantage in the conversation, "they see you clearly. Your faults, but also your strengths. I didn't find anyone among them harbouring such ill feelings that they would wish you physical harm. They see you as a whole. They see you for who you are."

Winnifred slowly raised an eyebrow. "Is that so?"

"That is my assessment, yes."

It was, of course, something of a vague assessment without concrete evidence. But then Winnifred's claim of being poisoned also seemed rather woolly. What felt more pressing and more dangerous than a murderer at Cullingslock Castle was the idea that Winnifred genuinely believed a member of her own family wished to harm her. Such division and suspicion within an already tense home was good for no one, and if Felicity could do anything to alleviate the situation, then she could be happy with her trip to North Devon.

Winnifred continued to regard Felicity with consternation. Lines deepened around her mouth. "And what are my faults, as you have learned about them from my family?" Her voice shook a little but was still commanding.

Felicity allowed silence to settle before continuing. "There are concerns about how you have used the proceeds from the land. There are worries about the upkeep of the castle." The question of the building's preservation had been a recurring theme across the discussions with Elfrida, Tristan, and Philippa. Felicity could comfortably share this feedback without pointing the finger at a particular family member.

Winnifred's lips pressed together into a thin line. "Go on."

"There are also concerns about your relationship with the other residents of the castle." Felicity swallowed. She had heard this only from Philippa, but she was curious to see Winnifred's reaction. "Concerns have been raised that you may be exploited."

Winnifred's eyebrows flew upwards. "Is that so?" The words emerged clipped with irritation.

"There is a great amount of respect for you," added Felicity quickly. "There would have been mutiny by now if the disagreement with your way of doing things had been so strong and the respect for your position weak. But you are held in high regard. Your decisions are still trusted as the best way to lead the castle." This was a rather broad interpretation of what Elfrida and Tristan had shared with Felicity about their mother, but it wasn't a lie. Reassuring Winnifred there was no murderer lurking among her loved ones felt like the most important priority in that moment.

Winnifred shifted again, her movement unmistakably awkward — her left side did all the work while her right remained still. Her jaw shifted slightly. She was struggling to maintain her imperious bearing. "Were these feelings across-the-board, or was there one person in particular expressing such forthright views about my performance?"

Felicity chose her words with care. There were only three adults she had spoken to, and Winnifred might deduce identities if she wished. "What I've reported to you is an amalgamation of the opinions I heard." Keeping to generalities was safest. The line between helpful intervention and harmful interference could be gossamer-thin.

Winnifred inhaled deeply and rather noisily through her nose. A faint wheeze betrayed the effort it cost her. "Well, I suppose I must thank you."

Felicity quirked an eyebrow. She hadn't been given too much choice in the matter of investigating — her great-aunt having practically strong-armed her into it — so it was refreshing to hear her gratitude. "I hope you find reassurance in knowing that I didn't uncover a scheme for your downfall, but I would still like to repeat my earlier advice," added Felicity. "If you genuinely feel at risk, you should contact the police." She was as certain as she could be that there was no would-be killer at the castle, but she could never be one-hundred per cent sure.

Winnifred tucked her chin. "I already told you I shall not do that."

Felicity shifted on the little stool. She had expected as much.

"But I do trust in what you've told me," added Winnifred with a solemn nod.

Felicity gave a little smile. "I'm glad." She was happy to have reassured her great-aunt.

"And I understand you took something of a tour of the Cullingslock Wastes today." Winnifred's eyes twinkled. "Become enamoured, have you? Ready to live up to your ancestral expectations and take the lot on?"

Felicity frowned. "Not exactly." She hesitated. Was it a wise plan to play with the expectations of what she might do with the land and its profits? She'd felt inspired by the idea while out on the moors and witnessing the arrogance of the land agent, but hadn't she meddled enough at Cullingslock?

She cleared her throat. There was another line of approach she could take. "I'm curious to know more about my ancestors on my mother's side. I realise the family archive was lost to fire. I was hoping some evidence might persist in the stories that have been told through the generations, although, as you know, my mother sadly did not live long enough to pass any such information onto me."

"Naturally, my child." Winnifred nodded sagely. "Would you like me to invite them to speak to you directly?"

"No," said Felicity, perhaps a little too promptly. "Thank you," she added with a smile. "I should just like to understand a little more about who these women were."

Winnifred nodded. "Very well, my child. I can't claim to know all the stories, but I shall do my best. Was there any ancestor you had in mind?"

"Who was the first woman in the family to take on the Wastes?"

Winnifred drew a deep breath. Her left hand traced patterns on the cat's silver fur. "Lady Katherine was the first to hold the land for the family. It was at the start of the Civil War. She was the younger daughter, and her brother was a fervent royalist. It was during a period when it made sense for a Devonian to maintain a royalist position — what were the chances of those parliamentarians sweeping that far down the country and taking everything over? Yet Katherine's father had something of a gift for seeing ahead. Perhaps he himself had the divine eye."

Felicity maintained a neutral expression at Winnifred's mystical interpretation.

"He saw the risks, and he didn't want bloodshed or destruction for the castle or for the people living on the surrounding land. So he ensured his son wouldn't gain control of the entire estate. The lad only got the castle. He left the land surrounding Cullingslock to his daughter via the clause about her being the first to marry before the elder brother. That clause is still in effect, as you well know."

Felicity nodded. The ancient and convoluted inheritance had shaped her own presence at the castle. "Were Lady Katherine and her husband not royalists, then?"

"My child, Lady Katherine was a pragmatist. It doesn't surprise me that you're in her direct line. Luckily for her and for the Cullingslock estate, she'd been matched in marriage to a man of similar temperament, which seems to be the case for you, too.

When the parliamentarians reached this part of the country, as Lady Katherine's father knew they would, Katherine and her husband were flexible about what happened to their land, allowing troops from all sides to manoeuvre. It meant the castle was taken without too much damage. It meant no siege and no farms laid to waste."

Felicity nodded. Katherine's diplomatic navigation of the Civil War spoke of remarkable political acumen. As her father had expected, the parliamentarians had triumphed, but Katherine had been able to uphold her father's wishes and vision for the future. It made it seem even more of a shame that the castle had fallen into such disrepair, but Felicity had already relayed Winnifred's family's thoughts on her performance as the castle's caretaker.

"Why was the tradition of the inheritance continued after the Civil War? Why not reattach the land to the castle?"

Winnifred gave a little sigh. "It worked out well for the family. I imagine they became afraid to change it, lest it alter their good fortune."

"Your daughter spoke of a curse," said Felicity a little haltingly. She didn't believe it herself, yet it seemed to affect Alex. "There were negative consequences for the marriage of a relative who refused the land, she said."

Winnifred's laugh was shrill and clear. "My daughter hasn't the faintest idea what she's talking about. That's not how curses work, my child."

Felicity felt an unexpected sense of relief.

"Now, if you'd be so kind as to excuse me." Winnifred shifted in her bed with visible discomfort. "There's much that needs to be done. Mrs Imrie!" Winnifred raised her voice and directed her appeal in the door's direction. "Miss Hartley!"

The door to the bedroom opened immediately, and the two spiritualist helpers appeared in the doorway. They'd been waiting just beyond the door.

Felicity felt her stomach drop. She had been overheard. How foolish had she been not to consider the possibility? She quickly ran through what she had shared with Winnifred. Nothing seemed immediately dangerous, yet the violation of privacy stung.

"Approach, please, ladies," said Winnifred, and the two women came closer to the bed. "I'm not disappointed in my great-niece's effort. She has done her best, but we are without a resolution to our problem. And the plan we discussed earlier must be put into effect."

"Yes, Reverend One," the two women said, bowing slightly.

Mrs Imrie's pale eyes glittered with something between devotion and calculation. "In the usual room?"

"Yes. And quickly — time is pressing."

Felicity was now thoroughly on the back foot. Her gaze jumped between her great-aunt and the helpers as the two women hurried out of the room.

"What's going on?" asked Felicity, unable to keep the edge from her voice.

"You carried out your investigation and found nothing," explained Winnifred. "That's normal and to be expected, as it's obvious now that there are greater powers at work. We shall have to use a different method to find whoever it was who tried to end my life."

"And what method would that be?" asked Felicity, a chill prickling along her spine. She had wanted to help, but had she succeeded? Or had her very presence at the castle only served to further stir matters within the household?

"Have patience, my child. And faith." Winnifred smiled in a way that said everything was going exactly to plan.

Yet Felicity had the creeping feeling she wouldn't care for what happened next.

Chapter Nineteen

There was to be another séance. Felicity might have guessed, only this one was to be much grander than the session she had witnessed on her first night at Cullingslock.

Mrs Imrie was charged with gathering everyone. She was instructed to do so on an individual basis and set about approaching people throughout the household and telling them of Great-Aunt Winnifred's request to join her in the grand turret room. Even the staff were invited.

Before Mrs Imrie could approach her, Felicity had slipped out of her great-aunt's bed chamber and hurried downstairs in the hope of finding Alex so that they might discuss how the meeting with Winnifred went before the séance began. She found him seated in a low-slung armchair in a chintzy salon, Pip held captive on his lap to prevent the Yorkie from harassing Lionheart, who was seated beside his master. It was thus that Felicity bore witness to Mr Kemp's response to Mrs Imrie's whispered request for his presence.

He laughed from behind his newspaper. "You know full well I don't have time for that mumbo jumbo."

Mrs Imrie looked oddly unfazed by Mr Kemp's reaction. A slight tightening around her eyes suggested she'd expected nothing more from the land agent. She approached the solicitor, who was sitting in the chair opposite, crystal tumbler on the table at his side.

"Very good," was his noncommittal response to Mrs Imrie's whispered approach.

The land agent frowned at the solicitor. "Not going along with it, are you?" he said, despite Mrs Imrie's continued presence in the salon.

The solicitor swirled the amber liquid around his tumbler. "The dowager baroness is paying for me to be here. I don't see the harm in going along with her requests."

The land agent shook his head and returned his attention to his newspaper, as though disapproving of the solicitor's attitude.

Mrs Imrie approached Felicity and Alex. Pip's tail began wagging at her approach, his small body quivering with excitement at the prospect of any diversion. "The dowager baroness kindly requests your presence in the turret room in the North Wing," she said gently.

"Thank you," said Felicity politely but also noncommittally.

Mrs Imrie gave a stiff nod and withdrew, leaving the room in search of further invitees.

Felicity gave Alex a sober look. "I believe my great-aunt's dissatisfaction with my report is the reason for the séance." She kept her voice low enough so the land agent and solicitor might not overhear. "You don't have to attend."

He raised a quizzical eyebrow. "This is the next stage of the investigation?" He kept his tone equally low, his eyes twinkling, "I've never been to a séance before, yet somehow I don't particularly want to miss it. Is that rum of me, considering I'm a nonbeliever?"

"Belief didn't seem to be an issue on the night we arrived."

Alex's fingers briefly found hers. "Shall we?"

Felicity's chest tightened slightly. Their discussion in the narrow stone staircase earlier still hadn't been resolved, but talk of a private nature in front of Mr Kemp and Mr Pope would not be comfortable. "Let's," she agreed.

Arriving in the turret room with Pip under her arm and Alex at her side, Felicity found they were not the only nonbelievers in attendance. The whole household, apart from the land agent, was present. Before the thick velvet curtains at the room's curved edge, the cook stood uneasily in her Sunday best — a black bombazine frock with jet buttons that had clearly seen many years of careful preservation. The footman and butler were in uniform and apparently still on duty, green aprons covering their livery, perhaps from the rearranging of furniture to accompany the larger gathering.

Mrs Imrie and Miss Hartley were busying themselves with preparations at the side of the room, overseen by Winnifred. Dressed in layers of amethyst silk that rustled with her every gesture, the dowager baroness seemed back to full power. Mr Silkstede was close by, proffering advice and direction which met Winnifred's approval and was acted upon by the two female helpers. The air hung heavy with amber and myrrh incense, the smoke pluming from ornate brass censers positioned around the room.

The rest of the household's inhabitants milled around the centre of the space, where the small table at which Felicity had sat on her first evening at Cullingslock had been replaced with a much larger table crafted from dark oak, its surface polished to a mirror-like sheen. Symbols had been expertly and elegantly carved into the table's edge — pentacles, moons, and stars that caught the candlelight. Around it were high-backed chairs in the same dark oak with burgundy cushions. Felicity had never seen a set of furniture quite like it.

Audrey was in conversation with Peregrine, her height and build not far off from his. They were both neatly dressed, Audrey in a practical navy wool frock and her cousin in a suit of light brown flannel. The boy's face was neutral, but he inclined his head attentively towards his cousin as he listened to Audrey talk effusively about a new planting scheme she was working on. Elfrida stood to one side, watching Winnifred and her helpers, her arms folded tightly over her chest. Her dusky mauve evening gown with its dropped waist and beaded hem suggested she'd made an effort for the occasion, although from Felicity's earlier conversation with her, she seemed not to be a believer in spirits even if she saw it fit to share her knowledge of curses.

Tristan stood beside Philippa. He wore a dinner jacket that hung loosely on his thin frame, while Philippa's emerald silk dress bore intricate embroidery but showed slight wear at the seams. The pair's expressions were glum, and they weren't speaking to one another. Solomon rested calmly at Tristan's feet, his black-and-white coat freshly brushed, ears alert to every sound. The Border Collie glanced occasionally in Pip's and Audrey's direction. The girl remained absorbed in her conversation with her cousin, but Pip whined, eager to play with his new friends, his nose twitching at the unfamiliar scents filling the room. Thankfully, the two cats weren't present, otherwise Felicity would have had a tough time hanging onto the eager little terrier.

The solicitor was the last to arrive in the turret room. The butler went to him and gently coaxed the crystal tumbler from his hand. The solicitor let go of the glass, but he didn't look happy about it.

Felicity glanced uneasily at Alex. In her view, the investigation into Winnifred's supposed poisoning was over. What was her great-aunt hoping to achieve?

Alex gave her a subtle wink. His ability to find amusement throughout their stay at Cullingslock verged on unsound.

Taking Alex's playful spirit as inspiration, Felicity thrust her shoulders back and approached Elfrida.

"I asked your grandmother about the curse."

Elfrida's brow rose a little sleepily. "Oh?"

"She said it was nonsense."

Alex lifted his eyebrows with pleasant surprise. Was it enough to dispel his worry?

Elfrida laughed gently. "We're all free to hold our own beliefs, are we not?"

Felicity regarded Elfrida carefully. It could be hard to tell where her joking ended. "Is it quite normal for the whole household to be gathered for a séance?"

Elfrida's fingers worried the beaded fringe at her hip. "It's hardly a weekly or even monthly occurrence, but it's not unheard of."

"I wasn't informed of the séance's purpose," continued Felicity, even though she knew it to be an extension of the poisoning enquiry — although how that would play out in practice was yet to be seen.

Elfrida watched her mother's helpers bustling with preparations at the side of the room. "We usually don't find out until afterwards. Or sometimes never at all."

Alex looked around. "It seems Mr Kemp is the only one who didn't feel like attending."

A hint of a smile returned to Elfrida's lips. "That man does what he wants. We might all take a little inspiration from him now and then."

It was a peculiar observation — to Felicity's mind the land agent was provocative but certainly not inspirational — but there was no time to dwell upon it.

"Thank you, everyone, for gathering," said Miss Hartley, addressing the group. Her rose-printed day dress had been replaced with a flowing gown in deep fuchsia that shimmered in the candlelight. "On behalf of the Reverend One, I kindly request that you take your seats."

There were the dull scrapes of the heavy oak chairs on the rugs that covered the floor and a little discussion about who would sit where. Winnifred was settled into her chair by her assistants. Mrs Imrie and Miss Hartley flanked the dowager baroness. Mr Silkstede took a seat beside Miss Hartley. Next to him sat Elfrida and Audrey, then Tristan and his family. The cook took her place beside Mrs Imrie, and the solicitor seated himself beside the cook. The butler and the footman remained standing at the side of the room.

Felicity found a seat beside Philippa, and Alex took his place beside the solicitor. At least they were together. She gave him a little smile, which he fondly returned. They would clasp hands soon enough, and the idea gave her a little shiver of pleasure, even if there wasn't much else to look forward to in the session.

"If you please, Mr Timpson," came the instruction from Miss Hartley.

The butler and footman went into motion, dimming the lighting in the room so that the only glow came from several candles dotted about in front of the heavy curtains. On a side table, a spray of crystal rods in a natural cluster caught the flickering light, sending rainbow prisms across the draped velvet. From somewhere in the room's shadows came a soft trilling sound — or was it simply the draught bothering the curtains?

"Please," continued Miss Hartley, "take the hands of those seated next to you and close your eyes. We shall begin."

When Felicity took Alex's hand, he squeezed her fingers tightly for a moment and they exchanged glances. The warmth of his touch amid the bizarreness of the séance was very welcome.

On Felicity's other side, Philippa's fingers were cool, the ring on her right hand pressing slightly against Felicity's palm. Felicity and Philippa exchanged polite smiles before closing their eyes.

A low, rhythmic murmur rose from the spiritualists, words in what might have been Latin or perhaps something even older. The air grew thick with frankincense, its sweetness mingling with the underlying notes of beeswax from the candles. There was more chanting, then an eerie keening that raised the fine hairs on Felicity's neck. There was that same swish through the air like the waving of a sword. Then silence.

Felicity cracked one eyelid, peering through her lashes. What created the swishing sound?

"Who is with us?" Winnifred's voice trembled with an operatic vibrato.

Everyone had their eyes closed, even the servants. The cook looked to be taking the session particularly seriously. The butler stood as steady as a sentinel in the shadows, while the footman shifted nervously near the door. The solicitor might have been asleep, though he still had hold of the cook's and Alex's hands. Elfrida seemed calm while Audrey's forehead was lined with concentration. Tristan's lips were down-turned with faint displeasure. Philippa's expression was also one of discomfort, though their son's features were clear and relaxed. Solomon lay perfectly still at Tristan's feet, only his ears twitching at each new sound. Even Pip was oddly calm on Felicity's lap.

Was she really the only one not taking it seriously?

Alex squeezed her hand again. She twisted a little towards him. He had both eyes open and gave her a sarcastic, wide-eyed look that said, *What on earth have we got ourselves into?*

She bit the inside of her cheek to suppress a laugh. With Alex, even the most absurd of situations became bearable.

"I shall ask again," continued Winnifred. "Who is with us?"

"I am," the voice that responded was female and young-sounding. There was something oddly hollow about it, as though it came from a great distance. There was no movement of lips among the women at the table. How did they do it?

"And who are you?" continued Winnifred.

There was a pause. "I am." The same answer was repeated in the same voice.

Audrey shifted in her seat.

The answer made little sense. Was everything going according to plan?

"Mrs Imrie, the board," commanded Winnifred.

Felicity closed her eyes to maintain the pretence of participation, but she heard the movements. After a while, curiosity got the better of her. Through barely parted lids, she watched Mrs Imrie — attired in austere grey wool — rearrange items on the table in front of Winnifred. An ornate spirit board emerged from a velvet-lined box, its polished surface gleaming with alphabetic characters arranged in perfect arcs with numbers below and the words *YES* and *NO* positioned at opposite corners. Felicity had heard about such things and even seen them for sale in the toy section of the big department store in Exeter. A heart-shaped wooden planchette with a small window sat atop the board, ready to glide across the letters under supernatural guidance.

Winnifred and the two helpers seated either side of her put their hands on the pointer and waited. For a while, nothing happened.

"Tell us who you are," commanded Winnifred, and the pointer

swung into action. The rest of the table remained with eyes closed as Winnifred, Mrs Imrie, and Miss Hartley watched with excitement as the pointer moved across the letters on the board. First one letter, then the next, and the one after that...

"Astraea." Winnifred looked at her helpers. "Astraea?"

"Goddess of justice," whispered Mrs Imrie, though her voice held a slight tremor, as if the name disturbed her.

Winnifred straightened dramatically. "Are you Astraea, goddess of justice?" she boomed.

There was a pause. "I am," came the disembodied female voice.

"Are you here to help us, Astraea?"

"I am."

"Are you the one who will deliver us from the threat lurking among us?"

Felicity watched for a reaction from around the table. It seemed there weren't any secrets between Winnifred and her spiritualist group, but her family members weren't aware of her suspicions about a murder plot, were they?

The solicitor's fingers twitched against the cook's hand, while Audrey's eyebrows drew together fearfully. A muscle jumped in Peregrine's jaw. Tristan and his sister's expressions held fast, though Philippa's grip on Felicity's hand tightened slightly. Was it perhaps not the first time Winnifred had gathered everyone to hunt a 'threat lurking among us'? Or were Winnifred's relatives so disinterested that their minds were elsewhere?

"Thank you, Your Highness," continued Winnifred, addressing the spirit she'd apparently summoned. "Mrs Imrie, the offering."

Mrs Imrie rose from her chair, her movements oddly stiff, and went to the side of the room. Felicity wasn't the only one sneaking a look now. She could see that Audrey had an eye open.

"Astraea," continued Winnifred, "tonight you are our protector, the benevolent force ensuring peace and wellness in this household. I hand over to you the reins that I do my best to hold. I hand to you my power and my insight so that you may use it for our benefit."

Philippa also had her eyes open now. She was looking at her

husband, her expression a mixture of concern and something towards irritation. Tristan still sat with his eyes closed. Was he immersed in the goings-on, or had he absented himself internally?

"Mrs Imrie?" urged Winnifred with a whisper, a note of impatience creeping into her voice.

The helper didn't reply. She was still busy at the side of the room. There was the sharp scrape of a match being struck, followed by the acrid scent of sulphur. Mrs Imrie returned to the table. She had in her hands a tray laden with a tarnished silver chalice, dried herbs bound with black ribbon, a small cluster of shimmering crystals, and what appeared to be an ancient stone carving of an Egyptian scarab mounted on a copper stand. Also on the tray were a cone of burning incense and several candles. Her hands shook visibly as she carried the offering towards the séance table, the flames of the candles trembling as she moved.

As the plume of incense smoke neared the table, the solicitor wrinkled his nose and opened one eye with the expression of a man who'd bitten into a lemon, although he closed it again rather quickly, perhaps keen to stay in the dowager baroness's good books. The incense was pungent, a cloying mixture that almost made Felicity's eyes water, but she felt compelled to keep watching. Even as a nonbeliever, she had to wonder if the ceremony might somehow help uncover the truth behind her great-aunt's sudden illness.

"Astraea, accept this offering from us," said Winnifred as Mrs Imrie set the tray down on the table in front of her. The shake of the helper's hands set one of the candlesticks swinging, and it fell. The flame touched onto a bunch of herbs which immediately caught alight, the dried plants crackling as orange flames licked upwards with alarming speed.

"Oh!" cried Winnifred, recoiling as the fire flared, her carefully maintained composure cracking, her eyes wide with panic.

Alex, who must have been watching, too, crossed the room in three swift strides, grabbed a carafe with a crystal stopper full of clear liquid from the sideboard. He sniffed it, then doused the flames with decisive efficiency, though a generous splash caught Miss Hartley's silk gown and Mr Silkstede's evening jacket.

Eyes flew open as gasps and exclamations erupted around the table, and the delicious-smelling scent of baked rosemary and sage lifted into the air. Pip, who had been dozing in Felicity's lap, sat up with an indignant yap, while Solomon rose to his feet, alert and ready.

"Awfully sorry," said Alex to the dampened spiritualists as he returned the empty carafe to its place. "But it was that or have the whole table go up."

"Not a problem, Mr Cooper. Not a problem." Mr Silkstede took a handkerchief from his top pocket and offered it to Miss Hartley with old-fashioned gallantry. She accepted with a grateful smile that seemed to linger a moment longer than necessary.

Mrs Imrie stood frozen, her face drained of all colour, her hands trembling at her sides. Winnifred was also rigid and pale, though whether from shock or carefully controlled fury was difficult to determine. Philippa let go of Felicity's hand and looked about the table as though awakening from a bad dream.

Whatever magic — real or otherwise — had been in the room had now dissipated like a reflection in disturbed water.

"I am," came the voice again, high and clear, with an odd whistling quality. Audrey looked upwards, her gaze both worried and questioning.

Elfrida cleared her throat. "Well, this is awkward."

Winnifred turned slowly towards her Scottish helper, her shoulders trembling. "Mrs Imrie, I would suggest that you go to your room and ask for help from your trusted guides." Her voice shook with barely contained emotion. "Ask them for help. When you've had their answer, you may come back to us."

Mrs Imrie's entire frame shook like a leaf in a gale. "Yes, Reverend One," she said and fled towards the door.

"How many times..." said Winnifred, leaning towards Miss Hartley, exasperation now clear in her lowered tone.

"It is most regrettable, Reverend One," said Miss Hartley, slipping a glance of unexpected satisfaction in Mrs Imrie's direction.

Mrs Imrie hadn't quite left the room. She paused in the doorway and looked over her shoulder. Her pale eyes glittered with hurt as she cast her gaze at Winnifred. She was suffering, yes, but beneath her pain burned something harder — resentment, perhaps even hatred, for an instant unconcealed.

Had Winnifred noticed the way Mrs Imrie had looked at her?

Felicity had. And she wouldn't forget it.

Chapter Twenty

The evening ended in rather a shambles. Winnifred sat sullenly as Miss Hartley swiftly did the work of two helpers in getting everything from the séance cleared up as the session's participants drifted away from the table.

Mr Silkstede offered words of condolence to the dowager baroness. "It's the nature of the spirits to deliver messages in ways that are not always straightforward."

"I know this, Mr Silkstede," said Winnifred. She was still seated, her elbow on the polished table and her fingers at her temple as she watched Miss Hartley at work. It seemed the butler and footman weren't allowed to touch objects related to the rituals.

Felicity and Alex lingered, not wishing to offend by being the first to leave the séance room. Elfrida left before anyone else, followed by Tristan, Philippa, and Peregrine. Tristan and his son seemed calm, as if nothing out of the ordinary had happened, while Philippa's brow was pinched with worry. Solomon also seemed less settled than usual, the Collie's intelligent gaze roaming over the room as he trotted at his master's side.

Almost everyone proclaimed they were retiring to bed except the solicitor, who invited anyone interested for a drink in the library. No one seemed keen, which did not prompt the solicitor to change his plans. Felicity and Alex, with a sleepy Pip tucked under Felicity's arm, were eventually among the last of the séance participants remaining in the turret room, along with Audrey, who hung back as though waiting to speak to Winnifred.

Discussing the poisoning in front of Winnifred's granddaughter would not have been appropriate, so Felicity wished her great-aunt good night and went to leave.

As Alex turned to follow Felicity, Winnifred took his hand and squeezed it hard. "Thank you, my dear. You did a wonderful job."

Alex's eyebrows shot upwards as though surprised that Winnifred had registered his quick reaction to the fire. Perhaps he thought the spiritualists had been in a trance-like state. "Happy to help," he said, modest and sincere as ever.

"You're a good man, Mr Cooper. A very good man."

Felicity smiled. He really was, and she was desperate to have a private conversation with him. It was therefore a relief to be out of the incense-hazed turret room.

As they descended the staircase, Mr Silkstede quickly caught up with them.

"Lady Felicity. Mr Cooper. Might I have a word?"

They halted and turned. "By all means," said Felicity, any trace of impatience hidden from her tone.

"It's about a business proposition," clarified the researcher, straightening his antique-looking dinner jacket and stroking his pointed beard.

"Neither Mr Cooper nor I are people of business, Mr Silkstede."

"But you're both journalists, are you not?"

Felicity and Alex looked at one another. They'd yet to have their privacy, but with matters at the castle still unresolved, this was potentially an opening it might be unwise to ignore.

"Perhaps we could talk in the morning?" suggested Alex, reading Felicity's look perfectly.

"Much appreciated, Mr Cooper. Good night, to you both." The spiritualist gave a polite but exaggerated little bow and passed down the turret stairs ahead of them. Even after his footsteps had disappeared into silence, Felicity and Alex only looked at one another. Not wishing to be overheard, they remained quiet along the labyrinth of passages and stairways until they reached the great entrance hall with its vast medieval chandelier, where they stepped outside into the coolness of the evening. Letting Pip have a sniff and attend to his business was essential before bedtime, but it was also a convenient moment for a private discussion.

"What did you make of all that?" whispered Alex as they neared the trees, the fresh air scented with damp earth and pine resin. Above the treetops, stars pricked the purple-black sky like scattered diamonds.

"You first," said Felicity, her tone equally quiet.

"If the spirits really were in control," said Alex as they followed behind Pip in the dim glow coming from the tall windows of the castle's ground floor, "I don't think they were very happy. I mean, why else would you set fire to your own offering?"

If Felicity hadn't been so preoccupied by what she'd seen at the end of the ceremony, she might have laughed.

"Did you notice how nervous Mrs Imrie was?" she said. "It was her shaking that sent the candlestick flying."

"So it wasn't a message from the spirits?" Alex seemed rather incapable of taking the topic of the séance seriously.

Felicity increased her pace to keep up with Pip as he snuffled through the bracken. "Did you watch Mrs Imrie after Winnifred corrected her?"

"No, but your great-aunt wasn't unkind, was she? She was clearly irritated, but she did her best to control herself."

Felicity frowned. "Did you not hear the exchange of comments between my great-aunt and Miss Hartley? It caused Mrs Imrie to pause by the door and give my great-aunt a stare full of..." She hesitated. "I don't usually like to jump to conclusions about this kind of thing, but I would say Mrs Imrie's stare was full of resentment. Perhaps even hate."

Alex widened his eyes. "Hate? That's rather strong, isn't it?"

Felicity shook her head, as though wishing to disbelieve it, too. "Yet it's what I saw."

"Winnifred told you her spiritualist helpers have her full trust."

"She did," said Felicity, folding her arms against the chill of the night air. An owl hooted somewhere high in the trees. "But what if she was wrong?"

Alex moved closer, his warmth a welcome shield against the evening breeze. "I sense our work here at the castle is not quite done."

Felicity turned to him. "If you wish to leave, I would quite understand. That article on smuggling in Cornwall that Jasper wants you to write sounded awfully interesting."

Alex stopped and put his hands in his pockets. "If you're staying, I'm staying."

A warmth spread through Felicity. Having him consistently at her side was a blessing of incalculable value, but there was still a knot in her stomach. She didn't wish to disrupt the calm intimacy between them, but there was unfinished business that would keep pricking at her conscience until it was resolved.

"When we spoke earlier while seated on the staircase," began Felicity.

Alex's eyebrows rose expectantly, as if he'd been waiting for her to bring the topic.

His reaction caused her to hesitate slightly. "We were talking about the plans for our wedding, and I gathered the impression that... That you were displeased with me."

He took a hand out of his pocket and stroked his jaw, saying nothing.

"Is that the case?" she pressed.

"If I'm entirely honest, I suppose I was, mildly. Yes."

Felicity's eyes flew wide. She'd asked, yet she'd not prepared herself for the answer. "May I ask why?" she said, controlling her tone.

"You seemed quite insistent on knowing my thoughts."

Felicity narrowed her eyes. "Why should that be displeasing?"

Alex put his hand back in his pocket. He dropped his head, then smiled. "Because I didn't wish to tell you."

"Why ever not?"

He huffed out a laugh. "Because I didn't wish to displease you."

Felicity looked into his earnest, dark-blue eyes. A smile cracked over her face. "And I only wished to know your thoughts to avoid displeasing you."

He smiled back at her. "Is this the kind of muddle that we can expect from being married?"

Felicity laughed. "I suppose it's best we learn to navigate such issues sooner rather than later."

Alex reached for her hand. "I ought to tell you what I think about the arrangements for our wedding, then," he said, wincing slightly.

"Only if you want to. I shan't apply further pressure."

His smile was full of affection and heart-meltingly handsome. "Perhaps we might discuss it properly when we're not standing in the damp with a Yorkie investigating something questionable?"

Felicity glanced down to see the little terrier nosing a toadstool with a bright red spotted cap.

"Pip, no!"

She scooped the Yorkie up and gently chastised him. The tenderness of the moment with Alex had dissipated, though they both agreed there was no rush to discuss their wedding planning. It was late and time for bed. There were also other, potentially more deadly matters at the castle that needed urgent address — starting with the spiritualists.

Chapter Twenty-One

The next morning, a telegram was delivered to Felicity's room along with her breakfast, this time from Lady Henrietta. Would Felicity be back at Bradley Court in time for their monthly appointment for tea with Lower Diddleton's vicar? That was her grandmother's question.

As Felicity finished her last bites of thick toast slathered with butter and chunky Seville marmalade, she was quite certain the appointment with the vicar wasn't to take place in the coming days but was scheduled for next week. Lady Henrietta was simply making a polite yet justifiably sharp point. Jasper's earlier telegram had been left unanswered, and it was insensitive to leave her family guessing at her whereabouts and potential for reappearance, but Felicity was unsure of when she might leave Cullingslock. As she dressed in a powder blue muslin day dress, she decided she would continue to hold off from sending her grandmother a response, at least for that morning.

Mr Silkstede was rather pleasantly surprised when Felicity and Alex, the latter in a sand-coloured linen suit and the former with Pip in tow, located him seated on a bench and writing in his notebook. The ancient stone parapet bore the scars of centuries, its crenellations softened by time and the pale morning light, while far below, the morning mist clung to the valleys like spun silver. In the distance, the moorland looked like a watercolour of purple and green.

The spiritualist researcher stood up energetically, both surprised and encouraged that his business proposition was squarely on Felicity and Alex's minds, prompting them to seek an audience with him so shortly after breakfast. It was, however, entirely Felicity's idea that they were paying an early call on Mr Silkstede, the glare that Mrs Imrie had given her great-aunt having haunted her restless night. If there were murderous intentions among the spiritualists at Cullingslock Castle, then they must be detected promptly. A repeat attempt must be avoided at all costs. It would also be handy if matters could be resolved quickly enough so Felicity could return home without worrying her grandmother or brother more than necessary.

"We're all ears, Mr Silkstede," said Alex, sounding authentically enthusiastic as he took a seat on the bench after Felicity had done so. Pip was allowed to explore the enormous stones that made up the floor and the walls of the battlement, the wind ruffling his fur.

"Right, yes, of course. This is a proposal in which I'm sure you will be most interested." Mr Silkstede shifted his weight nervously, his frock coat flapping in the breeze as he flicked through his notebook with ink-stained fingers. The presentation was essentially a pitch for a regular column for himself in the Western Daily News, the newspaper for which Felicity and Alex both worked — Felicity less now that she had her own regular obligation to the Gentlewomen's Gazette — and of which Felicity's brother was editor-in-chief. It was possibly not the first time Mr Silkstede had made the proposal, as it sounded professionally put together.

Alex and Felicity sat and listened, looking interested and nodding along, although it was practically impossible that a serious news publication such as the Western Daily News would want to publish insight into horoscopes and tea leaf reading. It was also rather out of the hands of both Felicity and Alex what features were added to the publication. Jasper discussed such matters with his senior editors and — business-minded as he was — his advertisers.

Mr Silkstede's enthusiasm built as he spoke, his hands sketching invisible columns in the air. "Imagine: *Messages from Beyond* or perhaps *The Ethereal Observer* — a weekly glimpse into the supernatural currents affecting your readers' lives."

As agreed prior to locating Mr Silkstede, Felicity and Alex responded appreciatively to the suggestion.

"That's very interesting, Mr Silkstede," said Felicity. "Thank you for sharing it with us."

"We will certainly give it some thought." Alex sounded quite genuine in his interest.

"Although I must say," said Felicity, preparing to take the discussion in quite another direction. "I hadn't been exposed to the world of spiritualism before coming to Cullingslock. May I ask how you got into the topic yourself, Mr Silkstede?"

"As many do, your ladyship." An odd little smile appeared above the man's pointed grey beard. "Through desperation."

Alex frowned. "Desperation?"

"After the sudden passing of my wife, I found myself quite unable to cope." His tone had become earthy and genuine, quite unlike the voice he'd used for his presentation. "Being able to once again contact her was enormously reassuring."

"I'm so sorry for your loss," said Felicity.

"Thank you, your ladyship, but she's in a better place now."

It was easy to imagine how grief tempted people to connect with the other side. "How did you meet my great-aunt?"

The researcher began pacing. "Goodness, how could I not? She was the most powerful medium in all of England." He flapped a hand. "Is the most powerful, I mean."

Felicity glanced at Alex. Both the slip and its correction were rather telling.

"So my great-aunt is something of a celebrity in spiritual circles?"

"Most definitely. Legendary, I would say." Mr Silkstede's eyes took on the gleam of a devoted admirer discussing his idol. "She could sell out a theatre within hours of the posters going up."

Felicity tipped her head. "Great-Aunt Winnifred was a stage performer?" The photographs that Felicity had seen of her great-aunt in dramatic costumes made sense now. Yet in passing on what he knew about Winnifred, Jasper hadn't mentioned a career in the theatre. Was Felicity's brother unaware? Or did he judge it better that Felicity didn't know? To sceptics, stage performances by mediums and fortune tellers could carry an air of vulgarity or unsophistication.

"She was *the* performer," continued Mr Silkstede. "She made a name for herself before the war. Then, of course, with so many not coming back from the conflict, she became very much in demand until... Until... Well, it was time for your great-aunt to take a break from all that as I'm sure you can imagine."

Alex twitched an eyebrow. "Did something happen?"

Felicity was happy for him to ask this. Hadn't Tristan hinted at something similar?

Mr Silkstede drew in his chin. "No, not at all. Why do you ask?"

Felicity's suspicions remained on high alert, but she wouldn't push the point further. Not when there were other more pressing topics to cover.

"Is that why you chose to write a new book about my great-aunt?" She clarified. "Because of her fame?"

The researcher winced slightly, adjusting his neck tie with nervous fingers. "It was actually the dowager baroness herself who approached me. But it was, of course, an opportunity I couldn't refuse."

Felicity nodded. It would have been improper to ask whether it was because of Winnifred's legendary status as a medium or because of the money she was paying him, money members of Winnifred's family would rather see spent on the upkeep of the castle — not that it mattered too much. Mr Silkstede wasn't the real object of Felicity's interest that morning.

"I can quite imagine," she continued, "but there's something that's been puzzling me. Perhaps you can help me understand, Mr Silkstede. What role is it that Miss Hartley and Mrs Imrie have, exactly? Are they paid as staff or is there some other arrangement?"

Mr Silkstede's brow lifted with relief at no longer being the topic of conversation. "Miss Hartley and Mrs Imrie are your great-aunt's apprentices. You might be surprised to understand, but there is a certain career progression among spiritualists. Being apprentice to a powerful medium such as your great-aunt is a tremendous honour." He straightened as if some of that honour reflected upon him.

Alex frowned, as though unable to fully understand. "Would an apprentice eventually take on the role of the medium to which they are apprenticed?"

"Not automatically, but that would be the ultimate honour."

"Do you expect Mrs Imrie or Miss Hartley to take over from my great-aunt whenever the time comes?" Felicity blinked innocently. There was hopefully no way that Mr Silkstede had of fathoming that her thoughts were on a motive for plotting and murder.

The spiritualist researcher laughed a little, but there was something hollow in the sound. "You would need to ask the dowager baroness herself about that. And she would likely need to consult beyond this realm for the answers. A medium such as your great-aunt would only hand over her powers once the transition had been agreed with her spirit guides."

"So it's not that, upon her demise, her powers simply flit off and settle into someone else?" said Alex doubtfully.

Felicity hid a smile. She was immensely grateful for Alex's dauntless interviewing style.

Mr Silkstede, too, suppressed amusement, though his manner was more one of patronising someone less knowledgeable than himself. "No, Mr Cooper. That's not how it works."

Well, that was one motive for murder eliminated.

As the morning sun climbed higher, the stones of the wall behind the bench grew warmer. Felicity shifted in her seat as Pip sprung up and lay down between her and Alex, ready for a nap. Somewhere below, a door slammed, the sound echoing up the castle walls like a pistol shot.

"As apprentices, what does the work of Miss Hartley and Mrs Imrie involve?" Felicity asked as though genuinely curious, which she was, although probably not for the reasons Mr Silkstede imagined. "I've witnessed their roles in the formalities of the séance."

Mr Silkstede nodded with the enthusiasm of a lecturer finding an engaged student. "They are developing their talents for reaching into the other realm. They each have their specialities."

Felicity raised an eyebrow. "Oh really?" This was a way in. If she was going to interview Mrs Imrie without the woman herself knowing, it would be best to do so either on common ground or on a topic about which Mrs Imrie was knowledgeable for which Felicity could feign interest or even admiration. "What is Mrs Imrie's specialism?"

"Palmistry." Mr Silkstede adjusted his neck tie, his manner professional. "She has quite the gift for it, though perhaps not the temperament for public demonstrations."

"How wonderful," Felicity looked at Alex with a delighted smile, which Alex didn't immediately return. He found feigning interest in spiritualist matters more trying than Felicity.

"Do you think Mrs Imrie might give me a reading?" Felicity continued.

Mr Silkstede's face lit up. "I'm certain she would be honoured, your ladyship." His eyes shone a little. "Indeed, if it is a glance into your future that you're after, I have a set of Greco-Egyptian crystals that you might be interested in."

"Thank you, but that will not be necessary, Mr Silkstede." Felicity stood up sharply from the bench.

So Philippa had been correct in her observation of the acquisition of mystical objects at the castle via Winnifred's spiritualist supporters. Yet until Felicity found a thread linking the sale of the items to the potential murder plot against her great-aunt, she wouldn't meddle in the matter. Exposing a conman meant more than the discovery of the sale of items. It meant digging into the beliefs and intentions behind the transaction, which was a whole separate topic that Felicity had no wish to get into. Not on that morning, anyway.

Alex rose beside her, Pip tucked under his arm as Felicity straightened her skirt.

"If you would simply be so kind as to tell me where I might find Mrs Imrie," she said, "I should be most obliged to you, Mr Silkstede."

Chapter Twenty-Two

Mr Silkstede indicated that Winnifred's two apprentices had their living quarters near the séance room. Not that he knew exactly where to find them, of course, him being a gentleman. Unfortunately, Felicity and Alex didn't come across the butler or the footman in order to ask for more specific directions, so they headed for the séance room for what would be the starting point for their search.

As they climbed the stairs, sounds drifted down from the turret, echoing off the stone walls. There was someone in attendance.

Felicity turned to Alex. He gave her an encouraging nod. It was absolutely possible that she might, within the span of the following conversation, be reassured that Mrs Imrie's glare at her great-aunt meant nothing at all, and they would be back on the road to Bradley Court by lunchtime. It might never be possible to settle all the frustrations at Cullingslock Castle — indeed, what household was utterly free of tension? — but it would be satisfying to leave reassured that there wasn't anyone wishing physical harm.

But it wasn't Mrs Imrie in the séance room. It was Miss Hartley, and she was alone.

The woman turned as they entered, her brown hair catching the light from the tall windows, the long velvet curtains now drawn back.

She wore a day dress in soft peach cotton with mending at the cuffs and a cream scarf with delicate tassels. Her pretty round face transformed with genuine delight — though her delight seemed quickly to shift to something more calculating.

"Your ladyship, Mr Cooper. What can I do for you? Have you come to see my letters?"

Felicity cocked her head. "Your letters, Miss Hartley?"

The spiritualist apprentice continued to smile brightly. "Mr Silkstede said he would mention my letters to you. Did he not do so?"

"We just came from a discussion with Mr Silkstede, but he didn't mention any letters," clarified Alex.

Miss Hartley looked distinctly disappointed, then brightened again. "I can show you them now if you like?"

Felicity and Alex looked at one another. Was this a necessary interaction? There were two apprentices, perhaps both vying to become the next powerful medium after Winnifred. Mrs Imrie had seemingly been humiliated at the séance the night before. Might further interaction with Miss Hartley help illuminate whether genuine danger lurked beneath the tensions between the spiritualists?

"Why not?" Felicity smiled politely. "If it shan't take long."

They followed Miss Hartley down the turret steps and along a narrow corridor. The cool breeze that blew through the gaps where glass ought to have been carried with it the mingled scents of moorland and sea.

"Here we are," said Miss Hartley, opening the door to a little sitting room decorated modestly with tasteful attention to colour. Various swathes of shimmering fabric had been draped around to brighten up the old wooden furniture, some of it perhaps dating from the medieval period when the castle was built. Dried herbs hung in bundles from the bare beams overhead, filling the air with the odour of lavender and rosemary. There was a collection of yellow and pink stones in a bowl on a side table, which gleamed like glass. Beyond that, the space was devoid of ornaments.

"Please, take a seat." Miss Hartley gestured gracefully yet humbly at a round table at the centre of the sitting room, which had a mismatch of chairs around it and a pretty embroidered tablecloth spread upon it. Felicity tucked Pip onto her lap as she and Alex settled themselves. Sun streamed through the sitting room window, which thankfully had glass in it, although a couple of the small leaded panes had been lost at some point and were now stuffed with rags.

Miss Hartley disappeared into the room next door and reappeared with a large satchel in faded brown leather. She opened it carefully and began removing pages, laying them reverently on the tablecloth in front of Felicity and Alex, smoothing them with her fingertips and speaking gently. "There we go." She left the satchel on the table and stepped backwards, clasping her hands tightly in front of her dress. "I will let you read them."

"Thank you." Alex's tone was respectful and appreciative, but there was a hint of wonderment at just what the blazes they had got themselves into.

Turning her attention to the paper in front of her, Felicity stifled a smile and rearranged her features into an expression of seriousness.

The handwriting was looping and formal and a little jagged in places. *My dearest George,* it began. The content was a description of daily activities, ranging from creating pastel sketches of beloved pets to singing and playing the piano. There was an odd line about meeting Shakespeare and discussing his works with him. Then Felicity saw who had signed the letter: *Your loving grandmother, Victoria RI.*

She drew back from the page and frowned. It was a letter to the current king from Queen Victoria. It was dated just a couple of years before, yet the Queen had passed away over two decades ago.

She glanced at the page that lay before Alex. The handwriting was different, although there were some similarities. This letter was addressed to a Mr Shaw. Felicity didn't take the time to read the content, but she could see it was signed by a *Mr C Dickens.*

Alex's eyebrows were raised in a most disbelieving fashion.

Felicity did her best to erase any trace of incredulity from her expression when she looked up at Miss Hartley. It wouldn't help matters to be impolite.

"This is quite..." It was a struggle to find the words for a fitting reaction. "It's uncanny."

Alex was more to the point, yet somehow still courteous in his manner. "Perhaps the fault lies with me, but I'm not sure I understand what I've just read."

"It's quite normal," assured Miss Hartley. Her voice carried excitement even as she intended to reassure. "When one is not accustomed to receiving messages from the other realm, it can be quite disorienting at first."

Felicity nodded. Miss Hartley's presentation was beginning to make an odd sort of sense. She felt she knew what might come next.

"I understood from Mr Silkstede," Felicity ventured, "that both you and Mrs Imrie have specific talents related to the spiritual world. Yours is, I suppose..." Inventing letters from famous people from beyond the grave? She hesitated, reining herself in. It was always Felicity's natural inclination not to offend, regardless of her own feelings on a topic. She also hoped to continue into some kind of discussion with Miss Hartley after the letters had been put away and perhaps gain some more understanding about Mrs Imrie. But that wouldn't be possible if Miss Hartley thought that Felicity and Alex didn't take her seriously.

"Automatic writing. Yes, that's my speciality." Miss Hartley's brown eyes sparkled with pride and continued excitement. "Of course, I shared the messages with the people to whom they had been written, but there was, up until now, little interest." She put a hand on the leather satchel as though it contained treasure. "But I do keep receiving the messages, and I do, of course, keep writing them down. Do you wish to read more?" She lifted the satchel, threatening to produce additional sheets.

Felicity raised her hand. "Perhaps later. Might you tell us how it works?" She was keen to move away from reading and onto talking.

Miss Hartley's cheeks flushed with pleasure. "Not everything can be explained in words, of course, but it's something that happens when I'm able to access a certain state of receptivity — a trance, I suppose you might call it. I place my hand on the paper with a pen. I can't say I fully understand what happens, but when I come out of it, the letter is there."

"Do you do this regularly?" Alex's tone suggested genuine curiosity, though Felicity detected the effort behind it.

"Most days," said Miss Hartley.

"And is it always a famous person writing to another famous person?" he pressed in a slightly less courteous manner. "This is the author Charles Dickens addressing the writer George Bernard Shaw, is it not?"

Felicity's shoe connected gently with Alex's. His scepticism was understandable, but there were practical benefits to avoiding rudeness.

Thankfully, Miss Hartley was oblivious to Alex's sarcasm. "It's the strongest personalities that tend to come through. I'm just a vessel allowing them to say the things they wish to say but no longer can. At least not directly."

Pip lifted his nose above the tablecloth and gave the letter a sniff. Considering Queen Victoria ruled the British Empire for several decades and her grandson George now occupied the same position, might Her Majesty not have more profound wisdom to share from the afterlife than reporting on the progress of her attempts at art?

"Mrs Imrie has quite a different talent, does she not?" Felicity asked, any hint of an ulterior motive to the question absent from her tone.

Miss Hartley's expression soured momentarily. "She does, but there's nothing to show for it, nothing that could be published in the newspapers, for example." She smiled winsomely at the pair.

So that was the crux of it. Like Mr Silkstede, Miss Hartley was essentially selling something — or attempting to.

"I would only expect a modest fee, of course, being just the vessel through which these messages are delivered."

Alex's eyes narrowed doubtfully. "You wish to publish what you've written?"

Felicity resisted another nudge of his foot. "Thank you for showing us your letters, Miss Hartley, but I don't think this is something for the Western Daily News," she said gently, choosing honesty over false encouragement. There was something about the female apprentice that struck her as more vulnerable than the spiritual researcher.

"Oh." Miss Hartley sounded crestfallen.

"You might try the Empire Examiner, however," continued Felicity. It was a far more salacious publication than her family's newspaper.

Miss Hartley brightened considerably. "Oh, I see. Well, thank you for the consideration." She carefully returned the sheets to the satchel, handling them like sacred texts.

"Forgive me if it's too personal a question," began Felicity, "but may I ask how you came to spiritualism in the first place?"

Miss Hartley's fingers worried the edge of her satchel. "My brother. He was at the Somme." The words emerged barely above a whisper. "The automatic writing began shortly after. His first letter came through on what would have been his twenty-first birthday."

The revelation hung in the air between them, yet it was a familiar story — the desperate attempt to maintain connection with the lost, to build meaning from grief, and a war that had scarred even those who had never seen the battlefields.

"I'm so very sorry."

"Very sorry indeed," echoed Alex solemnly.

Miss Hartley shook her head. "Don't be. He's not lost to me."

"Have you been an apprentice to my great-aunt for very long?" Felicity stood, tucking Pip under her arm, though she had no intention of leaving just yet.

"For two years now."

"Have you learned a great deal?"

"Oh, most definitely. The Reverend One has been so generous with her time and attention."

"Is it a paid position?" asked Alex.

Miss Hartley blinked. "We are housed and fed, and we are paid with the knowledge that we gather."

Felicity smiled somewhat sympathetically at Miss Hartley. While avarice might have been behind Mr Silkstede's motivations for desiring a paid newspaper column and for selling his esoteric items — for by his own admission, he was in receipt of a wage from Winnifred — Miss Hartley's position was more fragile. The world could be difficult enough to navigate without adding to that the burden of being a single woman without means. Her keenness to sell her letters was, in that regard, understandable.

"Is there a fixed end to the apprenticeship?" Felicity asked as Pip craned his neck to sniff further at the papers.

Miss Hartley shook her head, buckling the satchel firmly closed. "No, it's a rather fluid situation. I would say it's not up to anyone in this realm to define when the time is right for either myself or Mrs Imrie to pass on to the next stage."

"What is the next stage?" Alex came to stand beside Felicity.

Miss Hartley's smile grew strained. "Difficult to say, really. The Reverend One may take on a successor, or she may not."

"Is it possible that you and Mrs Imrie both become my great-aunt's successors?" Felicity ventured. "You needn't answer if that's too delicate a question."

Miss Hartley's head twitched sideways. "I don't wish to be unkind, but I would say not." She folded her arms. "You saw what happened last night. It's uncertain whether Mrs Imrie has the stamina or strength for the power that would need to flow through her should she be chosen as the Reverend One's successor."

Felicity maintained a neutral expression. If doubts about Mrs Imrie's abilities already existed, the séance stakes had perhaps been considerable. "Is that simply your view or the view of my great-aunt as well?"

Miss Hartley gave her head a prim little shake. "I wouldn't like to speak on the Reverend One's behalf."

An ominous picture was forming. Mrs Imrie had perhaps dedicated years of her life to an unpaid position hoping to ascend through the ranks of spiritualism only for her dreams to be quashed. Humiliated and frustrated, did she channel her anger in an act of revenge towards the Reverend One?

There was one way to find out.

"Mrs Imrie's particular skill is with palm reading, is it not?" Felicity kept her tone cool.

Miss Hartley nodded, superiority creeping into her tone. "She's extremely skilled in that area, although it has quite a limited scope in terms of reach." She scoffed a little. "Crowds don't flock to watch someone read a palm."

Felicity recalled what Mr Silkstede had said about Winnifred's renown and theatre appearances. Is that what the apprentices hoped to gain from their time at Cullingslock? Fame and adoration?

"We should like to procure a reading from her," continued Felicity. "Do you think Mrs Imrie would be amenable?"

Miss Hartley drew a deep breath. "Given what happened last night, I'm not sure Mrs Imrie is able to focus on interactions in this realm at the moment."

"I shall bear that in mind," said Felicity, ignoring Alex's incredulous glare. "Where might we find her?"

Miss Hartley somewhat begrudgingly provided directions.

As they prepared to leave, Felicity paused. "Forgive me if I'm prying, but what would your plans be, Miss Hartley, if you were not to be chosen as my great-aunt's successor?"

Miss Hartley fluttered her lashes and smiled. "I'm quite certain the spirits will guide me along the right path."

Chapter Twenty-Three

"For people supposedly more concerned with realms beyond this one, Hartley and Silkstede have a keen interest in the money of this world."

Alex's observation came as he and Felicity climbed another staircase, following Miss Hartley's directions to Mrs Imrie's quarters. Their footsteps echoed on the bare stone treads while Pip's claws scrabbled eagerly behind, Felicity's arms having grown weary of restraining the energetic terrier.

Alex lowered his voice further. "And financial difficulties can drive people to desperate measures."

"I believe you to be right on both counts," replied Felicity. "But how would doing away with their 'Reverend One' benefit either of them?"

Alex continued climbing ahead of Felicity. "Silkstede's book about your great-aunt might sell better." He cast a wry smile at her. "The public's tastes can be rather ghoulish."

"Again, you're probably right," said Felicity. "But weighing up the risks, aren't there easier ways to earn extra money than getting away with murder?"

"What about all those mystical artefacts?" suggested Alex. "Might they be worth something?"

Felicity nodded. "Possibly, and I suppose there's not much else my great-aunt has to leave behind." The castle was already Tristan's, and the land wasn't Winnifred's either, of course. "But would anyone truly kill for such trinkets?"

Alex halted on the steps, allowing Felicity and Pip to catch up, the little terrier stretching to navigate each of the ancient stone treads. "Desperation makes people behave oddly," he said as Felicity drew close. "What else explains writing letters from Queen Victoria and Charles Dickens?"

"I doubt Miss Hartley to be purely mercenary, despite her need for money." Felicity stopped on the step below and looked up at Alex, her breath coming fast from the climb. "Perhaps I'm overlooking something, but neither Mr Silkstede nor Miss Hartley strike me as desperately unhappy. And the risk of the act remains unconscionable."

"Attempting a poisoning in the presence of an esteemed detective, you mean?" Alex's smile held a gentle blend of mockery and pride as he needled her about her reputation.

Felicity shot him a glare and continued past him, now following Pip up the stairs. "I mean making such a move in front of the whole household — it shows a lack of clear-headedness. I believe we're looking for someone blinded by emotion."

Alex's footsteps tapped behind her. "You're not esteemed in your role as detective for nothing," he said quietly, any trace of mocking gone from his voice.

They emerged into a sun-drenched stone corridor with a faded Persian runner. Pip immediately investigated the carpet with intense concentration, but beyond the Yorkie's own sniffing came a more human sound. The soft whimpering drew them forward. As they approached the door from behind which the sounds emanated, sobs could be heard.

"Blinded by emotion, you said?" Alex murmured, eyes widening with wariness.

Felicity had been dismissive of the idea of her great-aunt having been poisoned, but were they about to enter the presence of a would-be assassin?

Felicity gathered Pip up and rapped upon the door.

The crying ceased abruptly. After rustling sounds and a pause, the door opened to reveal Mrs Imrie standing rigidly upright. Though her expression remained neutral, red-rimmed eyes betrayed recent tears. She wore the same grey woollen dress she'd had on at the séance, its severity softened only by delicate lace at the cuffs. Her ash-blonde hair, pulled into an unforgiving chignon, accentuated her hollow cheeks and the sharp line of her jaw.

The open door released incense smoke, the resinous scent of cedar wood mixed with something peppery like bay. Behind her, the sitting room appeared Spartanly furnished save for an elaborate altar occupying one corner. Upon it rested an array of crystals and semi-precious stones arranged in precise patterns around a silver bowl. Tarot cards lay spread in a cross formation.

"Your ladyship, Mr Cooper." She sniffed delicately. "My apologies for the delay in coming to the door. I wasn't expecting company. How may I assist you?"

Felicity offered her warmest smile. "Please forgive our intrusion, Mrs Imrie, but I understand you possess remarkable skill in palmistry."

A spark of interest flickered in Mrs Imrie's pale eyes, though she quickly suppressed it. "I wouldn't presume to call myself an expert," she said humbly in her Scottish lilt, "though I've studied the art for many years."

"Would you be able to perform a reading for us?" pressed Felicity. It wasn't that she wanted her fortune told. Far from it. The focus on Mrs Imrie's speciality would merely serve as a bridge to further conversation so that she might subtly get to know the woman better.

If Mrs Imrie showed even the slightest inclination towards wishing Winnifred harm, then Felicity would take further action — without putting herself or Alex at risk, of course. If there proved to be no reason for Felicity to worry about Mrs Imrie's intentions towards her great-aunt, then she could return to Bradley Court knowing she had done all she could.

"The Reverend One has instructed me to focus on my own energy and issues for the time being." Mrs Imrie dipped her gaze. "I'm not sure performing a reading would be appropriate."

Felicity allowed disappointment to colour her features. "How unfortunate. We depart soon, and I'd so hoped to experience a reading from someone of your calibre."

Mrs Imrie's teeth worried her lower lip. Internal struggle played across her features. "As you're the Reverend One's guest and time presses... I shall make an exception. Please enter."

"Most kind of you," Felicity said, exchanging a meaningful glance with Alex as he moved to follow.

Mrs Imrie's hand rose, barring his way. "One person only, I'm afraid." Her Scottish accent could be as clipped and abrupt as it could be gentle.

Alex's frown deepened. "Might I not observe?"

She shook her head firmly. "The spirits require focus. Your presence — and the dog's — would disturb the energies." She looked down at where, in Felicity's arms, Pip was working the air with his little black nose, enchanted by the incense.

Felicity turned to Alex. Entering a chamber alone with a potential murderess showed poor judgement. Was it a risk that could be borne if it meant a murder plot might be undermined?

"I'll remain just outside," Alex said, accepting Pip from Felicity, his brow only mildly crumpled with concern. He understood her reasoning as clearly as if she'd spoken it aloud. With Alex so near, Felicity entered the room with confidence but also wary alertness.

"Please, sit."

Mrs Imrie drew the curtains with deliberate ceremony, transforming bright morning into a mysterious twilight. She lit a beeswax candle, its warm, slightly sweet scent mingling with the lingering incense as she placed it on the small table. The table bore a cloth of extraordinary beauty — midnight silk shot through with silver threads, creating patterns like moonlight on dark water. The setting was enormously evocative.

Taking her seat opposite Felicity, Mrs Imrie set the candle in a simple pewter holder, its ancient surface worn smooth. She waited with perfect stillness.

"Your hands?" she prompted gently.

"Oh, naturally." Felicity placed her hands palm-up on the silk.

Mrs Imrie studied Felicity's face rather than her hands. "Your first reading, I presume?"

No point dissembling. "Indeed."

Disappointment flickered across the palmist's features — Felicity's earlier praise rang hollow now — but retreat was impossible.

Mrs Imrie nodded, closing her eyes. Her lips moved in silent prayer for a moment. Then she spoke. "I seek the guidance of spirits to bring clarity and truth. May energies from beyond illuminate understanding."

When her eyes opened, all frustration had vanished from her features, replaced by a serene focus. She lifted Felicity's right hand with surprising gentleness, her touch warm and soft despite her angular appearance. "Right-handed, yes?"

Felicity nodded.

"Square palm, long fingers — the practical hand." Mrs Imrie turned Felicity's hand, examining both sides. "A woman of intellect and action." She glanced up. "Though we knew that already, of course."

Felicity smiled awkwardly at the concentrated attention.

Mrs Imrie bent over Felicity's palm, fingers tracing lines with butterfly touches. She angled her hand towards the candle, its warmth joining the pleasant heat of human contact.

In the present context, it was extremely difficult to imagine Mrs Imrie harming anyone. In the cocoon of her sitting room, it was also difficult to imagine asking questions that might dance around such a topic.

"Your heart line runs strong and true, though this fork suggests challenges. Conflict between ambition and affection, perhaps?"

Felicity's mind flew to Alex. When they'd first met, they'd been rivals pursuing the same story. "Perhaps."

"Young as you are, loss has touched you. First as a child, then recently. Does this resonate?"

Felicity swallowed, thinking of her mother's death when Felicity was just an infant and her father's passing from the influenza just after the war. "It does."

Mrs Imrie nodded, returning her focus to the palm. "But you didn't come to me for what you already know. That gentleman outside — is he your intended?"

Excitement rippled through Felicity, the same thrill she often felt when imagining her and Alex's wedding day. "We've not finalised the arrangements, but yes."

"Shall I read your future together?" Mrs Imrie's gaze lifted hopefully.

Did Felicity want such knowledge? Mrs Imrie's accuracy thus far impressed, but what if it wasn't merely coincidence? What if she spoke unwelcome truths?

Felicity cleared her throat. "I'd prefer insights about my career."

"Of course." Mrs Imrie bent again over Felicity's palm, unperturbed. "Your fate line emerges from turbulence into clarity — dedication to your chosen path. Your well-developed mount of Moon indicates deep empathy. Your sun line promises recognition through service. Without presuming too much, you'll help many people for years to come, earning well-deserved acclaim."

Felicity breathed steadily. Every observation could apply to her torn loyalties between journalism and detection, her discomfort with fame, her desire to help. Was this Mrs Imrie's gift, or Felicity's ability to find meaning in vague pronouncements? Or had Mrs Imrie simply researched Felicity, anticipating a potential reading request?

It didn't matter. The reading wasn't Felicity's true purpose.

"Thank you, Mrs Imrie." She gently withdrew her hand from the palmist's touch. "Most enlightening."

Mrs Imrie inclined her head solemnly. “I hope the pronouncements prove useful to you.”

Felicity smiled. “As do I,” she said as she put the reading aside in her mind. Her goal was to learn about Mrs Imrie, not about herself.

Mrs Imrie extinguished the candle and moved to the curtains. Morning light flooded back.

Felicity blinked at the sudden brightness. “Might I offer payment?” she asked as she rose from the table. Her question was perhaps gauche, but she wished to probe for the same sensitivity the other spiritualists displayed.

“Thank you, but I have sufficient for my needs.”

“How gratifying to know that my great-aunt provides so well for those in her service.” The assumption was deliberate bait.

Mrs Imrie stiffened. “I’m no employee. I remain here by choice.”

“Forgive me — I didn’t mean to imply employment. You’re an apprentice, I understand?”

They stood awkwardly by the table as Mrs Imrie’s fingertips pressed onto the silk cloth. “The Reverend One has taught me much,” she said, her gaze dropping. “But perhaps my time here draws to a close.”

Felicity’s brow lifted. “What makes you say that?”

Mrs Imrie’s expression grew wistful. “I fear my usefulness to the Reverend One may have ended.”

“What prompts this conclusion, if I may ask?”

Bewilderment crossed Mrs Imrie’s face. “You witnessed last night’s gathering. You saw my failure. The fire that your intended gallantly extinguished.” Her pale eyes widened, as though distressed to recall the events. “I wish to help, not to harm. It’s important that I’m realistic about my limitations.” Her words indicated regret, self-awareness, and deep thought. Despite the glare Mrs Imrie had directed at Winnifred, the apprentice wasn’t rash or ruled by emotion. She seemed capable of understanding and even controlling her feelings. The glare was likely a moment of weakness she now regretted.

“You didn’t knock the candle over on purpose.”

A sad smile touched Mrs Imrie's lips. "So you were watching."

Heat reached Felicity's cheeks. She imagined no one had noticed. "Is curiosity wrong?"

"Not at all. It's how most begin their journey of interest in the other realm."

"May I ask how your journey began?" Even if Felicity now felt fairly certain Mrs Imrie hadn't poisoned her great-aunt, she remained curious about the woman.

"When my husband perished suddenly," Mrs Imrie's chin lifted, though her hands twisted together, "mere weeks after our wedding."

"How dreadful," Felicity murmured. It was another tale of grief drawing souls to spiritualism. Was there anyone involved in the field who had not been touched by loss?

"Please, don't feel sorry for me." A little smile appeared on Mrs Imrie's thin lips. "I've perhaps discovered more fulfilment since than I might have found as a wife and mother."

Felicity admired such resilience. "Mr Silkstede and Miss Hartley shared similar stories of loss leading them to their interests in the other realm."

Mrs Imrie's expression darkened. "Unfortunately, not everyone's intentions remain pure."

Whom did she mean? Miss Hartley? Mr Silkstede? Both? What might be gleaned if Felicity pressed a little harder? "What exactly are you—"

Crash!

The sound of shattering glass and a sickening thud cut Felicity short.

"By Jupiter." Mrs Imrie paled, her hand flying to her throat.

"Felicity!"

The door to the little sitting room flew open. Alex stood in the doorway, Pip under his arm, tail wagging. "Are you all right?"

"I'm completely fine. What on earth—"

A scream from somewhere down below pierced the air. A terrible, blood-chilling scream.

Chapter Twenty-Four

Felicity and Alex made no wrong turns as they raced downstairs to discover what had happened. The scream had come from outside, slicing through the castle like a blade through silk. They weren't the first on the scene when they emerged into the small courtyard enclosed within the castle's weathered walls. It was Audrey's flower garden.

Dahlias in crimson and gold nodded alongside towering hollyhocks as the roses released their perfume into the sun-warmed morning air. The contrast between such loveliness and what lay before them made Felicity's stomach turn.

The cook stood at the front of the gathering, her aged frame trembling like a blade of grass. Her weathered face was buried against the butler's dark jacket, her white cap askew. In her hand was clutched a bunch of sage, though most of it had fallen to the ground. Timpson held her with unexpected tenderness, his usually rigid posture bent protectively over the distraught woman.

Beside them, the footman looked pale as parchment, his prominent ears seeming even more pronounced against his bloodless complexion. The solicitor stood frozen, his pudgy fingers still curved around an empty crystal tumbler, amber liquid pooling in the gravel beside his polished shoes. Mr Silkstede was also present, clutching his left arm against his frock coat, his face a grimace. He was injured.

Felicity clutched Pip tightly under her elbow as she and Alex approached steadily. Every instinct urged caution. Shattered glass sparkled like deadly jewels across the paths and flower borders. Fragments of mullioned window and carved stone had rained down with devastating force. In the middle of the devastation, flattening a section of Canterbury bells still nodding in the breeze, lay a body.

Face-up among the crushed flowers, Mr Harry Kemp stared sightlessly at the sky. The confident swagger that had defined him was gone, replaced by a terrible stillness. His shirt, its collar partially unbuttoned, revealed a gold chain that caught the sunlight with inappropriate cheerfulness. His arms and legs lay at angles that implied an uncontrolled fall.

A shiver like ice water poured down Felicity's spine. During the reading with Mrs Imrie, she'd reached the conclusion there was no one at the castle with murder on their mind. Had she been catastrophically wrong?

"What happened?" Alex pushed through the trampled flowers to approach the fallen man, Felicity hanging back, Pip clutched tight to her chest, their movements careful to avoid disturbing more evidence than necessary.

"Mr Kemp appears to have had a very serious accident," the butler managed, his voice maintaining professional composure despite the cook's continued sobs against his chest.

"That's quite clear." Alex crouched among the ruined blooms, reaching for the land agent's wrist, then neck. His grave expression as he stood confirmed what they all suspected. "Are you hurt?" he asked, addressing the spiritualist researcher.

Mr Silkstede swallowed and nodded. "A scratch. F-from the flying glass."

"Did anyone witness what happened?" asked Alex.

"I... I..." Mr Silkstede appeared to be suffering from shock. "I was on that bench there, writing in my notebook. He just came flying out of the sky. Mrs Wiseley was kneeling down, collecting herbs. We're..."

He sighed deeply, catching his breath. "We're lucky he didn't land on either of us."

The cook howled into the butler's jacket, the memory of the incident no doubt raw in her mind.

"Did you hear anything preceding the man's fall?" enquired Felicity.

Mr Silkstede shook his head. "It was peaceful until..." His gaze travelled upwards.

Felicity looked up, following the land agent's doomed trajectory. Two storeys above the garden, a damaged window gaped like a wound in the castle's red sandstone face. Not merely the glass but portions of the ornate stone window frame had been torn away, leaving jagged edges indicating tremendous force. The white muslin of torn curtains fluttered in the breeze like ghostly fingers.

"It appears to be something more than an accident." Felicity spoke quietly but couldn't keep the sharp edge from her voice, though her frustration was at herself. No matter her misgivings over the man, Mr Kemp did not deserve this fate. She'd conducted an investigation to flush out a would-be killer and failed — with devastating consequences.

"An accident isn't out of the question, your ladyship," the butler replied, raising his trembling voice above the cook's keening. "Given the state of some of the castle's fixtures, it's not beyond possibility."

Alex looked at Felicity, clearly keen to gauge her reaction to this assertion, but movement at the shattered window caught Felicity's eye.

A hand — pale, quick, and decisive — reached out and plucked something from the jagged glass. The afternoon sun cast the room beyond in deep shadow, making it impossible to determine if the hand belonged to a man or woman. The fingers were slender and delicate in their swift retrieval.

"What room is that?" she demanded.

"The billiard room, your ladyship."

"Take me there immediately," Felicity commanded, her detective instincts overriding any other reaction. She couldn't afford to be passive now. It had cost a life already. “And someone must summon the police.”

“The police?” Winnifred’s voice cut through the chaos. She appeared at the garden’s entrance, moving with notable stiffness. Her left hand gripped the head of a shining black walking cane while her right hung awkwardly at her side, partially concealed by flowing purple silk. “Why should we summon the police? I will not have—”

The words died as her gaze fell upon the land agent’s form among the purple flowers. Colour drained from her already pale features. “Oh, merciful heavens.”

Tristan arrived at a trot. “I say, what’s—” He froze beside his mother, his slender face becoming mask-like in its stillness. What little colour he possessed fled entirely. “How... How did this happen?”

“Mr Timpson, please escort me to the billiard room immediately,” Felicity repeated, clutching Pip more tightly as the terrier strained to investigate the drama. “Or I shall have to find it myself. The footman should be sent to the village at once. The police must be summoned directly. Every moment we delay gives a potential murderer time to destroy evidence.”

“Murderer?” echoed Mr Silkstede.

“Is he...?” Winnifred couldn’t complete the question, her blue eyes fixed on the man who’d managed the Wastes with such ruthless efficiency.

Philippa arrived with Peregrine close behind, her primrose-yellow frock incongruously cheerful against the scene’s horror. “What’s going on?” Her question faded as she registered the land agent’s form among the flowers. “Oh my goodness. Peregrine, darling, don’t look.”

Despite towering over his mother, Peregrine allowed her to turn him away, his jaw tightening. “What’s happened?” he asked.

“It’s Mr Kemp,” said Philippa, a sob erupting through the word. “He appears to be...”

“Very well, I shall investigate myself,” Felicity declared, already calculating who’d been present in the garden at what moment and who remained conspicuously absent. Where were Elfrida and Audrey? Where was Miss Hartley?

“Should we not alert the police first?” Tristan’s voice emerged thin as paper.

Winnifred’s gaze remained locked on the body, as though willing it to rise and walk away. She made no further protest about contacting the authorities. This couldn’t be resolved with a séance.

Another glance up at the hole through which Mr Kemp had plummeted showed no further movement. Felicity’s heart thudded as time bled away. Whoever retrieved evidence from that window — evidence that might reveal accident or murder — could be destroying it even now.

“Of course,” Felicity conceded, though every investigative instinct screamed against delay. This wasn’t her case. She had no jurisdiction. Proper channels must be followed, especially now that death had visited Cullingslock. “The police must be summoned immediately. Mr Cooper and I will go directly to the local sergeant.” Felicity’s mind whirred as she catalogued the scene: who stood where, who was missing, who showed genuine shock versus mere surprise. In her motor, she kept a notebook where she could record these crucial first observations.

“No.” Winnifred’s voice cracked like a whip, sudden authority overriding her shock. “Tristan, you must go — you know the way.” She swallowed hard and met Felicity’s gaze across the garden. For the first time since Felicity’s arrival at the castle, fear flashed in her great-aunt’s eyes. There could be no more covering up of the fact that someone had already attempted murder at the castle.

“I’m on my way,” assured Tristan as he left the garden.

“I need to lie down,” Winnifred added, her voice suddenly quieter, as if even the small amount of exertion fatigued her.

Philippa went to her mother-in-law’s side. “Lean on me, your ladyship,” she said as she and Peregrine helped Winnifred back indoors.

Again, Felicity stared up at the smashed window. She felt almost dizzy, as if the ground were shifting beneath her feet. She’d been far too dismissive of the poisoning attempt reported by her great-aunt. Dangerously dismissive.

"Are you all right?" Alex stood close to Felicity, his voice warm and low.

"Mm-hmm," she nodded, but her mind was racing. For whoever had orchestrated Mr Kemp's fatal fall, slipping poison into an apple crumble would have been child's play by comparison.

"The police will arrive soon," assured Alex, finding Felicity's hand with his. "You've done what you can."

As the household began to fragment — some still frozen in shock, others withdrawing from the scene — one thought crystallised in Felicity's mind with terrible clarity. There was a killer at Cullingslock Castle, and their actions showed they would not stop at a single victim.

Chapter Twenty-Five

The police arrived from the nearby village of Brackenfold with remarkable swiftness, their boots crunching purposefully on the gravel drive as they descended from the constabulary motor, promptly followed by the return of Dr Marsh in his dark grey Humber. The police went straight to the flower garden where Mr Kemp still lay, their request coming via the footman for the household to gather in a single room and await questioning. Based mainly on Philippa's input, the grand salon was promptly designated as the appropriate gathering place.

Positioned to the side of the medieval entrance hall, the room was — like many of the castle's chambers — well past its prime. The floral motifs of a pink and taupe Aubusson carpet covered wobbling floorboards. Mismatched furniture in a jumbled arrangement gave the room a cluttered, cottage-like feel. The windows were tall and gleaming but gave onto a dark patch of woodland. The presence of mystical objects was restrained: only a set of Egyptian figurines and an astrological chart were present. Faint traces of wood smoke from the unlit fireplace still hung in the air, as did a rather palpable sense of shock.

The footman served tea from a Georgian silver service, his unsteady hands rattling the cups in their saucers. Without Timpson's reassuring presence — the butler remained below stairs, still tending to the distraught cook — the service couldn't offer the intended consolation. Steam rose from delicate Spode cups, some of which were chipped, most of which sat untouched on the various side tables dotted throughout the room.

Elfrida and Audrey, who had been conspicuously absent during the garden's awful revelation, emerged from the kitchens once the butler informed them of the tragedy. They entered the salon with a subdued air, their cheeks pale, their eyes downcast. Neither of them appeared to have been moved to tears by the news of Mr Kemp's passing, but the initial shock could take time to subside before any grief could be felt.

Elfrida wore a practical lilac day dress with mother-of-pearl buttons, while Audrey's navy pinafore bore traces of flour at the cuffs. The girl settled onto a worn settee, Solomon's sleek head resting beneath her gentle fingers while Pip, ever the opportunist for comfort, claimed her lap. Felicity gladly surrendered the terrier to Audrey's care. Having one of her cherished gardens transformed into the scene of the land agent's untimely end would have compounded any distress she felt.

Elfrida took up position in front of the window, her back turned to the room, her arms wrapped across her chest in a tight hug. Tristan stood beside the fireplace, a hand on the marble mantel as if to steady himself, his gaze slightly wide-eyed and fixed on the metal fire grate, his Adam's apple occasionally bobbing. His tweed jacket hung loosely on his frame.

Philippa and Peregrine occupied the leather-covered Howard sofa opposite the matching piece of furniture upon which Felicity and Alex were seated. Philippa sat upright on the edge of her seat, her hands clasped in the lap of her yellow dress, her chin held aloft as though refusing to give into her emotions, though her mouth was very much down-turned. Peregrine maintained his military bearing, his shoulders square and his back long. He leaned into the sofa's back and drummed his fingers noiselessly on the armrest as his gaze flicked around the room. He seemed as curious as Felicity about the various reactions to what had happened. Alex was also watching with subtle rigour.

Was it possible they were seated in the grand salon with a killer? It was not only possible. It was likely.

Felicity and Alex swapped solemn looks. They couldn't exchange thoughts, but some elements of the investigation were already obvious.

The list of people who couldn't have been in the billiard room with Mr Kemp at the time of his fall was small but definite. Felicity and Alex had been with Mrs Imrie at the time of the crash into Audrey's garden and the cook's scream. Mr Silkstede — whose wounds were currently being attended to by Dr Marsh — had been in the flower garden along with the cook and both had witnessed the man's unfortunate end. The butler and footman appeared on the scene before Felicity and Alex did — would there have been enough time for either of them to commit the crime and then race down to comfort the cook? Felicity hadn't yet been given the opportunity to calculate the distance between the billiard room and the little garden, but it wasn't essential. This wasn't her investigation. The police were in attendance. They would be thorough in collecting witness statements and alibis. But would everyone be as truthful as possible?

Winnifred remained sequestered in her quarters, her two apprentices hovering close. Would they tell the police about the poisoning attempt? Winnifred clearly disliked the constabulary, but it was dangerous to imagine the two incidents — Mr Kemp's fall and the poisoned apple crumble — weren't connected, even if it wasn't yet obvious what linked them. What if the wrongdoer were to strike successfully again? Even with the investigation out of Felicity's hands, she could still contribute. To ensure nothing was overlooked, she would tell the police about the poisoning herself. She'd promised her great-aunt discretion on the matter, but the situation had changed significantly since making the vow.

The solicitor, his usually florid complexion now ashen, joined the assembly of Tristan, Philippa, Peregrine, Elfrida, Audrey, Felicity, and Alex in the faded grand salon. The atmosphere hung heavy as wet wool, punctuated only by the relentless ticking of a carriage clock from the marble mantelpiece.

"What a terrible way to go." The solicitor shook his head as he lowered himself onto the sofa beside Audrey and the dogs.

Despite the defaults of Mr Kemp's character, the man's death inspired no rejoicing. Yet as an outsider to both family and spiritual circles, to what extent would the land agent be mourned?

"Quite." Tristan's jaw tensed, his posture at the fireplace rigid.

Elfrida's fingers plucked at an invisible thread on her sleeve. "I told Mother that Axminster in the billiard room needed replacing. It was positively a death trap."

Philippa's gaze sharpened as it fixed on her sister-in-law. The yellow of her dress rendered her complexion waxy in the filtered light, her dark eyes shining like onyx. Watching his mother, Peregrine pressed his hands between his knees, his brow furrowed. His father's face stayed mask-like while his mother's mouth remained clamped closed, as though fighting the urge to speak. Whether dark humour or genuine concern, Elfrida's observation about the billiard room carpet had been somewhat inappropriate.

But was it possible to be certain Mr Kemp's fall hadn't been an accident?

Felicity's mind churned through possibilities. She'd not visited the scene of the incident and hadn't witnessed the precise circumstances of the man's fatal plunge. To land on his back in the flower garden, he'd surely fallen backwards through the window. The force needed to break the stone window frame could not have been caused by merely a backwards stumble, and Felicity and Alex understood better than anyone save Winnifred and her apprentices the slim probability of coincidence. A poisoning attempt followed by a deadly fall — the pattern suggested malevolence rather than misfortune.

But who would target both Winnifred and her land agent?

Felicity had already ruled out Winnifred's relatives and even the spiritualists in wishing her harm. Motivations for wishing to do away with Mr Kemp were perhaps more obvious, although not to the point of being convincing as a motive for murder.

Was there a deeper conspiracy than first thought? Had Mr Kemp orchestrated Winnifred's poisoning, only to meet his end through some twisted act of revenge?

Felicity's questions multiplied like mushrooms after rain, made worse by the silence enforced by the grim mood dominating the grand salon. She turned again to Alex. He looked as desperate as she did to engage in a vigorous discussion of methodical deduction.

Relief came in the form of three officers of the Devon County Constabulary appearing in dark blue uniforms in the salon's doorway, a sergeant flanked by two constables.

Elfrida turned away from the window, examining the policemen with subdued curiosity.

Sergeant Norris presented himself as the leader of the investigation. He was a compact man with a dark moustache and eyebrows like fattened caterpillars. He surveyed the room with the sharp gaze of a ferret assessing a warren, his thick moustache twitching.

"I should like a word with the physician before I begin my questioning. Constable Fielding, you'll guard this room," he directed the older of his subordinates, a man whose lined visage suggested years of service. "No one leaves without permission. And Constable Dinsdale—" The sergeant turned to address the younger of the two constables. "—fetch the servants up. They're to wait with the rest."

The young policeman nodded and scuttled away.

There was further movement as Dr Marsh arrived at the grand salon, delivering Mr Silkstede to the room, his arm now bandaged, his cheeks wan above his pointed beard. He found a seat on the settee beside Felicity and Alex. He had the air of someone who had aged ten years within the space of a day.

"Been to see the body?" the sergeant asked of the doctor.

The doctor remained courteous, though he seemed somewhat irked by the senior policeman's informal directness. "Not yet. It's normal to first attend to the living."

"Take a look, would you? I'd appreciate your opinion."

The doctor's grip tightened on his leather medical bag. "As you wish, Sergeant." He exited the room.

The subsequent arrival of the cook, butler, and footman created further awkwardness. The servants clustered near the door, their discomfort palpable as they shared space with their employers. Mrs Wiseley clutched a sodden handkerchief, her weathered face blotchy from weeping. The footman blinked and stood uneasily yet upright. Timpson looked weary for the first time since Felicity had met him, though his posture was alert as he stood beside the footman. At the butler's side, on a lead fashioned from thin rope, sat Lionheart. The Old English Sheepdog shook as if cold, his grey-and-white fur trembling, head hanging low. It was thoughtful of the servants to take the sheepdog into their care, but the situation could surely not be permanent.

"Where's the lady of the house?" Sergeant Norris's abrupt manner grated against the room's subdued, genteel atmosphere.

"The dowager baroness is upstairs in her chambers, sir," Timpson confirmed gently.

"Fetch her down, would you? Need everyone where I can see them till we sort this muddle."

Felicity prickled at the sergeant's casual tone regarding her great-aunt, though she recognised his efficiency. At least this officer seemed to understand the importance of preserving evidence and controlling the scene and suspects.

"I'll see to that directly, sir," said Timpson with a nod.

"And I'll be wanting a look at that room the fellow tumbled from."

"Naturally, sir."

The butler dispatched the footman to summon Winnifred while he accompanied Sergeant Norris and Constable Dinsdale to inspect the billiard room. Constable Fielding remained at the door of the grand salon.

"This waiting is insufferable," Philippa murmured, her fingers plucking at the embroidery on her dress.

Felicity smiled tightly in acknowledgment of the comment. It wasn't so much the waiting but the inability to take action that unsettled her. Yet she ought not to be so unnerved. The police were taking everything in hand. There was nothing to do except wait to be questioned.

"Murder investigations require patience," the solicitor observed, then blanched at his own words. "That is, if it proves to be murder. Could well be misadventure."

Felicity and Alex traded glances.

Tristan shifted minutely, the first movement he'd made in minutes. "The police will determine that."

After a period with nothing but the tick of the mantelpiece clock to break the silence, voices drifted from the entrance hall, the doors of the grand salon having been left open so that Constable Fielding might watch the room while also being connected to his colleagues beyond it. The sergeant and the doctor were having a curt yet efficient discussion about the body's removal. Audrey's eyebrows drew together at the talk, which everyone could hear, her grip tightening on Solomon and Pip, her eyes darting to Lionheart, who continued to sit trembling beside the cook. Footsteps echoing across the entrance hall's stone floor indicated the practical yet rather grim discussion's end.

Felicity had reached her limit of sitting and doing nothing.

She rose with studied casualness, Alex's questioning glance following her movement as she went to the doorway of the grand salon, stopping short of passing beyond the constable on duty. From the wary look on the policeman's face, he disapproved of Felicity's actions but was unsure whether to issue a warning.

"Dr Marsh," she called softly before Constable Fielding could make up his mind. "Might I have a word?"

The physician glanced at the constable, who granted permission with a curt nod. Denying access to medical care would not reflect well on the sergeant and his constables.

Felicity stepped into the echoing entrance hall. "In private, if possible?" she whispered to Dr Marsh.

The physician again looked to the constable. After a little pause, the policeman gave a reluctant nod, and Felicity followed Dr Marsh to the large doors leading outside.

Once out in the fresh air, free from the fear of being overheard in the grand salon, Felicity seized her chance.

"Have you examined my great-aunt today?"

"Not on this visit, no. I understand she's refusing to leave her room." His professional reserve didn't quite mask his concern.

Felicity selected her words carefully. "The gastric distress she suffered when you were last at the castle — might there be alternative reasons for her symptoms?"

Dr Marsh's eyes narrowed. "Why do you ask?"

"Mr Kemp's death wasn't natural, was it?" She kept her voice low.

The doctor huffed. "I imagine you're even better placed than me to make that assessment, your ladyship."

Felicity gave a polite smile. It was flattery — perhaps even sarcastic, depending on the man's opinion of lady detectives — but it was also avoiding her question. "If you're aware of the choices I've made in my career, which I assume from your comment that you are, then I hope you understand my concern. What if we're not looking at one attempt at murder, but two — one successful, the other not?"

The doctor lowered his brow.

"Is there a chance, Dr Marsh, that my great-aunt was poisoned?"

"That's a matter for the police, your ladyship." His tone was tight. It seemed Felicity had succeeded in irritating him. "If you'll excuse me, I have the removal of the unfortunate fellow's body to attend to."

Disappointed to have failed in nudging the physician towards her theory, Felicity returned to the salon. She had at least already made some effort to contribute to the investigation, and she had made up her mind. Winnifred's poisoning could no longer remain a secret. Felicity's promise of discretion must yield to the investigation's demands.

Shafts of light had pierced the trees and now slanted through the salon's tall windows, casting long shadows across the assembled company. Alex cast a hopeful look in Felicity's direction. She gave her head a little shake as she retook her seat beside him. How many more hours might it be before she and Alex could depart? Would there be an opportunity to telegram Bradley Court before rumours reached them? The thought of her grandmother's worry added another layer to her discomfort.

"Lady Felicity Quick?"

Constable Dinsdale appeared in the doorway. Fresh-faced beneath his helmet, he couldn't have been more than Peregrine's age.

"Yes?"

"Sergeant Norris would like to speak with you."

Surprise bloomed in Felicity alongside satisfaction. Her reputation had preceded her — why else summon her first? Her mind, over-wound like a watch spring since the terrible discovery in the flower garden, welcomed the chance to share her observations with someone who might actually use them.

"Please, Constable," she said, smoothing her skirt as she stood. "Lead the way."

Chapter Twenty-Six

The room Sergeant Norris had commandeered for his interviews bore all the hallmarks of practicality over comfort. A plain table in warm brown elm, its surface scarred by decades of use, dominated the modest space. Two ladder-back chairs faced each other across its width. Sunlight streamed through mullioned windows, one pane bearing a spider's web of cracks that scattered prisms across the whitewashed walls. It was perhaps the only room in the whole castle without even a hint of esoteric decoration — either that or the sergeant had ordered any trace of mysticism removed from the space.

"Take a seat, your ladyship." The sergeant's commanding tone implied he didn't have time for pleasantries.

Felicity settled onto the hard wooden seat and sat up straight, unfazed at being without Alex's steadying support or even Pip's comforting presence. She was confident she could help the investigation, even if she wouldn't be the one to run it.

"Am I the first in the household you're interviewing?" She kept her tone pleasantly curious.

"Not exactly." Sergeant Norris lowered himself into the opposite chair with symmetrical precision. He was a compact man, certainly nowhere near six feet in his polished boots, but what he lacked in stature, he compensated for with an intensity that filled the room. His dark eyes darted, never quite settling, while his uniform had been pressed to knife-edge perfection, its brass buttons gleaming. A thick moustache, waxed to aggressive points, jumped as he spoke. "But I thought it best to start with you, your ladyship. Now. Let's not beat about the bush. I read the papers. I know who you are. I know how you operate."

Felicity's eyebrow arched delicately. "How I operate?" The phrase suggested something rather more antagonistic than she cared for.

"Let me be perfectly clear." The sergeant leaned forward, thick fingers splayed on the table's surface. "I've no interest in spectacle or publicity stunts. No patience for recognition-seekers or attention-grabbers. I'll keep the press coverage of this business to an absolute minimum until I determine exactly what's occurred." His eyes narrowed to slits. "And mark my words, I will uncover the truth." The words sounded like a threat.

Felicity had expected cooperation, perhaps even consultation, given her experience. The sergeant's hostility caught her off-guard, though she kept her expression carefully neutral.

"I've no quarrel with your methods, Sergeant. This is your investigation."

"Glad to hear it." His smile held all the warmth of a January frost.

"Though I confess myself puzzled by your concern regarding publicity."

The sergeant's bark of laughter was humourless. "I might ask the same of you, your ladyship. You're quite the darling of the newspapers and periodicals, aren't you? You clearly enjoy the limelight." He paused, watching her with predatory patience. "You've that in common with your great-aunt."

Felicity repressed the urge to shift in her seat. Would the policeman even give her the opportunity to aid the investigation?

"I don't choose what newspapers print about my activities, Sergeant. That's simply the nature of the press."

"But you choose to write for that ladies' magazine, don't you?

The Gentlewoman's Gazette, isn't it?" His tone dripped with contempt. "Forced into it against your will, were you?"

Heat crept up Felicity's neck. The man had done his research, and his point struck home despite its unfairness.

"I come from a newspaper family, Sergeant. My brother is a businessman, and I follow his guidance regarding our family's interests." If it were up to Felicity alone, she'd have perhaps not even started writing for the Gentlewoman's Gazette, but she wouldn't discuss family politics with the belligerent policeman.

"Is that so?" The sergeant's expression suggested he'd sooner believe pigs might sprout wings.

"What has my great-aunt to do with my journalistic endeavours?"

This time his laugh held genuine mirth, though not the pleasant sort. "First visit to Cullingslock, and you're claiming ignorance? I'd not have taken you for naïve, your ladyship."

"Naïve of what, precisely?"

The sergeant studied her for a long moment, as though weighing her sincerity against his scepticism. When he spoke again, his voice was quieter. More spiteful. "Some folk call your great-aunt a spiritualist. I call her a charlatan and a confidence trickster."

The accusation landed like a slap. Felicity's own doubts about spiritualism left her unable to mount an enthusiastic defence, yet neither could she be certain that anyone in Winnifred's circle was a deliberate fraud. They all seemed to believe in what they were doing.

Felicity tightened the clasp of her hands in her lap. "Have you proof to support such serious accusations?"

"I'm a man of the law." Sergeant Norris puffed his chest, brass buttons straining. "My word ought to be sufficient."

Felicity managed a tight smile. Her experiences had taught her that badges didn't guarantee wisdom or fairness, particularly where unconventional women were concerned.

"Would you indulge me with specifics, Sergeant? As you've noted, I'm new to Cullingslock. I should hate to proceed under misapprehensions."

The sergeant settled back in his chair, arms folded across his chest.

"Your great-aunt peddles services that don't exist. Charges good money for speaking to the dead and such nonsense. And not everyone's been satisfied with the results."

"Could you elaborate?"

His expression darkened. "You've never heard of the Kensington séance tragedy?"

Something cold settled in Felicity's stomach. She shook her head. She would have strong words with Jasper when she got back to Bradley Court. He may have wished to spare her feelings by hiding ugly truths, but it had left her vulnerable.

"November 1917. Your great-aunt was performing at some duchess's mansion in London. Theatrical production, by all accounts — special electrical apparatus, spirit lamps, the full spectacle." The policeman's moustache twitched with disgust. "The whole contraption went up in flames. Two society ladies badly burned, your great-aunt worst of all. Made headlines for weeks."

Felicity's mind raced. She'd perhaps flicked past the story at the time, but her brother had only recently revealed to her Winnifred's existence and the Quick family's connection to Cullingslock. As unpleasant as it was to be schooled by the unfriendly sergeant, the revelation explained so much — Winnifred's careful movements, her reluctance to involve the police when she suspected someone tried to poison her, perhaps even her retreat to Cullingslock at a point when spiritualism and the demand for the services of mediums was still gaining in popularity.

"The police in London investigated, of course. Questions about faulty equipment, dangerous practices. Some suggested she'd rigged the fire herself for dramatic effect, though nothing was proved." Sergeant Norris leaned forward. "But we country folk read the London papers, your ladyship. When she slunk back here to recover, I made sure she understood such dangerous foolishness wouldn't be tolerated in these parts."

Felicity cleared her throat, recovering from her surprise at the sergeant's revelations. "And has my great-aunt heeded your warning?"

"Been quiet enough. Until now." His eyes bored into hers. "Until you arrived."

Felicity's heart rate increased. She tucked her chin in a display of indignation verging on outrage. "Are you suggesting I had something to do with Mr Kemp's fall?"

"Interesting leap, your ladyship." His smile was as sharp as glass. "Though since you've raised the question yourself — did you?"

Anger flared hot in Felicity's chest. "Are you actually proposing I arrange suspicious deaths wherever I travel, simply to investigate them?"

"You do have a habit of being conveniently present when bodies drop. That can't be denied."

The accusation was so outrageous Felicity had to bite back several unladylike responses. The prospect of headlines suggesting her suspected involvement in the land agent's death made her stomach turn. There were always newspapers that published just about anything, no matter how far-fetched, but Felicity needed to remain in control. The sergeant already had a very low opinion of her. It wouldn't help to lower it further.

"You're treating Mr Kemp's death as suspicious, then? Not as an accident?"

"Come now, your ladyship." He rose from his chair, looming despite his modest height. "A grown man in full possession of his faculties doesn't fall through a window backwards with enough force to shatter both glass and stone." He paced beside the table. "I'm familiar with the drunkards that frequent our local inns, and Mr Kemp wasn't one of them. Someone was with him when it happened. Of that I am certain."

Felicity nearly mentioned the hand she'd seen retrieving something from the broken window, but the policeman's hostility suggested he'd dismiss any observation she made. Besides, he hadn't asked what she'd witnessed, and there were more important things she needed to highlight to the sergeant.

"Two people can attest to my whereabouts when Mr Kemp fell. I was in Mrs Imrie's quarters, with Mr Cooper waiting just outside the door."

The policeman laughed, clearly entertained. "Your interest in attracting sensation is one thing, but I didn't realise you were the type to fall for that hocus-pocus nonsense."

Felicity's eyebrows knitted with displeasure. She was on the edge of informing him she had been with Mrs Imrie to investigate a suspected poisoning rather than to see her future, but would it help? The policeman had no intention of taking her at all seriously.

"I had nothing to do with Mr Kemp's demise," said Felicity carefully and clearly.

The sergeant placed both palms flat on the table, leaning forward until she could smell the wax in his moustache. "Oh, I don't doubt your hands are clean, your ladyship. But let me be crystal clear — if you or your spiritualist great-aunt orchestrated whatever led to the only sensible person in this castle meeting such a violent end, there'll be very serious consequences indeed."

Felicity sat frozen, caught between disbelief and fury. She'd encountered difficult people in her investigations, but never had anyone made such preposterous accusations directly to her face. The sergeant's threat was baseless — she'd had nothing whatsoever to do with Mr Kemp's death — yet defending herself might have granted the ridiculous suggestion more credence than it deserved.

"Is that all you wished to discuss, Sergeant?"

"I've said what needs saying." He straightened, tugging his dark blue tunic smooth. "I'm a busy man with real responsibilities to real people. Not to say I don't take this seriously — my constables will gather statements today, and I'll review them in my own time. The truth has a way of revealing itself, doesn't it, your ladyship?" His tone was somewhere between mockery and disdain.

Felicity rose with careful dignity, smoothing her skirt with steady hands, though anger trembled beneath her skin.

"Then I shall bid you good day, Sergeant."

As she turned towards the door, his voice followed her. "One more thing, your ladyship. Best keep yourself available. Wouldn't want you disappearing before we've sorted this mess."

The implied threat — that she might flee like a common criminal — was the final insult. Felicity paused at the threshold, looking back over her shoulder with the serene hauteur her grandmother had taught her.

"I assure you, Sergeant, I've no intention of going anywhere until this matter is resolved."

Felicity swept from the room with her chin high. Inside, she seethed, her blood close to boiling point. What she had expected to be a relatively standard police interview had been a disaster, leaving her shaken and furious in equal measure. It was now clear why Winnifred had been so reluctant to involve the police. With Sergeant Norris's prejudices colouring his investigation, how could justice be delivered?

Chapter Twenty-Seven

When Felicity returned to the grand salon, every eye followed her progress past the constable standing at the door. Even Tristan looked up from his rigid stance at the mantelpiece, and Elfrida turned away from the window to watch her weave between the mismatched furniture, but Felicity maintained a serene composure. Concern etched Alex's features, but he didn't rush towards her, even if that's what he wished to do. It wouldn't have been helpful to create a scene.

Miss Hartley and Mrs Imrie had now also joined the gathering, although Winnifred was still conspicuously absent. The availability of seating in the grand salon becoming rather limited, Alex had given up his place on the settee and the two women were now seated beside one another, Mrs Imrie appearing serene, her eyes lowered to her lap, Miss Hartley rather more flustered, her cheeks pink and her brow creased.

Upon Felicity's re-entry to the sunlit, increasingly stuffy room, the solicitor gave up his seat on the sofa next to Audrey and went to stand beside the servants. Felicity thanked him as Pip crawled back onto her lap.

"That was rather brief," said Philippa, blinking nervously at

Felicity, her hands clutched tightly in the lap of her inappropriately cheery yellow dress.

Felicity gave a tight smile as she stroked the Yorkie's silky back, more for her own comfort than the dog's. "It was an introductory meeting rather than a full interview."

Alex's dark blue gaze found hers as he approached the worn settee with a studied lack of hurriedness. "Everything all right?" he asked softly, his hand brushing her shoulder for the briefest of moments.

"I believe so," she said, still wearing a polite smile he would undoubtedly recognise for the mask it was. This was hardly the audience before which to voice her indignation at the sergeant's preposterous accusations. Yet perhaps even more noteworthy than her own anger was the fact that, despite her intentions, Felicity hadn't told Sergeant Norris about the attempted poisoning of her great-aunt. She still had to make sense of the sergeant's report of the disastrous séance in London — to what extent did it alter Felicity's perceptions of Winnifred and the goings-on at Cullingslock?

Constable Fielding was replaced at the grand salon's door by Constable Dinsdale, the younger policeman casting a gaze across the salon's residents with the wariness of a gaoler charged with overseeing hardened criminals. One by one, the captives were summoned to deliver their testimonies to the older constable. Sergeant Norris had departed shortly after his audience with Felicity, leaving his subordinates to gather the remaining statements, although what business could be more pressing for a rural sergeant than a murder enquiry was unclear.

The interviews proceeded with methodical precision. Philippa returned from her interrogation with tears coursing down her powdered cheeks, her primrose dress catching the light as she trembled. Tristan maintained his granite facade, though Felicity detected a muscle jumping in his jaw. Audrey emerged sniffling, her freckled face blotchy with distress, while Elfrida appeared notably pale beneath her usual sardonic composure.

After a curt whispered discussion between the constables, the butler was requested to summon Winnifred.

"I believe her ladyship requires rest, Constable," came the butler's reply.

The older of the two policemen sighed. "We still need to interview her, I'm afraid."

"Understood, sir." The butler moved swiftly and silently from the room.

When Felicity's turn arrived, she found herself back in the same simple chamber where she'd faced down the sergeant, an oil lamp now glowing on the elm table as the light outside dimmed. Constable Fielding, however, proved infinitely more professional than his superior. His drooping, deeply lined features gave him a mournful air, but his questions were thorough and impartial.

Felicity recounted her observations with scrupulous accuracy, including the order in which the various personages had arrived in the floral courtyard and the mysterious hand she'd witnessed retrieving something from the shattered window. The constable's pencil moved steadily across his notebook, his expression revealing nothing of whether her testimony aligned with or contradicted other accounts.

"Is there anything else you feel might be relevant, your ladyship?" he asked, his tone carefully neutral.

The invitation hung in the air. It was an opportunity to speak of Winnifred's poisoning, of the séances and spiritualist tensions, of family resentments simmering beneath polite facades. Yet something — perhaps lingering indignation at Sergeant Norris's treatment, perhaps a need to understand more about what she knew before sharing it — held her tongue.

"Nothing that seems immediately pertinent," Felicity replied, though the words felt somewhat like ash in her mouth. It wasn't right to withhold information from the police, but she wasn't ready to share her most intimate insights into the case. Not yet.

Returning once again to the salon, she caught Alex's eye as she passed where he stood, still awaiting his own call-up for interview. His slight nod conveyed understanding. They would need to confer privately and soon.

As the golden afternoon light gave way to the blue shadows of approaching dusk, the gas jets in the wall sconces began their gentle hiss, offering a warm glow. Pip dozed on Felicity's lap, occasionally opening an eye to track Solomon's movements. The Border Collie paced restlessly near his master. The Old English Sheepdog rested his head on his paws but was unable to close his eyes.

The butler had returned to the grand salon, taking up his place along the wall beside the footman and the cook. There was no sign of Winnifred, however.

"Her ladyship is most weak, sir," explained Timpson to the older constable.

"But there can't be exceptions, can there?" The younger policeman looked at his older colleague.

Constable Fielding stroked his wrinkled chin. "Should the doctor be summoned?" he asked of the butler.

"Please, allow us to rejoin her." Miss Hartley had sprung from her seat, her hands clasped earnestly before her chest.

Mrs Imrie also stood. "We know what the Reverend One needs. We know how to care for her."

The fresh-faced Constable Dinsdale frowned his disapproval.

"Her ladyship requires peace and rest," assured the butler, still addressing the older constable. "Nothing more."

Constable Fielding's lips pressed together in a thin line. "Go to her and ensure that she remains well," the policeman instructed the butler. "If her condition deteriorates, let me know of it." The constable's consideration towards Winnifred was markedly different from that of his superior.

The butler gave a solemn nod and departed from the grand salon. The two apprentices continued to appeal to the older constable that they would be better suited to cater to Winnifred's needs, but he curtly dismissed their entreaties and summoned Alex as the next interviewee.

"Here we go," whispered Alex, giving Felicity a little smile as he followed the policeman to the door. That his mood remained lively was heartening. He'd perhaps feel differently if he'd also had an unpleasant run-in with Sergeant Norris, but then Felicity would also feel differently if she might just have a moment alone with Alex in which to share her thoughts. Simply recalling the tone the sergeant had taken with her drove her to dig her fingernails into her palms.

When Alex returned from his interview, which was relatively brief, just as all the others had been, he brushed past where Felicity was seated. Under the pretence of adjusting Pip's position, she caught his whispered words: "A blow to the head."

She gave an almost imperceptible nod and suppressed a satisfied smile. Alex had worked his magic with the older constable and reversed the flow of information. The police, or more likely the doctor, had found something significant: the man had suffered an injury to the head before he fell. The chances of Mr Kemp's demise being an accident had gone from slim to none at all.

Philippa approached the young constable stationed at the door. Her composure was restored though her eyes remained red-rimmed. "Constable Dinsdale, we must make arrangements for dinner. The cook needs to return to her duties."

The elderly cook looked up hopefully from where she still stood next to the young footman. After so long standing, Felicity would have preferred a sit down rather than a session working in the kitchen, but the servants' discomfort at being gathered with the castle's residents was perhaps not to be underestimated.

The fresh-faced officer frowned deeply as he swallowed nervously. "Yes. Um." He looked thoroughly out of his depth. "I'll need to consult with Constable Fielding. Don't anyone leave this room. Is that understood?"

During the policeman's absence, conversation tentatively resumed.

"Who among us was the last to see him alive?" Elfrida's question emerged barely above a whisper, her usual cynical armour cracked by a dose of seemingly genuine concern.

The solicitor shifted his considerable bulk from one foot to the other. "He stopped by the library after luncheon to smoke a pipe."

Philippa's hands twisted in her lap. "I passed him in the entrance hall. He was heading upstairs. That must have been shortly before he..." The words died unspoken.

Elfrida caught Philippa's gaze and held it. Something passed between the women — something uncomfortable that made them both look away.

"Will we be put in prison?" Audrey's voice quavered with adolescent fear.

Elfrida went to her daughter and rubbed her sturdy shoulders. "No, darling, of course not."

"But one of us might." Tristan's voice carried an eerie flatness, as though any trace of emotion had been drained from him.

Philippa turned sharply towards her husband. "Surely it might have been an accident?"

"The constable indicated—" Tristan's Adam's apple worked as he swallowed. "—that Mr Kemp bore injuries consistent with violence. A blow to the face, delivered by human hands."

Felicity and Alex exchanged worried looks. The older constable had become loose-lipped. Felicity and Alex's awareness of the detail was one thing. The consequences of such knowledge mingling with the tension, confusion, and distress permeating the household could be dire.

"Oh dear," Elfrida murmured, the words barely audible.

"You mean..." Miss Hartley shook her head. "Someone killed him? Deliberately killed him?"

Philippa reached for Peregrine and tugged his arm against her side, whether for her own comfort or her son's was unclear. The young man sat rigid as a telegraph pole, staring at his father with something approaching horror.

Tristan gazed back at his son, his expression quite blank. He had no words of reassurance to offer.

Felicity took a steadying breath. When considering who among the castle's residents would have a motive to wish both Winnifred and her land agent gone, Tristan's name appeared high on the list. The friction he experienced with both victims had been made obvious even to Felicity. His understanding for his mother made matricide unlikely, however, and even if he had expressed strong sentiments during the tour of the Wastes, he didn't seem the sort to strike out. Even if he was, his build was far less substantial than the land agent's.

The return of both constables curtailed further speculation. Constable Fielding's announcement was delivered with the flat efficiency of a man following protocol.

"The butler and cook may proceed to the kitchen to prepare the evening meal, which will be served here in the salon."

"Are we expected to sleep here as well?" Philippa's tone was sharp, her patience fraying.

The constable continued as though she hadn't spoken. "Following the meal, you will be escorted to your chambers, where you will remain until morning. Sergeant Norris will then return to review the testimony and determine how to proceed."

Felicity rose, her mind swirling with possibilities. "I'm expected at home — I'm merely a guest here, as you're aware. Might I contact my family to inform them of my well-being?"

The constables exchanged glances, the younger somehow irritated yet deferring to his senior colleague's judgement.

"We can arrange for a telephone call or telegram from the station tomorrow morning, your ladyship," Constable Fielding replied. "Would that be satisfactory?"

Felicity caught Alex's gaze. A slight twinkle in his eye implied other plans.

"It would, yes," she agreed, resuming her seat. It was best to cooperate for now and avoid drawing unwanted attention.

There was, however, no possibility of two constables keeping watch over the entire castle for the whole night. And Felicity wasn't one to tolerate imprisonment if there were other options available.

Chapter Twenty-Eight

The darkened castle corridors stretched before Felicity like the tunnels of an underground cave, with only the occasional gas-powered sconce or pool of silvery moonlight to guide her way. Pip's small body quivered with barely suppressed energy under Felicity's elbow so it wasn't a solitary journey, but he couldn't be trusted alone in her chamber. His protestations might have drawn unwanted attention from the constables on patrol.

Felicity had armed herself with explanations should discovery threaten. A lady might require any number of things in the dead of night — a sleeping draught from the kitchen, a book from the library, even simple reassurance after the day's grim events. The sergeant's opinion of her could hardly sink lower, rendering caution somewhat academic. Still, prudence demanded she forgo a candle to guide her way. Its telltale glow would beacon her movements to watching eyes, and the constables would certainly intervene. Not being caught was key to the success of this mission.

"I was hoping you might come for me," whispered Alex as he slipped into the corridor following Felicity's gentle knock at his door. In the moonlight-tinted darkness, she could just about discern his features — the determined set of his chiselled jaw combined with a touch of a smile on his lips. "I stayed put on that assumption, lest we both spend the night wandering the corridors looking for one another."

Felicity returned his smile, her hand finding his. "You know me reassuringly well." It had been far too long since they'd had a moment alone together.

Alex cast a glance over his shoulder at the closed door to his chambers. "I've been burning to ask you about your experience with Sergeant Norris." The corridor wasn't the subtlest of locations for a discussion, but being discovered together in either of their chambers before their wedding was beyond the risks even Felicity was willing to take.

She gave a little huff at the memory of the experience, though the sting of the sergeant's accusations — that she was involved in Mr Kemp's demise, a love of public attention as her motive — had worn away over the course of the day. Her thoughts had now crystallised into a plan of action. "Please be forewarned that you shan't like what I have to share on the topic."

Alex's face showed distinct irritation as Felicity recounted the sergeant's accusations, his revelations about Winnifred's past, and his unwillingness to take either Felicity or her great-aunt seriously.

Alex drew in a steadying breath, controlling his emotions. "So we are to act?"

Felicity's posture stiffened with determination. "How can we not?"

As she outlined her plan in hushed tones, his nods of understanding warmed her from within, increasing her conviction in her own deductions. Here stood a man who trusted her judgement implicitly, who recognised her capabilities without condescension or doubt. The contrast with Sergeant Norris's dismissive hostility could not have been starker.

Despite the animosity the senior policeman had created between them, Felicity had no wish to undermine his investigation. "I don't yearn to take action with a view of coming out on top," she clarified as they set off towards the castle's great entrance hall, Pip's curious eyes shining in the dark and Alex in the lead as the most experienced lookout of the group.

"You simply wish to help matters along in the proper direction." Alex flashed a smile at her over his shoulder. "There's no need to defend your decisions for my sake," he continued, keeping his voice low. "Not unless I directly challenge you upon them."

Felicity smiled. "How reassuring."

Pale moonlight filtered through the entrance hall's high windows. The distant call of an owl was the only sound that pierced the night. They clung to the elongated shadows cast across the worn the flagstones, careful to make as little noise as possible with their footsteps, minimising every chance of discovery.

Navigating the vaulted staircase — which gently creaked as they climbed, though thankfully not too loudly — and after several corridors, they paused at the base of a narrow spiral staircase. Felicity transferred Pip to Alex's waiting arms. The terrier went willingly, his tail wagging with the promise of adventure.

"Are you sure you're happy doing this?" She searched his face in the dimness.

"Happy might not be the right word," he said as he looked down at the Yorkie. The dog looked up at him and sniffed his chin. "But I want to help."

Felicity leaned forward impulsively, pressing her lips to his cheek. The warmth of his skin, the faint scent of his shaving soap, grounded her in the moment. "Good luck."

His free hand found hers briefly, giving a squeeze of reassurance. "You can count on me."

Shadows embraced Felicity as she pressed herself against the cold stone of a nearby alcove, watching as Alex climbed the narrow stairs. His invented need for a lantern with which to venture outside and walk the dog drew Timpson away from Winnifred's quarters with remarkable efficiency, though reluctance radiated from the butler's movements as Felicity watched him lead Alex and Pip back along the corridor whence they'd come.

Only when their footsteps faded to whispers did she dare ascend.

The door to Winnifred's chamber stood slightly ajar, the warm glow of candlelight flickering through the gap.

Carefully, she eased it open.

The room's heavy furnishings and thick carpets swallowed the sound of Felicity's approach towards the great bed, where candlelight created an island of amber warmth. Thoth and Ra regarded her entrance with feline disdain, their eyes sparkling like topaz in the gloom. Thank goodness Alex had taken Pip — the chaos of the little terrier meeting the cats in the middle of the night didn't bear contemplating.

"Timpson?" Winnifred's voice rang clear and commanding, belying any pretence of illness. "I should like another mug of cocoa if you'd be so kind."

As Felicity advanced into the light, her great-aunt's expression transformed from expectation to something harder to read. Fear? Calculation? In the candle's unsteady glow, Winnifred appeared diminished — her grey hair loose across her pillow, her complexion waxy beneath her voluminous white nightgown trimmed with fraying lace. A bed jacket of quilted pink satin hung loosely about her shoulders.

"My child." The words emerged cordial enough, but something lurked beneath. "What are you doing here? Did Mr Timpson not tell you I am not to be disturbed? I thought the police had taken control of the castle." Her voice trembled on the final words, from frailty or perhaps outrage.

Felicity continued her approach, noting the familiar stool beside the bed but choosing to remain standing. This was no social call, no time for the niceties that had so far governed their interactions.

"Have you spoken to the police, Great-Aunt?" She came directly to the point, acutely aware that they might be interrupted at any moment by the return of the butler or by one of the constables.

"My child, I simply haven't the energy to talk."

"Did you tell the police someone tried to do away with you?"

Fear bloomed unmistakably in Winnifred's eyes — not the

manufactured emotion of the séance room but something raw and real. "I have yet to speak to the police."

Felicity's eyes narrowed. However frail Winnifred might appear, surely she could not avoid official questioning indefinitely. "When you do, will you inform them you were poisoned?"

The older woman's nostrils flared. "I will not."

"I have witnessed the contempt with which Sergeant Norris regards you and your activities." Felicity kept her voice level despite rising frustration. "But you must understand the gravity of the situation. A man lies dead. What happened to you may illuminate what befell Mr Kemp." She leaned forward slightly, willing her great-aunt to see reason. "Please trust me when I say I have questioned everyone in this household, seeking any who might wish you or your circle harm."

"You've been speaking to my helpers and to Mr Silkstede?" Accusation sharpened Winnifred's tone. "I told you they are above suspicion."

Felicity refused to be diverted. "If you don't tell the police about the poisoning, then I will." The threat emerged more forcefully than intended, but desperation drove her now. Whatever her feelings about Sergeant Norris, this was murder. Truth could not be buried beneath family loyalty or spiritualist solidarity.

"Don't do it."

"Great-Aunt, you cannot stop me." There could be no more sitting about. No more dithering and protecting sensibilities.

"It's not true."

The air grew suddenly still. Felicity's certainty wavered. "What's not true?"

Winnifred's eyes closed, her expression pained. "No one poisoned me." She sighed deeply. "I poisoned myself."

The revelation struck Felicity like a physical blow. "What?"

"I'm sorry." The words emerged just above a whisper.

"How?"

"Administered a little foxglove to my pudding. It's not complicated."

"You might have died."

The older woman shook her head slowly. "I knew what I was doing."

"I don't understand. Why would you poison yourself?" Even as the question left her lips, Felicity's mind continued to race through the possibilities, none of them making any sense at all.

The bedroom door swung open with decisive force. "Your ladyship." Timpson appeared at Winnifred's bedside as though conjured by her need, his manner one of embarrassment and haste, perhaps realising he'd been played. Upon locking eyes with Felicity, only the briefest flicker of annoyance crossed his features before his professional composure returned.

"Your ladyship." His tone carried the unyielding deference of a servant accustomed to managing difficult situations with discretion. "Constable Fielding will pass through this wing soon. Allow me to escort you back to your room."

Winnifred raised a trembling hand. "Timpson, it's over. My great-niece knows now. She knows what I did."

The butler's gaze shifted between the two women, uncertainty creasing his distinguished features as he sought an appropriate response. "Very good, m'lady," he managed finally, a bow marking the beginning of his withdrawal.

"Timpson, wait." Winnifred's command halted him mid-step. "I have no secrets from you. And I realise now that I must have none from Felicity, either."

"Why did you poison yourself?" Felicity pressed, her mind still reeling from the confession. Nothing about this made sense — unless... The sergeant had been very wrong in his assumptions about Felicity. Might he have been right about her great-aunt?

Winnifred nodded slowly, her eyes raising towards the canopy of her four-poster bed. "My child, I realise you know what it is to live with loss. But I hope you never know what it's like to lose a husband, or to lose a child when he is in the prime of his very young life, then to have the worry of your son going to war, to have him come back and discover he's not the same man."

The butler's gaze fixed studiously on the carpet's worn patterns, his discomfort detectable even as he maintained his post.

"You have no doubt known much sorrow," Felicity conceded, though what bearing this had on the admission to poisoning oneself was as yet unclear. Wariness crept along her spine. Was she in danger? Had she miscalculated by coming here alone? Her awareness sharpened to the room's geography — the door, the distance to it, the butler's position between herself and escape.

"One makes decisions to look after oneself, to look after one's family. Some of these decisions have risks." Winnifred's voice gained strength. She sat up a little against the pillows, her movements stiff, the cats shifting slightly on the coverlet. "I saw an opportunity, and I took a risk, and now I'm afraid I have blood on my hands."

Ice flooded Felicity's veins. Was this confession extending beyond self-poisoning to murder? Had she walked willingly into a monster's jaws? Every instinct screamed at her to step back, to flee, but showing fear before a predator — if a predator Winnifred was — might only precipitate disaster.

"I can't understand it." Felicity forced steadiness into her voice. "Why did you poison yourself? Why do you have blood on your hands?"

Winnifred's sigh was heavy with remorse. "I'm more than aware of your connection to the newspapers, my child, and I'm afraid I was hoping to take advantage of that."

Felicity's jaw tightened. She hated to admit it, but Sergeant Norris had, to a certain extent, been correct.

"It was wrong of me and I regret it now. Of course I do, but you would understand, I think, if you were in my situation. You know, for example, that money can be scarce these days. The world isn't what it was like in Lady Katherine's time. Families like ours are no longer favoured as we once were. You know that, my child."

Understanding trickled through Felicity like ice water. Her dreams of family reconciliation suddenly appeared painfully naïve. With her newspaper connections and detective reputation, her arrival at Cullingslock had been interpreted as an opportunity to turn a profit. The intention had been to use her. Even her own great-aunt had seen her chance.

"How would poisoning yourself achieve benefits in combination with my newspaper connections?" Felicity kept her tone flat despite her continued confusion and a sense of disappointment so heavy it ached.

"You were trying to solve the case. You wouldn't be able to. And the conclusion would be simple." Winnifred's eyes glittered with something between pride and desperation. "It was a case of a poisoning from beyond the grave."

"And you would expect that to have been reported in the papers?" The sheer audacity of it was stunning, as was the miscalculation. "Have you ever read a copy of the Western Daily News or the Gentlewomen's Gazette?" She couldn't keep incredulity from her voice. The notion that respectable publications would print such sensationalist nonsense defied comprehension.

"It's a question of money, my dear." A cool hardness crept into Winnifred's tone now. "I don't like the ugly topic more than anyone else does, but it costs money to keep a household like this, to keep my loyal staff paid."

Felicity thought of the Egyptian artefacts, the mystical paraphernalia, the salary supporting Mr Silkstede's research. Both Elfrida and Philippa had hinted at it: priorities clearly required adjustment at Cullingslock.

"So you poisoned yourself, hoping it would develop into a story of supernatural attack." Felicity could barely force the words past her lips. The premise was so utterly ridiculous. "Was the hope that your reputation would be restored?"

Winnifred gave a little chuckle. "There's nothing the matter with my reputation, my child."

"Even after what happened in Kensington?"

Winnifred's mouth dropped open. The butler stiffened, his eyes wide and fixed on his mistress.

Felicity had touched a nerve. It wasn't satisfying to use what Sergeant Norris had told her in this way, but her great-aunt had sought to deceive her since her arrival at the castle, hadn't she? Felicity was at liberty to counter this with honesty.

"What do you know about what happened in Kensington?" Winnifred's voice was suddenly fragile.

"I know you held a performance that caused injury."

"The dowager baroness herself was injured," interjected the butler, taking the highly unusual step of breaking rank to join the discussion.

"Timpson, please. It's all right. I've no need for anyone to defend me." Winnifred shook her head, her hair catching on her pillow. "It's time for me to face the consequences of all that I've done."

"Is that what happened to Mr Kemp?" Felicity's own voice trembled now. Was this going too far? Was she putting herself at risk? Surely if she were to scream, the constables would come running. "One of your tricks gone wrong?"

Winnifred looked hurt. "No, my child. The land agent wanted nothing to do with my beliefs." Terror flickered across her features. "And trust me when I say I've paid the price for my past mistakes and changed my ways. Never again would I engage in such dangerous antics, such mechanical enhancements. The spirits prefer natural interventions, not electrical contraptions. They've made that very clear to me. But I must have upset them again. I must have triggered this whole situation somehow. I've made them angry, and they've taken it out on the household. On poor Mr Kemp."

Felicity blinked. She was struggling to understand what she was hearing. "You believe a ghost pushed the land agent out of the window?"

Winnifred's gaze sought Timpson's. The butler's carefully neutral expression cracked into confusion for just an instant.

The older woman sighed once more, her lungs whistling with the effort. "I've always had to make bold moves. I've held this whole place together. When my son came back from the trenches, I was hoping to hand things back to him, but he wasn't capable." Sadness crept into her voice. "You must have seen that he isn't capable?"

Felicity said nothing. She'd heard a great deal about Tristan's lack of ability to look after his own castle, but she'd seen little evidence of it other than his deference to his mother.

"Then when I heard you would come for the Wastes, just as they were coming into profit... You say you don't want them, but you could change your mind at any point, couldn't you? So I had to make other arrangements. I thought I could bring myself back out into the world, build back to prominence once more. Use the proceeds to look after my family and everyone here at the castle." The goal was admirable even if — given Winnifred's spending priorities — perhaps not realistic. "But I've gone too far this time. It wasn't my intention. But it's my fault, don't you see?"

The logic — if it could be called that — defied comprehension. How could one feel the need to fake a spiritual attack and then genuinely believe spirits had retaliated? Did Winnifred have faith in the supernatural or not? The contradictions made Felicity's head spin.

A tear slipped down Winnifred's cheek. "Indeed, the more I consider it all, the more regret I feel."

One thing was now clear, however. Further answers about what really happened to Mr Kemp would not emerge at Felicity's great-aunt's bedside.

"Thank you, Great-Aunt. I believe I've heard enough." Felicity kept her voice carefully neutral despite the turmoil within. She was now grateful she'd not informed the police of the attempt on her great-aunt's life, but that didn't mean she would refrain from doing so indefinitely. And she was not yet out of options for furthering her understanding.

Felicity straightened. "Might I ask for Mr Timpson's help with a task?"

Winnifred and the butler looked at one another with concern, but they couldn't exactly refuse.

"What is it you plan to do, my child?"

Chapter Twenty-Nine

Felicity's plan was elegantly simple.

The butler, Mr Timpson, would be the lure to distract the police constable on patrol. The officers were working shifts through the night to ensure none of the potential suspects escaped from the castle — and with even Felicity on his list of possible murderers, Sergeant Norris had made it clear he was casting a very wide net.

Fortune favoured them in the form of the older of the two policemen being on duty. Constable Fielding seemed more reasonable and less zealous than his younger counterpart. Based on his more flexible and even concerned attitude towards Winnifred's refusal to leave her bed, he was perhaps less committed than Constable Dinsdale to adopting Sergeant Norris's attitudes towards the household. Unlike his younger colleague, Constable Fielding also appeared to possess a developed palate and the wisdom to appreciate life's finer offerings when presented. The butler's proposal of a tipple from his pantry — where pre-war whiskies and cognacs from more prosperous generations lay carefully preserved — proved irresistible to a man whose usual evening entertainment likely consisted of weak ale at the village pub.

Despite insisting she had no direct hand in what had happened to the man, Winnifred remained racked with guilt at what had befallen Mr Kemp. Fearful of further spiritual retribution, Felicity's great-aunt had ceased further attempts to control the situation at the castle and gave her blessing to the butler's involvement in Felicity's plan. Felicity promised to do what she could to further the investigation so that everyone could be reassured — Felicity herself, above all — that the correct people would be handled by the police in the right way. It wasn't that she'd lost faith in the Devon County Constabulary, but if Sergeant Norris heard Winnifred's assertion that spirits had been involved in Mr Kemp's demise, it would be like throwing a spark into a hayloft. No one stood to benefit. Might Felicity discover something that would help steer events along a less perilous course?

Timpson had sworn to Great-Aunt Winnifred he would keep the policeman occupied as long as possible without raising suspicion. The dowager baroness had embraced Felicity's involvement with surprising enthusiasm, even leaping to the notion that her great-niece might solve the case by morning — thus sparing Winnifred the ordeal of facing Sergeant Norris at all. The idea of such a swift resolution bordered on ludicrous, yet Felicity hadn't corrected her great-aunt, just as she'd mostly bitten her tongue regarding the theory of vengeful ghosts pushing land agents through windows.

Timpson executed his role with his usual smooth professionalism. Felicity, now reunited with Alex and Pip, waited at a safe distance, pressed against a cold stone wall as the older constable's heavy tread followed Timpson's measured pace towards the butler's pantry. Once the footsteps had fully receded, Felicity and Alex hurried towards the billiard room, following the butler's precise directions. Pip vibrated with barely contained excitement under Felicity's arm. As foreboding a context as Cullingslock Castle was, and as grim as Mr Kemp's passing had been, it was still an adventure of sorts.

"Do you truly expect to solve the case by morning?" Alex's whisper carried both amusement and concern as they navigated the moonlit hallways.

"Of course not." Felicity counted the heavy oak doors along the side of the corridor upon which Timpson had said the billiard room would be found. A chill draught gusted along the worn stone flags with surprising enthusiasm. "But if Great-Aunt Winnifred tells Sergeant Norris she believes a ghost murdered Mr Kemp, it won't exactly enhance her credibility — or that of anyone associated with her."

...four, five. Felicity attempted to ease open the billiard room door, but the door pushed back stubbornly. An irrational thought swept through her mind — was it the work of ghosts? It was, of course, nothing of the sort.

"The wind through the shattered window is creating resistance," she whispered.

"Allow me." Alex lent his strength to the operation. With Felicity's skirt whipping at her calves and the flaps of Alex's jacket dancing in the wind, together they entered the room and closed the door behind them without much undue noise, other than a gentle whimper from Pip. Once inside, the little Yorkie desperately wished to be put on the ground, but Felicity kept a tight hold on him.

With the door closed, the power of the wind subsided, though a breeze still gusted through the damaged window that gaped like a monster's maw at the centre of the far wall. The light from the moon streamed in through the damaged window, casting everything in bright silver. Clouds scudded across the moon's face, plunging them periodically into velvet darkness before releasing them again to ethereal illumination, although the silvery light was never quite brilliant enough to examine the room in detail.

Click!

Alex's pocket torch — a sturdy brass model with a strong yellow beam — cut through the darkness.

Felicity flashed him a grateful smile. "Where would I be without you?"

He smirked a little. "Not safely at home tucked up in a warm bed, that's for sure." He squinted into the shadows. "What are we looking for?" Alex directed the torch beam to where Felicity indicated. Beside the door, there was a seating nook with a small sofa and two wingback chairs. Aside from a couple of old landscapes in oil hanging from the striped wallpaper, the room was uncluttered, the billiard table with its dusty cover had been untouched perhaps for many years, the cues in their wall rack equally disused. Mr Kemp hadn't come here expecting to play games.

"We're looking for understanding, primarily." She approached the window, where the air gusted inward with increasing violence. Moonlight caught on the jagged glass still clinging to the mullioned frame, shards of it still scattered on the parquet. Crime scene or not, Pip couldn't run about the room.

"If I can help the police reach the correct conclusion, I must do so."

"Do you intend to assist their investigation?" Alex clicked off the torch as they neared the hole in the wall, lest someone observe their light from a neighbouring window or the grounds below.

Felicity leaned carefully through the gap, doing her best to avoid the thigh-height points of broken glass as she peered down at the garden. A vast patch of crushed flowers still bore witness to Mr Kemp's final moments. The drop made her stomach lurch, and she stepped back, pulling Pip's head to her chest. "I'm uncertain Sergeant Norris is open to receiving my help — or any help, for that matter — but I'm certain we can think of ways around that if necessary. And if he mishandles this case, I'll have information for the Exeter detectives."

Alex's eyebrow rose in the moonlight. "Do you expect to have to call in favours?"

She met his gaze steadily. "I shan't stand for unfair treatment, no matter how uncommon a person's beliefs or what misdeeds they might previously have been involved in." Despite Winnifred's confession that she'd planned to use Felicity, she was thinking about Sergeant Norris's prejudice against her great-aunt, but he'd displayed intense bias against Felicity herself as well. Was she above calling in favours for her own sake? It would hopefully not come to that.

Returning her attention to the shattered window, she crouched to examine where she'd witnessed that mysterious hand retrieving evidence. Pip's nose quivered as he sampled the wild cocktail of scents on the night time air — jasmine from the garden, the earthiness of the moors, a pinch of salt from the Atlantic.

"In extreme circumstances," she observed, studying the window's position, "one might trip and fall through. A man of Mr Kemp's substantial build would certainly take glass and frame with him if the stumble was unrestrained."

Alex nodded, following her reasoning. "Yet there's nothing here to trip over. Not near the window. Ample space surrounds the billiard table for players to move freely."

"Precisely. And falling backwards with sufficient force to shatter not merely glass but the stone mullions themselves..." She let the implication hang. "That suggests something far more violent than accident."

"Dr Marsh found evidence of a blow to Kemp's head."

Felicity nodded, her expression darkening. "A blow delivered before the fall." She imagined a confrontation escalating — Mr Kemp struck, perhaps rendered unconscious or disoriented, then pushed.

She looked to where she'd seen a hand grasping at something caught on the broken window. "Dare we risk the torch?"

Alex leaned through the gap and scanned the surroundings. "Briefly, if you believe it worthwhile."

Felicity held out a finger. "There."

Click!

The beam illuminated their target. In the battery-powered glow, several threads of fabric danced in the wind like tiny angry ghosts, clinging to a shard of glass. In the combined torch and moonlight, their colour remained ambiguous, their material uncertain. But if they waited a moment longer, the relentless moorland wind might claim them.

She plucked the threads carefully, secreting them in her skirt pocket.

Alex's expression mixed admiration with concern. "Is it wise to interfere with evidence?"

"Would you prefer I leave it for the wind to take? I'll surrender it to the police — after I've examined it properly."

Click!

The torch died. Alex froze, raising a finger to his lips. *Quiet.*

Pip's nose worked frantically now, catching scents that made his small body tense.

Felicity's eyes widened. *What is it?*

Then she heard them. Voices, distant but growing clearer.

"...with her..." A woman's voice, tight with emotion.

"...so what..." A man's response, most of the words lost but the anger unmistakable.

They weren't alone in this seemingly abandoned wing of the castle.

Without speaking, Felicity and Alex moved as one towards the door, struggling against the wind's resistance to open it silently. Pausing to listen, they slipped into the corridor's darkness, fighting to close the door soundlessly as the wind whistled its protest.

Ting, ting, ting!

The faint sound might have been glass fragments falling or metal touching stone — it was impossible to determine in their haste to escape the billiard room's corridor.

Pip squirmed desperately, eager to investigate for himself, but Felicity held him fast as they navigated the winding hallways. Relief settled as they arrived under the great entrance hall's iron chandelier. They parted after a clasping of hands — but before they could move off, a low hiss emerged from the shadows.

Thoth or Ra — it was impossible to tell which of the two cats — materialised from beneath an oak settle, back arched and eyes glowing green fire at the sight of Pip. The terrier yapped once before Felicity could muffle him, and the cat's hiss escalated to a yowl that would surely draw attention.

"Go," Alex whispered urgently, already moving towards his wing as Felicity hurried in the opposite direction.

The evidence in her pocket seemed to pulse with possibility. She'd solved cases before. Might she solve this one? The inhabitants of

Cullingslock need not suffer the prejudice and scandal that Sergeant Norris seemed determined to inflict, and there'd be no telling what chaos would ensue once the less reputable newspapers got hold of the story. Success depended on so many factors, yet optimism lifted her spirits. It was difficult to sleep because of the excitement, but sleep she must. Daylight was needed to examine the threads.

Chapter Thirty

Morning promised a change from the previous day's sunshine, although the wind had yet to settle. Through the blotchy leaded glass of Felicity's sitting room window, treetops danced under craggy clouds tinted a foreboding shade of pewter.

With Pip still drowsing on the chintz-covered settee, Felicity drew a ladder-back chair close to the window, pulled back one of the slightly ragged lace curtains, and blinked in the pale grey light. Sleep had proved elusive, her mind churning over Great-Aunt Winnifred's shocking confession. Her breakfast tray — delivered at a characteristically erratic hour — sat untouched save for a triangle of toast with lemon curd and tea with a generous amount of milk now growing cold in its delicate, though chipped, cup. Felicity had awaited breakfast not because she'd been eager to eat, but because she couldn't risk interruption.

The threads collected from the billiard room lay across her palm. She picked them up, one by one, holding them towards the window between the pads of her forefinger and thumb. In the clear morning light, their colour revealed itself as bottle green or perhaps emerald — though it was possible the fibres might have been woven with darker or lighter strands to create a more complex shade.

The texture spoke more definitively. Tiny strands radiated from the threads, their form crimped and sometimes of uneven thickness. Felicity wasn't a vain person, but she enjoyed shopping for clothes and knew enough about the different fabrics to make her own judgements as to a garment's suitableness for her wardrobe. The threads in her palm were wool, or possibly a wool blend. Rolling the gentle coarseness between her fingers, she imagined the garment from which they'd been torn.

The image of Mr Kemp, sprawled face-up among the Canterbury bells, rose in her mind. She lacked the ability to memorise everything she saw — a deficiency she occasionally regretted — but certain details from the scene remained vivid. His typical country tweeds, his partially unbuttoned shirt, the gold chain glinting at his neck. There'd been no trace of green in his attire. Felicity was certain of that.

So whose clothing had snagged on that lethal glass? And did it happen during the action of pushing the man outside? Or in the aftermath, while leaning out to survey the results of their handiwork? Who had been in the billiard room with Mr Kemp at the time of his passing?

Who had been wearing green?

Felicity's stomach squeezed with a mix of concern and excitement. She could already think of several people she had seen wearing the colour around the castle, and her mind took off in multiple directions at once. But why speculate alone when Alex's steady pragmatism could temper her racing thoughts?

Felicity carefully folded the threads in a sheet of writing paper, creating a makeshift packet that she slipped into the pocket of her dark blue serge dress, the garment being both appropriately sombre given what had happened at the castle and practical, for who knew what sort of day lay ahead.

She found Alex pacing beneath the entrance hall's medieval chandelier like a caged leopard in a lightweight brown wool suit. The morning light streaming through the high windows caught his dark blond hair, lending him an almost golden aspect that made her heart perform a small, involuntary leap. Constable Dinsdale stood guard at the castle doors, his youthful face set in lines of exaggerated vigilance, his hands clasped behind his back.

"Ready for your constitutional, Master Pip?" Alex's enthusiasm for the terrier was more exaggerated than usual. It was likely a performance for the young constable, though he ruffled the dog's ears with genuine affection.

"It's very kind of you to agree to accompany Pip and I on our morning walk, Mr Cooper," said Felicity, playing along, "what with everything that's happened here at Cullingslock," she added with a dash of theatre as they headed together for the grand entrance doors.

"Wait!"

The policeman's command echoed through the great hall, though his voice cracked slightly.

Felicity and Alex paused mid-stride, turning with expressions of polite inquiry.

"My dog requires his morning exercise, Constable Dinsdale." Felicity allowed a hint of aristocratic frost to edge her tone as the young policeman approached them, his boots clomping across the worn stone floor. "Surely you don't wish to deny an innocent animal his necessities?"

The constable's brow was low with disapproval. "Doesn't take two people to walk such a little dog, now, does it?" His tone was too condescending to be taken seriously, the constable being perhaps younger than Felicity and not much older than Audrey and Peregrine.

"The dog is mine," Felicity replied, adjusting Pip in her arms as he squirmed. "I take full responsibility for him. However, he possesses an unfortunate tendency towards adventure. Mr Cooper kindly assists when retrieval from undergrowth becomes necessary." She glanced meaningfully at her T-strap shoes, their delicate leather and modest heels clearly more suited for tea and cake at Exeter's most well-respected hotels than for dashing about a moorland estate. "I trust you wouldn't expect a lady to wade through bracken? What if I were to disturb an ant hill?" She looked at Alex, her eyes wide with faux terror. "Or a wasp's nest?"

Alex returned a sympathetic and reassuring gaze worthy of a stage drama.

Constable Dinsdale's eyes narrowed at the pair, transforming his face into a mask of suspicion that might have been comical in less serious circumstances. His distrust — seemingly inherited wholesale from his sergeant — radiated like heat from a forge, encompassing not just Felicity and Alex but the entire household.

"Just as long as you're back for when Sergeant Norris arrives." Constable Fielding's more measured tones carried from a corridor doorway on the other side of the hall. Age and experience — perhaps lubricated by the butler's excellent whisky — had rendered him more philosophical about his duties. "The sergeant wishes to see everyone in the grand salon within the hour."

Felicity caught Alex's eye, a spark of satisfaction passing between them. It was more time than they had expected and a gift not to be squandered.

"Thank you, Constable Fielding," she said. "We shall certainly return before Sergeant Norris arrives."

After reluctantly assisting with the opening of the doors, Constable Dinsdale planted himself in the castle's entryway like a sentry, watching as Felicity and Alex crossed the gravel of the drive towards the tree line. Felicity offered the young constable a gracious smile that he pointedly ignored. Only when the grass beside the drive gave way to dappled forest light — and indicator that they were truly out of earshot from the castle — did she finally release Pip, who'd been struggling for freedom since they'd emerged into morning air redolent with the scents of damp earth and a sea breeze.

"So, is the case solved?" asked Alex as they strolled beneath the canopies of ancient oaks and beside patches of hart's-tongue fern, the glossy green fronds still holding droplets of dew.

"If you intend sarcasm, we might as well return." Felicity kept her own tone light, though she recognised his hunger for information. The reporter's instinct was one they shared.

Alex's expression shifted to mild affront. "I wasn't being sarcastic." His earnest blue eyes held such conviction that guilt pricked at Felicity. His expectations might be dangerously optimistic, but the faith behind them warmed her to her core.

She dropped any trace of remonstration from her tone as she recounted her analysis of the threads, which remained tucked in her pocket.

Alex nodded, his fingers stroking his chin in a gesture she recognised as deep thought. "So our question becomes: who wore green?"

Felicity watched Pip bound through the ferns after a cabbage white butterfly, his jumps knocking showers of dew to the ground and no doubt across his fur, which Felicity would later have to clutch to her dress. The butterfly danced, as butterflies always did, just beyond reach.

"Miss Hartley has a green scarf." The words emerged reluctantly. Even voicing suspicion felt like a betrayal of their brief acquaintance. "I saw it when we visited her room."

"Then she's our suspect?" Alex's eyebrows performed an athletic leap.

Felicity tipped her head thoughtfully. "She might have harboured anger towards Mr Kemp. He was openly dismissive of spiritualism. Perhaps my great-aunt's approval of the man wasn't sufficient protection against wounded feelings among her supporters."

"But surely he wasn't the household's only sceptic." Alex gestured towards a fallen oak that had created a natural bench, its bark soft with moss. They settled companionably, though Felicity remained aware of Constable Dinsdale's distant surveillance.

"He was the most vocal, though. The only one who refused to attend the séance." She paused, remembering his dismissive laughter. *Mumbo jumbo*, he'd said, although that had been in front of the other apprentice, not Miss Hartley.

"Is that enough to drive someone to kill?"

Felicity frowned. "What if she was in one of her trances? Like when she writes her letters?"

Alex gave his head a shake, his eyes settling on the young constable still standing in the now-distant doorway. "Trance or no trance, Miss Hartley couldn't toss Kemp out of that window. He was at least twice her size."

"Unless she caught him unaware." Felicity's voice faded as unwelcome possibilities intruded. "Or she has experience in jujutsu or something similar."

Alex turned a narrow-eyed gaze at her. "Miss Hartley wasn't alone in wearing green, was she?"

The question hung between them. Alex had noticed Felicity's rather farfetched attempts to decipher some manner in which the crime might fit petite Miss Hartley.

Felicity's fingers found the pocket containing the threads, their presence suddenly heavy. "No," she admitted. "She wasn't."

A wood pigeon's hollow call echoed through the trees.

"Who else?" Alex prompted gently.

Felicity's throat constricted. The name lodged there like a stone, unwilling to emerge. She hadn't wanted to believe it when she'd remembered the garment, and she still didn't.

Pip chose that moment to return, a specimen of bramble tangled in his coat and his pink tongue lolling with satisfaction. He butted against the skirt of Felicity's dress, leaving traces of the forest floor on the blue serge.

"Felicity?" Alex's hand found hers, warm and steadying. "Who else wore green?"

Chapter Thirty-One

With the sergeant's return to the castle looming, time was ticking before Felicity and Alex's movements would be curtailed. It was therefore a relief to return from their woodland excursion, Pip's coat still damp with dew, and find that the young constable had disappeared from his post, perhaps called away to duties elsewhere or simply grown weary of his fruitless surveillance. The footman was, however, on hand, his prominent ears seeming to prick forward with interest as he provided Felicity and Alex with their required directions.

Alex offered to tuck the damp terrier under his arm to save Felicity from getting a mark on her dress, and it was thus that the trio swiftly navigated portrait-lined corridors to arrive in a surprisingly well-kept hallway, its Persian rug fresh as though recently beaten, the handle and escutcheon on the intended door gleaming with polish.

Alex hiked the Yorkie up at his side. "Are you ready to do this?" he asked quietly, his eyebrows drawn low.

Felicity had been thoroughly honest with him about her uneasiness at the situation. "I believe doing nothing would feel infinitely worse," she said. She knocked at the door.

When Tristan answered her knock, genuine surprise flickered

across his long, angular features. Behind him, Solomon's tail created a blur of motion, the Border Collie full of joy at the sight of the visitors, particularly Pip. Mr Kemp's big Old English Sheepdog was there too, sitting behind Tristan and watching with curiosity — as far as the dog's gaze could be observed under his shaggy mane — but not panting or at all nervous. It was kind of Tristan to look after the orphaned dog, but it was nothing less than Felicity expected of her first cousin once removed, which made her feel even worse about her purpose for being at the baron's apartments.

The requisite pleasantries were exchanged. Tristan wasn't unfriendly, but he mumbled his greetings and blinked as if awoken from sleep, even though he was dressed in shirt sleeves and a waistcoat, his thin, reddish hair slicked to the side. The sitting room behind him revealed Philippa's tasteful influence — silk cushions in muted jewel tones adorned a velvet settee while watercolours of moorland scenes graced walls papered in a William Morris print. It was a haven of civilised comfort amid the blend of ruined museum and shamanic ashram that the rest of the castle had become.

"Is that the footman with the laundry?" Philippa's voice drifted from somewhere beyond the sitting room. "I wish to speak with him about the starching of your collars."

"Might I have a private word?" Felicity asked quietly of Tristan.

Philippa emerged from an adjoining room. Her morning dress of heather-grey crêpe de chine rustled as she moved. "It's simply unnecessary to use so much—" She stiffened when she saw who was at the door. "Lady Felicity, what a pleasant surprise." The words emerged clipped. "Under the circumstances, of course, but I understood we weren't to leave our rooms until the sergeant arrived."

Theoretically, such restrictions existed, but Felicity and Alex had successfully ignored them so far, and Philippa's gentle reminder wouldn't convince Felicity to change course, even if the mission in hand brought her no pleasure whatsoever.

"I should like a brief word with your husband," Felicity assured her, maintaining a gentle smile despite the weight settling in her stomach. "It shouldn't take long."

Philippa's gaze darted between her husband and their visitors. Her brow creased slightly, as though the sight of Tristan evoked in her a sense of pity. "Might I also join you?"

There seemed little point in argument, particularly with the risk of Sergeant Norris's imminent return to the castle.

"Very well." Felicity kept her tone light, though her pulse quickened. It was perhaps safest for everyone if the discussion happened with Philippa present as well and not just between Felicity, Alex, and Tristan, as Felicity had originally envisioned it might do. "There's no point in hiding matters, is there? We are family, after all."

As her words dangled with polite yet unavoidable foreboding, Felicity's smile faltered. Tristan's gaze had already dropped to the sitting room's Turkish carpet, studying its tangled roses with intensity. Philippa watched him with an expression that mingled sorrow with increasing protectiveness, like a lioness guarding a wounded cub.

Was this madness? The person who'd sent Mr Kemp through that window had maintained their silence through yesterday's police interviews. Was the wrongdoer wrestling with what they had done? Or was the intention to get away with it? Either way, if Felicity could expedite matters and spare the household a prolonged investigation, wasn't it better for everyone? Sergeant Norris had made it clear the hammer of justice would fall. It was best if it fell swiftly, cleanly, and precisely.

"Do come in," Philippa said after a pause, reaching to plump fringed cushions as they entered and took their places on the velvet settee.

"Where's your son?" Alex posed his question casually, though it further revealed that he and Felicity wished to discuss matters of import.

"Still in his room, asleep," Philippa replied, glancing towards a panelled door as she and Tristan sat on matching velvet chairs. The maternal concern in her voice twisted the knife of Felicity's unease.

She caught Alex's eye. He appeared calm, but she read the question in the slight raise of his brow. Should they proceed with

Peregrine potentially within earshot? If the lad's parents were fine with him overhearing, then what objection could she and Alex have? Not that Philippa and Tristan necessarily understood the purpose of Felicity's visit, although a somewhat urgent-seeming early morning call from a renowned lady detective directly after a suspicious death must have given some indication. Tristan certainly looked concerned, and although Philippa was doing her best to be polite, she was also clearly nervous.

Philippa attempted a hostess's smile. It trembled at the edges. "I'm afraid I can't offer refreshments. We're not in the habit of receiving guests here, as I'm sure you can imagine."

"It's quite all right." Felicity took Pip from Alex and settled the Yorkie on her lap, where she lightly restrained him, his neck craning towards Solomon and Lionheart, both of whom remained obediently seated at Tristan's side. "I hope you don't mind if I come straight to the point."

A dense grey cloud passed before the sun, casting the sitting room into sudden shadow. The air in the chamber felt thick. Tristan and Philippa were family, yes, yet virtual strangers. Still, the weight of that connection, the ties of blood and marriage, pressed upon Felicity's shoulders like a lead cape.

She wished to move the investigation along in the proper manner. Was this the best way of doing so?

"Please," Tristan's voice emerged a little desperate. "What is it you wish to say?"

It was too late to turn back now.

Felicity straightened in her seat. "As we all know, Mr Kemp met his end yesterday in... Suspicious circumstances. The police are naturally eager to identify the perpetrator. I want to be clear that they haven't asked me to involve myself. I'm not here in any official capacity."

Philippa's knuckles whitened as she gripped her hands together. This was now clearly not a social call.

Felicity glanced at Alex, but his gaze was fixed on the couple. Words were merely one method of communication. Gestures and expressions could also say volumes. And if anyone were to move boldly, Alex would be quick to react.

"When I toured the Wastes with you, Tristan, you mentioned disagreements with Mr Kemp." Felicity spoke carefully. "Conflicts over land management."

Philippa's gaze shot to her husband, her cheeks slightly flushed. Her lips parted as if to speak, but no sound came.

Tristan's fingers found each other in his lap, intertwining and releasing in a nervous dance. His hands were not the soft appendages of an idle aristocrat. These were hands that knew work. Long-fingered but strong, with calluses from reins and rough rope, they were powerful hands that could control a spirited horse — or push a man through a window.

The observation constricted Felicity's throat.

Granted, she didn't know him well, but she was already fond of Tristan and sympathetic towards Philippa. Their private hopes had already been dashed so many times, and now here Felicity was to deliver even more hurt and uncertainty. But as her faith in what she was doing wavered, Felicity continued to sit tall, her expression mild. She had reached the conclusion with Alex that this approach was the best of a series of terrible choices. Even as her own emotions whirled into a tumult, she couldn't undermine that evaluation now.

"I did disagree with him," Tristan admitted, still addressing the carpet. "Rather strongly."

His honesty came as a relief, but they weren't on safe ground. Not yet.

"Do you have an alibi for your whereabouts yesterday at the time of Mr Kemp's death?" Felicity asked Tristan.

Philippa's sharp intake of breath cut through the room. "W-what are you trying to—"

"Not unless you count Solomon as a witness." Tristan rubbed the back of his neck as he spoke over his wife.

The Border Collie's ears pricked at his name, his tail resuming its hopeful rhythm.

"Where were you?" Alex pressed gently.

"On my way to the stables when I heard that awful scream." Tristan's hand moved to his chest, fingers splaying over his heart. "I thought it was Mother."

Felicity exhaled slowly. So far, matters were going as well as could be expected. Tristan had arrived at a trot to witness Mr Kemp's body lying in the floral courtyard. The time between spotting the hand reaching out of the window and his appearance would have been tight — though not impossible — for a journey from the billiard room. But they were now coming to the nub of things.

"Forgive what might seem an odd question," she began, "but you wear a jumper with shades of green in it, don't you?" Felicity had noticed the multicoloured garment under Tristan's jacket when he'd arrived in the little flower garden.

The change in atmosphere was immediate. Tristan's head snapped up, meeting Felicity's gaze for the first time. Philippa's confusion bloomed into fear.

"I have, but what's that to do with—" Understanding dawned in Tristan's eyes. "Do you have reason to believe I'm the culprit?"

The pain in his voice made Felicity's heart tighten. She wished wholeheartedly to be able to retreat, but she couldn't. Not now. She needed to continue. She had to be sure.

She swallowed. "I went into the billiard room last night. What I retrieved indicated that someone wearing green was at the scene of the crime."

Tristan looked at his wife, but Philippa was staring with disbelief at Felicity. "But the police said..." Her voice trailed away.

"The disagreements between you and Mr Kemp were well known." Felicity continued to address Tristan while internally wincing at every word. "I believe you can understand how that might appear to be a motive."

His face crumpled, and he buried it in his hands, shoulders bowing as Solomon whined and pushed his muzzle insistently against his master's elbow. Even Lionheart stirred, padding over to rest his great head against Tristan's knee.

Philippa stared at Felicity, indignation smouldering like coals in her dark eyes. "How could you think such a thing?"

"It's not a conclusion," Felicity clarified, doing her best to remain gentle in her manner, even as doubt continued to claw at her. "This case's resolution isn't mine to determine. It rests with the police and with whoever bears responsibility for the crime. I came only to say that if — and I don't know that you did — but if you were involved, Tristan, it would be best to come forward now. Before the police's investigation takes its own route towards its inevitable conclusion."

Tristan raised his head slowly. Sunlight returned suddenly to the room and caught the moisture in his eyes, transforming him from suspect to suffering soul. "I didn't do it. Believe me when I say I was never in that room. And after what I saw in the war, the horrors I witnessed, I would never..." He blinked. A tear ran down his hollow cheek. "I couldn't. You must understand, I simply couldn't."

"We know you didn't, darling." As if suddenly regaining her senses, Philippa stood and flew to her husband's side, gripping his shoulders with fierce tenderness. "Her ladyship is merely voicing a theory. She isn't saying you did it, is she?"

Yet that was precisely what hung between them. Felicity hadn't wished it — she didn't want to cause the gentle, tormented man seated before her more anguish than he'd already suffered — but Felicity had made an accusation. The evidence she'd gathered left her no choice.

She found Alex's gaze. A subtle shake of his head confirmed her growing doubts. Something here didn't fit. Some piece of the puzzle remained stubbornly misaligned. She had come to make an appeal to the most likely murderer to turn himself in, to save the castle and the rest of the family from the discomfort and embarrassment of a drawn-out investigation. Yet the gambit had failed. Indeed, Felicity's initial misgivings about the conclusion had played out before them. Even if he strongly disagreed with much of what Mr Kemp had stood for, Tristan wasn't cold or calculating enough to have murdered the land agent and then lied to the police about it.

"We can't know with certainty what happened in that room," Alex offered carefully. "Perhaps there had been a misunderstanding. Perhaps it was some kind of accident. That's for the authorities to determine."

"But you mentioned the green jumper," Tristan said, his voice steady now despite the tremor in his hands. "You have evidence of some kind."

"I found threads," admitted Felicity, "caught on the broken glass of the window through which Mr Kemp fell. To my knowledge, they don't match any of the garments the victim was wearing at the time of his fall." It was a calculated risk to share details of the evidence she held with potential wrongdoers, as it might enable a story to be concocted to render the threads innocuous. But Felicity didn't wish to storm around Cullingslock making seemingly baseless allegations. By being honest with her relatives, she hoped to enable an outcome that would be best for all involved.

Yet in visiting Tristan and Philippa, she'd hit a painful dead end, hadn't she?

Tristan wiped at his face with the back of his hand. "Thank you for your honesty, Felicity. I know the truth will out," he said, a hint of confidence returning to his voice.

Philippa took her husband's hands in both of hers. "We shall get through this. We have already been through so much together." Would this whole grim affair present the couple with an opportunity to strengthen their troubled relationship?

Tristan nodded. He looked down at Solomon and patted the dog's head. Almost as if apologising to him.

"It's helpful that her ladyship has warned us of what's ahead, but you weren't the only one to disagree with Mr Kemp." Philippa turned, lifting her chin with defiance in Felicity and Alex's direction. "There were others whose disagreements were more... More personal in nature."

"The spiritualists?" Felicity ventured, remembering Mr Kemp's mention of mumbo jumbo and Miss Hartley's green scarf.

Philippa tucked her chin. “Not them.” Her voice was low, as if keen no one should overhear. “Have you not noticed?”

Felicity glanced at Alex. What had she missed in her brief time at Cullingslock? What currents ran beneath the surface she’d barely begun to navigate?

“Noticed what?”

Chapter Thirty-Two

Philippa's revelation hung uneasily between them as Felicity and Alex moved swiftly down the stone stairs, their footsteps echoing as they hurried. Sergeant Norris's return loomed, but there was an avenue of enquiry not yet explored.

"Philippa seemed most anxious that we not interpret her words as accusation," said Felicity as their footsteps softened but fell no less quickly along a carpeted hallway.

"Suspiciously anxious?" suggested Alex.

"Perhaps." Felicity shifted Pip in her arms as they rounded a corner where a suit of armour slumped wearily, a wreath of dried flowers dotted with runic symbols hanging across its tarnished breastplate. "Though I confess myself increasingly uncertain about just about everything. First, I believed Tristan innocent, then guilty, and now..." She trailed off, unable to articulate the gnawing doubt that had taken root during their morning interview.

"His manner didn't suggest guilt," Alex agreed, letting her precede him up a narrow spiral staircase. "Unless he's a rather talented actor."

Felicity frowned. "Or unless he's numb to ordinary feeling." During their tour of the Wastes, Tristan had recounted how his experiences in the trenches had changed him. Philippa had also highlighted her own experiences of this transformation. Had the effect of war on Tristan been so extreme he couldn't control or even remember aspects of his own behaviour?

They emerged onto a landing where the pale morning light streamed through tall windows. Gone were the trappings of an ancestral home full of mystical performances. Paintings cluttered the walls behind sculptures on pedestals of a style seen nowhere else in the castle. These artworks were thoroughly modern, the forms abstract, the angles and colours awkward and almost deliberately displeasing.

Alex touched Felicity's elbow and spoke gently. "You said what you needed to. There's no more you can do than that."

Felicity nodded as they approached the door at the end of the landing. He was right, of course, but that didn't make the lack of clarity on the situation any easier to bear. This next encounter might help explain matters, but there was the chance it might not. Just as in the build up to her confrontation with Tristan, Felicity harboured the contradictory hope that this next encounter would leave the situation still ambiguous.

Tap, tap, tap.

She knocked gently on the door.

Elfrida's stern expression melted into surprised laughter when she saw Felicity, Alex, and Pip in her doorway. "Trust you to have the police wrapped around your little finger and be allowed to circulate wherever you please."

Behind her, Elfrida's little sitting room was filled with colour and energy that positively glowed compared to the rest of the castle's greyness and faded grandeur. A bronze figure of a dancer, all sharp angles and impossible grace, stretched across a side table, while a loose, fluid sketch — just a few sweeping lines that somehow captured a woman in motion — hung slightly askew above a settee whose springs had long since surrendered to gravity. On a low lacquered table at the centre of the room, a vividly glazed vase burst with pale pink roses and magenta dahlias. A gramophone and a stack of records stood on a cabinet at the side of the room, next to a roughly chiselled bust of a woman with unrealistically large yet touchingly mournful eyes. Cigarette smoke, floral perfume, and the bergamot of Earl Grey tea mingled in the air.

"May we come in?" Felicity asked.

Elfrida gestured them inside with a theatrical flourish, her burgundy silk robe swirling about her as she moved and collapsed onto one of the worn-out settees. She didn't seem at all perturbed by the unannounced visit. She seemed to welcome it.

Alex moved to the bay window, pushed his hands into his pockets, and gazed outside. The sitting room overlooked another wing of the castle and perhaps one of the courtyard gardens. Felicity couldn't quite see, but Alex would keep her informed. One window was open, and the wind made a gusting sound, chilling the room slightly. A simple wooden table and chairs were positioned beside the open window, a jumble of scarves, cardigans, and jumpers piled on the chair backs. It reminded Felicity of what she'd seen at the girls' school she'd once worked at, where young women shared rooms together.

As Felicity rearranged the cushions on the matching sofa on the other side of the low table so that she and Pip might take a seat, Elfrida retrieved an ivory cigarette holder from beneath a cushion embroidered with a metallic blue peacock design.

"You don't mind, do you?" Elfrida didn't wait for an answer before lighting up, the match's sulphur tang briefly overwhelming the room's complex bouquet.

Felicity blinked at her hostess, smiling. There was something oddly enjoyable about Elfrida's rebelliousness. "It's your apartment. You must do as you please."

"It's mine and Audrey's, actually," Elfrida said, smoke pluming upwards from her pursed lips. "And Audrey disapproves of cigarettes. But the young woman has taken to spending rather long mornings in bed." She raised her voice pointedly on the last words, clearly intending them to penetrate the closed door of an adjoining chamber. After a pause filled only by the distant squawk of geese, she shrugged. "Dead to the world."

Felicity smiled, the coil of unease that had wound around her spine relaxing a little.

Philippa had said that Elfrida and Mr Kemp had a personal grudge. She insisted she didn't wish to accuse anyone of murder, but that if her own husband's dealings with the man were to be examined, then everyone with strong feelings regarding the victim ought to be put under the magnifying glass.

Having not found concrete answers with Tristan and Philippa, Felicity had agreed with Alex that Elfrida was worthy of a visit, even if neither of them could recall seeing her in green wool. Even if humour had always blunted the sharpness of their discussions, Elfrida and the land agent had engaged in some barbed interactions, yet Felicity already felt reassured by Elfrida's behaviour. Granted, Felicity hadn't known her first cousin once removed for very long, but she was the same as she'd ever been. To have done away with a man in such dramatic fashion, to have been questioned by the police, then the morning after, to be behaving as cool as a cucumber denoted either innocence or moral insanity.

Pip, however, was less relaxed. He wriggled with determination on Felicity's lap, his need for rest after their jaunt under the trees clearly ending.

Elfrida gestured at Pip. "You can put him down if you like. He can't do any more harm to my belongings than time and poverty haven't already accomplished."

Felicity released the terrier, watching anxiously as he began investigating the sculpture-bearing pedestals and cabinets. Some of the most modern-looking sculptures were displayed directly on the floor. The Yorkie's small form wove between a sinewy and abstract wooden figure and an assemblage of metal and wire that might have been art or something else entirely.

"Some fascinating pieces you've collected," said Felicity, a little lost for words to describe the art decorating Elfrida's apartment, her eyes lingering on the metallic monstrosity at rest on the floor.

Elfrida sighed. "That's one of my husband's. I suppose I

should've thrown them out after what he did to us, but somehow I'm rather fond of them."

Felicity tipped her head. She couldn't imagine the muddle of emotions her husband's abandonment had caused when he ran off to fight for the Germans. "This one is quite beautiful," she said of the shapely bronze on the sideboard.

Elfrida smiled warmly. "Oh, that's one of mine."

Felicity's brow raised. "One of yours?"

Elfrida drew on her cigarette. "I used to sculpt. That's how Otto and I met. Gave it up when our little one came along. Mistakenly believed abandoning my dreams to be romantic. Somehow never went back to it. Goodness knows I've made some regrettable decisions in my life."

Felicity re-looked at the room's art with fresh eyes. "You were an artist?" Her next question might have been, *Why not go back to it?* had Alex not been there to bring the discussion back to their reason for being there.

"Interesting view you have here," Alex observed from his post by the window, a splash of sunlight catching the gold in his hair and throwing his elegant profile into sharp relief.

Curiosity overcoming caution, Felicity joined him. The window overlooked the ornamental garden where Mr Kemp had met his end, the shattered window above the courtyard still gaping like a wound in the castle's flank.

"Goodness." The word escaped Felicity's lips as barely more than breath. "Did you witness what happened?"

Elfrida drew deeply on her cigarette, one eye closing as the ember glowed. "I heard it, then looked out and saw him lying there. Like a broken doll someone had tossed away." She tapped ash into a brass bowl and gave her head a little shake. "Rather dramatic end for such a prosaic man."

Felicity returned to the settee, mildly unsettled by Elfrida's casual callousness even as she recognised it as protective armour. Pip, having completed his initial reconnaissance, bounded up beside Felicity and burrowed into the cushions with a contented huff.

"And before you ask," Elfrida continued, smoke veiling her expression, "I lack what you'd call an alibi. Unless one counts Virginia Woolf—" She threw a sidelong glance to a book pancaked open on a side table. "—though I doubt she'd testify on my behalf."

Alex moved quietly from the window to stand beside Felicity's settee. She glanced up at Alex. He didn't seem at all amused by Elfrida. Was Felicity being too easy on her?

"As we're all quite painfully aware, Mr Kemp is no longer with us," said Felicity carefully, "and the police suspect murder."

"How terribly observant of them." Elfrida's tone hardened.

"Do you have any knowledge about what happened to the man?" asked Felicity.

Elfrida's movements remained tight as she continued to smoke. Her lips bore no trace of a smile. "You must have noticed yourself that he was not well liked."

"Disliked enough to be done away with?"

Elfrida watched Felicity through the smoke. "Apparently."

"Who disliked him the most, would you say?"

"Are you on the case?"

"Not officially," Felicity admitted.

Elfrida watched her carefully. "Did someone ask you to get involved, or is this your own endeavour?"

"No one asked me to investigate. I simply wish to help."

"Is that why you've come to my rooms this morning? To help?"

Alex put a hand on the back of the settee as Felicity inhaled slowly, steadying herself. "That is my aim, yes." But was she succeeding? She'd upset Tristan and now seemed to be irritating Elfrida.

Elfrida looked thoughtful for a moment. "My brother thoroughly disagreed with the man's land management methods. But you would have to be completely oblivious not to realise that."

Felicity quirked an eyebrow. "And what were your thoughts on the matter?"

Elfrida shrugged. "Not my business." She narrowed her eyes. "Didn't we already discuss this?"

"That was before the man passed away." Felicity paused. "Since then, I've heard you harbour some strong opinions."

Elfrida reacted sharply, leaning forward. "Where did you hear that?"

Felicity glanced at Alex. Divulging sources was something they didn't do as journalists.

"Wait." Elfrida closed her eyes and held up a hand. "Was it my brother's wife who made the accusation?"

Felicity swallowed. It seemed she had stepped into a briar patch. "I'd rather not say."

Elfrida let out a laugh. She sounded genuinely amused, albeit with an undertone of sadness and disappointment, the same subtle undercurrent that ran beneath most of her utterances.

"You don't have to say. I know exactly what's going on." She continued to chuckle as she stood up. "That woman." She went to the window, closed it, and began rummaging through the clothing piled on the back of one of the wooden chairs. "How delightful that she should suddenly develop an interest in my opinions. She's usually far too busy managing her husband and son to notice what anyone else thinks."

Alex gave Felicity's shoulder a subtle tap. He pointed, directing her attention to the floor beneath the chair from which Elfrida had retrieved a long purple shawl that she was now in the process of draping around her shoulders. Lying on the carpet, perhaps fallen during Elfrida's enthusiastic rummaging, was a woollen cardigan in bottle green.

Their eyes met, understanding passing between them like a bolt of lightning. Felicity hadn't remembered Elfrida wearing the cardigan, but that didn't mean she hadn't put it on to meet the land agent. What had passed between them that had led to his fall? What had Philippa alluded to that Elfrida was now so smoothly and convincingly holding back?

Elfrida flopped back onto her seat, pulling the shawl across herself and retrieving her still-glowing cigarette from the brass bowl. "It was bound to end up like this. Accusations flying like shrapnel, everyone scrambling to save themselves." Smoke curled from her lips as her head tipped languidly backwards. "I didn't do it. I don't care if you believe me. And as for the police — they have a disliking for pretty much all of us here. I'm quite certain they view everyone as a suspect. Even you. I'm sure it would be a different story if we all led normal lives, kept the place properly clean, and spent money on doing it up." Elfrida's facade cracked. She sank back onto the settee, her cigarette held away as she pressed the end of her shawl to her eyes. Her shoulders shook as she sobbed.

"Elfrida." Felicity's instinct was to go to her and put an arm around her — to comfort a murderer now feeling regret?

The door to the adjoining chamber flew open. Audrey emerged, the smile brightening her broad face faltering when she registered the room's occupants.

"Good morning, beautiful," Elfrida managed, straightening with visible effort and returning her daughter's smile.

"Morning, Mother." Audrey's natural cheer reasserted itself, though uncertainty flickered in her eyes. She wore a simple navy dress, the tight shoulders of which emphasised her sturdy build. Her reddish hair was woven into a thick plait that swung between her shoulder blades.

"Good morning, Lady Felicity. Mr Cooper. Oh, and there's Master Pip." Audrey crossed to the Yorkie, kneeling to wake him with gentle caresses between his ears. The terrier responded by attempting to wash her face with enthusiastic kisses.

"I'm sorry I can't dawdle," she told him regretfully, rising to approach the sideboard where breakfast remnants waited. "I've got mountains of work in the gardens."

Elfrida's carefully reconstructed composure threatened to crumble again. While Audrey's back was turned, she dabbed at her eyes. What was it that had upset her so? Regret at what had happened to Mr Kemp? Self-pity at her own situation? If Elfrida's daughter hadn't been present, Felicity would gently have probed.

"Audrey, darling, you can't simply wander about the place. The police insisted we remain in our quarters."

Audrey turned, hastily swallowing a mouthful of buttered toast. "But I must water the seedlings, and the tomatoes need pinching out, and Grandmama specifically asked me to—"

Elfrida waved a hand. "I shan't fight you, darling. You know best." She sounded utterly drained, but Felicity couldn't leave matters as they were. If Elfrida — for whatever currently obscure motive — had a hand in Mr Kemp's demise, Felicity had a duty to repeat to Elfrida what she'd said to her brother about the need to bring the investigation to a prompt end, even if it pushed the woman to the brink of what she could bear.

"Thank you, Mother." Audrey's smile bloomed again. The sight of it made Felicity smile, too, but it also made her sad. The girl was fatherless and had experienced homelessness. Was she about to lose her mother as well?

She crossed to the table and chairs with the piles of clothes. "Mother, where's my cardigan?"

A chill touched Felicity's shoulders.

"Which one, darling?"

"The green one."

Felicity looked up at Alex as ice flooded her veins. His dark blue gaze brimmed with alarm.

"*Your* cardigan?" Elfrida squinted over at the chair. "There it is, darling. On the floor. I must have knocked it off when I fetched my shawl. My apologies."

"It doesn't matter." Audrey retrieved the garment, shook it, and tugged it on. "I'm only going to work in the garden." The sleeve, Felicity noted with sinking certainty, showed signs of mending, the darning done with thread in a slightly darker green.

"Audrey, darling," Elfrida called, but her daughter had already slipped out of the room, her footsteps light in the corridor despite her solid build.

Alex and Felicity exchanged stricken glances. The implications crashed over them like a cold and drenching wave. That strong, gentle girl who communed with plants and animals, who cradled Pip with such tenderness. It simply couldn't be.

Chapter Thirty-Three

Glances snatched through corridor windows revealed gathering clouds, their tin-coloured bellies threatening rain as Felicity and Alex hurried after Audrey, Pip clutched at Felicity's side. The rounding off of their encounter with Elfrida had been hurried and somewhat awkward, but they'd left no trace of their suspicions about Audrey with her mother. The notion of the big, gentle girl as Mr Kemp's murderer remained unfathomable.

"I must have another look at that cardigan," Felicity murmured to Alex as dusty portraits and fading photographs of Cullingslock ancestors gazed down from hallway walls. "It's possible it's not wool. Cardigans can be knitted from all sorts of yarn these days," she added, though her own words were unconvincing. The bottle green cardigan with the mend on its sleeve — precisely where a wrist might have caught on a broken window — certainly looked to be woollen.

"Are you quite sure about your analysis of the threads?" asked Alex as they continued towards the vegetable garden. "Not that I doubt your judgement, but we haven't access to a magnifying glass."

"I could indeed be mistaken," said Felicity hopefully, the image of Audrey in that green cardigan haunting her thoughts. The girl possessed both the physical strength and stature to throw a man of Mr Kemp's size off balance, certainly more convincingly than her mother did, and perhaps even more than her Uncle Tristan. She was assuredly more physically capable than Miss Hartley. Yet everything in Felicity's experience rebelled against the conclusion.

It couldn't have been Audrey. Could it?

Yet what had drawn Mr Kemp to that dusty billiard room?

The question gnawed at Felicity with increasing urgency. If he'd arranged a clandestine meeting, what purpose had it served? What crucial element had she overlooked in her investigations? And how might she coax whatever secrets Audrey might hold out of the girl?

Arriving in the little courtyard garden where Audrey claimed urgent business awaited, the girl was nowhere to be found. Darkened clouds rolled overhead as the wind shook dried bean pods and the long papery leaves of sweetcorn as the sharp scent of onions lifted into the air.

Felicity's shoulders sank with a mixture of disappointment and relief. The castle being the maze that it was, there would be no time to both locate Audrey — wherever she had disappeared to — and conduct a delicate conversation about murder with the girl ahead of Sergeant Norris arriving.

"Well, I suppose that's it," said Alex, standing with his hands on his hips as he surveyed the garden. "It's for the police to deal with now, yet I still can't conceive of it."

Felicity released Pip, who went bounding between the neat rows of plants. "Our inability to imagine something doesn't render it impossible." She glanced up at the gathering clouds. A low, leaden pressure settled on her. She had failed to identify a convincing murderer among the castle's inhabitants. What had she missed? "I suppose in fairness we ought also to have spoken to—"

"Your ladyship? Mr Cooper?"

The voice startled them both. From the garden's shadowy entrance, Miss Hartley stepped out onto the gravel path, her leather satchel clutched beneath her arm. In the gathering gloom of the approaching rain, she appeared smaller than ever, her brown hair escaping from its pins to frame features marked by exhaustion and something else — fear? Desperation? Her rose-printed day dress might have appeared cheerful, but the fabric was creased as though she'd slept in it — or hadn't slept at all.

Felicity and Alex exchanged glances of mild alarm, their shared disbelief in clairvoyance a little shaken. Miss Hartley was precisely who Felicity was about to say they should speak to, though the spirits hadn't guided her to appear wearing her green scarf.

"Miss Hartley," said Felicity, regaining her composure. "What a surprise to see you here."

The stone arch of the doorway framing Miss Hartley emphasised her small stature. Besides frequently bed-ridden Winnifred and the elderly cook, Miss Hartley was perhaps the least physically capable among the castle's inhabitants of tossing a grown man out of a window. But just because it couldn't be imagined, didn't make it impossible. And out of Miss Hartley and Audrey, it was surely the older and less naïve of the two who was more likely to have developed the bitter resentment and cold resolve necessary to take the actions that led to the man's demise.

Pip lifted his nose to sniff the air as Miss Hartley advanced slowly towards Felicity, her fingers unbuckling the satchel. "I wondered if you'd had the opportunity to reconsider the letters I showed you?" Hope coloured her voice despite the dark circles beneath her eyes. "I know you expressed reservations, but surely a publication of your family's standing might appreciate their unique value?"

Felicity's heart sank. She'd believed herself quite clear regarding the impossibility of publication, yet Miss Hartley felt driven — by desperation or by delusion — to make a final appeal.

"Miss Hartley," Felicity began, her tone kind but firm, for there was nothing to be gained from engendering false hope. "I believed we reached an understanding on this matter."

"Publication remains quite impossible, I'm afraid," Alex added, his tone even gentler than Felicity's. He clearly recognised the distress beneath the woman's persistence, but was it only her need to make a sale that had driven the apprentice to seek Felicity and Alex?

"I received another letter." Miss Hartley fumbled for her leather satchel, almost dropping it, her movements clumsy with uneasiness.

"Just this morning, as I sat in meditation. The spirits were most insistent that I share it with someone who might understand its significance."

Felicity gave Miss Hartley a tight smile. Time pressed — the sergeant would arrive soon enough to draw his own conclusions — but the threads Felicity had found potentially linked the petite apprentice to the crime. Might engaging with her further provide fresh insight?

"Very well," Felicity conceded with a glance in Alex's direction to check he had no objection. "We shall take a look."

Miss Hartley's relief transformed her features, and she withdrew a sheet of paper with reverent care, her hands trembling.

The now-familiar angular script sprawled across the page, though this letter's formation appeared more hurried and less carefully crafted than its predecessors. The addressee made Felicity's breath catch: *Lady Winnifred Cullingslock*. The signature at the letter's end sent ice through her veins: *Mr Harold Kemp*. The date — today's date — seemed to mock the very notion of rationality.

Felicity's gaze met Alex's over the paper's edge. His expression mirrored her own scepticism and unease.

"Are you quite serious about this, Miss Hartley?" Felicity kept her voice level, despite the impassioned response building in her chest. Was this a desperate attempt to manipulate a murder investigation? Or was any sense of reality slipping from Miss Hartley's grasp?

The petite woman blinked in genuine confusion. "Whatever do you mean, your ladyship?"

"A man lies dead," Alex stated with quiet force. "The police are conducting a murder investigation."

"How do you imagine this will be perceived?" Felicity's tone was softer than Alex's.

Understanding dawned slowly across Miss Hartley's features, followed swiftly by panic. "Oh, but I wouldn't dream of showing it to them. I know how violently non-believers can react to evidence from the spirit realm. I only thought you might..." She trailed off. "I'm so sorry. I've made a mistake." She went to take the paper back.

"There's indeed no need to show it to the police," said Felicity reassuringly, her curiosity piqued against her better judgement. "May I read it?"

Miss Hartley bit her lip. She nodded. Felicity and Alex studied the paper.

> To Lady Winnifred Cullingslock, Dowager Baroness of Cullingslock Castle,
>
> Time grows short in this place of judgement. The weight of my wrongdoing presses upon me like rocks too heavy to bear. I must unburden myself. My behaviour in your household was dishonourable, yet my arrogance prevented me from seeing my mistakes.

The prose continued in this vein, with Mr Kemp's supposed spirit confessing to various vague misdeeds at the castle related to overstepping boundaries and a lack of respect. The text concluded, however, with an extraordinary claim:

> You were right all along. The afterlife is real, and it's not pleasant for wrongdoers like me. Though I fell out of that window by myself, I realise it's caused tremendous trouble for you and your people, and I want to apologise for my clumsy accident in the billiard room.

Felicity exchanged a look with Alex. She lowered the paper. "What do you hope to achieve by showing us this, Miss Hartley?"

Miss Hartley blinked. "You're a detective, are you not, your ladyship? I thought you might be able to make use of such evidence."

"Evidence?" Felicity's chest tightened. "Were you in the billiard room with Mr Kemp? Did you witness what happened to him?"

Alex's posture tensed. He was ready to take action if Felicity's questions prompted an adverse response.

"What?" Miss Hartley grew pale. "Of course not. I would... I would never."

"Then how do you know what happened to him?" asked Alex.

With shaking hands, the apprentice slid the letter slowly from Felicity's grasp. "I am merely a vessel for communications beyond our understanding. If the spirits choose to reveal uncomfortable truths—"

"But do you know what happened to him, Miss Hartley?" pressed Felicity. "You personally. Not the spirits."

Tears gathered in Miss Hartley's eyes as she clutched her satchel close. "The Reverend One's reputation is already damaged, and this whole mess won't help. We will all be marked by it. And what do you think will happen to me if I'm forced to leave here?" A tear slid down her cheek. "Not that I suppose either of you cares."

Felicity's compassion stirred. Miss Hartley's worries were the same as her own — that the deadly incident involving the land agent would further isolate Cullingslock's inhabitants from the world. If Miss Hartley was innocent of murder, she was simply a woman who'd lost her brother to war, found solace in spiritualism, and now faced an uncertain future with only her supposed gift as currency. And just like Miss Hartley was now attempting — albeit in a most unorthodox manner — Felicity, too, had swung into action to try to find a neater, less painful solution to the situation.

"Miss Hartley." Felicity placed a steadying hand on the woman's trembling arm. "We're all struggling to make sense of yesterday's tragedy. But truth must prevail, however painful. The police will uncover what happened—" And they would be aided by the threads in Felicity's pocket, but there was no need to highlight that to Miss Hartley. She wasn't Mr Kemp's murderer. "—and justice will follow."

Miss Hartley pulled away from Felicity's touch with surprising force. "Justice?" Her gaze hardened. "There's no justice for people like us. Only survival, by whatever means necessary." She backed away, wiping her eyes with her sleeve, her satchel held before her like a shield. "I'll manage alone. I always have." As she turned to flee through the doorway, she stopped and stepped backward.

Constable Dinsdale emerged from the shadows of the corridor, his youthful face set with stern authority, the brass buttons of his uniform gleaming as his boots crunched onto the garden's gravel.

The first drops of rain landed, splatting onto cabbage leaves and the dry earth mounded along the potato rows. Pip lifted his nose skywards.

Had the young policeman overheard their exchange? Felicity's mind raced through the implications as Miss Hartley shrank back from the constable's presence. It was too late to retract anything now.

"Sergeant Norris has arrived," the constable announced, his tone commanding but his voice cracking slightly. "All household members are required to gather immediately." His gaze swept impatiently over the small group. It was possible the trio in the garden wasn't the first gathering he'd had to fetch from unauthorised locations despite the apparent requirement for everyone to remain in their assigned quarters.

Miss Hartley's desperate eyes met Felicity's one final time, a plea for salvation that Felicity couldn't answer. Whatever fantasies the woman had woven about messages from the dead, they paled beside the solid reality of police authority and impending judgement.

"Excellent," Felicity said, forcing brightness into her tone as she scooped Pip into her arms. "I should like very much to speak with the sergeant on an urgent basis."

Miss Hartley widened her eyes at Felicity.

The constable's stern expression flickered with curiosity before reasserting itself. "Is that so, your ladyship?"

Thunder rumbled in the distance as Felicity surged towards the corridor doorway, her determined progress — Alex close behind her — causing the policeman to step aside. "Indeed, it is, Constable. I wish to be the first to speak with Sergeant Norris before any conclusions are drawn."

Felicity hadn't solved the case as she had secretly and rather too optimistically hoped, but she hadn't emerged empty-handed from her investigations. The green threads that still sat wrapped in paper in her pocket might prove decisive. What Felicity had set in motion, the police would see through to its end — whatever the outcome.

Chapter Thirty-Four

Felicity, Alex, and Miss Hartley followed the young constable to the great entrance hall as the rumble of thunder continued its approach. Rain tapped against the tall windows beneath which the cook and footman had already assembled, their expressions pinched. Even the solicitor appeared nervous — or perhaps merely discomfited by the absence of his customary glass. Miss Hartley went to stand beside Mr Silkstede, whose complexion had taken on a greyish tint, as though the previous day's injury and shock continued to weigh heavily upon him. Elfrida stood with arms folded, while Audrey hovered uncertainly at her mother's elbow, still wearing the bottle-green cardigan over her simple navy dress.

Hugging Pip to her chest, Felicity exchanged glances with Alex. Even if this was no occasion for a private discussion, it was clear they both harboured doubts about practically everything. Felicity had certainly been misled more than once since her arrival at Cullingslock, even discounting her great-aunt's deception. It was, however, clear what must happen next.

She raised her voice slightly, addressing the young constable. "Is the sergeant in the interview room?" She gestured towards the chamber where Sergeant Norris had subjected her to his peculiar brand of interrogation and where the older constable had later conducted his more civilised interviews.

Constable Fielding materialised from the grand salon's direction, his drooping features giving him the air of a gentle yet mournful walrus. "Looking for Sergeant Norris, are you, your ladyship?"

"Indeed. I wish to speak to him as a matter of urgency."

A murmur of surprise fluttered around the gathering in the great hall. Miss Hartley cocked her head and blinked hopefully, perhaps imagining her letter had prompted Felicity to take action. Elfrida narrowed her eyes at Felicity, her expression a blend of curiosity and wariness. Audrey looked to her mother, her freckled forehead puckered with confusion.

"You'll need to wait your turn, I'm afraid, your ladyship. The sergeant's engaged at present."

"May I ask who he's speaking to?" Felicity's pulse fluttered. Was she too late?

The older constable's expression remained professionally neutral, though something flickered behind his eyes — sympathy, perhaps, or simple resignation to his superior's methods. "I don't think it would be appropriate for me to say, your ladyship."

"Is he conducting an interview or has the investigation already moved onto another phase?" asked Alex, raising his voice as a volley of hailstones clattered against the windows, thunder now rolling directly above the castle.

Another round of muttering passed through the great hall. Pip whimpered.

"Heaven help us," whispered the cook, looking up to where the pellets of ice threatened to smash through the ancient window panes.

"I'm afraid I can't share that information." The constable's jaw tensed almost imperceptibly. "I'm certain all will be revealed in due course."

"Felicity, my child!"

Winnifred's voice cascaded down the staircase, rising above a theatrically timed clap of thunder. She descended with surprising vigour for one supposedly prostrated by shock and old vulnerabilities, the butler supporting one elbow while Mrs Imrie flanked her other side. Her cats accompanied her like a pair of minor royals attending their queen, but the felines paused mid-descent at the sight of Pip tucked beneath Felicity's arm, their amber eyes narrowing and smoke-coloured tails flicking.

"That you remain here means everything." Winnifred's voice swelled with operatic emotion. "Your presence, supporting the family through our darkest hour — such loyalty, such devotion!"

The servants and spiritualists gathered on the stone flags of the entrance hall looked up admiringly at Winnifred, hope shining in their eyes.

"Our Reverend One is restored," whispered Miss Hartley. Mr Silkstede nodded in agreement.

Elfrida was the only member of the group to regard her mother with an expression that mingled exhaustion with incredulity, her arms still firmly crossed over her chest as the hail and thunder continued their barrage.

"Are you feeling better, Grandmama?" Audrey's voice lifted with genuine pleasure at seeing her grandmother mobile.

"I am stronger, my darling." Winnifred's gaze swept over the assembly. "We shall weather this storm together. And with Felicity's help."

Both constables turned towards Felicity. Constable Fielding seemed confused, while Constable Dinsdale wore an expression of intense scepticism.

Heat rose in Felicity's cheeks. In telling Winnifred she'd do what she could to help ensure a swift and smooth rounding off to the investigation into Mr Kemp's demise, she hadn't expected it to be announced in such grand terms to the household. Indeed, as long as the threads sat in her pocket and she hadn't been given the opportunity to share her observations with the police, she'd contributed nothing of any practical value to the official investigation. Yet every eye was fixed upon her like an audience awaiting a conjurer's grand finale.

Elfrida lifted a cynically amused eyebrow.

"There appears to be some misunderstanding," Felicity managed, her voice steady despite the scrutiny. She wouldn't allow any form of misunderstanding to pervade for too long this time. "Not that I don't wish for a peaceful resolution to matters here at the castle," she added hastily, seeing hurt flicker across Winnifred's features.

Elfrida's head tilted. "I believe you've been here long enough to know that peace and harmony would be a long way off even if Mr Kemp hadn't met his untimely end."

The interview room door swung open, and Sergeant Norris strode forward. His thick, dark moustache twitched with obvious satisfaction.

"Sergeant Norris." Felicity stepped forward, hope brightening her voice. Was there still time to make a difference?

The sergeant raised a hand that stopped her in her tracks. "In a moment, your ladyship." The irritation in his tone suggested her intrusion had disrupted some carefully orchestrated performance. "Constable Fielding." He beckoned with a finger, and the older policeman approached.

"Your handcuffs," the sergeant commanded, pointing to the constable's belt.

Felicity's heart flew like a caged bird against her ribs. She looked at Alex, but his eyes were fixed on the policemen, his brow drawn low with concern.

The older constable's movements remained unhurried as he unclipped the restraints, though Constable Dinsdale's eager expression faltered, replaced by something between unease and envy at being excluded from whatever drama was unfolding.

"Is there to be an arrest?" said Felicity, swallowing down the lump of fear that had lodged in her throat.

Philippa was first after the sergeant to emerge from the interview room, a lace-edged handkerchief pressed to her eyes. Peregrine followed, his youthful features drained of colour, his usually upright posture slightly bowed.

Finally, Tristan appeared in the doorway, Solomon and Lionheart flanking him like mismatched guards. The Border Collie's intelligent eyes darted between the assembled faces, his muzzle prodding at his master's hand, while the Old English Sheepdog pressed close to his temporary master's leg. Tristan's gaze found Peregrine's, but his son looked towards his mother. Philippa's handkerchief stilled against her cheek as she stared at Elfrida, some silent communication passing between the women before both looked away, Elfrida still hugging herself.

"Constable, if you please." Sergeant Norris's voice boomed above a crescendo of hail and thunder, the wind whistling under the big entrance doors.

The older policeman had been hesitating, whether from uncertainty about the sergeant's target or from simple reluctance to participate in what was unfolding. The sergeant solved the dilemma by seizing the handcuffs himself.

"Mother, what's happening?" Audrey's voice climbed towards panic.

"Sergeant Norris," Winnifred descended the remaining stairs with remarkable speed, Mrs Imrie struggling to maintain pace while the butler did his best to remain close at his mistress's side. "What exactly do you think you're doing? I will have no one in my household—"

"It's not your household, though, is it?" The sergeant's words cut through her protests with surgical precision as he strode past Philippa and Peregrine and stopped before Tristan. "This is the lord of the manor. And he also happens to have confessed to being Mr Harry Kemp's killer."

Felicity's stomach plummeted.

No. It can't be.

This couldn't be how her visit to Cullingslock would end.

Alex took her hand and held it tight.

"What?" Winnifred's voice cracked like a whip. She stumbled on the final steps, saved from falling only by Timpson's steady presence. "Mr Pope?" Her panicked stare shot to the solicitor. "Will you not do something?"

"I—" began the solicitor, his hands trembling as he held up his palms. “I’m not sure what I can do, your ladyship.” His voice wavered. He was thoroughly out of his depth.

Elfrida’s carefully maintained cynicism shattered. “Is this some kind of awful joke?” She searched the policemen’s expressions, alarm clear in her gaze.

“Had a little falling out about some land, apparently,” added Sergeant Norris.

Felicity had considered Tristan innocent, then guilty, then innocent again — ultimately she hadn’t believed him capable. She remembered Tristan’s gentle hands with the animals, his passionate defence of the land. How had she been so wrong? Yet her presence at Cullingslock must have had an influence. All that talk about the Wastes and the treatment of the land, the disagreements between Tristan and Mr Kemp brought into painful focus.

“No!”

Winnifred’s cry was accompanied by a boom of thunder so loud it shook the castle to its foundations as the sergeant fastened the manacles around her son’s wrists. The metal snapped with horrible finality. Tristan lifted his gaze towards his mother but couldn’t maintain the connection, his attention dropping to his shackled hands.

“My boy, my boy!” Winnifred broke free from her supporters, crossing the hall with desperate energy to clutch at her son. “Tell me it’s not true. You can’t have done this. You didn’t do this.”

Elfrida approached with uncharacteristic gentleness. “Mother, it’s all right.” She took Winnifred’s elbow. “It’ll be all right. What’s done is done.” She glanced at her brother, something unreadable flickering across her features. Resignation? Understanding?

“Mother, what’s going on?” Audrey’s voice was becoming shrill with fear.

Felicity went to her and put her arm around the girl’s shoulders. “It’ll be all right,” she said gently, echoing Elfrida’s words, but would it? How could it be?

Audrey glanced at Felicity, but her attention quickly returned to her mother, as though only Elfrida’s words could soothe her. The cook sobbed. The butler attempted a professional mask, but the shock of the revelation had turned him pale. The footman pressed himself against the wall as if he wished to be absorbed into the stone. Mr Silkstede, Miss Hartley, and Mrs Imrie watched in disbelief, although none of them seemed particularly stunned or upset. This was a family issue, one from which they were keen to keep their distance.

A sickening smile spread beneath the sergeant's moustache. "Do you still wish to speak with me, your ladyship?"

Felicity shook her head mutely, her arm still around Audrey's broad shoulders, Alex standing solemnly at her side, her prepared observations about green threads suddenly meaningless. What more could anyone say?

"See how we solved it? Just us lowly local policemen, plugging away." Sergeant Norris's chest puffed with pride. "We don't need help from the likes of you."

Felicity frowned deeply but didn't respond. It was over.

The hail gave way to a drenching rain that splashed like a waterfall against the windows, the thunder rolling into the distance.

"Take him to the van, Fielding."

The older constable placed a hand on Tristan's elbow with surprising gentleness. "Come along, your lordship."

Tristan kept his eyes fixed on the floor ahead, unable to meet his wife's stricken gaze or his son's bewildered stare. Peregrine's hand rose to wipe away a tear in a gesture that was more boy than soldier. Solomon whined and moved to follow his master, tail low and ears flattened.

"Back!" Constable Dinsdale interposed himself between the dog and the prisoner, attempting to push the Collie away with clumsy authority. Lionheart remained beside the spot where Tristan had stood. The Old English Sheepdog had resumed his anxious panting.

Solomon's whine escalated to a warning growl, his loyalty to his master transforming him from gentle companion to potential threat.

"Solomon," Felicity called softly, her voice cutting through the mounting tension and raising above the sound of the rain against the windows. "Good boy." She knelt despite the impropriety of the gesture, setting Pip carefully on the flagstones. The Yorkie trotted directly to the distressed Collie and administered a gentle lick to his muzzle. Solomon's growl subsided into a confused whine as he sank to his haunches, still watching his master's retreating form.

Audrey crouched and petted Pip and Solomon. "Good dogs," she said gently, the innocuous mend at the cuff of her green cardigan connecting with the Collie's tufted ears as she stroked him, eager to lose herself in the company of animals. Was Audrey's innocence a consolation? Of sorts, though it certainly didn't feel like any sort of relief.

The older constable opened the castle's entrance doors. The hiss of the rain and cool damp air filled the great hall.

Tristan paused at the threshold, turning with visible effort. His gaze found Felicity. "I'm sorry," he said, the words rasping in his throat. Then to his mother, whose tears carved her powdered face with loss. "I'm sorry, Mama." He looked back at Felicity. "I lied to you. I lied to everyone."

"Come along now, your lordship," Constable Fielding urged respectfully.

I'm sorry. I lied to you. I lied to everyone.

The words hit Felicity like a bucket of icy water. She released a breath she hadn't realised she'd been holding. Her investigations had perhaps made a difference — not through the evidence she'd gathered, but from the pressure she'd applied.

Winnifred's keening filled the hall as she pulled against Elfrida and Timpson's restraining hands. The sight of the dowager baroness reduced to raw maternal anguish made Felicity's chest constrict. Whatever Winnifred's faults, whatever manipulations she'd attempted, this pain was genuine.

Alex's hand found Felicity's shoulder. He pulled her gently towards him, the warmth of his firm presence a comfort and an anchor. "You did what you could," he murmured.

Felicity nodded. But had she done too much? The day after she'd arrived, she'd been worried about making a scene over luncheon.

How naïve that concern seemed now, the family lying in ruins at her feet.

"The blame isn't with you," continued Alex, as though reading her thoughts.

A lump rose in Felicity's throat. This was catastrophically distant from the reconciliation she'd envisioned. Her brother had been right. She should never have come to Cullingslock Castle.

Chapter Thirty-Five

The police having left, the castle fell into an eerie stillness, everyone withdrawing to their own corners of the vast edifice. After all that had passed, there was no chance of matters returning to normal, yet it was clearly the end of something. And it was certainly time for Felicity, Alex, and Pip to leave. Might they ever come back? The matter of the land could be resolved via solicitors, as had always been the case, but what hope did Felicity have of reuniting the estranged elements of her family if the bonds between the Cullingslocks themselves had been shattered?

Felicity and Alex met under the grand iron chandelier of the great entrance hall, rain still pattering on the windows, and waited as the footman made a trip to bring Felicity's luggage down from her rooms, Alex having carried his own. There was no one to say goodbye to them, but it didn't feel appropriate to make social calls. Hadn't Felicity meddled quite enough in the household's affairs?

So as not to seem entirely uncouth, she'd left a message with the butler for her great-aunt, who was feeling deeply unwell and could not be disturbed. She'd also written a note for Elfrida, although from the looks Elfrida had given her during Tristan's arrest, their relationship seemed to have soured.

Felicity hugged Pip to her chest and stroked his warm little head.

"I can't help wondering what might have happened had I not come here at all." She spoke quietly, remembering how tensions between Tristan and Mr Kemp had simmered then practically erupted during their tour of the Cullingslock Wastes.

Alex wrapped a hand around Felicity's upper arm, his clasp gentle but firm. "You mustn't blame yourself." His dark blue gaze bored into her with utmost seriousness. "Whatever passed between those two men in that room had roots far deeper than the few days we've spent here. Their conflict would likely have come to a head, regardless."

Felicity stared at him, blinking. Part of her knew he spoke the truth. But part of her couldn't accept any of it. In the pit of her belly, something felt wrong. Entirely wrong.

The footman's tread echoed on the main staircase as he returned with the last of Felicity's bags. As she and Alex separated from one another, Alex ready to assist the footman with the luggage, she turned to her fiancé with sudden resolution.

"Would you oversee the loading of the motor?" Her voice held a note of urgency. It was now or never, for there was a risk they would never return. "There's something I must do before we leave."

Understanding flickered in Alex's gaze. "Shall I look after Pip?" It seemed he knew what she wished to do. She had his unwavering support.

The journey had grown familiar over these few tumultuous days. Up the winding staircases, under portraits whose painted eyes seemed to follow with cold judgement, past framed photographs capturing moments of happiness never to be repeated. With each step, the scent of sandalwood incense grew stronger. At the bedroom door, she knocked with gentle insistence. Silence greeted her, but she turned the handle, anyway.

The chamber lay shrouded in artificial twilight, heavy curtains drawn against the afternoon's pale brightness as rain tapped at the window. The air hung thick with incense and the tang of camphor. The two silver cats, Thoth and Ra, maintained their vigil from the counterpane, amber eyes gleaming at Felicity's intrusion.

Great-Aunt Winnifred lay amid her fortress of goose-down pillows. Without the protective armour of purple silk and dramatic gestures, she looked as fragile as a broken bird in her faded nightgown, impossible to imagine as commanding orchestrated supernatural performances. Her face, pale as parchment in the glow of a single candle at her bedside, bore the ravages of genuine grief. Tears had washed away her powder and rouge, and her mouth hung slightly open in the manner of exhausted sleep, grey hair spread across the pillows in dishevelled waves.

Felicity's heart clenched at the sight. Whatever Winnifred's machinations, whatever deceptions she'd practised — and goodness knew she'd gone to great lengths to pull the wool over Felicity's eyes — her great-aunt's suffering was real. Decades ago, she'd survived the loss of a husband and of a young child. Now, at this later stage in life, how would she overcome the loss of her only surviving son?

Felicity hesitated. Was disturbing Winnifred worth what she had to say? Was it not for her own benefit more than for her great-aunt?

"Felicity?"

Winnifred spoke without opening her eyes, her voice emerging as barely more than a whisper.

"Yes, Great-Aunt." Felicity approached the bedside.

"Did I dream it?" Winnifred's eyes remained closed. "Please tell me it isn't true."

The dagger of guilt twisted deeper into Felicity's heart. To witness one's only remaining son arrested and led away in handcuffs to face the possibility of the hangman's noose — no mother should endure such horror, whatever her faults.

"I need to apologise," Felicity said, her voice catching on the words.

Winnifred's eyes fluttered open, confusion clouding their faded blue depths. "Whatever for, my child?"

"I feel an amount of responsibility for this whole situation."

The older woman struggled to sit upright, the right side of her body moving with particular stiffness, a marker of the true extent of her injuries from that long-ago séance disaster. Felicity stepped forward to help, adjusting the mountain of pillows and settling her great-aunt against them, wafts of old incense emanating from the bedsheets. The older woman's skin was papery but warm to the touch. The cats observed this disruption with displeasure but maintained their posts on either side of Winnifred's outstretched legs.

"And how, pray tell, are you responsible for my son's downfall?" Winnifred's voice held more than a hint of disbelief.

"If I hadn't come here, if I hadn't stirred emotions about the Cullingslock Wastes..." Felicity sank onto the little stool beside the bed, swallowing hard. "The confrontation between your son and Mr Kemp might never have reached such a terrible conclusion." It was a relief to admit her remorse to her great-aunt, but what did she expect as an outcome? To be absolved? There was nothing Felicity could do to take away her great-aunt's suffering.

Winnifred studied her with an intensity that belied her weakened state. "So you believe my Tristan to be guilty?"

Felicity tilted her head, puzzled by the query. "He confessed to the crime, did he not?"

Winnifred held her gaze with unexpected steel before melting into sobs, fresh tears wetting her cheeks and her nightgown.

Felicity fished a handkerchief from her pocket and offered it.

"I simply cannot believe it," said Winnifred, dabbing at her streaming eyes. "He doesn't seem capable. Not my gentle boy."

Felicity had questions about the family's lack of faith in Tristan's practical abilities, yet she shared Winnifred's assessment of his essential nature. This was not a man one could easily imagine committing murder, especially not such a forceful assault upon someone like Mr Kemp, who hadn't seemed easy to subdue.

But then many men had gone off to war and come back changed in ways they themselves didn't even understand. Tristan was perhaps no exception to this.

"It can be surprising to know what lies dormant within a person," Felicity offered. The comment perhaps wasn't reassuring, but it was truthful based on her experience. "Or within any of us."

"If fault lies anywhere, it rests upon my shoulders. I knew of

Tristan's objections to Mr Kemp's methods, heard his pleas for the land's gentler treatment. But the money, you see. The money was so necessary." She paused, her breath catching in her throat. "I never imagined it would lead to this. I saw no warning."

For once, Winnifred's speech contained no theatrical flourishes, no references to the other realm. Would there not be a séance to get the answers from Mr Kemp? It was perhaps not just her son's arrest that was coaxing Winnifred towards less outgoing behaviour. There was her failed poison plot as well, and the newspapers would likely feast upon this tragedy — a baron murdering his land agent would provide sensational copy for weeks.

Felicity and Alex had already discussed how the Western Daily News might handle the delicate matter. Given the family connection, coverage would be minimal unless public interest demanded otherwise. Less reputable publications would show no such restraint. And though Winnifred had schemed to use Felicity's press connections for publicity, this was assuredly not the attention she'd sought. Her plans for a triumphant return to the stage, for readers queueing to purchase copies of her new book — all of it lay in ruins as beyond repair as the castle's crumbling curtain walls.

Yet it wasn't simply about fame and attention, was it? Money lay at the core of seemingly all the castle's ills.

As the rain's steady patter increased against the window, Felicity reached for her great-aunt's hand, adorned with rings that now seemed too heavy for such fragility. "The blame belongs to no one save Tristan himself," she said gently, echoing the sentiment Alex had expressed to her in the great hall. If she wished to absolve her great-aunt of feelings of guilt, then Felicity must offer herself the same reprieve.

"He returned from that awful war so altered," Winnifred continued, her voice gaining strength from anger at a situation that couldn't be changed. "I thought he would be relieved to have the Wastes off his hands. He didn't object that I'd hired a land agent in his absence. He just said, 'Whatever you think is best, Mama.' He had faith in me, and I let him down. I could see that Mr Kemp riled him. Goodness, I even found the fellow quite unpleasant at times myself."

The candle at the beside spluttered.

Wishing to allow Winnifred to talk as much as she needed, Felicity left a pause before responding. "Did your son develop a temper after he came back from the war?" If her final visit to Winnifred couldn't offer a sense of resolution, it could help develop her understanding.

Winnifred looked at Felicity with curiosity. "Quite the reverse, my child. Before Tristan's service in the army, I might have believed him capable of striking out in anger. He was a powder keg awaiting a spark. But the man who returned? Something changed my Tristan. He wouldn't tell any of us what he saw as a soldier, but he was rendered as gentle as a spring lamb."

Felicity frowned. The revelation was entirely unexpected. She'd glimpsed hints of suppressed emotion beneath Tristan's placid surface during their tour of the Wastes, yet he'd always regained control of himself. "Before the war, would you have believed him capable of striking Mr Kemp?"

"Oh, most definitely," said Winnifred. "Not that he was a thug. He knew how to behave himself, though his temper could be quick. But now... No. I cannot see it. I suppose that's what makes this so very hard."

Felicity nodded, her mind whirring with ideas flying off in different directions. She rose from the stool.

"Must you leave so soon, my child?" The question emerged plaintive as a child's plea. "Your presence brings such comfort."

"I'm afraid I must," said Felicity, although she certainly needed to speak with Alex before they set off in the Alvis. What she had learned from her great-aunt didn't quite make sense. "Perhaps conversations with your daughter might ease your burden?" she suggested carefully, still faintly hopeful that she might prove useful towards the building of bridges within the family. "I'm sure Elfrida would welcome the chance to understand you better."

Winnifred's chuckle was soft, yet wistful. "I lost my daughter's respect years ago, I'm afraid. She merely tolerates my presence. Though I confess, I've given her ample cause for such feelings. Too many promises broken, too many priorities misplaced."

"It might not be too late. People can surprise us with their capacity for forgiveness."

A ghost of her former theatrical smile touched Winnifred's lips. "Always eager to help, aren't you, my child?"

Felicity blinked at what might have been a compliment or gentle criticism. "If I believe I have a reasonable chance at leaving a situation improved, then I shall endeavour to make it so." She knew by now it wasn't possible to erase this wrinkle in her character.

"I must say..." Winnifred's expression sobered. She reached for one of her cats, stroking its tail, her gaze avoiding Felicity's. "I'm sorry, my child. Sorry for the deception with the poisoning, sorry for attempting to use your reputation for my own ends. You came here with such pure intentions, hoping to mend what was broken, and I..." Her voice broke. "I treated you as merely another opportunity to grasp at fading glory."

"You have known great suffering, Great-Aunt," said Felicity earnestly. "And you continue to do so. I understand your desperation. I do not wish you ill."

Winnifred raised her pale blue gaze and blinked hopefully at Felicity. "You forgive an old fool her follies?"

"What's done is done," asserted Felicity, gently side-stepping the request for forgiveness. She'd arrived in her great-aunt's chamber seeking absolution for herself, yet she could never approve of her great-aunt's actions in plotting to misuse her visit to Cullingslock. Felicity had developed an understanding of the older woman's motives, however. Understanding and forgiveness were two sides of the same coin.

Winnifred nodded slowly, as though she had expected Felicity's forgiveness might remain elusive.

"Is there anything I might do to ease your situation before I depart?"

"Send Timpson to me, please, my child." Winnifred settled

deeper into her pillows, her eyelids drooping with exhaustion. "Tell him to bring cocoa — prepared by his own hand, mind you, not Cook's. Dear Mrs Wiseley means well, but Timpson knows precisely how I prefer it. Extra bitter, with just a touch of cinnamon." She was like a child seeking the comfort of familiar rituals.

Felicity said she would pass the message to the butler and gave her great-aunt's frail hand one last squeeze. She moved softly towards the bedroom door but paused at the threshold, one hand on the heavy stone doorframe. The cats blinked slowly in her direction. This might be her last opportunity to satisfy a curiosity that had nagged since her first evening at Cullingslock.

"Great-Aunt?"

"Hmm?" Winnifred sounded half-asleep, perhaps already dreaming of her cocoa.

"Those voices during the séances — how do you do it?"

Winnifred's eyes snapped open. She turned her head slowly on the pillow, studying Felicity with unexpected sharpness. "Where do you think they come from, my child?" Her words were a challenge. Would Felicity voice her doubts in her great-aunt's beliefs at a time when the older woman lay wounded and vulnerable? The revelations about the disastrous séance in London had made it clear the powerful medium wasn't against using props for her spiritualist displays.

"Some sort of recording mechanism?" Felicity offered honestly.

A deep sigh escaped the older woman, stirring the cats. Had Felicity overstepped? Would they now part on bitter terms?

"I suppose you could call them that." A fond little smile crept over Winnifred's lips. "After Kensington, I swore off those treacherous electrical contraptions, but nature has its own ways. Are you able to guard a secret, my child?" A hint of her old theatricality crept back into her tone. "To never tell another living soul?"

A shiver of anticipation trickled down Felicity's spine as she gave her solemn promise. Would one final truth balance against all the deceptions that had marked her stay at Cullingslock?

Chapter Thirty-Six

Felicity hadn't received the specifics from Winnifred — only directions to a section of the castle that Elfrida had declared forbidden due to structural conditions during her tour. The narrow turret staircase glistened with dampness where the rain gusted in through open slits in the ancient stone walls. It was where Felicity and Alex had once sought refuge for a private discussion, including talk of wedding arrangements. How distant such concerns felt now.

Alex cast a glance over his shoulder. He was leading, Pip still tucked under his arm. He'd shown no hesitation in wanting to accompany Felicity and follow Winnifred's instructions, but as they reached the end of the narrow staircase, his half-smile hinted at scepticism. "What do you suppose your great-aunt has sent us to see?"

The thick oak door at the top of the stairs appeared to be locked, a rusted padlock hanging from old ironwork. As Felicity played with the mechanism, she discovered — just as Winnifred had said — that the lock was merely for show. It wasn't holding the door closed.

The door swung slowly open with a creak.

"I expect to find at least one answer to my myriad questions," said Felicity as they eased through the narrow doorway.

Closing the door behind them, as instructed, they were plunged into a murky gloom. But as more stairs carried them upwards, daylight filtered from above, pale and grey, and strange sounds drifted towards them — clicks and whistles, the rustling of what might have been paper.

As they climbed, Pip's nose worked frantically, his small body stiff with excitement. The sounds grew louder, more distinct. Definitely whistles now, and something that might have been — laughter?

Alex heaved open a caged trap door overhead, its chicken-wire frame revealing their destination. The papery sounds exploded into a cacophony of fluttering wings. Squawks and whistles filled the air as dark shapes launched themselves upwards.

"Good heavens," Felicity breathed.

The circular chamber soared above them, its stone walls rising to a peaked ceiling crossed with ancient beams. More chicken wire covered the slender windows, transforming the space into an enormous aviary filled with light and air. Mirrors, bells, and various perches decorated the walls, and there were places to sleep and feed. The windows offered views of the rain-soaked, heather-covered hills stretching away into greyness.

The birds — six of them — regarded the intruders with bright, intelligent eyes.

Ting, ting, ting!

One bird, bolder than its fellows, tapped a small bell with its brilliant orange beak. The sound rang clear and purposeful through the tower room.

"Magnificent," Alex whispered, and Felicity had to agree.

The birds were striking creatures. Their sleek black plumage caught the muted light with iridescent hints of green and deep blue, as though dipped in oil. Yellow markings encircled their throats like exotic necklaces, flexing as they twisted their heads to better examine their visitors. Bright orange beaks and legs provided shocking splashes of colour against their dark elegance.

With her.

The voice emerged clear and human, though oddly hollow. Felicity's breath caught.

Good birds. Good birds.

Another voice, different from the first.

"So that's how she did it." Alex's words held equal parts admiration and disbelief. "These creatures are the voices of the séance spirits."

The aviary answered a question Felicity had harboured since her first night at Cullingslock. It did little to undo any of the terrible misfortune of her visit, but the animals' beauty and obvious brilliance were among the lighter, more welcome impressions she would take away from the castle.

Gradually, the birds descended from the highest perches, hopping from branch to branch with acrobatic grace. Two approached quite close, their movements a blend of avian caution and almost human boldness.

I am. I am.

The phrase heard during the first séance emerged from one bird's throat, its beak barely moving. The effect was fascinating but also unnerving.

"Incredible," Felicity whispered. She extended a tentative finger towards the nearest bird, which cocked its head to regard her with a bright eye. Its gaze held an uncanny intelligence.

"Good birds," she echoed softly.

Good birds.

The responding voice was realistic yet tinny, not unlike a mechanical recording.

Pip squirmed desperately in Alex's grip, eager to investigate the fascinating winged creatures. Gently, Alex tightened his hold on the little dog, unwilling to risk chaos in the aviary.

With her.

This voice was different to the others — mature, feminine, but with a windswept quality, as though heard from a distance.

"They don't know what they're saying, do they?" Alex watched as the bird's neck and chest puffed with the sound. "They're just repeating what they've heard."

So what.

A man's voice now, rough with irritation and equally windswept.

"They're Winnifred's recording devices," said Felicity, watching the talking bird.

So what. So what.

Alex laughed at the timing of the animal's response, but the repetition of the words sent a chill down Felicity's spine. These weren't simply trained phrases. The birds were capturing and repeating actual conversations.

She turned to Alex. "Don't you recognise the voice?"

He looked at her with a quizzical expression.

Ting, ting, ting!

The bell rang again, and the birds began flapping and jumping about. Pip craned his neck.

Felicity and Alex had been so charmed and distracted by the discovery of the aviary they hadn't heard the footsteps on the tower stairs. And there was no way out other than through the wire-covered trap door, which was now slowly lifting.

"What are you doing here?"

Audrey emerged through the trap door like an avenging angel, her usually gentle gaze blazing with protective fury. Her reddish hair, normally so neatly plaited, had worked loose in wisps that framed her face. In the pale grey light filtering into the aviary, she appeared larger and less delicate than previously, her green woollen cardigan tight over her broad shoulders.

The birds erupted at her appearance, wings beating the air in a frenzy of welcome. Several landed on her shoulders and arms, their enthusiastic cries and whistles creating a chaos of sound, their heads bobbing in arrhythmic motion. The basket of fruit hanging on the girl's arm was no doubt the source of much of the excitement.

"Audrey," began Felicity, holding out a calming hand. "I can explain."

"No one must be here. No one but me." Her voice trembled between anger and distress. "If my grandmother finds out—"

"Your grandmother sent us here." Felicity kept her voice steady despite the girl's obvious agitation. It was a twist on the truth because in reality Winnifred had given directions to the aviary only to Felicity, though making the trip without Alex had been unthinkable. "She gave us permission."

Audrey's chest heaved with emotion, her sturdy frame trembling. She wasn't always the first to comprehend things, but her understanding of matters important to her was profound.

The birds sensed her distress, their cries growing frantic. One bold creature clung to her basket, pecking at the strawberries and plums she'd brought for them.

"So there's no secret anymore?" Audrey's words emerged as a wail. "Everything I've done, all that work, all those hours of training were for nothing?"

"Your secrets are safe with us," Alex assured her. His positioning had shifted subtly, ready to pass Pip to Felicity and to move decisively, if needed. But beyond her green jumper, was there any foundation to their suspicions about the girl's intentions and capabilities? Were such concerns not voided now that Audrey's uncle had confessed to the dreadful crime?

"We promise," Felicity added, acutely aware of their isolation in the tower. One door. One exit. And Audrey blocking it.

The girl's breathing remained laboured, her face working through emotions perhaps too complex for her years. Pip whined and struggled in Alex's arms, desperate to greet his young friend. Alex handed the struggling terrier to Felicity, but she wouldn't release him. The birds continued to flap about, chattering and whistling, desperate to attack the food Audrey had brought with her but too well trained for a full-scale assault.

"Are these your birds?" asked Felicity in an attempt to diffuse the stand-off. She'd not imagined Audrey capable till now, but if the indignation she was displaying in the aviary had occurred in the billiard room, then a man's untimely demise might have been the result.

"They're my grandmother's birds. I just train them." Some of the fire dimmed in Audrey's eyes, replaced by a vague flicker of pride.

"You have an enormous talent with animals," continued Felicity, relief flooding her veins as she noticed the girl's cheeks flushing at the compliment, though Audrey was doing her best to continue to look angry.

"You mustn't tell anyone."

"We won't," assured Felicity.

"Not even my mother."

So Audrey had her grandmother's confidence where Elfrida perhaps didn't, and the girl was comfortable keeping secrets from her mother.

"We shan't tell anyone," promised Alex, his posture also relaxing.

"Would you like to feed them?" suggested Felicity, as the birds continued their flapping and whistling, one even landing on the crown of Audrey's head. "They seem rather desperate."

Audrey glanced between them, her gaze still touched with suspicion, then she moved to the feeding troughs, the birds following in a flutter of black feathers.

"What type of birds are they?" asked Alex.

"*Gracula religiosa*," she said without looking up from her work. "The common mynah. From the East Indies." After emptying half the basket, she took it to the trough on the other side of the room, placing items of fruit on some of the perches as she went. "The Latin name comes from how they used to be taught to repeat prayers."

"How fascinating." Felicity spoke sincerely, even if what she'd heard some of the birds saying continue to worry her. "Do they mind being trained?"

With the food all given out, the sound of pecking and the occasional squawk of joy replaced the chattering and whistling as the birds set about eating their food.

Audrey held out a plum for one of the shyer members of the troop. He pecked gently at the flesh. She kept her eyes on the creature as she spoke. "They don't seem to, as long as there's a reward." Her voice had returned to its usual gentle cadence.

"Food, you mean?" said Felicity, Pip still scrambling in her arms.

A little smile touched Audrey's lips as she continued to watch the feeding bird. Its sharp, slender toes gripped the cardigan at her wrist, but its claws didn't catch or damage the wool. "There's not an animal on Earth who can't be swayed by a morsel of food they adore."

"That's certainly the case for me," Alex offered, earning an amused glance from the girl.

"How does their involvement in the séances work?" Felicity pressed carefully.

"They're transported in cages to the location." Audrey seemed calm now. She held out another piece of fruit for the bird, inviting it to hop onto her shoulder, which it happily did. "They respond to specific prompts, always from my grandmother. She comes here sometimes to work with them, but I train them to say what they need to. They're not all good for the performances—" Audrey shook her head. "For connecting with the other realm, I mean." She had clearly been schooled by her grandmother on how to talk about the séances. "Only four of them can be used at the moment, but I expect to have all six of them trained soon."

Good birds.

I am.

Some of the birds had finished eating and were hopping about the aviary again, firing out various utterances. One of them even did a very good rendition of the cage door over the stairs banging shut.

"Is it always your voice they're mimicking?" asked Felicity.

"Not always," replied Audrey. "Sometimes it's my grandmother's. Sometimes I'll use my mother's gramophone. We have recordings of all kinds of speeches and plays."

With her.

It was a woman's voice, mature, agitated.

So what.

This was the voice of a man, and not just any man.

Felicity shivered and looked at Alex. His eyes flashed with concern. He heard it now, too.

Felicity raised a finger as the windswept voices were repeated amid an increasing flurry of different sounds.

With her.

So what.

"Did you teach them that?"

Audrey frowned a little. "Oh no. That's a new one. They pick up all kinds of things. Anything they can hear, really."

Felicity gave Alex a meaningful look. He went to one of the wire-covered windows and looked outside.

"New since when?" asked Felicity.

Audrey blinked. "I don't recall hearing the words while we were getting ready for the last séance."

"Thank you for explaining so much to us," continued Felicity, not wishing to dwell too much on her suspicions in the young girl's presence. "We're very grateful to you."

Audrey nodded her acceptance. "I'm sorry I was so angry when I arrived. I've seen no one else in here except my grandmother. I can't say I understand why she told you about the birds, but I suppose I should trust her. It's her secret, after all. Not mine."

Felicity smiled a little sadly. She may not have been at fault, but Audrey was definitely caught up in something, wasn't she?

"The cardigan you're wearing," Felicity said carefully, for she was venturing out onto thin ice now — with the risk of becoming entangled once more in what she'd just escaped. "It's quite a striking shade of green."

Colour flooded Audrey's cheeks. She touched the wool self-consciously, her fingers finding the carefully mended section at her wrist. "Oh, it's actually not mine."

Alex turned and looked with seriousness at the girl. A cold, damp breeze passed through the wire-covered windows.

"Whose is it then?" Felicity kept her voice light, though her pulse raced.

The answer was already quite obvious.

Chapter Thirty-Seven

The scent of proving dough and cinnamon drifted up the kitchen stairs, a deceptively homely welcome that did nothing to ease the knot in Felicity's stomach. Alex hung back as she descended into the castle's great kitchen, where scuffed pots gleamed on the walls and bundles of dried herbs swayed gently from the ceiling. They agreed Felicity should handle this confrontation alone, though she kept Pip tucked firmly beneath her arm, so that Alex could act quickly if needed.

The terrier wriggled when Solomon and Lionheart came into view.

The two herding dogs lay beside the unlit range, neither fully at ease. Solomon's intelligent dark eyes tracked their approach, his black-and-white coat sleek in the pale light that slanted through high windows. His tail gave a cautious wag. Lionheart, Mr Kemp's orphaned sheepdog, watched cautiously from beneath his fringe of grey-and-white fur. He'd seemed happy at Tristan's side, but now both dogs were masterless and under the care of the house's domestic staff for the time being.

Thump. Roll. Thump.

The rhythmic sound drew Felicity's attention to the great oak table at the kitchen's heart, the same scarred surface where she'd first witnessed the cook's tears over Winnifred's poisoning. Elfrida stood there now, wielding a heavy marble rolling pin with rather more vigour than any pastry required. Flour dust hung in the air like a thin mist, catching the light and settling on every surface.

Elfrida wore a practical linen apron over a day dress of soft heather wool. The colour brought out the copper tones in her hair, wisps of which escaped to frame her taut expression. A smudge of flour decorated a cheekbone, and her sleeves were pushed up to reveal forearms surprisingly muscled for a woman of artistic temperament, her long fingers gripping the rolling pin with the same intensity she might have once reserved for chisels and clay.

Thump. Roll. Thump.

The pastry before her had long since passed the point of workability, yet Elfrida continued her rhythmic assault. She didn't look up as Felicity approached, though the slight stiffening of her shoulders betrayed her awareness.

"Thought you'd left without saying goodbye." Her voice was frosty. She must have seen the footman loading the Alvis.

"I admit that had been my intention." There was no point in being anything but honest at this stage.

Elfrida's hands stilled on the marble pin. Slowly, she raised her head. Her sardonic mask had slipped, revealing eyes red-rimmed from crying. She'd seemed to handle her brother's arrest more calmly than anyone, but emotion had clearly caught up with her. "Understandable." Her laugh was brittle. "As if the séances and theatrics weren't enough. Was my brother's confession to murder a step too far for you?"

The hurt in her gaze struck Felicity with unexpected force. This wasn't merely Elfrida's customary cynicism — this was the anguish of a woman who'd already lost her husband, her home, her artistic dreams, and now faced losing her brother.

Felicity's chest constricted with heartfelt concern for everyone trapped within Cullingslock's crumbling walls even as wariness prickled along her spine. Elfrida's knuckles had whitened around the rolling pin's handles, and there was something unsettling in the way she hefted its considerable weight.

Felicity suppressed the urge to swallow nervously. "May I sit down?"

Elfrida held her gaze, something unreadable flickering behind her pain. She nodded but did not relinquish her grip on the marble implement, nor did she take a seat herself. She returned to her pastry dough with renewed violence. Each impact sent small halos of flour into the air, creating a fairy-ring of white dust on the table's surface.

Thump. Roll. Thump.

The cacophony made conversation nearly impossible, but Felicity waited with patience, the kitchen's familiar scents enveloping her — rosemary and sage from the herb bundles overhead, the yeasty tang of bread rising in the proving cupboard, the faint sweetness of vanilla and nutmeg from whatever had emerged from the ovens earlier. It was no wonder Elfrida had sought solace in the kitchen. She was someone who liked to keep her hands busy.

Solomon had crept closer during the pause. He now sat beside Felicity, cocking his head and looking at Pip, the Yorkie whimpering with a yearning to join his black-and-white pal.

"Where's the cook?" Felicity ventured, stroking the Collie's silky ears.

"In her room. I sent her away." Elfrida attacked a fresh section of dough with particular gusto. "It's all been too much for her these past days. She's older than my mother, you know."

"That's kind of you to take on such responsibility."

Elfrida's laugh held no humour. "It's not a choice." She abandoned the rolling pin for a moment to scatter more flour, though the work surface hardly needed it.

"Who's forcing you?" Felicity kept her tone gentle. She remained acutely aware of how Elfrida's fingers had returned to the marble handles of the heavy rolling pin, and of the distance between the kitchen table and Alex waiting on the stairs behind her.

Thump!

The rolling pin struck the table with a force that made Pip cower.

Elfrida's chest heaved. "If you'd had the misfortune to marry a German who abandoned you and your child to fight against your own country—" Her voice cracked. "If you'd been turned out of your home with a child in your arms, treated like a traitor when you'd done nothing wrong—" She pressed a flour-dusted hand to her mouth to contain her emotion, leaving white streaks across her cheeks. "You would do everything you could to cling onto the last remnants of civilised living that remained available to you." Another bitter laugh escaped. "Wait, what am I talking about? Of course you wouldn't. You wouldn't have to. You were born into a family with money, with respectability that couldn't be stripped away by one man's choices." She gripped the rolling pin again, her movements sharp with anger. "And I was born here. To this."

Thump. Roll. Thump.

The blows came harder now, more erratic. Elfrida wasn't as sturdy as her daughter, but she certainly had power in her arms. If she chose to wield that marble pin as a weapon rather than a kitchen tool, Felicity's position at the table left her decidedly vulnerable. Rising now would only heighten the tension, yet remaining seated felt increasingly exposed. But she couldn't back away now. She had to know for certain, to understand the details of what led to Mr Kemp's demise, no matter what emotions got stirred to the surface.

"How did you feel when you learned your brother had confessed?" Felicity steered the conversation carefully towards the purpose of her visit to the kitchen.

Elfrida's hands stilled. She glanced at Felicity with a mixture of anger and longing. Was Felicity the first to ask about Elfrida's experience of the situation? Several heartbeats passed before she returned her attention to the ruined pastry.

Thump. Roll. Thump.

"How do you think I felt?"

Felicity let the silence stretch. *Guilty?* she thought but didn't voice it. The marble pin looked heavier with each crushing roll across the table.

Felicity stroked a hand over Pip's back. "I went to the billiard room."

Elfrida's rhythm faltered briefly.

"The night after Mr Kemp was found."

Thump. Roll. Thump. The tempo increased.

"I'll be honest. I was concerned about the integrity of the scene. I'm not usually dismissive of the police, but Sergeant Norris seemed behind the times in more ways than one." Would an attempt at levity bring Elfrida closer to her? "Rather like one of those fossils who still believes women shouldn't have the vote."

A thin smile flickered across Elfrida's flour-dusted features, a reminder of their earlier camaraderie, but it vanished as quickly as it had appeared.

Lionheart rose from his spot by the range, padding over to lean his considerable bulk against Elfrida's legs. She paused to run floury fingers through his thick coat, and Felicity saw her shoulders tremble. She was struggling to maintain the toughness of her exterior.

"It turns out I was right to be concerned," continued Felicity, a little more casually, as though confiding in a friend. "There were elements of evidence the police had overlooked." She paused. "Did you go up to the billiard room yourself? Did you have a look?"

Elfrida's gaze snapped up. "Of course not."

"Well, you can perhaps imagine it. Where the poor fellow smashed through the window, taking mullions and all, it was simply open to the elements. I've no idea what traces of the incident got wiped away. I don't like to be critical of the police, but the sergeant and his men ought at least to have attempted to cover the hole and shield what evidence there was."

Another glance, sharper this time. "So you found nothing?"

"Oh no," said Felicity. "I found something. Not that it matters now, of course, with your brother having made his confession."

Elfrida glanced again at Felicity but said nothing.

"Indeed, what I found rather confirmed Tristan's involvement, if my memory serves correctly."

There was a long pause. Felicity didn't want to drag things out or play games with anyone, but if Elfrida did not wish to be open, then Felicity had her own methods for understanding what was galloping through the agitated woman's mind.

"What was it you found?" Elfrida didn't look up from her pastry dough, but the question emerged strained, as though forced through clenched teeth.

"There were threads caught on the broken glass. Green threads."

Thump. Roll. Thump. Thump.

Elfrida's work intensified. She was interested.

"Your brother often wears a jumper with some green in it, I noticed."

"Did you inform the police?"

"No. There's no need, is there? We know who did it. That Tristan left behind threads from his jumper makes sense, and I wouldn't want to embarrass the police."

Elfrida paused her rolling to sprinkle flour. She let out a little sigh, as though tired from intense effort.

"But you know what's rather odd? I've seen your daughter wearing a cardigan in exactly the same green as the threads I found. And not only that—"

Bang!

The rolling pin clattered onto the table. Elfrida gripped its edge, her knuckles white as the flour coating her hands. Lionheart whined softly and backed away.

"The cardigan's not hers, it's mine! Audrey has nothing to do with any of it. Do you hear me?"

"Felicity?" Alex's voice carried down the stairs, carefully timed.

Elfrida's eyes widened, darting between Felicity and the stairway. She'd given more away than she'd intended. Her whole body shuddered, perhaps struck suddenly by the realisation and the consequences of her outburst in defence of her daughter. Sinking into a chair, she buried her face in her hands, shoulders shaking with sobs that seemed to come from somewhere deep and long-buried.

There was no confession yet, but there was now an opening.

Lionheart rested his great head on Elfrida's lap. He'd become quite a different dog since his owner left him, and the simple comfort he offered seemed to break something in Elfrida, making her sobs come harder.

Alex looked at Felicity with raised eyebrows, a silent question about his timing. She gave him a subtle nod. His appearance had defused Elfrida's growing agitation, but more importantly, it had cracked her defensive shell.

He stood aside. His presence was now obvious, but he would not interfere in the discussion.

"Audrey is not in any trouble," Felicity said gently, drawing her chair closer to Elfrida. "You don't need to worry about that. She told me herself the cardigan was yours. That's why I came to you."

Elfrida raised her face, flour and tears mingling on her cheeks. "You think I did it? You think I pushed Harry out of the window?"

It was the first time Felicity had heard anyone at the castle use the land agent's given name. The familiarity of it was striking.

"You were in the billiard room, though, weren't you?"

Elfrida gasped. "How could you know this?"

Felicity had her sources — Elfrida's absence from the garden in which Mr Kemp landed, the caught threads, the mynahs' recorded fragments. *With her*, the woman's voice had said. *So what*, came the man's reply. Winnifred and Audrey had sworn Felicity to secrecy about those remarkable birds, but that didn't mean she couldn't use the information gleaned from them.

"Did you and Mr Kemp have a disagreement? Not about the land, but about something else?"

Elfrida rubbed her forehead, leaving a new streak of white.

"About someone else?" Felicity pressed gently.

Elfrida bit her lip. A tear rolled down her cheek, cutting a channel through the flour dust.

"You were in the billiard room when Mr Kemp fell, yet it's your brother who'll spend tonight and likely many more nights in a prison cell before he's sentenced to—"

"No!" The word tore from Elfrida's throat. "Do you think I'd let my own brother hang?" The anguish in her voice was real. This wasn't calculated deflection — this was genuine terror.

"Yet you know that's what he's facing."

Elfrida sniffled, absently stroking Lionheart's patient head.

"If there's more to this than what the police understand, then please, Elfrida, you must tell me. If others were involved in whatever happened, we need to make that known. Any mercy from the judge or jury depends on having all the facts."

The kitchen fell silent save for Elfrida's ragged breathing and a gentle whimper from Pip. Felicity reached into her pocket, producing a handkerchief. Elfrida stared at it but didn't take it.

"Very well." Felicity rose, tucking Pip under her arm. "I shall leave you to your secrets and your brother to his fate."

"We met most days." Elfrida's words emerged small and whispered. "After lunch, in the billiard room. In the beginning it was thrilling — like being alive again after so long of feeling dead. But by the end..." She shook her head. "I wasn't even enjoying it anymore."

Felicity sank slowly back into her chair. "You had an intimate relationship with Mr Kemp?" she asked, her tone hushed.

"Not that afternoon." Elfrida's fingers found Lionheart's ears, drawing comfort from the repetitive stroking. "I came up from the kitchen later than expected. Cook hasn't been her usual self since that lunch made Mother ill, and I've been picking up the work. I changed in my apartment, then went to meet him. I hadn't heard any commotion. Only Cook's scream." She paled at the memory. "The wind was gushing through the broken glass. I looked out and saw him there, among Audrey's flowers. Like a giant had tossed him away." She sniffled. "I pulled back, but the sleeve of my cardigan caught. Only Audrey mostly wears it now. I'd thrown it on in a rush..." She shook her head dolefully. "I tried to remove all the threads that had caught. Seems I didn't do a good enough job."

So it had been Elfrida's hand Felicity had seen reaching out of the window above the flower garden.

"You didn't see Mr Kemp in the billiard room that day?"

"We were supposed to meet, but someone got to him before me."

Felicity studied Elfrida carefully. The mynahs had recorded an argument between a man and a woman. If the man was Mr Kemp, but the woman wasn't Elfrida, the list of suspects narrowed considerably.

Elfrida continued to weep, her tears falling onto Lionheart's patient head. The dog pressed closer.

"I wasn't doing it for myself," she whispered. "I was doing it to spite her."

"To spite who?" Felicity frowned. "Your mother?" she said, remembering what Winnifred had told her about losing her daughter's respect.

Elfrida looked up, blinking through tears. "No. Not her."

Felicity leaned forward in her seat. "Who, then?"

Chapter Thirty-Eight

Elfrida hadn't told Felicity everything. She hadn't needed to. Felicity could fill in the gaps herself. It wasn't just the land — it perhaps wasn't the land at all.

As they made their way along one of the castle's darker passageways, where neither external windows nor gas lamps offered relief from the gloom, Felicity's mind reeled with the implications. Mr Kemp had been more of a destructive force at the castle than previously realised. A cold weight settled in her stomach as she considered the full scope of his behaviour. Miss Hartley and her freshly written letter from beyond the grave had hinted at this, but Felicity missed the clues. Had Mr Kemp attempted to lay hands on the spiritualist apprentice as well?

"But it was Tristan, wasn't it?" asked Alex, his voice echoing slightly in the narrow hallway.

"I'm not convinced the police have the full picture," said Felicity, clutching Pip tightly as they navigated the shadows, the terrier's warm body providing comfort against the chill that had nothing to do with the castle's draughty corridors.

"But it was definitely him, wasn't it? Otherwise why confess?" Alex wasn't in the habit of reining Felicity in, but caution edged his voice. Was she becoming over-involved in a situation that was not only complicated but also fraught with intense emotions — emotions that could pull a person under?

"The motivations are just as important as the method," she asserted. There might still be a chance of uncovering something that would change the way Tristan was viewed during his trial — not that anyone should escape punishment for wrongdoing. But to understand that more people were involved than just Tristan and Mr Kemp — and it was already clear Elfrida had a hand in the maelstrom of misdeeds swirling around the final deadly act — could make the difference between the gallows and a lesser sentence. The stakes could not have been higher.

"Do you expect to convince everyone to come clean to the police about the whole sorry situation?" whispered Alex.

They emerged into the brightly lit corridor with its freshly beaten Persian runner and stopped outside the familiar door.

"We have to try." Felicity knocked, the sound sharp in the hushed hallway. Pip squirmed under her arm, sensing the tension. As much as the Yorkie had wanted to stay with Solomon and Lionheart in the kitchen, she couldn't leave him there. If she and Alex needed to leave the castle in a hurry, she must have her dog at her side.

Alex stepped forward. "Shall I?" he said, gesturing to Pip with understanding in his eyes.

"If you wouldn't mind." Despite the gravity of the moment, warmth blossomed in her chest. Alex had such an uncanny knack for reading her thoughts that he may as well have been psychic.

Pip didn't look overly excited to be transferred to Alex's arms, his small body stiffening slightly, but he didn't actively resist. Just as well, as the door to the apartment opened.

Philippa stood in the doorway, her posture upright, her chin lifted. She was dressed primly in travelling clothes — a tailored suit of charcoal wool with jet buttons that caught the light, a white blouse with a high lace collar, and a small velvet hat perched at a fashionable angle. Yet the ensemble's elegance only emphasised the strain in her features. The shadows beneath her eyes hinted at sleepless hours, and her mouth was set in a hard line that aged her.

Behind her, trunks and valises cluttered the usually orderly sitting room.

Peregrine was visible through the doorway, slowly folding clothes and placing them in the trunks with mechanical precision. He looked over his shoulder towards the door. Something in his expression — a flicker of fear, perhaps — made Felicity's pulse quicken.

Philippa offered a smile that never reached her eyes. "Your ladyship, are you here to bid us farewell?"

Felicity seized upon the opening. "Indeed. May we come in?"

Philippa's smile faltered. "I'm afraid we're in rather a hurry. Peregrine has a train to catch to get back up to Sandhurst." She glanced around the apartment with jerky movements, her fingers plucking at the buttons of her jacket. "I don't think we're in the right state to be receiving visitors, especially with everything that's happened with my poor husband."

Felicity's eyebrow rose at the peculiar ordering of priorities — first the train, then her husband. Although what a confession to murder might do to one's affection for a person was unimaginable.

"I quite understand," said Felicity, her tone gentle and courteous. "We can say our farewells here at the door. In fact, it's a little more than a goodbye that I wish to say to you." She softened her tone further. "I wish to express my sadness at your husband's position. I didn't know him well, but I found him to be a very gentle, thoughtful man. He must've been under enormous pressure to have behaved the way he did in the billiard room."

Philippa's entire body tensed, her shoulders drawing up towards her ears, her hands clenching into fists.

Felicity was onto something.

"Peregrine, please go to your room."

The young man looked between his mother and the visitors, something unreadable passing across his features. Without a word, he withdrew, though the door through which he disappeared closed with deliberate slowness, the click of the latch taking longer than necessary.

Philippa tugged at her jacket. "That's very kind of you to say." Her voice was barely above a whisper.

"I imagine you share my disbelief at the situation," suggested Felicity, her tone deliberately soft. The dance had begun, and she must lead carefully.

"Of course. Of course I do." Philippa's dark eyes darted about like a trapped animal's. "It's an extremely unfortunate situation."

"Have you given a full account of your side of things to the police?" asked Felicity.

Alex cleared his throat softly. Was it a gentle warning? Was she moving too fast? Perhaps, but instinct surged through her. They were so close to the truth. So very close.

"I am not sure I..." Philippa edged closer to the corridor, pulling the door of the apartment towards her back like a shield. "I wasn't involved in the... Just what do you mean, exactly?"

Felicity allowed sadness to colour her expression. "Regretfully, I'm rather well acquainted with cases of unnatural death and with people confessing — and even being found guilty. I should just like to offer you some advice, if I may?"

Philippa swallowed nervously, the movement visible above the lace of her collar. She looked back into the apartment, then at Felicity. "You may do so, your ladyship," she said in a tone that suggested she'd rather face a firing squad.

"I think it was evident to everyone — certainly to me, and I arrived only recently at the castle — that it was the matter of the land about which Mr Kemp and your husband disagreed."

"That is correct. Indeed, my husband mentioned this in his confession to the police, which I witnessed. It was quite a terrible occasion, as you can imagine, and I am still very shaken by it." The words emerged rather hurriedly and rang quite hollow. Whatever emotion Philippa claimed, it wasn't present in her voice — only a desperate need to maintain appearances.

Felicity pressed on, choosing her words with precision. "Naturally. And I feel a certain amount of responsibility. If I hadn't come here and brought up the topic of the Wastes, then things might not have come to a head. My brother advised me that the inheritance ought to be dealt with by solicitors, but I wanted to meet the family. I didn't know..." She let her voice trail off, watching Philippa's face. "Now that I look back at everything that happened, it was rather silly of me, don't you think?"

"Your ladyship, please. I don't think anyone would ever consider you silly."

Philippa's defence of Felicity against her own self-criticism was touching, but there was something tight in her tone. Had she perhaps given rather a lot of thought to Felicity's abilities?

"I will speak to the police about the possible influence of my presence at the castle," continued Felicity. "I don't believe that what your husband did to Mr Kemp should go unpunished, but there can be mitigating circumstances in even the most violent of situations. This can lead to quite a different outcome for a case." She paused, letting the implication sink in. "While I'm, of course, not guilty of being directly involved in the crime, I will tell them the responsibility I feel I must bear in triggering the situation. Had I not come to Cullingslock and brought the topic of the Wastes to the fore, who knows how matters might have developed? It's possible my influence might be borne in mind during the proceedings concerning your husband and what he has done."

Felicity paused again, scanning Philippa for a response. The woman's mask held firm, her grip still tight on the apartment door.

Felicity would have to go further.

"But then I expect you have feelings similar to my own regarding responsibility."

Philippa's face drained of colour. "I beg your pardon." She practically spat the words.

Felicity stared calmly at her as the silence stretched between them. Alex shifted his weight, adjusting his hold on Pip. He was ready if needed.

"Do you not?" pressed Felicity.

Philippa's laugh emerged high and strained. "I'm afraid I don't know what you're talking about," she said, her gaze skittering demurely away from Felicity's stare.

Felicity leaned forward, lowering her voice to barely above a whisper. "I shouldn't like to be too specific, standing here in the corridor. It's an extremely delicate topic, of course, and I quite understand your desire for discretion."

The accusation was oblique, yet targeted enough for the words to strike with devastating precision.

Philippa swayed slightly, grasping the door for support. Crimson splashed into her cheeks. "How did you..."

Felicity said nothing. The mynahs' recorded fragments echoed in her memory.

With her.

So what.

The quarrel in the billiard room hadn't been between Elfrida and Mr Kemp. It had been between Philippa and the land agent — likely about Elfrida, perhaps about their daily assignations in that very room.

"You can't..." Fear warred with anger across Philippa's features. She gripped the door.

Alex stepped forward, standing closer to Felicity now.

Matters in the billiard room had clearly escalated beyond control. But how? Philippa had been involved with the land agent, just as Elfrida had been. What had driven these women into the arms of such a man remained unclear. What was in it for Mr Kemp was obvious — the thrill of conquest, the sense of power. But the stakes for Philippa were infinitely higher than for Elfrida. It was possible the desperation that led to Philippa being unfaithful to Tristan would never be fully understood. Perhaps Philippa didn't quite understand it herself. When had her husband found out? What had pushed him into taking action?

"You..." Philippa's voice was a growl, but she was unable to finish her words.

Was supporting Tristan worth destroying Philippa? The consequences of murder versus those of manslaughter on the grounds of diminished responsibility could mean the difference between the hangman and a prison sentence. Why had Tristan first proclaimed his innocence, then confessed to the police? Why had he given disagreements about the land as his excuse, knowing the difference his motive might make?

Felicity took a step backwards as a new possibility crystallised in her mind.

The green threads had been a distraction.

What if Tristan had never been in the billiard room at all?

In retreating, she bumped Alex. He put a hand to the small of her back, his touch reassuring, protective.

Had the thought occurred to him, too?

"I believe I've said all I need to," said Felicity with a tight smile.

Philippa took in a deep breath and straightened, tugging at her jacket with trembling fingers, the fine wool bunching under her grip. "Thank you for your visit, Lady Felicity, but I have to get on." She seemed relieved to have the opportunity to behave as if the discussion regarding her impact on her husband's guilt had never taken place. "There's the train to catch."

Behind Philippa, the door through which Peregrine had disappeared swung slowly open. The boy's face appeared in the gap, eyes wide with something Felicity couldn't quite determine. "Mother—"

"I wish you safe travels back to your respective homes. Good day to you."

Slam!

The door to the apartment shut with such force the sound echoed through the corridor like a gunshot. Alex stepped forward instinctively, positioning himself between Felicity and the closed door, though no physical threat remained.

"Do you think you've made a difference?" he whispered, concern clouding his dark blue gaze as Pip's glistening black nose worked the air.

"I had to—" Felicity stopped, her eyes widening as she raised a finger to her lips.

Beyond the door, voices rose. At first low and urgent, then sharp with anger. Mother and son were locked in heated disagreement.

Crash!

The sound of furniture overturning made Felicity's heart leap. Something heavy had been sent flying.

A scream pierced the air, shrill with terror.

"Philippa," breathed Felicity, her stomach plummeting.

What had she done? What forces had Felicity unwittingly unleashed? In her determination to uncover the truth, had she pushed too hard, too fast?

The questions would have to wait. Action was needed now, and there could be no hesitating in a crisis.

Alex thrust Pip into Felicity's arms. "Stand back," he commanded, and using all his considerable strength, he shouldered open the door.

Chapter Thirty-Nine

The elegant sitting room had transformed into a battlefield. An overturned rosewood table blocked the immediate entrance, its delicate legs pointing skyward like the frail limbs of a toppled doll. Shattered picture frames littered the Turkish carpet, their glass catching the greyish afternoon light in dangerous glints. A vase lay in pieces near the window, its painted roses now fragments among the wreckage.

At the room's heart stood Philippa, her back to the doorway through which Alex followed by Felicity and Pip had burst. She had one arm extended. In her trembling hand gleamed a silver letter opener, its blade long and the point dangerously sharp. The weapon was aimed directly at her son.

"No," she growled. "You shall not. I will not allow it."

Peregrine's face had darkened to a shade that spoke of barely contained fury. His chest heaved as his breathing came fast, his hands clenched into fists at his sides. The carefully maintained bearing of a future army officer had cracked. Beneath was a young man pushed beyond endurance.

"Throw all the furniture you want. You can't stop me." The words emerged as a rumble from deep in his chest, his gaze locked so tightly on his mother it was as though Felicity and Alex hadn't burst through the door at all.

Felicity tried to analyse the scene without taking her eyes off mother and son. It sounded as if Philippa had been the one to throw the table. But which of them had begun the violence? And why?

Philippa's hand juddered, the letter opener's blade dancing in the light. Tears streaked down her cheeks. "You mustn't—" Her voice cracked. "I won't let you destroy everything."

Alex moved slowly and calmly, his hands raised in a gesture of peace. Each step was measured, his shoes finding purchase between scattered photographs and broken porcelain. "Let's all take a breath, shall we?"

Felicity clutched Pip to her chest. The scene before her — a doting mother threatening her beloved son with a household implement — was wrong. Utterly wrong. Was Philippa defending herself? Or had she launched the initial attack? What had Felicity missed?

"Stay back!" Philippa whirled, the blade now aimed at Alex's chest. Her onyx eyes were wide with fear, unravelled strands of her elegantly pinned hair falling onto her face. "You don't understand what's at stake."

Alex halted, maintaining a careful distance beyond the letter opener's reach. His stance remained ready, weight balanced on the balls of his feet.

"My father's life." Peregrine's voice cut through the tension. "That's what's at stake." The boy lunged.

"No!"

Philippa's shriek pierced the air as she swung the blade in a wild arc towards her advancing son.

Alex moved with fluid yet powerful grace.

"*Gngh!*"

His shoulder caught Peregrine mid-stride, sending the young man stumbling sideways into a stack of shelves. Books tumbled to the floor, pages fluttering.

For a heartbeat, Philippa stood frozen, her mouth agape at what she'd nearly done. Without Alex's intervention, her son might have charged onto the point of her blade. The letter opener trembled in her grip, its angle wavering.

Felicity seized on the moment of hesitation. Setting Pip carefully on the carpet and trusting the Yorkie's instinct towards self-preservation, she stepped forward with deliberate calm. "There now," she murmured, extending her hand as one might to a frightened horse. "Let me help you with that," she cooed, slipping her hand under the knife's hilt.

Philippa's fingers loosened for a moment, her dark eyes finding Felicity's. The look she gave her was one of sadness, of desperation, of a longing to be understood.

Was this Mr Kemp's killer?

The grip tightened around the ivory handle, and Philippa's hand snatched away from Felicity's. She pressed the blade to her own throat. "If my son speaks another word, I'll do it. I swear I will."

The air turned sharp and still. Philippa was intent on containing her son and would stop at nothing to succeed.

Peregrine recovered his balance against the bookcase and went rigid. "Mother, please." His baritone shook. "Don't."

Alex caught Felicity's eye. Any sudden movement could trigger catastrophe. From his position near the door, Pip watched with unusual stillness, his tail lowered.

"Lady Cullingslock." Felicity's tone was soothing. She and Philippa had spoken of marriage arrangements, of household management, of the burdens carried by women of their station. Could the connection they'd once had form a bridge in this moment of crisis? "Tell us about the sacrifices you've made."

Philippa blinked at Felicity, taken aback by the question. The point of the blade slackened at her throat. "My sacrifices?"

"Your life has been one of struggle, hasn't it?" Felicity took the smallest step forward, cataloguing every tremor, every flicker of emotion across Philippa's features. "Perhaps your son doesn't fully understand what you've endured."

The words found their mark. Philippa's gaze darted to Peregrine, something desperate and pleading in her eyes. "I don't like to complain."

"Of course not." Felicity took another careful step. Could she do it? Could she encourage Philippa to talk and calm herself but also keep Peregrine settled enough so that they might diffuse the situation entirely? "We're taught to bear our burdens in silence, aren't we? To maintain that brave face regardless of our circumstances." Felicity implied shared understanding with her tone. "But you're among those who care for you now. Your son especially wishes to understand."

Felicity glanced meaningfully at Peregrine. She didn't yet fully comprehend his role in all of this, but she willed him to play along. Even if he had misgivings about his mother, he surely wished her to lower the blade from her neck.

The young man's jaw worked as he struggled with conflicting emotions — fear, outrage, perhaps even a growing comprehension.

Philippa glanced nervously at her son. "Don't say a word, Perry." She pressed the tip of the knife harder against her own throat. "Not a word."

"But it's time for Perry to hear from his mother, isn't it?" pressed Felicity gently. "It's clear he doesn't understand everything about the decisions you've made."

"I want to understand, Mother." The boy's words emerged strained but sincere.

Felicity's heart lifted a little. Peregrine saw her purpose.

The letter opener lowered fractionally. Philippa's free hand rose to touch the small wound she'd made at her own throat. "You can't imagine what I expected when I married your father. Such dreams I had — balls in the great hall, gowns from London, a box at the opera." A sorrowful chuckle escaped her. "I was just your age, Perry. Barely out of the schoolroom. So certain I understood the world."

"You weren't born to this life, were you?" Felicity prompted gently, recognising the signs of a woman ready to unburden herself.

"Not at all, your ladyship. My family were merchants. Respectable, certainly, but trade nonetheless." Philippa's voice grew distant with memory. "When Tristan began courting me, I thought I was living a fairy tale. A baron! Can you imagine? I'd be Lady Cullingslock, mistress of an ancient castle." She gestured weakly at their surroundings. The apartment was perhaps the best kept in the whole castle, but the crumbling walls beyond couldn't be forgotten. "This wasn't what I'd pictured."

Peregrine's fists had uncurled, though tension still corded his neck. "You believed Father cheated you?"

"At first, yes." The letter opener trembled in Philippa's loosening grip. "I was furious at him for the deception — though truly, he'd never pretended to wealth. I'd simply assumed. But then you came along, my darling boy, and everything changed. You gave me purpose beyond my selfish, childish dreams."

"Then why?" The question tore from Peregrine's throat. "Why did you betray Father with that man?"

So Philippa's son knew about her relations with Mr Kemp.

The blade jerked upwards again. Philippa's face crumpled. "I'm so ashamed. I can't... There's no excuse that would satisfy you."

"Please, do try." Felicity kept her voice steady despite her racing pulse. Behind her, she sensed Alex shifting position, ready to intervene if needed. "Sometimes we do things that seem inexplicable even to ourselves. But there's always a reason, even if we can only see it in hindsight."

Philippa's shoulders shook with silent sobs. "Harry made me feel... Noticed. After years of your father returning from his rides, more interested in bird calls than his wife, of watching him drift further into his own world after returning from the war." She shook her head. "No, I won't blame Tristan. The fault is mine alone."

Peregrine's chest was heaving, his fists tight at his sides as he stared at his mother.

"But you didn't have Mr Kemp's full attention, did you?" Felicity spoke softly. "You discovered he was also carrying on with Tristan's sister, did you not?" She let the question hang in the air.

Understanding dawned on Peregrine's face. "That's why you went to the billiard room?"

Philippa nodded miserably. "He was preparing for her. Loosening his collar when I entered. The look on his face when he saw me instead—" She choked on the words. "All those pretty lies, all those promises. I was just another conquest, no different from any trollop who caught his eye."

Felicity's thoughts flew to Miss Hartley. Her letter purporting to be from the deceased man had noted multiple vague misdemeanours but stopped short of specific allegations. Had Winnifred's apprentice had to fend off Mr Kemp's advances? The secrecy under which such men operated could be part of their allure, but it could also be part of the power they wielded over often desperate women.

"So you argued." Felicity guided the narrative gently forward, aware that every moment the letter opener remained at Philippa's throat was another moment of danger.

"I called him terrible things. Things a lady shouldn't know, let alone speak." Philippa's gaze found her son's. "And then you arrived."

Peregrine's shoulders rolled back, his bearing straightening. "I heard you through the door. The way you begged him. The way he laughed." His voice hardened. "I was angry at him for the way he'd treated you, but more than that, I was angry about the betrayal of Father."

Peregrine's chest rose and fell in sharp breaths. Felicity exchanged a wide-eyed glance with Alex. The picture was becoming clearer by the moment, but the danger in the sitting room had far from passed.

"Perry, no," Philippa sobbed, the letter opener still at her neck jerking with the motion. "Please, no."

The young man hung his head. "I only meant to bloody his nose. One good punch to teach him respect."

"No." Philippa's voice was a whisper.

Alex adjusted his stance, ready to get the knife out of her hand by any means necessary.

"But Mr Kemp fell backward." Felicity's voice remained gentle as her own realisation took form. She could see it clearly now. Mr Kemp, perhaps already off-balance from the confrontation with Philippa, stumbling from the unexpected blow from the angry son. The window behind him, the frame — likely in desperate need of upkeep like the rest of the crumbling castle — giving way as he fell into it.

"That sound." Peregrine bent further forward, his breath coming fast, his palms clamped to his temples. "I can still hear it. The glass, the stone shattering. That scream from below."

"An accident." Philippa lowered the letter opener at last, her arm falling limply to her side. "Just a terrible accident, but who would believe that? My son, defending his father's honour from his mother's lover?" She laughed bitterly and sniffled. "The scandal will destroy us all."

"So you convinced Father to confess instead." The accusation in Peregrine's voice had given way to a deep, aching sadness.

"He insisted." Philippa turned to appeal to Felicity. "When Peregrine told him what happened, Tristan said it was his duty as head of the family to protect us both. That his life was already half-lived, but that our son's was just beginning."

"You suggested it." Peregrine's voice broke entirely. "You were willing to let him hang for my mistake. I didn't want it. I wanted to confess, but you forced Father to go along with it. He would never have thought of such a deception if you hadn't proposed it."

"It wasn't supposed to be hanging!" Philippa's control shattered. "Manslaughter, perhaps a few years' imprisonment. Your father said he could bear it if it meant preserving your future."

Alex widened his eyes at Felicity. She felt the same astonishment. Did Philippa truly believe these to be the terms of her husband's false confession? With the information the police currently had, there was every chance he would be found guilty of wilful murder and be sent to the gallows. Was Philippa engaging in wishful thinking, or was she actually willing to exchange the life of her husband to maintain her son's unblemished prospects? She'd suffered much disappointment, yet the thinking behind it defied logic. But then Felicity had herself never been driven to such desperation.

“My future?” Peregrine spoke the words as though they tasted of ash. “Built on lies and my father’s sacrifice? How do you think I could survive with such a weight around my neck?”

Philippa pressed both hands to her face. The letter opener fell to the floor. Alex moved smoothly to kick it beyond reach, the blade spinning across the carpet to rest harmlessly beneath a side table.

“One lives,” Felicity said quietly, “by choosing truth over lies. Not through silence, but through honesty.”

Peregrine’s gaze found hers, something desperate but also hopeful in his eyes. “Even if it means...” He couldn’t say the words, but he seemed to look at Felicity for permission. Permission to tell the truth.

Philippa shook her head and sobbed. In her prim charcoal-wool travelling suit, she was a sorry figure. She’d betrayed her husband and attempted to control her son. It had been Peregrine who’d caused Mr Kemp’s fall, but Philippa would be punished for her mistakes for the rest of her life.

Yet of the options available, continuing with the plans she, Peregrine, and Tristan had somehow set in motion would be the worst possible outcome.

“The weight of your secrets would eventually crush you both,” said Felicity with a note of sadness but also deep sincerity. She’d witnessed tortured souls torn apart by lies. “It’s better to face the consequences of one’s actions with one’s integrity intact.”

For a long moment, mother and son stood frozen, the wreckage of their sitting room, their decisions, and their deception scattered around them.

Peregrine crossed the distance to his mother in swift strides.

Alex went to step forward but hesitated.

Philippa’s son caught her as her knees buckled.

“I’m sorry,” Peregrine whispered into her hair as she sobbed against his chest. “I’m so sorry, Mother.”

“My boy, my brave boy.” Her words were muffled against his jacket. “I only wanted to protect you.”

“I know.” His arms tightened around her slight frame.

Felicity's shoulders dropped with relief and exhaustion. Pip came to her heels and put a paw to her ankle, and she scooped him into her arms. She met Alex's gaze across the wreckage of the room. His expression mirrored her own, a mixture of gratitude and sadness.

It was over.

Chapter Forty

So profound was the relief that washed over Felicity when Chief Inspector Luscombe arrived at Cullingslock Castle, she might have embraced him like an old friend — had propriety allowed. The senior detective from Exeter had responded to her urgent telegram with admirable swiftness, his motor arriving just as the last rays of evening light painted the castle's red sandstone walls a deeper crimson.

His weary demeanour and the cynical arch of his eyebrow as he greeted her in the entrance hall brought her back to earth.

The Exeter detective now sat across from her, Alex, and Pip in the small interview room that had witnessed Sergeant Norris's hostile interrogation, rubbing his temples as he studied his notebook. An oil lamp cast warm shadows across the scarred elm table and whitewashed walls, its glow catching the shine of Chief Inspector Luscombe's balding head — his hair even thinner than Felicity remembered. Outside the narrow window, bats swooped through the purple twilight and the scent of the forest beyond permeated the draught-prone frame.

"So you didn't know it was the son until his confession?" The chief inspector's voice held a note of gentle reproach.

"I suspected it was the mother." Felicity's hands lay calmly folded beside where Pip was curled in her lap, but she longed to shift in her seat. The weight of her miscalculation pressed upon her shoulders, even though she'd fathomed out most of the intrigue before knocking at Philippa's door.

"I believed Lady Cullingslock had taken action against Mr Kemp after discovering his involvement with another woman in the castle."

The pieces had fallen into place after Elfrida's revelations in the kitchen. Her affair with Mr Kemp had been undertaken purely to spite her sister-in-law. Philippa had everything Elfrida had lost — a husband, a home that was truly hers, respectability. Philippa also seemed intent on undermining Tristan by supporting the land agent's approach to his beloved Wastes and by regarding the compassion he showed for his and Elfrida's mother as nothing but weakness.

Elfrida hadn't put all her motives into words, but the extrapolation was straightforward.

How Elfrida discovered Philippa's liaison with the land agent was still unclear. Elfrida's role as something close to domestic help meant she likely heard and saw things she oughtn't, but the revelation presented her with limited options. A direct confrontation with either Philippa or Mr Kemp would have humiliated Tristan, something Elfrida's protective instincts wouldn't allow. Instead, she'd chosen a crueller path. She stole what Philippa thought belonged to her alone — the exclusivity of Mr Kemp's attentions.

The policeman's pencil paused over his notebook. "Mr Kemp's involvement with Mrs Brand, you mean?"

Felicity pressed her lips together and put a hand on Pip's silky back. "I'm afraid I can't confirm that."

The Exeter detectives had already interviewed both Philippa and Peregrine extensively. Their confessions had likely laid bare all the sordid details, including Elfrida's role in the tragedy. Elfrida would likely not face charges — merely more social consequences for her choices — but Felicity didn't wish to be the source of any further suffering for the household. She'd intruded quite enough for one visit.

"Very well," said the policeman, folding his notebook closed.

"Both Lady Cullingslock and her son are en route to Exeter," Luscombe continued, his tone carefully neutral. "They'll be reunited with Lord Cullingslock there. All three face charges of perverting the course of justice. The boy will probably face manslaughter rather than murder. His youth and circumstances benefit him, as I'm sure you can imagine."

Felicity nodded, grateful for this small mercy. The trial would devastate them all. The familial bonds may have been irreparably damaged, and Peregrine's future military career was in tatters. But they would at least all come through the ordeal alive.

"And your witnesses were..." Luscombe glanced at his notes, a hint of amusement creeping across his features. "Talking birds, your ladyship?"

Alex, who had maintained a respectful impartiality throughout the interview as he took notes for what would be a sober and fact-based report for the Western Daily News, allowed himself a small smile. It was perhaps the most unusual element of any case in which Felicity had been involved, but she didn't dare return his smile. Given their occasionally fraught history, maintaining professional composure with Chief Inspector Luscombe remained paramount.

"Mynahs, to be precise. *Gracula religiosa* is, I believe, the Latin name for the species." She kept her tone matter-of-fact. "They're kept in an aviary in a turret adjoining the wing in which the billiard room can be found. One might say that they're rather like parrots in their ability to reproduce human speech, though they don't comprehend meaning, of course. Their recordings — if one might call them that — revealed Mr Kemp had quarrelled with a woman before his fall."

The chief inspector nodded knowingly. He knew the details now, too.

After the devastating confrontation in their sitting room, Felicity had gently encouraged mother and son to share their truth. The butler had been summoned and the footman dispatched to the post office with an urgent telegram. The full story had emerged between sobs, silences, and tea sipped from trembling hands.

Philippa had found Mr Kemp's behaviour towards her cooling, a development that shook her deeply as she'd come to rely on the man's attentions as a way of bolstering her own self-worth. She'd watched his behaviour closely for signs of what might be wrong but found nothing particularly telling. Following him on that fateful day towards the remote and disused wing where the billiard room was situated, Philippa hoped for the opportunity for a private discussion with Mr Kemp. Instead, she found him with a loosened collar and a lascivious gaze that quickly shifted from surprise to guilt at Philippa's arrival in the billiard room, all of it pointing to another woman's imminent arrival. The discovery of the deceit pushed Philippa over the edge. The confrontation turned ugly, with accusations flying and raised voices.

"And it might have stopped there," added Felicity, "if Lord and Lady Cullingslock's son hadn't been investigating his mother's behaviour."

Peregrine had watched his mother's relationship with the land agent develop over years, first during the war while his father served — which somewhat undermined Philippa's insistence that it was Tristan's post-conflict coldness towards her that drove her into Mr Kemp's arms — and then after his father's return, shattered by his experiences in the trenches. At first Peregrine was too young to understand what he noticed — the subtle looks, the absences together — but as he matured, he understood.

To verify what he suspected, he'd followed his mother to the billiard room. When he heard his mother's distress through the door and the contempt in Mr Kemp's laughter, something snapped. He felt indignation on behalf of his father but also a desire to defend his mother. It was a dangerous cocktail of emotions in a man too young to fully understand or control them.

I only meant to bloody his nose, Peregrine had admitted in the sitting room. He was tall, broad-shouldered, perhaps more powerful than he himself imagined. It was the first punch he'd ever thrown in anger. What jury in the country wouldn't have sympathy with the lad?

The Chief Inspector set down his pencil, leaning back in the hard wooden chair. "A tragic series of events."

"Indeed," agreed Alex.

"Made all the more tragic by Lord Cullingslock's false confession," added Felicity, her stomach twisting slightly. Her visit to Tristan and her confrontation with him regarding the green threads had indeed prompted his confession. But not in the way she'd imagined.

Philippa had sworn Peregrine to secrecy, to not even tell Tristan about what had occurred in the billiard room. Her plan was first to wait and see how the police would come to understand things. But Peregrine blurted out his confession to his father after Felicity's visit, fearful that Felicity — although distracted by the green threads — was, with her instincts and experience in detection, close to discovering the truth.

According to Peregrine, Philippa had promptly suggested the ruse of Tristan taking the blame for his son's error, indicating that it had perhaps been her plan all along. Passions had threatened to flair once again in the little sitting room as they awaited the arrival of Exeter's detectives, but emotions were settled when Philippa's version of events — that she and Tristan jointly took action to defend their son — was allowed to be the final word on the matter, at least in the little sitting room. Mother and son would, of course, be interviewed separately by the police.

The chief inspector sighed deeply. "It's quite incredible what some parents will do for their children."

Felicity's throat constricted. She thought of Tristan's gentleness with dogs and horses, his passion for the land that wasn't even his. A man already hollowed out by war, willing to empty himself completely for his family, and suffering the shock of not only his son's deadly actions but also of his wife's infidelity. Felicity remembered Tristan's frailty, his apologies in the great hall when he was arrested. The grim surprises of everything he'd learned about his wife and son in the wake of Felicity's visit must have been a blow that restricted his ability to think clearly.

"I don't believe any party in this tragedy has made sound decisions recently," said Felicity quietly. She had told no one about her great-aunt's self-poisoning plot. Winnifred's actions ultimately had no bearing on Mr Kemp's demise, and matters at the castle were wild enough without the dowager baroness's input.

Alex raised an eyebrow. "Including the deceased."

Felicity's foot found his under the table. "Unacceptable though it is to speak ill of the dead," she added, keen for the policeman not to take offence at Alex's comment, even though he was, to a certain extent, right.

Mr Kemp had paid the ultimate price for his wrongdoing, not that his affairs or even his arrogance warranted such a payment. Felicity continued to be confused about what could possibly drive smart, capable women like Philippa and Elfrida into the arms of a man such as Mr Kemp. She hoped never to feel the loneliness and lack of validation the two women seemed to share and that pushed them towards a man who cared for no one but himself.

"It's all right, your ladyship." Chief Inspector Luscombe tucked his notebook into his jacket pocket. "Mr Cooper may speak his mind. The dead aren't always thoroughly worth our sympathy. Although I gather you took rather a different view while in London not too long ago." His tone held equal parts exasperation and grudging respect. "I must admit, your ladyship. I can't quite fathom how it is you pick your cases."

Felicity managed a polite smile. "I simply endeavour to do what's right." There was no other way she had to explain her actions.

"And yet wrongdoers find you with remarkable consistency." He studied her with sharp eyes that had seen too much of human nature's darker corners. "Though I confess, your instincts prove sound more often than not. Without your intervention here at the castle, an innocent man might have hanged."

Felicity drew in her chin. Alex smiled at her. The policeman was paying her a compliment.

A knock interrupted before she could respond. The door flew

open without invitation, revealing Sergeant Norris in full uniform, his moustache practically vibrating with indignation.

"Chief Inspector." His voice boomed through the small room. "My constable informed me you're conducting interviews in my jurisdiction without proper consultation. I insist on being present for all proceedings."

Chief Inspector Luscombe's expression remained admirably cool, though Felicity detected a tightening around his jaw. The city detective had clearly encountered his share of territorial local officers, but Sergeant Norris's particular brand of self-importance seemed to test even his patience.

"Sergeant Norris." Each word was carefully measured. "I appreciate your diligence. However, this investigation has been formally transferred to the jurisdiction of myself and my fellow detectives in Exeter. Your help, while noted, is no longer required."

The sergeant's face flushed an alarming shade of purple. "Exmoor is my patch. Has been for fifteen years. You city types swan in here—"

"Sergeant." Chief Inspector Luscombe's voice carried quiet yet firm authority. "This is a murder investigation, not a matter of stolen chickens or public drunkenness. The complexities involved require resources beyond a village constabulary. In the future, I trust you'll contact us immediately when faced with suspicious deaths, rather than attempting to—" He paused delicately. "—manage matters locally."

Sergeant Norris's face darkened further, his thick fingers clenching into fists. For a moment, Felicity feared the sergeant might strike the chief inspector, although Alex was suppressing a smile.

"I won't have you telling me how to run my station!" Spittle flew from Sergeant Norris's lips. "You city boys down in Exeter—"

The chief inspector raised a hand in a gesture so commanding even the sergeant fell silent. "This discussion is concluded. You are dismissed, Sergeant."

Sergeant Norris looked ready to explode. He turned on Felicity, jabbing a thick finger in her direction. "This is your doing. You haven't heard the last of me." He spun on his heel and stormed out, slamming the door with such force that the oil lamp flickered.

"Charming fellow," said Alex.

"Should I be worried?" asked Felicity of the senior policeman, her brow arched.

Chief Inspector Luscombe sighed. He shook his head. "I gather he suffered a change in character after losing his only son in the war. He'd been an officer of admirable character up till then."

Alex's expression turned solemn. The conflict had left no one untouched.

"Norris's background helps explain his behaviour," continued the chief inspector, "but it doesn't excuse it. And you needn't worry about his threats, your ladyship. We're aware of his shortcomings, and he knows where the line is. He'll want to be able to collect his pension when the time comes." The policeman's high forehead creased a little. "What's more concerning to me, your ladyship, is your own insistence on putting yourself in danger on repeated occasions."

Felicity might have groaned with boredom. Instead, she batted her eyes. "Chief Inspector, whatever do you mean?" She was rather tired of hearing this complaint from various quarters.

The detective maintained his rumpled brow. "Confronting a suspected murderess or two?"

"I would like to ensure you, Chief Inspector," said Alex, gallantly stepping in, "that I'm dedicated to Lady Felicity's welfare and safety."

Felicity smiled her gratitude at him. "And this wasn't just any investigation, was it? These people are my family."

The policeman gave her a look as if to say, *Rather you than me.* "In any case," the chief inspector continued, rising from his chair, "I believe we're finished here. My men will complete their enquiries, though your testimony has proven illuminating, to say the least, your ladyship."

There was thankfully no sign of the volatile local sergeant when Felicity, Alex, and Pip emerged from the little interview room and into the great entrance hall. Indeed, there was no sign of anyone, although candles had been lit in the grand medieval chandelier, casting a warm, dancing glow on the stone walls and on the ancestral antiques and mystical trinkets that decorated the space. It was practically dark outside, but staying another night at Cullingslock was surely unwise. Lady Henrietta and Jasper would by now be desperate for Felicity's news, and she'd undoubtedly outstayed her welcome at the castle.

"I suppose this is the end," said Felicity in low tones, blinking as she looked around the entrance hall, Pip's alert gaze following hers from under her arm. Would this be the last time she glimpsed the castle's interior? She'd come to Cullingslock to build bonds with long-lost relatives, but would she ever return? Would they wish to see one another again after everything that had happened? How might matters have played out had Felicity not come to Exmoor?

Alex's hand found the small of Felicity's back, his touch warm and reassuring. They stood in thoughtful silence for a moment.

"Do you still regret coming here?" It was as if he was attempting to unravel her thoughts with her.

"I'm not—" began Felicity, but a sound on the vaulted staircase stole her attention. "—sure," she murmured.

Descending the great staircase, like an apparition from one of her own spiritualist performances, was Great-Aunt Winnifred. And she looked very unhappy indeed.

Chapter Forty-One

In the flickering candlelight from the medieval chandelier and the blue glow of the twilight sky through the great hall's leaded windows, Winnifred appeared diminished. Gone were the layers of purple silk, the theatrical jewellery, the elaborate coiffure. She wore a dress of black crêpe, high-necked and severe, that rendered her almost spectral in the gloom. She descended the staircase with painful deliberation, one hand gripping Timpson's steady arm while the other clutched an ebony walking stick that clicked against each step.

"So." The single word carried none of her usual projection. "You haven't left."

Felicity's throat constricted. What response could suffice? "Not yet, Great-Aunt."

Behind Winnifred, Audrey hovered on the stairs, her broad shoulders hunched beneath a practical grey wool dress. The girl's freckled face was blotchy from crying. Her sturdy frame looked crumpled.

"I should like everything settled before you go." Winnifred continued her descent, each movement an effort, the weight of old injuries and familial drama weighing heavily on her form. "The land. Sign it over properly. Before you leave us."

Felicity caught Alex's eye. In the chaos of arrest and confession, she'd forgotten entirely about the five hundred acres of moorland that had brought her here in the first place.

"That's kind of you to think of, Great-Aunt, but it's something our solicitors can contact one another about."

Reaching the bottom of the staircase, Winnifred drew in her chin. "I'm afraid, my dear, I can't let you leave without signing the land over to you."

Felicity tipped her head, regarding her great-aunt with a mixture of curiosity and frustration. "I'm not sure why you insist I must have it." Had she not made her wishes regarding the land abundantly clear? "Is this about the curse?" Her tone was perhaps a little curt, but she had no desire to rake that dubious topic back up.

Winnifred chuckled. "Curse? No, my child. This is because I'm afraid that if you leave this place, you'll never come back."

The accusation hung between them. When all was said and done, what was there at Cullingslock for Felicity? Who among her relatives at the castle could look at her and not be reminded of the terrible events of the past days?

"That land is yours," continued Winnifred, her cane tapping as she shuffled towards Felicity, "and I want you to have it. I want you to have a tie to us."

Felicity exchanged glances with Alex as Pip squirmed in her arms, excited by the appearance of Audrey. Felicity still didn't want the land. That definitely hadn't changed. But did the inhabitants of Cullingslock really wish for Felicity to remain in their lives?

"Thank you, Great-Aunt, but I fear you may be alone in that sentiment."

"Nonsense," said Winnifred, a hint of her theatricality returning as she stood before Felicity, flanked by Audrey and Timpson. "You've helped my son. I realise he's not out of the woods yet and that my grandson will also face certain consequences. I even feel for Philippa — to an extent. That woman's been unhappy for a long time. But you've treated them all with dignity and respect. You've helped the truth come through. You've even treated me much better than I deserve."

"Great-Aunt," began Felicity, but Audrey cut her off.

"You've been so very nice," the girl added.

Even Timpson gave a subtle nod, visible only to Felicity and Alex.

Felicity fought a blush. "I simply did what had to be done."

Winnifred reached out and grasped Felicity's hand, her grip weak but warm. "No, my dear, you've gone above and beyond. You've done more than anyone else in your position would have done. You didn't have to get involved. You could have jumped into that sporty little motor of yours and ridden away at the first sign of trouble. But instead you stayed, and you involved yourself. You saw injustice, and you took action."

Felicity looked at Alex. He was wearing a satisfied expression that very much proclaimed, *I told you so*. She had indeed heard similar encouragements from him throughout her time at Cullingslock. But hearing them now from Winnifred was unexpected.

"Do you not consider me to bear some responsibility for how things ended?" asked Felicity. She didn't want to pour her anxieties onto the older woman. Winnifred no doubt had worries enough, but Felicity's mind was stuck on how her confrontation with Tristan had triggered Peregrine's confession, which had prompted his father's lies to the police. Felicity could not be blamed for their actions, but her role in the drama could not be undone.

"Do I blame you?" Winnifred laughed. "My child, if you had not come here, goodness knows where we would have ended up. I have been turning a blind eye to the tensions in my own family for far too long. You've highlighted that support is needed. I am now ready to give that support, with the help of my closest allies." Winnifred put an arm around Audrey and pulled her close. She looked warmly at the butler, who gave a blink of acknowledgement but kept a professional posture.

Footsteps echoed on the vaulted staircase. Miss Hartley and Mr Silkstede appeared, both carrying suitcases, the footman behind them struggling with further luggage. They looked ready to spend more than just a few days away.

Felicity felt alarm. "Are Miss Hartley and Mr Silkstede leaving?"

she asked of Winnifred. "Where are they going?" Had her great-aunt somehow seen it fit to clear them out? Were they to be made homeless?

As Miss Hartley and Mr Silkstede arrived on the stone flags of the entrance hall, they embraced Winnifred warmly. "We wish you all the best," said Miss Hartley.

"Me too, my dear ones. *Au revoir*. Mr Timpson?"

The butler bowed to his mistress. "This way, Miss Hartley and Mr Silkstede. I've already brought the Napier to the front. I shall be glad to take you to the station for the last train to Exeter."

Felicity and Alex exchanged confused glances. Why were they leaving in such a hurry?

"Your ladyship. Mr Cooper." Mr Silkstede shook their hands, Pip watching with interest as the man slipped business cards into both their palms. "I look forward to hearing from you."

"Good luck," said Miss Hartley, grinning at Felicity.

"You too," said Felicity, a little uncertainly. What exactly was going on?

They were all smiles and waves as they left. A chill breeze whipped around the entrance hall as the butler opened and closed the castle's big entrance doors, the footman following Miss Hartley and Mr Silkstede outside with their luggage.

"What prompted them to depart?" asked Alex.

"And to seem so happy about it?" added Felicity.

Winnifred sighed deeply, her posture deflating. "I paid them. A handsome sum. I didn't force them out. It was an offer. I said I felt my energy was leaving me."

Audrey looked at her grandmother with concern. "Is that the case, Grandmama?"

The older woman hugged the big-shouldered girl to her. "Not where you are concerned, my dearest one."

"Where are they going?" asked Felicity.

Winnifred shrugged. "They can go wherever they please. I believe they have enough for a year or so."

Felicity was able to control her expression. Alex's eyebrows shot up.

Winnifred pressed onto the top of her cane with both hands. "I know what you're both thinking — that I don't have the money to spend. And perhaps you're right. But some things need to be rounded off neatly. Sometimes you need a clean start."

"What about Mrs Imrie?" asked Felicity.

Winnifred smiled with hints of both amusement and pride. "I'm afraid Mrs Imrie isn't as tempted by money. She remains in her room. She says she needs time to ask the spirits what it is she should do. She's welcome to take all the time she needs, but she understands there's nothing more she can gain from me. There will be no more books, no more shows."

"Yet you wish to sign the land over to me. Where will the financing come from for the upkeep of the castle?"

Winnifred gazed around the entrance hall. "Perhaps to you they may not appear to be of any worth, my child, but I've amassed a fair few treasures over the years, and I'm ready to sell them. Mr Pope will look into which are the best auction houses, and we shall see how much we can raise."

"I shall seek work as a gardener," said Audrey. "Or a trainer of animals."

"You shall do no such thing, my girl. There will be no need for you to work. I shall speak to your uncle about how we will continue just as soon as he..." It was unclear how long Tristan would be detained by the police in Exeter, although at least he would no longer face charges for Mr Kemp's demise. "As soon as your uncle is available."

Felicity smiled a little, lifting Pip higher under her arm. "There's nothing wrong with a woman earning her own money."

Audrey smiled. "See?" she said to her grandmother.

Winnifred shook her head, unwilling to say anything further on the matter. "Now, my child, if we could just get that land signed over to you before you leave, then I will be happy to allow you to depart. Mr Pope has drawn everything up for us. All we need to do is sign."

Felicity smiled uncomfortably. It seemed Winnifred and Audrey were eager to stay in touch, and though Felicity had come to the castle on a mission to gain new family members, after everything that had happened — not just Mr Kemp's untimely demise but her great-aunt's poison plot as well — did Felicity's original mission still make sense?

"What if I said I would stay in touch even if I didn't allow you to sign the land over to me?" she offered diplomatically.

"I would say that I trust you, my child — your intentions are good and true. But Exmoor is a long way from Lower Diddleton. I would need more reassurance than that, I'm afraid."

Felicity looked at Alex. His dark blue eyes narrowed. "It's getting rather late, isn't it? Perhaps it's wise to wait until the morning to depart." He could sense she needed more time to think.

Which was true, but it wasn't everything Felicity needed.

She turned to Winnifred. "Do you know where I might find Elfrida?"

The soft orange glow from the surrounding windows lit the pale gravel paths of the courtyard flower garden. The devastation among the plants had worsened. There was the great gouge in the bed of Canterbury bells into which Mr Kemp had fallen, but the surrounding geraniums and catmint had now also been trampled into mulch, glass fragments still glittering among the leaves, although someone had done their best to clear the mess. Elfrida wasn't visible at first, but a plume of smoke emanating from the shadows of a rose-covered arbour gave her presence away.

As Felicity approached — alone, Pip left in Audrey's care — Elfrida stepped out of the shadows, her feet crunching in the gravel, the orange light from the windows making the purple of her woollen dress appear rust-brown. Her cheeks looked hollow in the dim light.

She wiped at an eye, yet her mouth bore an odd little smile. "Come to pay your respects?"

Felicity halted her advance. The loss that Mr Kemp's demise would inflict upon the world — although certainly thoroughly regrettable — was far from her mind. "I came looking for you."

"Oh, I see." She shook her head, still smiling. "To gloat?"

The idea of it stung. "Is that truly how you see me?"

The smile fell from Elfrida's lips. "Why, then?"

"To apologise."

Elfrida frowned deeply. "Apologise? To me?"

Felicity nodded. She couldn't look into the future to see how her relationship with her Cullingslock relatives might evolve, but she remembered clearly why she had come to the castle. The gulf between her original intentions and what she would leave behind were she to depart that night had grown almost irreconcilable. The events could not be altered, but might she soften the edges of their impact by acknowledging the part she'd played?

"I was rather heavy-handed with you the last time we spoke. As a result, not just your brother but also his wife and son will spend the night — most likely longer, in Perry's case — in an Exeter police station. That can't be easy for you, and I had a role in it all."

Elfrida's smile returned. "You — heavy-handed?" She drew on her cigarette, hugging herself and tilting her head back to look at the indigo sky as she exhaled. "I knew what kind of man Harry was. Knew he collected women like my mother collects mystical ornaments. But when I discovered Philippa had fallen for his charms..." She looked at Felicity. "I could have spoken to her. I could even have told Tristan. Instead, I chose revenge. I took what she thought was hers." She tipped her chin towards the spot where Mr Kemp had landed. "And look where we ended up." A bitter smile twisted her lips, then faded. She put a knuckle to the corner of her eye, stifling a sob.

"You mustn't blame yourself," said Felicity, offering advice she could do better to take on board herself.

Elfrida straightened. "You have nothing for which to apologise. Without your intervention, where would my brother be? I, on the other hand..." She gazed at the mangled gap in the bell-shaped purple flowers as a cool breeze set the remaining blooms nodding. "I would never say I loved the man. Far from it. But his demise will haunt me. My role in it perhaps more than the fellow himself."

Felicity was quiet. What could she possibly say to ease Elfrida's suffering? They had all played a role in what happened, and each of them had their own conscience with which to reckon.

"Audrey doesn't know," Elfrida said suddenly. "About Harry and me." Her eyes flashed in the dimness, vulnerability flickering across her features. "I'd prefer to keep it that way, if possible."

"Of course," said Felicity softly. In apologising to Elfrida, Felicity had taken a step needed for her own healing, even if Elfrida hadn't found the gesture necessary. It wasn't up to Felicity what Elfrida or anyone else in the household might need in order to find their own form of peace with what happened. But there was one more thing she had to say.

"Your daughter is a remarkable young woman," Felicity continued. "She clearly has a gift." She cast a gaze over the remains of the garden, the musky scent of roses mingling with the sweetness of honeysuckle. "My grandmother has established a horticultural school for women and girls. If you'd like a place at the school to be arranged for Audrey, please let me know and I shall see to it."

Felicity hadn't discussed this yet with her grandmother, but Felicity could be extremely convincing when she needed to be. Lady Henrietta would doubtlessly be charmed by Audrey and her talents for growing impeccable flowers and vegetables. It was also a more comfortable way to maintain relations between Cullingslock and Bradley Court than Felicity becoming a landowner, which was still something she had no desire to add to her already overcrowded list of obligations.

Elfrida blinked at Felicity, confused. "Do you not want to wash your hands of us?"

"You're family," said Felicity, offering a sad smile. "I would like to imagine that might mean something even after—" She hesitated. "Even after all this unpleasantness."

Elfrida regarded Felicity for a long, searching moment.

Felicity met her gaze. She'd felt a deep affection for Elfrida and had even dared believe it to be reciprocated. But could such a bond survive all that had transpired? Family was a powerful force, capable of driving both noble deeds and terrible misjudgements. Elfrida had gone to extraordinary lengths to punish her sister-in-law's adultery, with disastrous consequences. Tristan had made his quiet yet cataclysmic sacrifice, while Philippa had been fierce, possibly brutal, in her defence of her only son. Even Winnifred's self-poisoning and attempt to manipulate Felicity had sprung from a desperate urge to protect her home and those within it.

"I shall think about it," Elfrida said.

"Please do," replied Felicity.

Chapter Forty-Two

SEVERAL WEEKS LATER

The period after Felicity's fateful visit to Cullingslock Castle passed in a blur. Their duties as reporters required Felicity and Alex's most immediate attention. They kept her great-aunt's poison plot from the spotlight, but there was no hiding Mr Kemp's demise, and when the link between Winnifred and the Kensington séance disaster could no longer be withheld from the press, the Gentlewoman's Gazette insisted on Felicity for the front page. Yet everything they delivered to their editors was respectful in their regard for their readers and for the often unwitting participants in the tragedy.

Given their interest in newspapers, as expressed to Felicity and Alex, the spiritualists themselves were surprisingly absent from the coverage. Winnifred's payments seemed to have done their trick — for a while, at least. After a lull in attention on the story, a letter purporting to have been written by Mr Kemp from beyond the grave was delivered anonymously to one of the more scandalous tabloids. The newspaper in question duly published it, and the issue of Winnifred and her erstwhile supporters' practices at Cullingslock were thrown needlessly into the limelight once more.

But even before the dust of the scrutiny had settled, Felicity's attention had shifted elsewhere. Ahead of arriving at Cullingslock, her mind had been unsettled regarding the organisation of her and Alex's wedding, her attention torn between her own desires, her imaginings of what Alex's wishes might be, and the pressure from Lady Henrietta and Jasper to do the right thing by society's expectations — and by the needs of the family business.

Upon returning from Cullingslock, Felicity's focus was sharpened. Her own wishes now stood clear in her mind, and after consulting only with Alex — who was no longer remotely evasive about his preferences — a detailed plan was made for the couple's nuptials, incorporating everything dear to them and starting with a party to announce their official engagement.

On the fringes of this glamorous yet intimate event, Felicity stood beside the tall mullioned windows of Bradley Court's drawing room, looking out across the drive and the lines of towering oaks, their leaves a glorious blaze of yellows and oranges against the crisp blue afternoon sky. Despite the joy brought by the many well wishes from her guests, she welcomed a moment of quiet contemplation.

The engagement celebration had become a larger event than Felicity anticipated, but when she and Alex concluded on the list of invitees — none of whom could responsibly be excluded — the decision had been to employ several spaces within the Quick's ancestral home to accommodate everyone.

Fires crackled in the drawing room and connecting library, warming against the coolness of autumn and tinting the air with wood smoke. Both rooms had been decorated with floral arrangements fitting the season: deep red dahlias, chrysanthemums in golden yellow, shining rose hips, and dried hydrangeas in muted pink. Doilies and lace runners lay across tables offering towers of finger sandwiches — cucumber, smoked salmon with dill butter, and egg and cress — sausage rolls, cheese straws, scones with clotted cream and blackberry jam, and slices of lemon drizzle and Victoria sponge. A young woman sat at the piano in the drawing room corner, playing light and popular airs, while waiting staff circulated with offerings of elderflower cordial, cloudy apple juice, and services of tea and coffee, with champagne on standby for the toast.

Connecting to the drawing room was the iron-framed conservatory, its doors opened onto the terrace as long as the sun continued to shine. Woollen lap rugs had been scattered on benches as the guests mingled both indoors and outside. The atmosphere was refined but relaxed, the society women dressed in afternoon frocks in rich jewel tones of forest green, plum, and deep orange, the men in lounge suits and polished balmorals. The women from the village wore practical wool and linen dresses decorated with brooches and home-knit cardigans, the men in well-worn Sunday best. The journalists with whom Felicity and Alex worked had donned loose ties and checked trousers for the occasion, the secretaries in fashionable dropped-waist frocks.

The presence of two of Alex's sisters was especially moving. Though his parents couldn't attend the engagement party, preparations were well underway to ensure their attendance — and comfort — on the big day. Any hesitation or disagreement between Felicity and Alex regarding the wedding planning had been resolved. They were quickly learning about the honesty and patience required to work as a couple on such a personal project.

The smiles on their guests' faces and the gentle laughter that accompanied the clinking of china as people enjoyed the refreshments made Felicity sigh. She felt an intense gladness tinged with fatigue but also relief that she and Alex had done things their way.

Apart from organising the floral displays, Lady Henrietta had very little involvement in the event's organisation. Far from being disappointed with Felicity taking control, her grandmother actually seemed relieved. Beside a couple of comments about expenses — Felicity's brother's mind put to rest when she confirmed Bradley Court as the venue — and a reminder or two about certain newspaper contacts needing to be on the guest list, a number so paltry Felicity conceded with ease, Jasper had also seemed satisfied with the arrangements. With the event in full swing, they were both busy in their respective circles. Lady Henrietta was in the conservatory in an ankle-length tea gown made of silk crêpe in soft mauve, Pip tucked under her arm, discussing the remarkable endurance of her jungle of potted ferns with interested listeners from the local plant and floral society. Jasper was with his business contacts at a small station for sherry, port, and whiskey that had been established in the library.

Everyone present seemed most satisfied. Yet invitations had been sent that hadn't been answered either by the invitees' presence at the event or via polite letters of decline. Somehow, amid the happiness, Felicity's chest squeezed at the thought, and her fingers worried the delicate seed-pearl beadwork at the cuff of her sapphire silk engagement dress. There was a plan she wished to discuss. She had hoped her own engagement celebration might provide the apt moment for it.

"Still watching the drive?"

Alex appeared at Felicity's elbow. The azure of his tie made his dark blue gaze sparkle, and the familiar scent of his cologne — the fresh smell of meadows — mingled with the sharp autumn air drifting through the open conservatory doors. He was always so dashing, always so handsome, yet the sight of him never failed to make butterflies erupt inside her.

"Was I watching the drive?" She smiled as she glanced outside. From her position by the drawing room window, she could see both Bradley Court's drive and the revelries indoors. "I wished merely to take a pause." She lowered her voice. "I have no regrets about our invitation list, but the volume of well-wishers has been a little overwhelming."

Alex's brow lifted, highlighting the scar on his forehead. "I hadn't realised you wished to rest. In that case, I shall come back when—" He took a step backwards, but Felicity caught his hand and pulled him gently towards her. Since they'd sent the invitations to their engagement party, their physical demonstrations of affection had become more certain and less hidden, their status as married-couple-to-be now more official and public.

"I always have time for you," she reassured with a smile.

Alex beamed at her, the warmth and contentment in his gaze making her legs melt a little. He reached into the pocket of his jacket and withdrew two small boxes, one round and covered in dark brown leather, the other square and of blue satin.

Felicity's pulse jumped. She hadn't expected this. But why two?

Alex turned towards the window and touched his elbow to Felicity's so that they might have more privacy as he carefully opened both boxes. Within sat two rings.

Felicity's intake of breath was sharp as the low autumn sunlight made the gems sparkle.

On cream silk within the leather box, an emerald the size of a shirt button sparkled in a yellow-gold setting, surrounded by a crown of elegant diamonds. Resting in green velvet in the satin-covered box was a more modest offering — a platinum trilogy ring, the sapphire at its centre not much bigger than a match head, the two diamonds flanking it as delicate as sugar crystals.

"I didn't think..." began Felicity, her eyes still exploring the beauty of the jewellery held in Alex's broad palm. "I imagined we wouldn't..." The topic of an engagement ring hadn't come up, and Felicity hadn't given it too much thought. It was a common enough gesture for courting couples preparing for marriage, but there was much about her and Alex's relationship that was decidedly uncommon.

Alex swallowed, the motion visible above the starched collar of his shirt. "I admit it felt rather queer to avoid the whole matter of a ring till now, but please believe me when I say I had no intention of allowing you to go without."

"They're both so... So..." It was clear neither piece was recently fabricated. "Beautiful." Both rings had to be heirlooms, but from where? Before she even understood their provenance, Felicity was moved almost to tears.

She looked up at her betrothed. "Where did they come from?"

Alex smiled with relief. "This one," he said, pointing to the emerald cluster, "belonged to your mother. Your grandmother gave it to me to present to you at the toast."

A tear rolled down Felicity's cheek. She wiped it briskly away, not wanting to burden Alex or anyone else at the party with her grief.

Neither her mother nor her father would be present at her wedding, but they would be in her thoughts. And they were always in her heart.

Alex pointed to the sapphire trilogy. "And this one only just arrived from London." He glanced at where his sisters were being served at the refreshments table. "It was my mother's, and her mother's before her. I realise it's rather a trifling thing compared to your own mother's piece, and I swear that neither myself nor anyone in my family will be offended if you don't choose my mother's ring." He took her hand and rubbed it with his thumb. "We all understand the importance of your mother and her memory. But seeing as my parents couldn't make it to our engagement party, I'm afraid I got rather strong-armed into at least offering you the option of my mother's ring." There was a depth of emotion in Alex's voice that surprised Felicity. It perhaps surprised him, too. He cleared his throat a little. "So here it is."

Felicity looked between the rings on Alex's palm and his earnest blue eyes. "Oh, Alex," she whispered.

"It's all right," he said. "We all know which one you'd prefer to wear, and I will be more than happy to present it to you. By Jove," he continued, squeezing her hand, "I'm happy just to be in your presence. Everything else is a bonus."

Felicity tried to smile but sobbed, wiping away another tear.

"Your ladyship?"

Felicity turned. Kitson, the Quick family's butler, had approached without notice to gently yet urgently interrupt Felicity and Alex's tête-à-tête.

Alex swiftly closed the ring boxes and replaced them in his jacket pocket as Felicity composed herself.

"I'm terribly sorry to intrude, your ladyship, but you asked me to inform you when we were approaching the moment of the toast, and that moment has now nearly arrived. Do you wish us to prepare the champagne?"

"Well," said Felicity, still experiencing the swirl emotions of what

Alex had shared with her. Yet she was already entirely clear on what her choice would be. “I suppose we can—”

“Felicity,” Alex interrupted. “Look.”

The old-fashioned Napier limousine with its landaulet top had appeared on the drive. As the late-comers stepped out onto the gravel, Felicity’s breath caught.

Chapter Forty-Three

Audrey arrived first in the drawing room, looking girlishly pretty in a pleated frock of mulberry-purple serge with a white Peter Pan collar, eyes wide and blinking at the guests and decorations. Directly behind her came Elfrida, gazing about with wonder but more subtly, the silver embroidery on her forest-green crêpe dress sparkling in the sunlight streaming through the drawing room's windows.

Having asked the butler to wait with the champagne for the toast, Felicity took Alex's hand and surged forward to meet the unexpected yet hoped-for guests, still dabbing her eyes from her husband-to-be's gesture with the heirloom rings.

"This is exactly what you wanted, isn't it?" whispered Alex as they navigated through groups of villagers and family acquaintances.

"Almost." Felicity had sent an invitation to Cullingslock, though not just for Elfrida and Audrey. Not that the mother and daughter's arrival was at all disappointing.

Felicity greeted her young second cousin with an embrace. Audrey's broad frame was at first stiff, perhaps taken aback by Felicity's enthusiasm, then warmly accepting.

"How wonderful that you're here." Felicity stepped back, her gaze moving to Elfrida. "I was very much hoping to see you both today."

Upon meeting her first cousin once removed, Felicity had immediately liked Elfrida. Despite everything that had happened at Cullingslock, Felicity still harboured a desire to reunite the estranged branches of the family, but was the ambition selfish? Simply the pedantic need for her original mission to Cullingslock to be declared a success? Given everything the family had been through, would Elfrida even wish to nurture a relationship with Felicity?

It was enormously encouraging that she and her daughter had come to the party.

Elfrida hugged herself. Her reddish hair, painstakingly styled into finger waves, shone copper in the afternoon light. Her eyes continued to shift around the room even as she smiled at Felicity, though with no trace of the wry confidence she'd often displayed at Cullingslock. The pair perhaps rarely attended such lavish events, not that Felicity and Alex's engagement party was over the top. Elfrida had maybe been unsure whether to attend and was already regretting her decision.

"Sorry that we didn't RSVP. There's been rather a lot going on, and it wasn't entirely clear which of us would make it." Elfrida placed a hand on her daughter's shoulder. "I'm afraid only Audrey and I can be here to wish you and Mr Cooper all the best."

"Congratulations." Audrey knitted her fingers in front of her dress and swung her shoulders. "You're such a lovely couple." A touch of red bloomed under her freckles.

Alex smiled warmly. "Thank you both."

"No need to apologise." Felicity took Elfrida's hand. "I'm so very happy you're here."

The corners of Elfrida's mouth tugged briefly downwards as she met Felicity's gaze, as though fighting back tears. The last time Felicity had seen them was on the final day of her visit to Cullingslock. Audrey seemed to have moved through the drama without too much damage, the machinations between the various parties involved perhaps too adult for her to understand. But her mother felt some weight of responsibility for what happened.

While Felicity's own remorse at her role in the tragedy had lessened significantly — her only desire had been to help — Elfrida was still struggling with her regrets, with the things she wished she'd never done yet could never take back.

"I'm very happy you wish us to be here," she said, struggling to smile, her eyes full of a tentative gratitude and no trace of sardonic undertone.

Apart from the engagement party invitation, there had only been a smattering of communication between Felicity and her Cullingslock relatives via letter. The missives had been rather formal, mainly concerning the family's welfare, although Winnifred had been diligent about adding repeated requests for Felicity to hasten matters with their respective solicitors regarding the Cullingslock Wastes.

But some things couldn't be expressed by letter.

"Why would I not wish you to be here?" Felicity took Elfrida's hand. "We're family, are we not?"

Elfrida nodded, swallowing. "We are." The relief in her voice gave Felicity an ache of tenderness in her chest. "We've something for you both." She flashed a little smile at Felicity and Alex. "Audrey?"

Audrey straightened and plunged her hands into deep pockets on either side of her dress. When she withdrew them, she held two ribbon-finished boxes, each not more than palm-sized.

Felicity drew a hand to her chest, her heart skipping at the echo of what Alex had presented at the drawing room window. But this was something else.

"Go ahead, Audrey," urged Elfrida.

Audrey handed one box to Felicity and the other to Alex. Felicity's was heavy for its size. The couple looked at each other — Alex lifting a quizzical brow — before pulling on the carefully tied ribbons.

"They're your engagement gifts," clarified Audrey, watching as they lifted the lids. "Mother made them."

Set in crushed tissue paper lay an identical item in each box.

Carved from bluish limestone with subtle marble was a bird — a swallow, flocks of which were common in both North and South Devon throughout the summer — its form rendered in a gently flowing abstract style. It swooped in flight, forked tail trailing, wings tucked back to form a teardrop shape.

"They're paperweights," continued Audrey, "and they fit together perfectly."

Alex held his box towards Felicity's. Indeed, the two delicate carvings were formed to nestle into one another.

"Just like you both," added Audrey with a giggle, her hand covering her mouth.

Felicity looked up at Elfrida. "You made these?"

She nodded, some of her usual confidence returning.

"They're stunning," said Alex, still examining the carvings.

"Quite wonderful," agreed Felicity, her soul uplifted not just by the thoughtfulness of the gift but by a once-defeated woman returning to her life's calling. "So you've taken up art again?"

Elfrida nodded. "It was always there, waiting for me. It's helped me work through many of the feelings I've been battling with since, well... You know."

"If you've anything you'd like to highlight in the newspaper," said Alex, still admiring the artwork in his hand, "just let me know, and I'll put a word in with our arts columnist."

Elfrida drew in her chin and blinked at Alex. "Th-thank you."

Felicity adored Alex's passion to help, but perhaps it was too soon for a woman with so much from which to recover.

"Does this mean you're spending less time in Cullingslock's kitchen?" asked Felicity as the gentle hubbub of the party continued around them.

"It does indeed," said Elfrida, unable to stifle a grin.

"Grandmama's hired extra help," said Audrey. "She said we all must have time to pursue what makes us happy, although I insisted we don't need a gardener."

Felicity smiled. It was heartening to hear the girl's fondness for plants was as strong as ever.

Alex frowned. "I thought finances at the castle were rather tight."

Felicity spun towards him, her real urge to elbow him in the ribs. Winnifred's management of the castle's resources had been questionable, but to bring the matter up so bluntly was rather uncalled for.

Mother and daughter seemed unfazed.

Elfrida leaned in, a wry smile beginning to dance on her lips. "Remember all those esoteric trinkets? Turns out they were not so worthless after all. Mother's been selling them off and investing the proceeds in the castle."

Felicity kept her mouth from falling open. It was a development she hadn't envisaged. Even if Winnifred had spent her money unwisely — a fault she appeared now to be rectifying — it seemed Mr Silkstede hadn't been a swindler, after all.

"We've even got glass in all the corridor windows now," added Audrey with delight.

"And where is your mother?" asked Felicity. Winnifred had been sent an invitation for the engagement celebration, but Felicity and Winnifred's relationship was more complicated than her bond with Elfrida. Perhaps it was best that Winnifred had been invited but had not attended. There would be future occasions when great-aunt and great-niece could be reunited, when past misdeeds would feel less raw.

"Mother sends her regrets. She's actually in Scotland at the moment."

Felicity's eyes flew wide.

"Scotland?" echoed Alex.

The last time they saw Winnifred, she needed help navigating the stairs and struggled even then.

"Do you remember Mrs Imrie?"

"Of course," said Felicity. The woman had given Felicity her first and, likely, last palm reading.

"She's established a centre for spiritualism in Inverness. A rather modest operation, by all accounts. Certainly nothing theatrical. Mother's gone up there for a spell to lend her 'powers'. There's no money in it, apparently, just donations of whatever people can afford." Elfrida's sardonic smile returned. "Mother said it's high time she 'cleansed her soul'."

Felicity and Alex exchanged glances. It was surprising but also most pleasing to hear of Winnifred's progress. Her energy for new endeavours and desire to do better verged on inspirational.

Alex winced slightly. "Did she take her birds?"

"Oh, no." Audrey beamed. "The mynahs are still with me. We'll be building an even bigger aviary for them, but they're enjoying their retirement so far."

Felicity smiled at the girl. Among the merriment of the engagement party, the news from Cullingslock all sounded so positive. Yet a rather less cheerful element was glaring in its absence.

"May I ask how your brother is getting on?" Felicity asked of Elfrida.

Felicity hadn't seen Tristan since the day of his false confession. After the revelations from Philippa and Peregrine about what really happened to Mr Kemp, Tristan had been released from custody, though he'd still faced punishment for his deception. Felicity had hoped to see him at Bradley Court. There was even something quite specific she wished to discuss with him, but his absence from the celebration was understandable. He was a shy fellow at the best of times, and he might even bear Felicity ill-will. He might have preferred to face the hangman rather than have his son's future destroyed. Felicity couldn't know for certain. Perhaps she never would.

Elfrida sighed deeply. "As well as expected, all things considered. He rides out across the moors every day, though he still spends rather a lot of time at the prison."

"I can quite imagine," said Felicity, Alex also nodding.

Tristan had been prosecuted for perverting the course of justice with his false confession. He'd spent only a month in prison, the jury very much moved by his desperate act on behalf of his son. Peregrine also garnered sympathy in the courtroom and was now serving a relatively lenient two years for the manslaughter of Mr Kemp. Not that a prison sentence for such a young man was anything but disastrous. There was certainly no hope of a military career now.

"Tristan and Perry's bond has become all the stronger for what they've been through," continued Elfrida. "My brother says Perry speaks frequently of his desire to ride out across the moors with him."

Felicity offered a sorrowful smile. Even if he rebuffed her approach, she would have to speak to Tristan at some point. There was no getting around it.

"Do you have news from your sister-in-law?"

Alex's question made Felicity simultaneously grateful and anxious. Grateful because she wished for news of Tristan's wife, and anxious because Elfrida and Philippa had something of a fraught relationship.

Elfrida's expression darkened suddenly.

Crash!

Her gaze skittered away. It sounded as though a whole tray of drinks had been dropped in the conservatory.

"What the..." Alex surged towards the noise, Felicity close behind as gasps went up.

Baff, baff, baff!

Woof! Grrr... Woof!

Alex was gentle but firm as he forged a path for himself and Felicity through the engagement party guests, all craning their necks to see what was happening, the valiant pianist somehow playing on. Felicity recognised one of the barks — Pip, of course, but there could be a fine line between excitement and aggression.

Baff! Baff, baff!

Woof! Woof!

The other dog's bark Felicity couldn't recognise. Pip's presence was acceptable — he was part of the family — but who had brought the other uncontrollable canine to the engagement party? The situation had to be resolved promptly, as it was clearly at risk of escalating.

Chapter Forty-Four

The dogs stood in the doorway to the conservatory.

Pip was positioned just indoors, his little jaws snarling with every bark, Lady Henrietta not far behind him, wide-eyed with shock at the terrier's behaviour. Beside her, household staff swiftly attended to a tray of empty glasses upset in the tumult.

Baff! Baff baff baff!

"Pip!" Felicity called as she and Alex raced towards the scene.

In front of the Yorkie, in a space cleared for him by startled guests who had been enjoying the autumn sunshine on the terrace, stood a slightly unkempt Old English Sheepdog.

Woof! Grrr... Woof!

The sheepdog lowered its chest to the ground, grey-and-white tail flapping with excitement.

"Lionheart! Terribly sorry. So very sorry."

Tristan appeared on the terrace, silhouetted against the golden October afternoon. Though his dark suit hung loosely on his tall frame, he moved with purpose through the startled guests.

"Excuse me. So sorry. We got rather lost, you see."

At his side trotted the ever obedient Solomon, the Border Collie's intelligent gaze sweeping the scene, his tail lifting as he spotted Pip.

"Ended up in the village. Walked the rest of the way. Let the dogs run off ahead, only I didn't realise we were so close to the house. Lionheart! Oh, dear. So terribly sorry."

Felicity smiled. So Tristan wasn't avoiding her. Might they be able to have that discussion she had on her mind? Not if the canine stand-off continued unchecked.

Baff baff! Baff!

"Pip," said Felicity, warningly.

Alex raised a doubtful eyebrow.

"Felicity, dear." Lady Henrietta's voice wavered. "Shouldn't we do something?"

Lionheart pounced.

"Goodness!" cried Felicity's grandmother, but Felicity's attempt to grab Pip was too late.

The shaggy sheepdog cavorted with puppy-like abandon, charging between the conservatory and the terrace. Pip, thrilled to have a willing playmate, darted between the larger dog's legs with impressive agility. They wove through groups of guests and under the terrace furniture, Lady Henrietta's carefully arranged floral displays trembling in their wake.

"Heavens," said the dowager, fanning herself a little.

Audrey and Elfrida arrived on the terrace. Audrey laughed. "Lionheart has really come out of his shell since my uncle's been looking after him."

"I do apologise," Tristan panted, attempting unsuccessfully to intercept the long-haired sheepdog as he flew through guests from the Lower Diddleton Plant and Floral Society. Thankfully, there was as much laughter as gasps of surprise.

Elfrida folded her arms and sighed with exasperation and affection. "You told us you weren't coming."

"I didn't think I was." Tristan was becoming breathless as he chased after Lionheart. "They needed help at the Crocker farm. I was as quick as I could be, realised I had no option but to bring the dogs, but then I missed my turning..."

Alex stepped forward decisively and plucked Pip from the fray, holding the squirming terrier aloft. Lionheart sat below his dangling playmate, tail wagging hard. The gathering on the terrace gave a gentle applause. Solomon, who had been seated obediently throughout, whimpered with disappointment. The fun was over before he'd joined in.

"Thank you, Mr Cooper." Lady Henrietta accepted the Yorkie with regal composure. "And how very rude of you, Master Pip," she scolded, though amusement glittered in her lavender-blue eyes.

Tristan secured Lionheart, snapping a loose lead to his collar as the fluffy sheepdog's tongue lolled with satisfaction. This was indeed a very different dog than the one commanded by Mr Kemp.

"The Baron of Cullingslock, I presume?" Lady Henrietta stepped forward, her silk crêpe gown rustling, her manner a little haughtier than Felicity would have liked, but Tristan had made rather an entrance, coming from the village on foot with two loose dogs. "How delightful to make your acquaintance at last."

Tristan shook her hand, still seeming overwhelmed. "You're welcome to call me Tristan, your ladyship."

"And this is Mrs Elfrida Brand, the baron's sister." Felicity stepped aside so her grandmother and Elfrida might shake hands. "And Mrs Brand's daughter, Audrey."

"How do you do?" Audrey curtseyed.

"Miss Audrey?" Lady Henrietta paused. She blinked at the girl, then turned to Felicity. "Is this the same Miss Audrey you've been telling me about?"

Felicity nodded with satisfaction as Audrey and her mother exchanged confused glances.

"Then you must accompany me right away, my dear." Lady Henrietta looped her arm through Audrey's. "I hear you have a phenomenal success rate when propagating delphiniums and quite some interesting ideas on companion planting, particularly with legumes."

Audrey's freckled face illuminated as the dowager whisked her away. Elfrida followed, her confusion replaced with tentative maternal pride, Pip's tail wagging at the dowager's side. It would take a miracle for Lady Henrietta not to offer the girl a place at her horticultural school.

Alex exhaled, sweeping a hand over his dark blond hair. "Did that go well? I admit I find it difficult to tell with your grandmother sometimes."

"There's nothing to worry about," said Felicity, watching the three women stroll towards Bradley Court's rose garden. She turned to Tristan, both dogs now sitting calmly beside him. "I'm so very pleased you're here." If she was as bold as her grandmother, she might have led him immediately away for a private discussion. But relationships could be fragile things, warranting as much if not more attention than the most precious rose bushes.

Tristan's Adam's apple bobbed above his askew tie. "I wasn't certain... After everything..."

"You're family," Felicity said, repeating her words to Elfrida. A shared bloodline didn't excuse every wrong, and it was always tempting to retreat when things grew difficult, but staying the course often proved more rewarding.

"Speaking of which," she lowered her voice as the party's chatter continued around them. "Have you any news of Philippa?"

During the period when her husband and son were both incarcerated, Philippa had sent letters to everyone touched by the tragedy. Her letter to Felicity and Alex expressed regret and sadness at her contribution to what happened, especially what had been taken from her son and from Mr Kemp's relatives, particularly the man's mother and father, the only members of his family to have attended the court hearings. She didn't ask for absolution — she said she would carry the blame forever — but she asked that her son be forgiven.

Many of us make mistakes in the heat of youth, the letter had read. *It is truly unfortunate that my son's error of judgement led to a man's passing.*

"She's well. Staying with family." Tristan rubbed his neck, his gaze downcast. He stroked Solomon's head. "I miss her."

Felicity glanced at Alex. He looked as sorrowful as she felt. Might

Philippa and Tristan ever be reconciled? A couple's love had to be strong to survive such mistakes. Any rapprochement would depend more on Philippa's ability to forgive herself than on Tristan's ability to forgive her.

"Elfrida tells me you're spending a lot of time outdoors," said Felicity, guiding the conversation away from his pain.

Tristan nodded. "As much as I can. I suppose Elfrida told you about Mother selling her belongings? That can only go so far. I believe I'll have to return to the Ministry of Agriculture. Perhaps even move back to London."

Felicity raised her brow. "Is that what you want?"

"What one wants and what one must do are not always the same thing, I'm afraid."

Felicity shot an excited glance at Alex. "Forgive me for a sharp change in tone, but would you object to remaining at the castle and managing the Cullingslock Wastes?" She could barely contain her excitement. In her letters, Winnifred had accused Felicity of dragging her heels on the land ownership question, but the topic had never been far from her mind.

Tristan frowned. "I certainly wouldn't object. But how might I earn the money needed for the castle's upkeep?" He was clearly against continuing Mr Kemp's practices.

"My brother has had his solicitors examine ways of reconnecting the land to the castle. It's not straightforward, but there's an alternative."

Tristan looked a little warily at Felicity and Alex. "What would that be?"

"I shall become the land's owner and employ you as my land agent." Becoming a landowner still felt unnatural, but if she could help her family, then it was what she wanted.

Tristan's mouth fell open. Solomon whined and nudged his hand. "You wish to employ me?"

Felicity glanced indoors. Her brother stood with a group of men she didn't recognise but who were of no doubt great importance to the smooth running of the Western Daily News, the exponential growth of which Jasper was keen to prolong. When he'd asked her what she desired as an engagement present, Felicity had requested an investment in the Cullingslock Wastes, to buy the time needed for Tristan to return the land to a more natural style of management. The mention of Tristan's qualification in agriculture from Oxford helped conclude the arrangement. The profits wouldn't be immediate, but a balanced environment would allow both wildlife and people to thrive, including the Cullingslocks.

"I would be honoured to employ you," said Felicity. "What do you say?"

Tristan smiled, his shoulders relaxing. "I would be honoured to accept."

"I say."

Jasper had appeared on the terrace and was heading towards them.

"Hullo, Jasp," said Alex, side-stepping his friend's determined approach with a look of amusement and wariness.

"Is this one of our relatives?" Jasper's voice boomed a little too hard, his chestnut moustache twitching as he thrust a hand towards Tristan. Something had irritated him.

"This is Lord Tristan Cullingslock," explained Felicity hastily. "You remember, dear brother, our discussions of the Cullingslock Wastes?"

"Yes, yes. Very good." Jasper leaned towards Felicity, lowering his voice. "The toast, old girl. When's it happening? I've got several important advertisers quite desperate for champagne."

It wasn't just Jasper's business contacts who'd been left waiting.

Felicity's gaze flew to Alex.

Goodness.

After their intimate moment with the two rings, she'd left him hanging. He looked calm and relaxed, but it wouldn't do. It simply wouldn't.

Felicity excused herself from Tristan — they could discuss the details of their arrangement later — and found the butler. With pleasing alacrity, flutes were distributed and everyone gathered in the conservatory, where the last rays of slanted sunlight glowed orange through polished glass. Felicity and Alex stood beside a pristine three-tiered fruitcake covered in marzipan and white icing, sugar paste delicately formed into cascades of flowers in autumnal shades. Lady Henrietta was fetched from the rose garden, where she'd been having a riveting time learning from Elfrida's daughter. Jasper stood at the dowager's side, Pip happily ensconced under Audrey's elbow.

Felicity stared deeply into Alex's eyes. There wasn't a shred of impatience in his gaze. She wished never to cease bathing in the warmth of his companionship.

"To the happy couple!" announced Jasper, prompting everyone to lift their glasses.

"To family!" added Felicity, also raising her glass.

Alex smiled as their gazes locked. Reuniting with the Cullingslocks was just part of it. There was the joining of the Quicks and Coopers to look forward to, regardless of who could attend which event.

"If I may..." Alex set his glass aside and reached into his pocket, withdrawing the small leather box. He revealed Felicity's mother's engagement ring, the emerald sparkling in the late afternoon light.

A wave of admiration passed through the gathering, followed by gentle applause as Alex slipped the ring onto Felicity's finger.

"And the other one," she whispered.

Confusion flickered across his face. "Really?"

Felicity nodded. "Please."

He retrieved his own mother's sapphire trilogy ring and slipped it onto the same finger. The gathering's applause was more hesitant than the first round. Two engagement rings were hardly normal, but when had Felicity and Alex ever worried about being perceived as normal?

Felicity pulled him gently towards her and kissed him on the lips in front of the whole crowd. He tasted of elderflower cordial.

As they pulled back, his dark blue eyes sparkled. "I never imagined such happiness was possible."

"This is only the beginning," she whispered.

They were able to linger alone for barely a few moments, as a deep, dejected sigh drew their attention.

Lady Henrietta had stepped away from the cake queue, looking vexed.

"Grandmama." Felicity retreated from her beloved but kept hold of his hand. "I trust you had a pleasant discussion with Audrey?"

"Indeed. A charming and very clever young woman," said the dowager, though her brow remained puckered.

"You will offer her a place at the horticultural school?"

"Without question, my dear. Without question."

"Then what's troubling you, Grandmama? And don't pretend there's nothing. Is it the two rings? I assure you I shan't be taking either off."

Alex squeezed her hand. He was with her, whatever Felicity decided to do.

"My dear, you can wear as much jewellery as you like. It's not that, it's..." She trailed off. "An acquaintance of mine is, unfortunately, rather ill. It's likely she will recover, but she must travel for a rather lengthy treatment."

Felicity frowned, full of sympathy. "Oh, how terrible. Can we help?"

Lady Henrietta's gaze brightened. "Are you aware of the winter gala in Sweetbrooke? The fundraising event for the village's orphanage?"

A small sigh escaped Felicity's lips. Even with the wedding preparations to consider, refusal was hardly an option. "Yes, Grandmama. I can give a speech or present a prize or whatever it is you wish me to do."

"You misunderstand, my dear. The poor orphans depend on the gala funds, and my ill acquaintance usually organises the event. I should like to replace her myself, but I've got the horticultural school to think about now, and well... No, I couldn't possibly. I can't ask that of you."

Felicity and Alex exchanged glances.

"Are you suggesting I—"

"Oh, would you, my dear? I know you have your wedding to consider, and I feel so awful raising this on such a special day, but those little children need help."

Alex frowned, concern in his dark blue gaze. "Isn't there someone else?"

"I'm afraid not, Mr Cooper. I just exhausted my last option in the cake queue. There's no one else to organise the gala this year. Simply no one else."

Alex looked at Felicity. The concern in his eyes was for her becoming overburdened — yet he was obviously touched by the plight of the parentless children.

Felicity stared back at him, her heart equally moved. Lady Henrietta was certainly a smooth operator.

But how hard could organising a charity event be?

Claim your free Lady Felicity Quick ebook!

Sign up for my email newsletter and you'll get **Murder at Afternoon Tea** absolutely free.

This exclusive story isn't available anywhere else.

As a newsletter subscriber, you'll also receive writing updates, special offers, and peeks behind the scenes...

Sign up and claim your copy today:

https://BookHip.com/XMGPNZC

The Lady Felicity Quick Mystery Series

Murder at Afternoon Tea

(Novella | Exclusive for Newsletter Subscribers)

Murder on the Village Green

(Book 1 | Available Now)

Murder at a Country House

(Book 2 | Available Now)

Murder at the Tea Rooms

(Book 3 | Available Now)

Murder at the Ball

(Book 4 | Available Now)

Murder on the Coast

(Book 5 | Available Now)

Murder at a Boarding School

(Book 6 | Available Now)

Murder at a Flower Show

(Book 7 | Available Now)

Murder by the Thames

(Book 8 | Available Now)

Murder in the Castle

(Book 9 | Available Now)

Murder at the Winter Gala

(Book 10 | Coming Soon)

About the Author

Rosie Hunt is a British author of cozy mysteries both puzzling and historical. Her books include the Lady Felicity Quick mystery series set in the green and pleasant countryside of southwest England in the 1920s.

A history addict and former journalist, Rosie grew up immersed in the worlds of Poirot and Miss Marple. This early exposure to baffling murder mysteries rather coloured her outlook on life, and it was only a matter of time before she began writing her own.

Rosie loves clotted cream, knitting, and Golden Age crime fiction, and she'll never miss an opportunity to visit a National Trust property. She lives with her husband and their four-pawed overlords on a river in Northern Europe.

Join Rosie's mailing list:
bookhip.com/XMGPNZC

Follow Rosie on Facebook:
facebook.com/RosieHuntAuthor

Made in the USA
Las Vegas, NV
07 September 2025

27530758R00218